THE HARMONY

MARK STELLAN

Thank you to my family, who endure my madness and quite a bit of silliness, but still find it in their hearts to love me. None of this was possible without your love and support.

Thank you to my friends, those both near and lurking in parts unknown. Your encouragement has helped more than you can know.

A special thanks to my literary heroes: Albert Camus, Frank Herbert, Kurt Vonnegut, Isaac Asimov and many others. I would never have made it here without your immortal words to guide me.

For Joy, for everything.

It matters not how strait the gate,
How charged with punishments the scroll,
I am the master of my fate,
I am the captain of my soul.

William Ernest Henley
Invictus (excerpt)

And you, my father, there on the sad height,
Curse, bless, me now with your fierce tears, I pray
Do not go gentle into that good night.
Rage, rage against the dying of the light.

Dylan Thomas
Do Not go Gentle into That Good Night (excerpt)

Contents

Prologue – A History

Excerpt from the History of The Harmony

By Therus Everfield

Esperlin Chronicler of House Carchel

A.D. 3579

The task of chronicling the lengthy and vibrant history of the First Imperial Empire, informally known to its inhabitants as the Imperium, becomes a binary division; a simple before and after delineation concerning the pivotal event of human history. This event, universally referred to as The Harmony, stems from the role of the Cognitive Harmonization Device. Used by the Imperium at the instruction of Emperor Rakeus VII of Karmarch, House Imperiatus—the Emperor of the Known Universe—it will undoubtedly serve as a reference point on the timeline of all historical events. The recorded chronicles of humanity will henceforth classify events as having occurred either pre-, or post-, Harmony. The future generations' perception of this proverbial line marking the entirety of human history is inconsequential. Whether it's seen as the genesis or the culmination of all history is similarly irrelevant. The fact remains that it happened, and the involved actors navigated the situation as if there were no alternative options, as if destiny guided them. To question the validity of these assumptions now is futile.

Comprehending the significance of The Harmony, as jailer and liberator, creator and annihilator, only uncovers half the story. It would be negligent as historians to overlook the vast strides our species has taken to avert destruction over the aeons. Our real strength has always lain in our eerie knack for finding places to prosper, both in the universe and within ourselves. The birthplace of humanity, Earth, or 'Origin' as we now refer to it, was an unremarkable third planet in orbit around its star. Comprising three quarters of non-potable, hypertonic water, Origin was a small planet whose finite natural resources, after enduring millennia of human civilization, were on the brink of exhaustion, unable to support an expanding population. Our earliest records relating to life on Origin cite a peak population of about 12 billion people—meager by contemporary Imperial standards.

Historians have yet to fully comprehend how the resources were depleted, or what events transpired, to catalyze an enigmatic crisis known as The Calamity. Theories regarding the nature of The Calamity vary. Some attribute it to an oxygen crisis induced by mass deforestation, while others point towards radiation poisoning from the utilization of archaic atomic weapons. The Imperium has long banned these weapons, though some insist, without admitting, that such practices persist. Others propose that the exhaustion of all viable resources, as rivers drained away and relentless storms ravaged the skies, caused it. A select few suggest a combination of these catastrophes. Regardless of the underlying cause, the early inhabitants of Origin found themselves at a crossroads, similar to the one faced millennia later by the Emperor and Imperial Council during The Sequence crisis. The choice was either survival or extinction.

In our history, survival triumphed. The most sophisticated civilizations on Origin were entrusted with the building of gigantic spaceships, each capable of transporting thousands of people to the farthest reaches of known space. Over several years, fleets of these vessels, named Arks (in reference to a popular tale from a regional religion of the area), embarked on their journeys into the deep recesses of the galaxy. These ships were the pioneers of a technology known to us as FTL, or Faster-Than-Light travel. Powering the first generation of FTL ships were unpredictable tachyon drives. Several of the ships that left Origin during this period were reported missing.

Despite these challenges, the inaugural vessels miraculously reached the uninhabited planets of the Virgo cluster. Graced with the title of the First Settlers, these pioneering spacefarers discovered the pivotal habitable planet and star system of Coursius-7 (now Nimbus) and Terisus Prime (now Archlon), the first world suitable for human habitation. Although the first settlers initially grappled with numerous adversities on this strange world, over time and with waves of immigrants from Origin, Archlon became the new home of humanity. It was a stroke of luck that the First Settlers meticulously maintained extensive data archives eventually forming the foundation for a society later known across the 97 inhabited worlds as the Imperium.

If the story of Origin and humanity's debut in interstellar travel imparts any wisdom, it is that the human spirit is endowed with an invincible will to survive. The actions taken during the era of The Harmony echo this sentiment and, should this record of events survive, may serve as an invaluable guide for our species should we again find ourselves cast into the abyss, seeking to transcend the confines of our biology and the fears clouding our collective consciousness. If there is a hidden message to be gleaned from the First Settlers' data archives, it might be that these fears have always been an integral part of human consciousness. The Era of Chaos has undoubtedly facilitated our evolution, and perhaps, the future holds further evolution for us. If a new dawn truly beckons in the stars of our destiny, it is worth remembering that throughout history, survival has often called upon our basest instincts, however unsightly.

CHAPTER 1
Has It Come To This?

T he dying rays of the setting sun bathed over the shimmering metallic structures of Archlon. Ribbons of rainbow light cascaded over the gleaming buildings, scattering prisms of color across the cityscape. For newcomers on their first day in Archlon, the sunset over the capital was an unforgettable spectacle. The sight was especially mesmerizing from behind the sprawling skyline of Kadzer, a colossal metal metropolis that dwarfed the antiquated pre-Imperial cities of legend. Archlon was the largest planet in the Capricorn system, nestled deep in the Virgo Cluster on the fringes between the Milky Way and Andromeda galaxies. The fourth world orbiting the blazing crimson star Nimbus, Archlon was the central planet of the Imperium and home-world of House Karmarch, the imperial dynasty that ruled the Known Universe.

Archlon was among the wealthiest planets in the Imperium, with abundant reserves of vermacite—an exotic superalloy metal found only on Archlon. Vermacite was a naturally occurring organic alloy, many times stronger than iron yet lighter than steel. The gleaming skyscrapers that dominated the skylines of cities like Kadzer were constructed from this remarkable metal. Vermacite was utilized for everything from building foundations, to the exterior hulls of interstellar starships. Its most striking visual characteristic was the way vermacite shimmered when illuminated, writhing as if the metal itself was alive. At sunset, buildings coated in vermacite seemed to dance with ribbons of color, as if the city was a living being swaying to an unheard rhythm.

Archlon was a highly industrialized world, perhaps the most mechanized planet in the Imperium. Most of its vast surface was enveloped by urban sprawl, mining installations, and manufacturing hubs. Little agriculture existed here, with staple crops like grain imported from breadbasket worlds across the Imperium. Each Imperial world had a vital role, providing specialized goods and services that allowed the far-flung civilization to function in symmetry. Archlon's cosmopolitan population of executives and elites controlled the most powerful organizations in the Imperium. Industry barons, diplomats, emissaries, and manufacturing titans called the metallic jungle of Archlon their home. The Imperium's interstellar warships, weapons, and other military material were manufactured in Archlon's factories. From here, commercial goods like hovercraft, farming equipment, and mechanical servants were exported across the Imperium to its most distant colonies.

The Imperium itself stretched across much of the known galaxy. It could take a Starcruiser traveling at sub-luminescent speeds many months to travel to the world's furthest from Archlon. These far-flung worlds on the very edge of explored space, referred to by most as the colonies, were considered the frontier of the Imperium. The farther one traveled from the core systems, the more disparate these worlds became, no longer conforming to the regimented Imperial system. Yet all played a role in the delicate balance of civilization. The Imperium had endured for over three millennia, with each world interdependent on the others.

It was difficult for visitors to behold Archlon's sublime sunsets and not feel a sense of awe, even envy. The resplendent metal architecture, the enormous crimson sun, the endless cityscape stretching to the horizons—all reinforced that this was the undisputed center of the civilized universe. It was as if all other worlds existed in service to Archlon's glory. Archlon is where the powerful came to rule.

As the dying embers of daylight illuminated the city below in ethereal radiance, Emperor Rakeus VII reclined on his balcony terrace overlooking the capital. Rakeus III was Emperor when the

Palazzo de Cournia was constructed off the east wing of the palace. Rakeus III enjoyed watching the city below from the elevated vantage point of Kral Markhan. Kral Markhan, commonly known as 'The Mark', was the imperial palace and the ancestral home of House Karmarch, and had served as the seat of power in the empire for hundreds of years.

Rakeus VII often spent evenings alone at the Palazzo de Cournia, sipping warm liquors as he observed the world he dominated. Watching the people below scurry about, living and dying at his whim. The thought sent a chill through him, as if the doors to the outside had swung open. As Rakeus watched the beautiful metal city of Kadzer sparkle in the fading rays of light, he stretched his leathery hand across his knee and let out a small sigh.

Beneath the glittering skyline was a rot that had taken deep root. Decay was settling in the dark cracks of the world. Whispers and hushed voices. Restlessness. More than that, it was the prevailing feeling that the end was nearer than perhaps it had been since the first of humanity's starships left the original human home world of Origin. When the first travelers ventured out among the stars searching for a new place to call home. Insurrections carry on the wind like seeds, darting around just seeking a place to plant.

Is it even insurrection, though, if the true enemy is not the dissent of our minds but the devils in our blood?

"Has the time finally come?" he murmured aloud. For decades, concern for the future had driven the Imperium's leaders to this pivotal junction, a crossroads that would determine the destiny of human civilization. Events were speeding towards a resolution, one way or another.

His private council had convened to decide how best to persuade their emperor to endorse whatever scheme they'd concocted to address the threat. Soon they would meet with him to discuss Zarena Denamonte's progress on the cure. But rumors suggested the cure came at significant cost, if the whispers held any truth. Rakeus knew what to expect. The solution would be almost as dire as the disease.

Could they ever be forgiven? He chuckled bitterly. *Would forgiveness even matter anymore?*

"Has it really come to this?" he sighed, as the sun dipped below the horizon.

"Sire," a steward interrupted, jolting Rakeus from his reflections.

"Yes, Jesper?"

"The council has concluded its meeting and requests an audience to present their suggestions."

"Of course they do. Let's not keep the saviors of humanity waiting."

Rakeus stood and gathered himself up, expelling a sigh that seemed a mixed of frustration and anticipation. He smoothed his clothes with the palms of his hands, looking down at his feet for a moment before raising his head high and proud before bringing his gaze to bear on the placid and indecipherable face of Jesper.

"The council chamber awaits, your Majesty," Jesper said evenly, a hint of coolness in his tone.

"Very well. And Jesper, is my daughter with them?"

"No Sire. She is returning from a diplomatic mission to House Collette. The princess is expected back by sunset tomorrow."

"Off-world! It is not safe for her to leave the palace. Our enemies are everywhere. Even at the gates, Jesper." Rakeus looked at him anxiously. "Contact the Intercession immediately and demand her return. I will need her by my side for what is to come. The council may be wise but they are still blunt instruments. We require a more nuanced perspective on the sacrifices asked on behalf of those we aim to protect."

"Of course, Sire. I will relay your request right away." Jesper gave a slight bow then silently slipped through the portcullis into the atrium. Tall and slender, with closely cropped hair, he moved with serpentine grace, footsteps whisper-quiet on the polished marble floors. His deep brown eyes glinted with flecks of crimson in the sunlight, like the glassy stare of a viper lurking unseen in the brush.

The boy unsettled him. *You never knew where Jesper might materialize*, Rakeus thought with unease. Yet his talents have always proved useful. No one under his command was more efficient. His methods, however unsavory at times, have protected the Imperium for many years in ways most would never fathom.

Rakeus took one final look at the dazzling city as the sun sank below the horizon. He closed his eyes, picturing the sprawling capital before him and all the lives unfolding below. With a hard sigh, he opened his eyes. The path ahead would be arduous, enough to crush a weaker man beneath the weight of so many worlds, so many souls. He must remain resolute. The decisions to come would forever mark his reign, shaping the course of events for generations to come.

Hopefully to come, he thought.

As Rakeus contemplated the burden of leadership, a faint buzzing sound approached from his right. The palace was secretly protected by a PGen field, an ancient technology that existed long before the Karmarch dynasty took control of the Imperium. It was almost a novelty that they were still used as part of the Mark's defense protocols. One was installed a few years prior, as the escalating tensions began to boil over. Originally developed as a starship defense system, they used a negatively charged ion field to negate the transit of matter traveling within a certain speed threshold from passing through. They were never able to successfully miniaturize the technology, and the cost to activate them was prohibitively high. Nowadays, they are mostly used as a passive defense system for Cruiseliner starships or as fortifications for landmarks such as palaces whose occupants could afford such lavish protections. The shield was invisible to the naked eye, but prevented any object moving faster than a slow trot from penetrating. It vaporized a projectile and redirected the molecular wave of exploding atoms to divert away from the shield, keeping the inhabitants sequestered behind the field safe from fallout.

He turned his head just as a projectile slammed into the shimmering PGen field encasing the palace, detonating in a violent explosion. The blast sent concussive shockwaves through the entire palace.

Rakeus stumbled, chair skidding beneath him.

Before he could react, the Krakeis Guard surrounded him, hustling him off the terrace. Guarded on all sides, he threw his arm over his head as they briskly escorted him inside, caring more for his safety than decorum. As they hurried along, Rakeus peered back at the smoke-filled sky. Shrapnel from the explosion burned up in the protective field, which had redirected the blast's energy up and away from the palace. To Rakeus, it appeared the very world was aflame.

As he was ushered through the atrium, Jesper came bounding down a side corridor, lazgun in hand. He fell in with the phalanx of guards surrounding the emperor.

"Your Majesty! Are you harmed? I heard the detonation from within the palace."

"I'm fine, Jesper," Rakeus panted. "Let's get to the bunker. These fools have no idea what they're doing. Stunts like this are nothing more than pissing down the backs of their only hopes."

Jesper's mouth curled into a slight grin. "We're still but primates in the jungle after all. What more can be expected of us?"

Rakeus scowled. "I'm pleased you find assassination attempts so amusing. Perhaps I ought to toss you into the PGen field."

"Then who would bring you those delectable tarts you adore so?" Jesper replied somberly.

They continued on in silence through the maze of corridors toward a rust-eaten metal door at the base of the stairwell, incongruous with the surrounding opulence of the palace. As they approached, Commander Levitz, the Emperor's Chief Military Officer, radioed the guards ahead.

"We have the emperor. Open the door." With a groan of metal, the doorway slowly swung open, revealing a passage sloping down into the earth. Shadowy and dim, the tunnel was lit at intervals by sputtering electric lamps. Levitz shouted orders to his men. "Send units to the council chamber, the Councilors may be in danger. Batten down until we assess the situation."

Flanked by guards, Rakeus and Jesper entered the stairwell as the doors boomed shut behind them. Moving swiftly, they passed ancient stone carvings etched with archaic symbols lining the granite walls. These tunnels had once been used by a rebel faction that nearly toppled imperial rule, hiding under the noses of the authorities seeking to bring them to justice. After their defeat, Rakeus I constructed Kral Markhan atop their former stronghold. This moved the seat of power of House Karmarch, and thus the Imperium, from the city of Gadize on the Southern Continent to the eastern side of the great city of Kazder. Rakeus I appointed Kazder as the new capital, with The Mark standing in its shadow as a warning to all would-be revolutionaries. It was the equivalent of planting your flag in the hearthstones of your conquered enemies. The council that served Rakeus I urged him to remove the symbols in the underground corridor, fearing they were dangerous code. After his crypto team assessed they were harmless, he opted to leave them on the walls as a reminder to his heirs of the dangers of rebellion.

At the tunnel's end, sprawled into the bunker itself, sat a colossal cylindrical chamber with a diameter of eighty meters. Inside were barracks, armories, and assembly rooms encircling a central computer hub. From here the emperor could command his empire, impervious to the chaos above.

"Comm systems are online, Sire," announced Commander Levitz. "All military units await your orders."

"How grave is the threat, Commander? Are we in danger?"

"Our intelligence indicates Rakur extremists launched the attack using a X571 skid rocket with dovetails, firing from approximately 450 yards outside the northwest corner of the Palazzo de Cournia, near Kremore Plaza. They fled after firing. We have multiple units scouring the area and will soon apprehend those responsible."

"Dovetails?" Rakeus asked.

"Yes, Sire. Dovetails allow a mid-flight course correction to bypass defenses. We believe they tried to bypass the PGen field by looping the rocket in at a slower speed than the approach. They miscalculated the field's perimeter, detonating the warhead prematurely."

"Would that have allowed it to successfully penetrate the barrier?"

Levitz stiffened. "No sire, but even so, the attack was disturbingly well-coordinated for such… feral dissidents. But their efforts are meaningless. We will hang every last Rakur from the spires of Kremore, Sire."

At that moment, Levitz's radio crackled. "Sir, we've located the terrorists and are engaging. The council has been evacuated to the bunker and will join His Majesty shortly. The complex is secure, but no one should attempt to exit yet."

Rakeus took the transmitter from Levitz. "This is Emperor Rakeus. Well done. These traitors will suffer for their crime against the empire."

After a pause, the voice returned, now less steady. "Yes, Sire… they will face imperial justice."

"Keep Commander Levitz informed." Rakeus returned the radio and turned to Jesper. "Intercept the council. I want a read on the situation before we confer. It may be useful. Tread gently."

Jesper bowed. "Of course, my emperor. The old goats may be more candid with me than with you. I suspect the course of action they've come to discuss will be equal parts exciting and unpleasant to them." Jesper then bowed to Rakeus, gently cradling his arms to his chest as he did so.

As Jesper turned to leave, Rakeus called out. "Bring my daughter home, Jesper. Whatever it takes."

Jesper paused, meeting the emperor's gaze. "She will be here before sunset, Sire. You have my oath." Then, turning to Levitz, Jesper spoke coldly, but with an eerie calm that others always found unsettling. "Guard your emperor well. Should any ill befall him in my absence, you will not leave this place alive."

Without another word, Jesper turned on his heels and silently glided out into the hallway as the doors shut behind him.

CHAPTER 2
God Wants Us To Die

J esper glided silently down the dim corridor, lost in contemplation. The predicament worsens. What the council is about to propose is anyone's guess, but Jesper had an inkling he already knew. Archlon has not endured *the affliction* as long as many of the outer worlds. Most of the smug old crones reside in The Mark, and many have not departed the palace in years. The few who have usually embarked for diplomatic reasons and are off-world attending stately feasts with one of the Great Houses, never venturing farther than the interior. It's more dire on the fringe. The plights there progress faster.

Perhaps it correlates to the water, he mulled. Typically, the fringe worlds don't utilize the same level of sophisticated purification. *Maybe the quality of the water accelerated it, coupled with coarser living conditions and less wholesome nutrition.*

He nearly cracked a smile as he pondered the various rationales. It's impossible to ascertain, beyond the feeble speculation of puffed-up academics and thinkers. It's as if the fate of the human race was to conclude as such. Like a fail-safe mechanism embedded in our DNA, limiting the duration of our civilization. Our very own meteorite, like the ones that annihilated the grand lizards of Origin. History is an endless cycle of demise and brutality, but perhaps the universe had decided it was time for the loop to finally close. Not that it mattered, of course. Jesper served the Imperium, and the Imperium was mankind. History would persist on his watch.

As he neared the door at the corridor's end, it started to open. Through the door, he saw a small platoon of armed guards, positioned in various locales around the atrium. Two particularly bulky guards stood on either side of the door. They barely acknowledged him as he passed, their eyes peering straight ahead, weapons clutched tightly at their sides. The atrium was a massive hexagonal edifice carved nearly entirely from marble and bedecked with gold and silver garlands that stretched up four stories to the passageway linking the Cournia. A colossal spiral staircase descended each floor from the eastern entrance. Gardens and hedge art were scattered across the bottom floor, interspersed with marble statues, most of them the Emperors of the Karmarch dynasty.

He observed the councilors descending the stairs with an armed escort. Four of them were men in their 60s and each wore a petite silver crown adorned with gilded golden leaves. They were mostly stale crusts of bread, sycophants who obeyed the Emperor without providing the necessary counterbalance demanded of their office. The other two were women.

The shorter of the two was Madame Kaia Dorsetta. Kaia was a woman in her fifties, short and slight of build with raven hair and a tan complexion, wearing an ivory robe with a gilded sash. Her round face smiled pleasantly as she walked, the ornate gold spiral earrings she wore swinging from side to side with each step.

The taller one was Madame Zarena Denamonte. Zarena was tall, with slender arms and legs, and hair the color of deep auburn with subtle natural highlights, so at certain angles her hair appeared almost blond. Her face was softly framed around the wisp of her swaying hair. Her skin was caramel and her eyes were a lovely shade of bright brown with barely perceptible flecks of gold, which complimented her delicate features. Zarena was attired in a similar fashion to Kaia Dorsetta and was by far the youngest of the group. The most juvenile councilor in recorded history, in fact. She became a councilor at age twenty-eight, after a distinguished academic vocation in neurobiology and engineering, in which she developed computational neural networks for martial applications. Now at thirty-six, she unofficially spearheaded the council on affairs of The Sequence and pioneered the devising of countermeasures. You might say Denamonte was the architect of the Imperium's salvation. She was also the bosom companion of Princess Raeka.

Thinking of Princess Raeka, he reached into a buttoned pocket on his vest and extracted a comm. He raised it to his ear and muttered in a hushed voice, "This is Jesper, the Emperor enjoined me to patch a message through to General Hausier. Princess Raeka is to be summoned home immediately. Her father requires her to attend him presently."

A response reverberated from the other end and Jesper uttered, "See to it then" and returned the comm to his pocket.

As he did this, the councilors reached the bottom level. As Jesper sauntered toward the entourage, they saw him approach and stopped walking. With an affable smile, he bowed to the councilors, and they nodded their heads in reciprocation.

"Your graces, I'm relieved that the council is unharmed after the morning's festivities."

"Thank you, Jesper, I'm equally relieved that you seem well after this entire unpleasant affair. Were you on the Cournia when the assault occurred?" Zarena inquired in a conversational tone.

"I was within proximity at the time. I rushed back to the balcony, but the Guard had already secured His Majesty. I accompanied him to the bunker with Commander Levitz, after which he requested that I intercept you and escort you down."

"I see," remarked Zarena. She seemed constrained today. Preoccupied with the tasks ahead. The other councilors sauntered in silence, either wholly disinterested in their discussion or at least feigning it.

"Is there something you wish to know, Jesper, before we convene with His Highness?" Zarena uttered, matter-of-factly.

"Not in the slightest, Madame Denamonte. Today's proceedings have imparted in us all a few bees buzzing around our heads, no doubt. If I wished to ask you something, I'm confident I would just ask you, my Lady."

She's impatient to convene with Rakeus. Her exterior is composed, but underneath there's a nervousness. They are endeavoring to lead us down the garden path after all, thought Jesper.

As they neared the door, Jesper circled around Zarena's flank and shuffled past the armed guards to stride in front of the group. The guards merely grunted as Jesper slipped past them. The party proceeded in silence the remainder of the way down the dimly illuminated passage until they reached the central bunker. Jesper sauntered through the bunker doors first and immediately caught Rakeus' eye. He maneuvered his right arm up steadily to the lapel of his vest, gently touched the collar and slid his hand down the front in a smoothing gesture. Rakeus flash an imperceptible wince only Jesper noticed. He comprehended the message.

"Greetings, my friends," Rakeus said to the company as they drew near. They reciprocated the salutation with a profound, ceremonial bow. Rakeus bestowed them a benevolent smile, and said, "Thank you for arriving here, under these circumstances. Unfortunately, what we accomplish here today may be the only prospect we possess to save the Imperium, and with it, all of human existence. This could not linger a moment longer."

Since Jesper had departed and returned, a circular table had been situated in the center of the comm room. The Emperor gestured for everyone to be seated as he assumed his chair.

Jesper bowed to the Emperor and declared, "Your majesty, if you require anything, I will be in the barracks." He sauntered through the door and Rakeus shouted after him.

"You may wish to avoid Commander Levitz, he didn't embrace your menace lightly." "Neither did I, Your Majesty".

"Remain on standby until I summon you". With that, Jesper relinquished the council to its task.

"My friends," persisted Rakeus. "We all know why we are here. Today's proceedings further prove the jeopardy we are all in. The hazard not only to us but to the Imperium as a whole. Since my predecessors' initial discovery of The Sequence, our biologists, geneticists, neuroscientists, and sociologists have been toiling in secrecy to uncover a cure. Since that time, the decay has proliferated.

More of the population has activated. Violence, abuse, jeopardy, and turbulence is widespread in the outer system. We have reached the boiling point. If humanity does not discover an answer to this abomination, we will enter a crucible that we will not emerge from. What we accomplish here today dangles the fate of our world in the balance. I am aware that you all have taken the matter as gravely as I have. We now must discuss serious solutions. Time is expiring. For all of us."

The council sat mutely, their visages resolute, as the Emperor spoke. After he finished, there were a few moments of silence. The councilors all swiveled to face Madame Dorsetta. She surveyed her colleagues with a wan expression.

Kaia Dorsetta appeared to have matured several years in the duration of a few minutes. She mildly cleared her throat and uttered, "Your Majesty, here is what we are aware of: the genetic mutation, codenamed The Sequence, first materialized in human DNA approximately 67 years ago, though that was simply when it was first identified by Imperial scientists. In actuality, it may have appeared much further back. The allele responsible for The Sequence is encoded as X217. A typical gene is composed of a regulatory system, which is customarily accountable for activating and deactivating the gene's transcription. This is accomplished at precise intervals during development, and the coding region filters out the potential for anomalies. In this instance, the intended function of the gene failed, you could say." She looked around the room at their stern faces, listening intently to every word. Taking a short breathe, she continued.

"This specific gene underwent a point mutation, severing it into a mutated gene with previously unseen coding. Essentially, the mutation lies dormant, and in the majority at least, does not activate. Activation is characterized by a surge in testosterone, cortisol, sentiments of anger, aggression, a predilection for violence and, in some cases, extreme fury. Subjects who become activated still retain their cognitive facilities. the reason centers of their brains that differentiate right from wrong, but many times cannot adhere to a system of logic or reason. They become effortlessly agitated, distraught, and most dangerously perhaps, paranoid.

"To exacerbate matters, there are some unprecedented attributes to the mutation that have rendered it virtually impossible to eliminate. Things we've, well, frankly have never witnessed before," she said with clear exasperation. "These are the most vital and confounding obstacles. First and foremost, every single living human possesses the mutation. Mutations usually impact a minor subset of a species' population. In this case, we have absolute, one hundred percent adoption. We all have it. Every one of us. Nothing like this has ever been witnessed before."

She hesitated for a lingering moment, before continuing less assuredly as before. "As if that weren't enough, the gene appears entirely immune to manipulation therapies. Our geneticists have discovered that the gene cannot be redacted through cloning or any other variety of genetic manipulation. It can't be expunged, and it can't be altered. We utilized a genetic cleansing process, akin to chemotherapy, to eradicate the mutation in an activated host. It is possible to completely eliminate it from a code sequence. But..." and with that Madame Dorsetta trailed off.

Rakeus, his demeanor impenetrable, uttered sternly, "But what, Kaia?"

"It returns, Sire." Silence befell the room. After a few heartbeats, Rakeus enunciated, "What returns?"

"The gene, Your Eminence. It reappears. The mutation springs up again in another allele, another mutated gene. And it's not always the same secondary gene. There is no way to halt it. It's as if...". She trailed off and looked down at her hands pensively.

"As if what, Kaia?"

"As if God wants us to die."

CHAPTER 3
It's Merely Its Nature

The Emperor chuckled. It was a peculiar and unsettling sound.

"We abandoned the archaic convictions for this very reason, Kaia. Only we, above all species, are the masters of our fate. We've never encountered another form of life with our reason, intellect, and capacity for knowledge. And you are going to be seated here and inform me that, unfortunately, it's *just our time?*"

"Your Majesty, the reason, intellect, and capacity for knowledge that distinguishes humanity is the very thing that is being imperiled. Torn apart from within. There is no question in my mind that we are maybe one generation away from total chaos, possibly less. A breakdown of government, of production, of travel, of commerce. Entire planets will begin to succumb. Technological and scientific progress will ultimately come to a standstill. The Great Houses will collapse, and the Imperium will no longer be able to maintain order, severed from the rest of the worlds and that's if we survive.

"Sire, there was an attempt on your life just this morning. Not much is being uttered about it, but I have an inkling this is the closest the insurgents have ever come to you. What if they had prevailed? Your daughter is apparently off-world, there would have no continuity in the chain of command, The Mark would have been in complete disarray. The Imperium could have begun to fall this very day.

"The days to come will be worse. Estimates for the activation of The Sequence is around 4% of the population of Archlon. You've seen the footage; riots in the streets, uprisings. There is even word you've had to supplant some of your military personnel and palace guard because of a few errant activations. Archlon, by all accounts, is the most secure planet in the system. Estimates from our scientists in the outer worlds are even more dire, with 6 to 7% of the population already activated. The last census positioned the population of the Imperium around five hundred and fifty billion. At even a 4% conversion, we are talking about twenty-two billion affected at present. That's almost twice the size of Archlon. Assuming that the gene entered the human population sixty-seven years ago, though I believe that's an incorrect estimate, it could signify that we are looking at a total system-wide collapse potentially within the decade."

The dim light flickered overhead, casting elongated shadows across the table. The Emperor and the Council sat motionless, their faces drawn and tense. At first, silence reigned, broken only by the distant hum of the air filtration system. Eyes darted from one person to another, suspicion and frustration mounting with each passing second. Fingers drummed anxiously on the scarred wood. Artis shifted in his seat, his jaw clenched tight. Zarena arrowed her eyes, arms folded defensively, but said nothing. The air felt thick with unspoken accusations and mounting impatience, each glance exchanged sharper than the last. In the close quarters of the bunker, vexation simmered, threatening to boil over. No one dared even so much as a glance in the direction of the Emperor. Kaia, pretending not to notice the sullen change in atmosphere, resumed speaking.

"These numbers, of course, are uncertain. We can't be certain if all the quote unquote "affected" are experiencing side effects from the mutation triggering, or if they are simply joining the bandwagon of revolution. Information about The Sequence is being leaked everywhere despite our best efforts. The population is aware that there is some existential menace, some unknown illness that causes a form of insanity. There are myths and legends already surrounding the outbreaks. There are also some profoundly disturbing reports of House Militia secretly executing those they suspect of being "infected". Most planetary authorities believe that it is an airborne illness. Few have even considered the possibility the threat is in their blood. If that information were disclosed, we could be talking about endless panic and riots and brutality."

Dorsetta and Rakeus were acquainted for many years, and the Emperor could depend on Kaia to give him an honest assessment. Still, the bleakness in her words stung everyone present.

She continued.

"Many affected believe we were the ones to engineer this sickness. The typical fringe conviction is that we created a pathogen that manifests fear and violence as a means of control. Countless people believe this madness. The paranoid has begun to influence the sane. What I'm saying is that this epidemic may be morphing from the purely physical into a social nightmare. There are reports that even some Great Houses are starting to suspect we are behind this. There may even be attempts to secede from the Imperium. Fortunately, most of them fear a direct conflict with House Karmarch. Our fleets, troops, and weaponry exceed the entirety of all the Great Houses combined. But they don't need to attack us head on. Most of them are juggling skirmishes and civil unrest on their own worlds. They don't have the time or the resources to mount a direct offensive, but that means we may not be able to rely on them for support. The weaker we get, the simpler it will be for the survivors to pick us off. Scavenge our bones like crows. All they have to do is attempt to secure their holdings and withhold support from us. A pivotal time will come where if enough of them turn on us, we'll be sitting ducks, severed from the rest of the empire. At that point, they might get brazen enough to come at us head on, but by that point, we might have already succumbed."

The last of her words lingered in the air. Rakeus just gazed at her, his stare cold. The crows feet around his eyes started to narrow. He peered around the table. Each councilor was perched there, pensively surveying each other, going from face to face, uncertain what to say or do next.

Rakeus had enough.

He arose and inhaled deeply. It was all he could do from slaughtering them all. Right here. He contemplated it for a second too long. His right hand casually touched the side of his robes. Underneath, he could feel the hilt of his lazblade. He could use it to slice through these simpletons like butter with a warm knife. The urge was so intense he immediately started to wonder if his mutation had activated. His mind raced a bit as he thought back through his past few days, his emotions, his thoughts. He had been in control, in as much control as he has always exerted. No, this was just fury. Like being angry at fire when it's dwindled to nothing more than dying embers. It's not the fire's fault, it consumes all it touches, then fades. It's merely its nature.

At least a portion of this must have materialized on Rakeus' face. He peered around the table and nothing but wide eyes riddled with trepidation peered back at him. They were frightened, genuinely frightened. This was not helping matters.

He straightened his vest with the palm of his hand, and positioned his hand to the bridge of his nose and closed his eyes. Rakeus rolled his neck in a stretching gesture and sat down again. He didn't make any sudden moves.

Once seated he exhaled a long, frustrated sigh then uttered, "I'm sorry my friends. Our situation is dire, as the esteemed Madame Dorsetta has explained to us in her very rousing oration about the end of days. We have the finest minds from across the galaxy toiling on this day and night. I believe she's right of course. A collapse is imminent, and maybe sooner than we are prepared for."

Rakeus had heard quite enough of the doom. He was promised a solution.

"In all your assessment, Councilor Dorsetta, there was not a single word to explain the solution I had been promised. In fact, you stated, quite plainly, that there is no way to halt this pandemic. No way at all. Is that correct?"

Kaia shot a furtive glance over to Zarena, who was perched stoned faced in the seat nearest the Emperor.

"No, there must be another choice," she said aloud and to no one in particular.

Her words dripped with exasperation, the weariness of the moment weighing her down like lead. She avoided Zarena's probing gaze, fixing her eyes on the polished marble floor.

"No, Sire, there is something. It's just…" and she looked around at her peers before continuing, "more complicated than we anticipated."

"Complicated, how?"

Dorsetta was interrupted by the high, clear voice of Zarena Denamonte, who finished the thought for her.

"The solution is ready, it's just there are side effects, your majesty."

Rakeus sat silently. They expected him to start asking questions, but instead he just sat there, waiting.

"Your Majesty, as you know, the other councilors and I have been working on strategies to counteract The Sequence for years and what we've accomplished was built on the backs of those before us. The Imperium has been trying to understand and ultimately repair The Sequence for decades. After countless hours of research, testing and trial and error, we have come to the conclusion that was so eloquently expressed by Madame Dorsetta. There is no way to cure The Sequence genetically. It seems to be a kill switch of sorts that was baked into our earliest genetic code, waiting for the day it would wake and send us into an age of despair. I know that it sounds like we are ascribing it to some erroneous religious plague, something sent forth by an ancient God to humble his children. We speak of it like that because, well, no one has ever seen anything like it. Ever. Not one of our brightest minds can crack its code. It's natural selection simply making its selection. I believe that perhaps it was never meant to be solved. And it hasn't been. But…"

"But *what*, Zarena?"

"But, it can be bypassed."

"Bypassed? Bypassed how?"

"It's a new branch of science. We call it Cognitive Harmonization. It's founded on a basic principle; the brain functions as the control center of the body and the central processing center of the mind is imbued with certain failsafes. Protections that can be, shall we say, unlocked? Harnessing these firewalls may allow us to short circuit the desires of our genes, or at least prevent them from realizing their goal. Specifically in the instance of The Sequence, a technique has been developed that rewrites the brainwaves of an individual, triggering a series of countermeasures that seem to entirely offset The Sequence's effects. Reduction in testosterone, cortisol, as well as reduction of parasympathetic stimulation, lowering of heart rate, and blood pressure. Essentially full reversal in activated individuals, regardless of how far into the mutation they are. It also acts as a prophylactic. It prevents activation in non-affected patients. It doesn't cure the mutation, mind you, but it bypasses the mutation to cure the symptoms."

"How successful is this process?"

"In all of our trials, we have found it to have nearly 100% efficacy. We've yet to encounter an individual during our testing that was immune to the process. However, the margin for error we are reporting is approximately .0001%. So, efficacy is expected to be about 99.9999%."

"How would we implement it?"

"We've created a device that can spread it in mass distribution. The process relies on the manipulation of harmonic frequencies, which radiate out from the device. Within a certain perimeter, every single person who is within range experiences a tonal shift in the patterns of their brain. The device is silent, the targets unaware what's even happening to them. It can be deployed with the utmost discretion and, as far as we can tell, the effects are irreversible. The patient stays cured indefinitely. We don't know what the genetic markers may be, whether the immunity will pass from generation to generation. We can say that if it is implemented on a wide scale, it would eradicate The Sequence from this generation."

"To use your religious analogies, it sounds as if we have been bestowed a miracle."

Madame Dorsetta spoke up again. "It's not quite that simple, Your Majesty. The process, though miraculous, has certain side effects. Severe side effects."

"What kind of side effects?"

"Well, it seems like the process doesn't just cancel The Sequence, it reverses it in the other direction. Successfully immunized subjects become docile, compliant. They will occasionally struggle with independent action or the ability to produce independent thoughts. Their personalities become malleable, weaker. In some cases, they lose their ability to self actualize. Essentially, they become like cattle, easy to herd. As far as their brain functions go, they more or less retain normal brain states, but there are changes to the parietal lobe, the amygdala, and the pathways between the amygdala and the hypothalamus, specifically the way they transmit aggression. It's as if the aggression impulse becomes entirely muted."

It was impossible to tell what Rakeus was thinking. He just sat there impassively.

Finally, he said, "How is that a problem? We would be ensuring the safety of billions. Would the population still be able to work? Would we be able to maintain our infrastructures? Could the Imperium still operate if everyone was subjected to this treatment?"

"Well, in a word, yes," Zarena responded. "The treatment does not remove the innate survival drives, or many of the instincts we've evolved over several millennia. Self-preservation is still prioritized in decision-making. The subjects have full use of their reason faculties. They feel pain, love, joy…"

"But not anger?"

"No, anger and rage, including all violent inclinations, simply disappear. They don't process them."

"So, we would be creating a utopia?" Rakeus smirked, a fire lit under his eyes.

"I don't know if that's what we could call it, Sire," said Dorsetta. "We would be making an empire of happy children. No anger sounds like a dream, but in reality it may be much different than we hope."

"I'm not certain I follow your concern, Kaia".

"We're taking away their free will, Your Majesty. We would be fundamentally changing the human condition, rewriting ourselves in ways that are hard to predict. Ways that may benefit the Imperium but disadvantage all of its people. We'd be taking away *choice*." Kaia Dorsetta sounded exasperated. She could feel Zarena's eyes on her, but she didn't meet them.

"Yes, it's true that humanity is faced with a biological crisis it can't cure. But this, Your Majesty? This… treatment, well, it wouldn't be a cure. Not really. We would be fundamentally changing humanity, possibly forever. We're talking about the annihilation of the human identity. No one would be who they are any longer."

"Would they be happy, Kaia? Would the treatment remove their pain, their fear, their desperation?"

"Yes."

"But your concerns are ethical ones? You fear that by saving humanity, by changing it even to save it from itself, somehow makes all people less than?"

"No, sire, not 'less than.' But maybe not exactly people anymore, either."

Rakeus seemed to take the concern seriously. He turned to the councilor sitting to Dorsetta's left, Elias Ardenot, n aging man, with thinning hair, in the customary formal wear of a councilor of the Imperium. "Master Ardenot. What are your thoughts on the matter?"

Ardenot gathered himself up a bit and said, "I share councilor Dorsetta's concerns, Your Eminence."

"Indeed. Does everyone agree with Madame Dorsetta?"

As he asked this, he looked at the faces of each councilor in turn, every one responding with a solemn nod of agreement. All but Madame Denamonte, who sat silently.

"I see." Rakeus let out a thin breath. A few moments passed, The length of a handful of heartbeats. Rakeus was about to speak when Councilor Ardenot suddenly spoke again.

"It doesn't mean it isn't necessary, Sire. However distasteful this may be, whatever price we may pay, we are frankly out of options. There is no way I can see to save the Imperium, to save humanity, without using Madame Denamonte's treatment. I've seen the results, Sire. Yes, people are changed, but the changes in almost all cases seem to be positive. It can simplify the mind, but it can also free people from their burdens. They may need more guidance, more support, more resources than they did. It may be harder to take care of themselves, of others. The alternative, however, is death. For some, a quick death. For most, a long and painful demise as the very pillars of our civilization collapse around them. When faced with the potential extinction of the human race, by its own hand no less, it's not really a choice at all."

"Yes, humanity faces an incurable biological crisis that threatens our very survival", Kaia interjected forcefully. "But this proposed 'treatment,' Your Majesty, is no panacea. It would irrevocably transform humanity, obliterating the essence of our identity. We risk annihilating the human spirit itself."

"You fear that in rescuing humanity, even changing our nature to spare us from oblivion, we sacrifice our souls?" asked Rakeus. It was a genuine question; there was no trace of ridicule in his voice.

"Not sacrifice, Your Eminence. But we may no longer be truly human anymore."

"Very well." Rakeus exhaled thinly. He pondered for a moment all that had been said. Finally he asked, "does this solution have a name?"

Madame Denamonte said, "Sire, we refer to the project by its codename. It's called The Harmony."

CHAPTER 4
The Harmony

"So, there's a way to prevent exposure to the treatment?" said Rakeus, the weight of the day's discussions bearing down on him like an anchor.

They had been cloistered in this oppressive bunker for endless hours debating how such an outrageous plan could possibly come to fruition. Rakeus was starting to wilt under the unrelenting talk, but their work was far from finished. So much more still needed to be done.

He shifted in his chair, the hard metal digging into his back.

"Yes, sire, the dampening devices need to be implanted in the ear canal," explained Zarena, her voice strained from the marathon discussion. "It absorbs the frequencies emitted by The Harmony like a sponge, acting as a barrier between the sound waves and the person. Once The Harmony activates, the dampener may cause disorientation, a swirling vertigo, but the side effects only linger for a few minutes. After The Harmony stops transmitting and the dampener is removed, the user returns to normal," she continued, "though it can induce drowsiness."

"Sire, we've thought of every countermeasure conceivable. This is the easiest and most elegant solution," said councilor Earham.

Markus Earham was sitting next to Rakeus on the side opposite of Zarena. Mark Earham was short and round, with a pleasant face that looked like a tan rug stretched across his wide cheekbones, and wrinkled with the weathered lines of a man who spent his life in service of others. His hair was always slightly tousled, which stood in sharp contrast to the impeccably tailored garments he wore. Rakeus always considered Earham to be a mouse of a man, timid and placating. Tiny in the ways some of his other esteemed colleagues loomed large, but Rakeus insisted he had his uses. If Earham, with all his skepticism at novel ideas, was comfortable enough to put this damn thing on his head, then it probably was as safe and easy as Zarena made it sound.

"And there is no risk to the user?" probed Rakeus.

"Correct, apart from the accompanying nausea, it's completely safe and entirely effective." Zarena's confidence oozed with every word.

Rakeus admired her steadfast belief in her audacious plan to halt The Sequence. Yet as he pressed her with question after question, the more he secretly feared this *Harmony* embodied every single gut-wrenching decision every Emperor ever had to face combined.

"Would we even need to inoculate the military forces?" Rakeus asked. Everyone just stared at him quietly. No one had even considered the alternative. Rakeus continued.

"Without the unending need to protect us, without the threat of future wars, would we even require a military? Perhaps a smaller peace keeping force is all that would be required."

Councilor Ardenot spoke, "Sire, despite the attraction of shrinking our military force, the reality is we have no way of knowing what threats we may face in the future. If something goes wrong, the Imperium needs to be ready."

"I suppose you're right, Elias. Best not to leave ourselves vulnerable. But it may be difficult to control them if we don't inoculate them. What if a Commander activates and turns on us? We could be in danger of The Sequence backfiring if we leave too large a force."

Rakeus contemplated this a moment. He was uneasy about diminishing the military in any capacity, let alone during the crisis they faced. Still, keeping a military force of hundreds of thousands from receiving The Harmony could work to undo all the precautions they were taking now. Maybe there was a compromise? Dorsetta had been quiet for a while. Rakeus thought that perhaps now was a suitable time to engage her.

"Kaia, what do you think about the military problem? Do you have any ideas on how best to approach it?"

Kaia hadn't expected to be called on. Still, she was prepared for anything. "Sire, the best course of action may be to find a middle ground. Take your most loyal men. A handful of squadrons, comprised of the most elite forces. Have them subjected to regular testing and continuous monitoring. We'd be looking for any symptoms that coincide with known Sequence triggers, which admittedly are scant. The ones with the highest risk should be immediately removed from service and inoculated with The Harmony.

This force should be trained to man all of our most advanced weaponry. We will need to rely on small, elite teams that can access our full array of weapons. That way, if there are complications during the process then we stand ready to provide a military response. The remainder of the forces should be subjected to The Harmony and given their discharge. Perhaps some of them can be evaluated for duty. Suitable ones may still be able to provide assistance in maintenance and mechanical repair. The rest can retire to civilian life. Once all the Imperial worlds are harmonized, the need to fight will be eliminated. That is the point of The Harmony. To eliminate anger, aggression, paranoia, and the associated violence most of all. What need will we have for instruments of war?"

One of the other councilors, Artis Fermonte, was speaking with Elias in a private sidebar. Artis was a tall, thin man, with a crooked pointy nose, and sharp ears. His complexion was like a cream colored paste, as if his pale skin was always moist from sweat or doused with a spritz of misty water from a spout. Most of his colleagues thought he looked like a bird, though no one would ever be so disrespectful as to point it out.

The group had moved from the comm room to a lounge area in the barracks, where there were more comfortable accommodations. The lounge was lit more dimly than the comm room, the walls a ruddy mud color. There were several large brown couches upholstered with animal skin and cushions made of feather down. Small serving tables littered the room and there was a circular dining table near the corner. Artwork on the walls depicted previous battles, exalting the glory of the Karmarch dynasty. Artis, concluding his conversion with Elias, began another surreptitious chat with Earham while while Kaia opined about the military to Zarena and the other councilors.

"…Maybe a medium-sized force would be better," said councilor Alfonse Cornado to Kaia and Zarena. "I don't see the point of creating unnecessary risks, My Lord," said Kaia. "We should prepare for peace, not waste resources on a hypothetical war that will almost certainly never come," said Zarena, with an exasperation building over hours of debate.

As the conversations continued, it was Artis Fermonte, who had to this point contributed nothing of value apart from agreement and support, who shot the first arrow.

"What about the Great Houses?" said Artis.

Everyone stopped and looked at him. No one had expected him to speak up. The Emperor turned his head and looked at Artis.

"What *about* the Great Houses?"

"Why would we need them anymore?" asked Artis. He was surprisingly confident with such a bold assertion, and that piqued Rakeus' interest.

"I'm not sure whether I follow you, Artis. The Great Houses have been an integral cog in the Imperial machine since the early days of the Empire. It wasn't always House Karmarch that ruled the Imperium. The Great House entrusted us with their future when they elected House Karmarch as House Imperiatus after the Cornastre Rebellion centuries ago. We have always repaid that faith."

"But, it has been mentioned repeatedly that ending war is the point of The Harmony. With all the worlds Harmonized, there will be no need for the Houses. A governor from House Karmarch could be installed on each world to maintain order, whatever little that may entail. If we include the Great Houses in this debate, it could rage on for much longer than we want. Maybe for longer than we have. Not all of them may consent. What if one or more of them oppose us? It could create further conflict, during which time millions of more lives may be lost."

"What would you suggest, Artis?"

All the voices quieted. Artis stood up from the couch he was sitting on with Elias and spoke to the room.

"I am suggesting that we do not include the Great Houses in our plan to unleash The Harmony on all Imperial worlds. Instead, I believe the safest course of action would be to allow all the members of the Great Houses to be harmonized. Their leadership, their staff, their military forces, their doctors, their warriors, even their gardeners. Everyone. Allow them to experience the Emperor's peace first hand; live out their lives, free of troubles and worries, free of the burdens of ruling. We must start to think of what the universe will look like once we've enacted this plan. The Great Houses would no longer serve a purpose. Perhaps it's best to keep them in the dark and eliminate their threat along with all other threats to the Empire." He tapped his foot at the end, to emphasize his point.

"So we should repay our allies with treachery?"

"No, Sire." This time it was Zarena. "We repay them with unending peace."

"We would be repaying them the same way a butcher repays the obedience of cattle. If we are going to do such a thing, it's best not to pretend, even to ourselves."

"No one is pretending, Sire. We are taking away their choice in the matter. Everyone's choice, if we are to avoid pretending. But humanity has had the power of choice for ten thousand years, and what did it give us? It led us to this."

Rakeus only wanted to feel like the weightiest verdict of his rule was not a hopeless dilemma, that there could be hope in the aftermath. Zarena's self-assurance placated his concerns more than any of the others could. She wholeheartedly believed in her work and the lives it would spare. Such unwavering faith can be contagious, and they desperately needed that kind of solace in these dark times.

The debate continued on as they hammered out the minutiae. Rakeus watched Zarena intently, noting the glint of excitement in her eyes when she spoke of her creation. He knew the excitement was not for what they planned to do, but for the chance to see her life's work implemented on such a grand scale. For giving humanity a sliver of hope amidst encroaching doom.

As the hours dragged on, the fluorescent lights above flickered erratically, buzzing like an angry hive. The stale recycled air of the bunker clung to Rakeus' skin, making him yearn for a breeze. He shifted again on the rigid chair, wincing as it bit into his thighs. The spartan barracks lounge offered no relief for his aching joints after being confined for so long.

Rakeus scrutinized Zarena's face, noting the dark circles under her eyes and the worry lines that creased her forehead. Even her normally tidy auburn hair was beginning to look disheveled after the lengthy debate. Her confident facade was starting to show cracks under the pressure. She was a coiled spring, ready to burst.

When she finally spoke again, desperation tinged her typically composed voice. "It's already lost, Your Majesty. Human civilization will crumble. We cannot stop it or even delay it. The 'when' hardly matters. The Sequence has beaten us. We are mutants, all. There is only one path forward where our civilization can hope to endure. Only one that we can foresee, Sire."

Her somber words hung ominously in the air.

Kaia Dorsetta shattered the uncomfortable silence, her pragmatism rising above the oppressive gloom. "This is the lesser of two great evils. Inaction is a death sentence. The Harmony, however flawed, is a more merciful end than what nature has in store for us."

Rakeus surveyed the faces of each council member, seeing his own sorrow reflected back at him. "So it is your belief that inaction would only quicken our demise?"

"Yes, Your Eminence," Kaia replied bluntly. "Eventually The Sequence will overtake too many and nothing can stop the inevitable. The Harmony is our only chance of survival, however slim."

Rakeus fixed his penetrating gaze on Zarena Denamonte, his eyes boring into hers with laser-like intensity. "Speak to me as if your life hangs by a gossamer thread. Is there truly no other path forward?"

Zarena met his stare unflinchingly, her voice smooth as silk. "There is no other way, Your Majesty."

Rakeus let out a resigned sigh, the weight of it all pressing down on his chest. "So be it. I will not make this choice alone. We shall take a vote, and each accept the consequences."

One by one the council cast their votes, voices heavy with regret. When all had spoken, Rakeus solemnly intoned, "The die is cast. May the universe show us mercy for what we've done here today."

His words echoed through the bunker like a funeral dirge, underscoring the bitter resignation all present felt. There was no celebration, only mournful acceptance of their fate.

"How shall we proceed, Zarena?"

"The Harmony devices can be deployed soon. With ninety-seven worlds in the Imperium, I estimate we'll need one hundred and thirty in total. To minimize retribution risks, they must be activated simultaneously regardless of local time.

"We must prepare our forces to synchronize The Harmony across planets. And we'll need an ample number of dampeners. It's a massive undertaking, but working day and night we can be ready in one hundred days."

"Make it happen, Zarena. I expect daily reports. Now go, all of you."

They bowed formally, arms across their chest, and departed. As the meeting concluded, the comm room radio crackled to life. "Sire, Princess Raeka's ship will arrive within the hour."

"Thank you, Jesper." Rakeus turned to Zarena. "You should greet her in the hangar. Best if this comes from you first."

"Of course, Your Majesty." Zarena hurried off towards the bunker exit.

CHAPTER 5
You Have To Run

The rosy fingers of dawn crept over the rolling fields of Eden, scattering dappled sunlight across the swaying stalks of wheat. Eden was as provincial a planet as any in the Imperium, just a simple mining colony until its brackish marshes were found to contain vital nutrients that seeped into the soil. Soon it became a critical outpost for farming, with corn, maize, beans, rice, wheat and more blanketing the plains of this little world.

Hydroponic stations grew edible plants in aquatic environments, recycling the nutrients to fertilize more delicate crops. Most of the Imperium's staple grains were grown on Eden, and planets like Archlon relied on it to help feed their massive populations. Transport ships left daily from the central hub of Saldana, ferrying goods to ports across the empire. For centuries, Eden had sustained the Imperium with its bounty, the fertile land never lying fallow. Thanks to agricultural innovations, it may have grown more verdant than when its richness was first tapped.

Each day on Eden was like the last. Most inhabitants worked the farms, factories and plants, or shipped the crops off-world. All were cogs in the machine that produced the Imperium's vital foodstuffs. And the Imperium didn't just rely on Eden's crops, but also its fuels and textiles from agricultural byproducts. Eden was known for its bright lavender skies, sunrises of rose gold and sunsets of deep amethyst. Dense oxygen in the atmosphere refracted the bright sunlight in violet hues, bathing the land in twilight beauty. For outworlders, as beautiful as the rose-colored sunrises were, Eden's dusky sunsets were the true marvel to behold. Even lifelong residents would pause in wonder at the peaceful transition between day and night. It was perhaps the only thing it had in common with a place like Archlon.

At least that's what Evard Roost thought as he sat in a hovercraft idling on a dusty road amidst endless seas of corn.

Evard was a lanky young man, with straight dark hair long enough to muss sloppily around the edges of face. He was lean but toned from working the fields. His face was the color of cream with reddish sunburns across his cheeks and brow. His eyes were a deep mahogany brown and his smile, a vestige of his childhood that plastered across his round face, could beam like the sun when the mood struck him. He ran an idle hand through his hair, letting it fall like feathers around his head.

"Should be just down this row. Maybe two rows down and one across. There's a sign by it," sighed Evard to his partner Jecab.

"Got it. I'll be back soon. I'll comm you when I find the condenser," Jecab replied.

The hovercraft dipped as he jumped out, his boots thudding on the ground below. No need to lower the ladder for such a quick stop. He strode through the rows of corn to find the condenser stationed in a bare patch of land, its lid agape.

"Found it, Ev. Lid's open so something might've gotten in. I'll take a look," he said over the comm.

"Sounds good. Holler if you need me. Otherwise, I'm gonna catch up on some sleep," Evard chuckled. "Not that you'll need help you're the condenser wizard around here."

He grinned and reclined his seat, eyes closing as he rested his head back. It was too early for him to be out in the fields. Their shift started before dawn, though most days they finished by midday when the sun began to beat down and dew-kiss the land. Unfortunately, he had an inkling today would be a long one.

As his mind wandered, the fields of crops stretched endlessly in all directions. Just another day in paradise. He stretched his lanky frame, the frayed ends of his dark mop of hair bobbing with the motion. His mother always said he'd be a *holovid* star if he just gained some weight and muscle. He usually responded by flipping her off with a grin and heading to the bar with friends—smoking, drinking and chatting up the handful of pretty migrant worker girls in town for the season. None ever stuck around long, the relentless rains of the wet season eventually chasing them off-world until the next harvest. But life was good enough on Eden, or so he told himself, when the loneliness crept in. With his family all holding down solid jobs they lived better than most out here in the wetlands. This backwater planet was good for them, he reassured himself, as if repeating it often enough would make it true.

He knew he'd never leave Eden. He figured he'd find some local girl to marry, work the fields and have a few kids to repeat the cycle. It wasn't glamorous but it was honest. There were worse fates than boredom and small town life. The wider universe was changing, and fast. Word of some new disease was spreading — a sickness that turned people feral. Rumors said it afflicted an old man in the next settlement. They had to shoot him dead in order to stop him. Evard didn't know if it was true — gossip thrived out here — but the idea was chilling.

Just then, Jecab's voice crackled over the comm. "Ev, someone's trying to reach you from the home station. Patching it through."

"Sure, patch 'em through," Evard replied, confused.

"Evard, it's Willet Fog. How are you, son?" said the gruff voice.

"Hi, Mr. Fog, I'm fine. What can I do for you?"

"There's been an accident in your settlement. Just came over the wire. Sounds like your dad's been hurt, on the way to the infirmary at the power station. Take the rest of the day and go check on him. Jecab will drop you off, he can handle today's tasks alone."

Evard jolted upright as if stabbed. A chill crept down his spine. His dad's job was the safest around — how could he be hurt?

He stammered into the comm, "Thank you sir, I appreciate the day off. I'll let you know how he's doing. See you in the morning."

"Take care young man," Fog replied solemnly. The line went dead just as Jecab came trudging back through the corn.

"Sorry for the wait. Heard you and Fog — hope your dad's okay. Let's get you to the infirmary," Jecab said as he climbed aboard.

"Yeah, sure, thanks Jay," Evard muttered, trying to sound less shaken than he felt.

"Don't worry bud, I'm sure he'll be fine. Just a precaution, ya know?" Jecab said with a fumbled attempt at a comforting grin. Evard smiled but he had a nagging feeling this was something more concerning than anyone was letting on.

"See you tomorrow, Jay," he said half-heartedly as the hovercraft arrived at the power station.

He had no idea his life was about to unravel.

Evard entered through an ornate rear entrance. The power stations always sported more technology and polish compared to the rest of Eden's worn, rural facade. The sleek halls glowed coolly, austere metal juxtaposed with softly illuminated walls. Through glass doors was a pristine reception area.

"Hello, I'm Evard Roost, here to see my dad, Verner," he told the nurse behind the desk. She was pretty, with long brown hair and mossy eyes. He was sure he knew every beauty in the wetlands, yet she was unfamiliar. He realized she looked a bit harried at the moment as she regarded him anxiously, murmuring into her phone.

"Yes, he's here. I understand. I'll tell him," she said softly, giving Evard an inscrutable look. "Mr. Roost, please wait here — someone will escort you back shortly."

Moments later two security officers emerged from the hallway, broad-shouldered and imposing — militia, not the usual rent-a-cops.

The one on the right approached Evard. "Mr. Roost, we're with station security. We'd like to ask you some questions before you see your father, if that's alright."

The hair on his arm prickled, but Evard simply said, "Of course, how can I help?"

"Let's talk somewhere more private. This way please." They led him down the hall to a nondescript door, entering a corridor lined with identical portals. Stopping at one, the guard placed his palm on the sensor pad and the door whisked open. Inside was a stark room with a table and chairs along the far wall. An interrogation room. They motioned for Evard to sit against the wall and flanked him on either side.

"Mr. Roost, I'm Officer Januse and this is Officer Kento," said the one on the left. Kento gave a slight nod. "We have some questions about the incident with your father. First, do you know the whereabouts of your brother Lester?"

Evard's thoughts scattered like startled birds. "What does Lester have to do with this?"

"We believe he was involved."

"Involved how? In my dad's accident?" Evard asked incredulously.

The officers shared a grave look. "Your father was assaulted at home before his shift. He's in critical condition in the ICU. We have evidence your brother fled the scene covered in blood. Your mother is protecting him, claims he was trying to help. Either way we need to speak with him immediately. His disappearance looks highly suspicious. If you know where he is, you need to tell us."

Evard reeled as if gut-punched. "This can't be… it can't be true," he stammered. "Lester idolizes Dad, he'd never hurt him. Why would he do this?"

"There are reports of a disease circulating that drives people violently mad. You've likely heard rumors. We've had cases reported here recently. It may have been a factor."

"You really think this crazy disease made him attack our dad?" Evard asked, incredulous. He couldn't believe any of this was real.

"We can't discuss an ongoing investigation. But it may have played a role, yes."

Evard took a shaky breath, head spinning. "I don't know how I can help you. I need to see my dad."

"Of course. But time is critical in cases like these — we needed to speak with you before you saw him. I hope you understand."

"Yes, please, take me to him."

Januse led him back to the infirmary entrance and down the hall. "Your father's in room 17," he said solemnly, ushering Evard through the doors. Inside the room, his mother was keeping vigil at his father's bedside, clutching his hand. His face was a patchwork of livid bruises and gashes, one eye swollen shut, bandaged hands, and tubes snaking around him. But he was awake.

"S-son," Verner wheezed through his oxygen mask, breaking into a fit of coughs.

"Hush now Vern, rest," Rita soothed, smiling weakly at Evard. "So glad you're here — he's been drifting in and out."

"Will he be okay, Mom?"

"The doctor says with time he'll be good as new. He needs at least a week or two here before he's healed enough to come home, but he will come home." Evard hesitated. "It's not true, right, Mom? Lester didn't do this?"

Rita's eyes clouded with sorrow, belying her words. "Of course not, dear. Just a misunderstanding."

"So, where is he? Why isn't he here?" Evard pressed.

"I'm sure he'll come clear this up soon enough." She embraced him fiercely. Placing her head on his shoulder she whispered into his ear so Verner couldn't hear. "Lester's dangerous now. He's sick. You need to stay away from him, at all costs. Don't go home tonight." Then she pulled back, her smile strained. "Dad will be better soon, I'm sure of it!"

"Yes, Mom, I know he will," Evard muttered, reeling. He could scarcely believe what was going on. Nothing felt real.

Just then, an announcement rang out overhead. "Please remain in your rooms, there is an emergency..." Then silence.

Moments before, a tall, slender man with dark hair had entered the infirmary, dressed in dusty work clothes, hands in his pockets. He now approached the front desk. "Excuse me, I'm looking for Verner Roost's room?" The nurse eyed him warily. "One moment please." She furtively glanced down the hall as she murmured into the phone. Two burly officers emerged, sizing up the man. "Lester Roost?"

"Why, yes, officers, what can I do for you?" said Lester as he quickly approached. Smiling pleasantly, Lester produced a concealed gun, pressing it to the nearest guard's temple and fired. The bullet exploded Januse's head like a grapefruit, scattering gore everywhere. Lester calmly wiped flecks of blood and brain from his face and turned to the stunned Kento, drawing a sharp homemade blade from his pocket. Before Kento could react, Lester plunged it into his neck, blood erupting in crimson spurts as he gurgled wetly, lungs filling with fluid.

Lester regarded the terrified nurse behind the glass. As she bolted towards the exit he raised the gun casually and shot her in the back. Moving behind the desk, he scanned the terminal until he found it — Room 17. He sauntered down the hall, whistling softly, a malevolent smirk playing about his lips.

"What the hell's happening?" Evard exclaimed. His mother's face looked as blanched as a cob of corn in the baking sun.

"He's back to finish the job. Quick, run! That thing's no longer your brother — it's a demon in his skin. It'll kill us all. You must flee, now!"

Evard's pulse raced, adrenaline surging wildly. This can't be real, he thought desperately. He frantically looked for a weapon as a knock came at the door.

"Knock knock, it's your son, Lester, here to see dear old Dad," came an unctuous, threatening voice.

"Please, leave us be!" Rita pleaded, shielding Verner's body.

The door crashed open and Lester strode in, grinning sadistically.

"Hello, Mommy! So much to discuss. But first — Evie! Hoped you'd be here too. We should catch up on why you were always the favorite. It really… pisses… me… off." His face contorted with seething rage, eyes crazed.

He lunged at Evard with blinding speed, punching him savagely in the face. Pain exploded through Evard's skull as he crashed into the nightstand. Clinging to consciousness, he saw Lester reach for his knife as Rita hurled herself at him with a scream. They tussled violently for the gun as another guard charged in. Lester viciously head-butted Rita before grabbing the pistol and riddling the guard with bullets. Blood and bits of viscera spattered the walls as the guard's body crumpled to the floor.

Through the haze of pain Evard stumbled to his feet and turned to his father, paralyzed in fear. His mother lay dazed on the floor, blood dripping from her face. Lester's own face was scarlet, chest heaving raggedly as if possessed by some demonic presence. Evard had never seen anything like it.

With demented fury Lester suddenly shrieked at their father, "You did this! You hurt Mom! I just wanted to hurt you! If you only loved me like you loved them! I hate you!" Verner's eyes were wide with mortal terror.

Rage oozed from Lester's pores, transforming him into a wild beast beyond remorse or reason. He stared malevolently at the knife, as if it was far too clean a death for the likes of Verner. With a guttural cry he pounced, stabbing repeatedly, Verner feebly trying to shield himself from the onslaught. Blood sprayed from the fresh wounds, as Lester's face became slick with the blood of his father. Eventually Verner's arms fell to his side as the awful sound of his gargled screams filled the room. Though only lasting seconds, it was as if time had slowed and each stab took an epoch to hit its target. Verner's body twitched convulsively then finally fell limp. Lester seemed not to notice, continuing his assault as if he was squeezing every ounce of rage from his body in this horrifying display of violence.

When the frenzy finally passed, Lester gazed down at the ravaged corpse, realization dawning. Tears flowed as guttural sobs wracked his body. "No! Why did I do this? What the fuck is wrong with me? Why?"

At that moment, Evard pounced. In all the chaos, he'd been able to pull the cord out of the bedside lamp. He had wrapped the cord around both his hands like a makeshift lariat and threw them over Lester's head. He squeezed as hard as he could, cutting off the air to his windpipe.

Lester screeched and bucked like a wild banshee. Evard, who was a bit smaller and less physically powerful than Lester, held on for dear life. He just kept pulling and pulling with every bit of strength he could muster until Lester began to give less and less resistance. His arms started spasming, his legs kicking outward involuntarily. Finally, they both crumpled to the floor. Evard let out a long sigh that sounded like the howl of a wounded animal, tears leaking from his eyes in waves.

When Evard was finally sure that Lester was either unconscious or dead, he let go of the cord and began to crawl over to his mother on his hands and knees. He brushed her face lightly with his fingertips, weeping with a flood of uncontrollable sobs. Just as his tears began to drip onto her lifeless face, his mother started coughing. He held her face in his hands and said in a breathless, raspy voice, "Mom… Mom, are you okay? Please be okay!"

She looked at him with bloodshot eyes, her voice a ragged whisper. "You're not safe here. You have to run."

CHAPTER 6

Nothing Was Your Fault

An hour later, Zarena stood in the opulent waiting area of Launchpad 12. It was a capacious, comfortable room outfitted with buttery leather couches and ottomans, adorned with antique paintings rendered in chalk and oil and exquisite ivory statues carved into the sensuous forms of nymphs and cherubs. Zarena looked around, musing that the era when such creative genius flourished may now be at its twilight. She banished the thought as swiftly as it arose. Still, a slight, reflexive shudder rippled through her.

"Best not to dwell on things beyond our control," she murmured to the empty room.

She watched as a small imperial cruiser glided through the wide launchpad doors and landed on the broad helipad at the hangar's core. The cruiser was a royal L15 starship, designed to ferry the Imperial family and other eminent dignitaries in luxury. Though outfitted with cutting-edge lazcore weaponry, it had still traveled cloaked in a military envoy, scout ships encircling its perimeter as it descended through Archlon's dense atmosphere. These were uncertain times. The ship landed with a hiss of steam from the landing hydraulics as a ramp extended from its flank. The bay doors swung open and a phalanx of bodyguards in black and green armor marched out, weapons at the ready.

Once the all-clear was given, Princess Raeka of House Karmarch stepped through the hatchway onto the exit ramp. A delicate silver crown bejeweled with shimmering gems adorned her auburn hair, arranged in tight braids that cascaded down her back. She was clad in a scarlet evening gown trimmed in gold at the flared hemline. Over it she wore a sash similar to the one Zarena wore, a small gold medallion emblazoned with the imperial seal clasped at its front.

Subtle yet regal, mused Zarena.

Raeka walked with eyes downcast across the landing area, encircled by guards who awaited her at the base of the ramp. Once her entourage reached the waiting room, Raeka saw Zarena and beamed.

"Welcome back, Your Highness. I hope your journey was fruitful," Zarena intoned formally.

Raeka disregarded the pleasantries and grasped Zarena in an embrace, both women smiling over the other's shoulder. "Zarena, things must be dire if you were dispatched to receive me," said Raeka, her voice lilting and sweet. "But I'm overjoyed to see you."

"Your father requested I welcome you home, but I was happy to oblige. He will need to speak with you urgently, but I think it must wait until tomorrow. It's been a long day, Your Grace."

Raeka's face shifted from cheerful to inscrutable, though precisely gauging her change in mood was difficult. "Zarena, if you insist on formality, I'll instruct that guard to slap you," she threatened mildly.

"Of course, Your Grace. I mean, of course, Raeka. Though assaulting a Councilor does constitute treason."

"As does insulting a Princess," Raeka volleyed back.

They held each other's gaze solemnly before bursting into laughter. When their laughter subsided, Zarena scanned the room surreptitiously before continuing in a hushed tone. "Raeka, there's no gentle way to tell you this, so I'll just say it plainly. There was an attempt on your father's life today on the Cournia. He's unharmed, they tried to assassinate him with a skid rocket but the PGen field activated. That's why he was so eager to have you home, for your safety."

Raeka was much shorter than Zarena, so she had to crane her neck to meet her eyes. Even so, she cultivated a talent for rendering her face utterly inscrutable, betraying not a flicker of joy or sorrow. Impossible to discern her inner thoughts when she wore that mask, Zarena knew. Best press on.

"Furthermore, as you might expect, it caused something of a panic. An emergency council meeting was convened as a result. At the meeting, the Council voted to deploy The Harmony." She paused before continuing, a hint of defiance coloring her tone. "That is the Emperor's command. The plan is to start immediately."

Raeka's expression remained impassive as marble. "Was the vote unanimous?" she inquired evenly.

"Yes."

"Anything else of note?"

"Perhaps one thing, a heads up: Jesper was nosing around. I'm uncertain why."

"I see."

Raeka simply gazed at Zarena wordlessly for a small eternity before speaking again. "What are your dinner plans?"

"Nothing, I planned to just grab a bite from the kitchen before bed."

"I haven't eaten all day. Let's dine in my private quarters in an hour?" Though her face was still unreadable, warmth had entered her voice. Zarena relaxed slightly.

"That would be lovely. I'll see you then."

Raeka turned and glided down the corridor, her retinue of guards instantly forming around her. Zarena was struck by the precaution taken within the palace itself. Another disquieting notion flickered through her mind. *The end of days is upon us. Nothing will ever be the same.* She dismissed the thought like swatting at an insect.

I will save us, she resolved silently. Immodest perhaps, but she knew it was true. She felt it in her bones. A new world could rise from the murky chaos once humanity walked the path of peace. Maybe this would spark a renaissance to uplift the ages, minds and souls united in harmony. It could be beautiful.

Zarena watched Raeka disappear down the hallway before making her own way back to her quarters, turning over the puzzling interaction in her mind. Raeka was clearly disturbed but wouldn't publicly denounce the plan now that her father sanctioned it. Yet she likely expected dissent, perhaps even from Zarena herself. Instead the vote was unanimous. Dorsetta's capitulation was likely an unwelcome surprise. In any case, the wheels were in motion. No stopping it now.

An hour later, Zarena knocked at the door to Raeka's private chambers. The royal suites sprawled through a secluded wing of the palace, though only Rakeus and Raeka resided there now. With no Queen or other children, the capacious quarters echoed emptily. Rakeus' rooms were separated from Raeka's, allowing ample space even from each other. Though close, their relationship allowed for independence, Zarena thought. Rumors had once persisted that Rakeus had tried to assassinate Raeka to choose a more malleable heir, but there was never any proof. Zarena doubted them to be true. He seemed to hold genuine affection for his daughter. Theirs was a relationship built on mutual respect, if not overflowing warmth. As his sole offspring, Raeka was groomed to rule from childhood. Rakeus seemed to take pride that she would someday succeed him, whatever may remain of the empire by then.

Rakeus was a capable ruler, Zarena reflected. He cared for his subjects, worked to maintain order and peace. He sought not to force submission from the worlds under his control but to help them stand on their own, for the good of all. Yet he clung to imperialist delusions of manifest destiny, as if the universe itself charted the Imperium's purposeful course regardless of obstacles. At times it obstructed solutions to The Sequence. Many inside Kral Markhan thought nature itself would right things before human intervention was required. But the crisis only deepened, and he came to view it as his ordained burden to shoulder. A more rational mind might have conceived The Harmony sooner.

Raeka lacked such imperialistic notions. She was learned, her interests in science and math far beyond her father's. She studied history voraciously, seeking insights from humanity's failures on Origin. Zarena felt that when Raeka finally ruled, she would be the greatest Emperor in generations. For now, she was one of her father's most trusted advisors, though not a Councilor herself. He didn't just love her, he trusted her.

The door swung open and Raeka appeared, clad in a diaphanous white sundress embroidered with The Imperial crest at the waist. Her unbound auburn hair cascaded over her shoulders, and open-toed sandals graced her feet.

"Come in, Zarena," she said breezily, leading the way into an expansive circular foyer. At its center loomed an imposing marble statue. Crimson carpets lined the floors and the walls were festooned with imperial pageantry in purple, gold and scarlet. Spaced between plush benches, doorways ringed the perimeter, leading off in all directions to Raeka's private domain.

She headed towards the dining hall, Zarena following apace. They proceeded down a corridor studded with paintings and classical busts ensconced in oval alcoves. It resembled a museum. The passage opened into a grand dining room anchored by an immense table hewn of emerald jade, gleaming silver place settings flanked by cream silk napkins lined its edges. Raeka settled into the head seat nearest the door and beckoned Zarena over.

"Here, next to me. This isn't a state affair." She smiled impishly as Zarena sat down beside her.

"So what delights has the chef prepared this evening, Your Majesty?"

"It had better be delectable. Quality ingredients are scarce with civilization's collapse underway."

Raeka eyed her pointedly, blatantly angling for a response. Zarena was too weary for verbal fencing, even with Raeka.

"I know you're upset. But there's no other way. The Council unanimously agreed, as did your father. All voices concur that however distasteful, this is a mercy we could not have granted in the past."

"I understand, Zee. But rationalizing it doesn't absolve the choice. Going out of our way to justify this doesn't make it any less wrong. Apart from a miracle, there's no other way to save us. That still doesn't make it right. Without intervention, the Imperium may fall, most will die, and any survivors might take thousands of years to even resemble humanity again, if ever. But at least we'd be following nature's course. Throughout history, we've tried to defy nature's laws. It never lasts. Each time we try, the universe grows worse. Our vision has narrowed to only see death, oblivious to how The Harmony will shape us in twenty years, or two hundred. We may only be providing one last analgesic as civilization awaits the end."

"You may be right, Rae. But I cannot accept violent death as the likely fate for those I love, at the hands of some lunatics whose twisted biology drives them to kill. I know it's nature's way, but nature is barbaric. Humanity encompasses both angels and beasts. Now the beast rises up to consume us. We must try to appeal to our better angels before becoming the generation that finally destroys humanity after ten millennia of survival."

Raeka looked wistful, almost sad, but still smiled as she squeezed Zarena's hand. "You mentioned Jesper earlier. Any inkling what he's up to?"

"Hard to tell with that weasel. I suspect he was sniffing around to see if The Harmony was ready before the Council convened, but it's difficult to know his agenda until your father wants us to, if ever."

"Tread carefully around Jesper. He may seem a fawning sycophant carrying out my father's bidding, but he's dangerous. Maybe more dangerous than anyone."

"I'll be vigilant," Zarena said, with a weary smile.

Liveried servants emerged from the kitchen bearing the first course on silver trays — lemongrass soup with lentil fritters and crispy chicken. They dined mostly in silence through several sumptuous courses, served one after another, until the head server approached. "We have prepared a special dessert tonight, Your Majesty. Would you care to partake?"

"Of course, Deven. One never knows when such delights may come again." She beamed at him disarmingly and he gestured towards the table. Two other servants appeared with a covered silver cart, a saccharine aroma wafting from beneath the lid.

As they finished the last morsels of caramel soufflé, Raeka finally shattered the long quiet. "When will The Harmony be activated?"

"In a few months time. The plan is to Harmonize all worlds simultaneously to maintain control and minimize losses."

"That makes sense. Time is no longer our ally. On House Collette's home world Vergarden, The Sequence is appearing at an alarming pace. Their scientists only know what we disclose, but there is genuine concern for public safety."

"They still think it's airborne?" Zarena asked with mild surprise.

"That's the party line, but many suspect something else is at work. Baron Collette tried to needle me for information. They wanted to learn our plans for stopping this scourge. I claimed we were months away from a cure, and that the Emperor would convene the Great Houses when the time came. It was odd though, Collette has an older son who would be a more suitable match if he sought a marriage alliance, yet he brought his younger boy. He's only about seventeen years old. I suspect the elder may have triggered and was kept hidden. They want to strengthen alliances before their ranks also begin to decay."

"It was only a matter of time before it infected their upper classes as well." Zarena observed.

"Indeed. In some ways it makes this all the more real. And yet..." Raeka trailed off as the thought sadly deflated the conversation.

"Yes. I know", said Zarena mirthlessly.

"What happens next?", continued Raeka.

"We finish producing The Harmony devices and dampeners, then coordinate deployment. Archlon will be harmonized concurrently with the rest of the Imperium. The royal family and Council will likely convene with the scientists to ensure the dampeners function properly throughout. We're still finalizing details."

"It seems you've prepared thoroughly. I suppose certain things are fated to transpire." Raeka lifted a glass of plum wine off the table. "A toast — to humanity's last days. And to new beginnings… for all of us." She chuckled softly. "May the universe bless us for trying."

Zarena felt heartened that Raeka could voice her misgivings in private. She would never publicly denounce the plan now that her father sanctioned it. The wheels were turning.

After dessert, Raeka walked with Zarena back to the foyer. At her chamber door she said, "You're my oldest, dearest friend. No matter what happens, I love you. Remember, come what may, nothing was your fault." She rose up on her toes and lightly kissed Zarena's lips, then smiled with such warmth it melted Zarena's core. "In the days ahead, you may doubt yourself. Don't. You've given us our only chance to survive. Remember that." With that, she gestured for Zarena to go.

As the door closed, Zarena glimpsed Raeka's parting image. She stood motionless a few moments, her mouth in a tight smile, before slowly making her way back to her quarters, puzzling over the strange encounter.

CHAPTER 7
Shadows in the Hallway

The Imperial Palace of Kra Markan loomed majestically against the twilight sky, its spires piercing the clouds like the claws of a great beast. Inside, the marble halls echoed with the whispers of history, as each step taken by Emperor Rakeus resonated through the empty, quiet spaces. He strode purposefully, his dark robes flowing behind him like shadows, his mind heavy with the weight of responsibility.

At the end of the corridor, Councilor Kaia Dorsetta awaited him, her expression a mixture of concern and determination. Rakeus admired her resolve. She didn't have the confidence of Zarena, or a talent for political machinations like Elias Ardenot, but she wasn't a blunt instrument either. She was fair and just, wiser than most of the council. Where Zarena could sometimes seem brash, mostly on account of her youth, Kaia was measured. That had its uses.

"Your Majesty," she began, her voice steady as she fell into step beside him. "The reports from Verenthia are troubling. Our intelligence suggests an unusual amount of violence in the major cities. The unrest is spreading faster than we anticipated. We must address the concerns of the citizens before it escalates further."

"House Verenius?", Rakeus said with a grimace. "Has Baron Lucan contacted us?"

"Yes, Your Majesty," Kaia replied. "He is demanding an audience, here, on Archlon. He wants you to agree to see him within the fortnight."

Rakeus glanced at her, his eyes narrowing slightly. "And what do you propose, Councilor? Another round of empty promises? The people are restless, and their fears are warranted but we cannot allow this to distract us from the course."

Kaia met his gaze, unflinching. "They are not merely doubts, Rakeus. If we do not confront it, we risk losing control of the entire Imperium. The Harmony may quell their fears, but it cannot erase their memories of suffering."

He paused, considering her words. "We don't know that, Kaia. Despite all of Zarena's efforts, there is no way to predict what is to come. Even she is unsure whether or not long term memories will be impacted."

He stopped walking and turned to Kaia, a wistful look passing as a shadow over his face. "Our minds are the enemy. As much as I want to reassure the Houses about the future of the galaxy, nothing we can say or do will make any difference. Once Verenthia is Harmonized none of Lucian's concerns will matter. Collette is also getting bold with us, pushing for answers. If we told them the full scope of the truth it would only cause pandemonium and I'm tired of giving empty platitudes. We're almost ready for mass deployment. Everything else waits."

As they continued down the hallway, a young guard stationed nearby shifted uneasily, his hand twitching at his side. He was tall and muscular, like most of the Imperial guards assigned to the Mark. He was facing forward but broke formation and turned his head, looking in the direction of Rakeus and Kaia. Rakeus noticed the movement out of the corner of his eye, but before he could react, the guard's expression twisted into a mask of rage.

"Your Majesty!" Kaia shouted, her voice cutting through the tension as the guard lunged forward, his weapon drawn.

Instinctively, Rakeus stepped in front of Kaia, his posture shifting to a defensive position.

"Stop!" he commanded, his voice low and dangerous. The guard paused, his lip curled in a snarl. He glared at the Emperor with an expression of disgust that Rakeus had rarely seen directed at him, certainly not by any who still live.

He put out his hand in a "stop" gesture and said, "Just relax, son. I'm the Emperor of the Imperium and this can be forgiven. You have to fight your urges."

The guard stared at him, a half-crazed expression of blood-lust crossing his face, shining through his very eyes. Rakeus knew in an instant that he was beyond reason, The Sequence had triggered an uncontrollable surge of aggression. The guard charged, letting out a bestial scream as he did so. In that moment, Rakeus felt a rush of adrenaline. In a split second, he reached for the guard's weapon, deftly disarming him with a swift movement.

The guard stumbled, momentarily disoriented, but Rakeus didn't relent. With a calculated precision that would have been scarcely possible for most his age, he struck the guard's throat with a sharp blow, sending him crashing to the ground, gasping for breath. There was a squishy sound as the larynx ruptured, the guard grabbing his throat as he crumpled to the floor, spasming.

Kaia gasped, her hand flying to her mouth. "Rakeus! You didn't have to use such force."

"Didn't I?" he interrupted, his voice cold and steady. "This is the reality we face, Councilor. This is the enemy. We cannot be weak against the enemy. Weakness breeds chaos, and chaos breeds death. I will not allow my Empire to fall to the whims of those who cannot control themselves, I don't give a fuck what the reasons are."

As the guard writhed on the floor, Rakeus straightened, his expression a mask of poised determination. He turned to Kaia, who looked both horrified and impressed. "We must show strength, Kaia. We must make an example of those who allow The Sequence to take hold. Force must be met with force."

Kaia's eyes narrowed, and she took a step closer, her voice low but fierce. She was reminded of a moment during the last council meeting when Rakeus flashed a moment of anger. It had scared her then, and this had scared her now.

"These people are innocent, Your Majesty." Kaia voice was low and steady. "Please, just remember that."

Rakeus regarded her for a moment, the tension palpable between them. "The Harmony is unavoidable, Councilor. After today it must be all too obvious why we need it. I won't be there to protect all of our citizens, as I protected you today."

As they stood in the dimly lit hallway, the guard's gasping breaths echoed in the silence, a stark reminder of the brutality that lay just beneath the surface of their skins. Rakeus felt a flicker of satisfaction at having asserted his dominance, but deep down, a nagging thought lingered at the edge of his consciousness. What if he, too, was not immune to the chaos he sought to control?

Kaia's expression softened, and for a moment, she glimpsed the compassion that lay beneath his fierce exterior. "You are not just an Emperor, Rakeus. You are a man. And, for as long as I have known you, a good one. Thank you for protecting me."

As they spoke, guards came rushing down the corridor, weapons drawn. They surround the triggered guard, who still lay twitching on the floor.

"Your Majesty,' the lead guard shouted. "Come with me, we will get you to safety!"

He turned towards the guards, waving them off. "I'm fine, I'm fine. Get rid of this," he said pointing at the convulsing body. "Dispose of it, and clear the hallway. I think it will be safer for us to finish our walk in solitude." He turned to Kaia.

"We will need to discuss this with Zarena and the council. For now, we may have to limit personnel with access to the palace. I will not tolerate any more incidents. The emperor of the Imperium will not jump at shadows in the hallway.

They strode onward down the hall, as the guard who attacked them was dragged away gurgling, the squad of guards kicking him over and over again into submission.

As they moved deeper into the palace putting distance between them and the incident, he couldn't shake the feeling that the true battle had only just begun. A battle that would test not only his resolve but also the very foundation of his rule.

CHAPTER 8
The Day Arrives

The palace bustled frenetically in the days preceding Harmony Day. Zarena was so consumed with preparations and endless meetings, she scarcely remembered when she had last slept more than a handful of hours. Amid the controlled chaos, Raeka was conspicuously absent. When Jesper questioned her most recent encounter with the princess, his dissatisfaction was evident as he promptly glided away. Since the attack on the Emperor by the triggered guard, Dorsetta had been heavily involved, meeting privately with the Emperor as well as the full Council, lending guidance however she could for the monumental event. In a way, it was peaceful. All who knew the truth were singularly focused; the hours flew by uncounted.

Zarena flitted in and out of strategy meetings with Commander Levitz and the Emperor himself, synchronizing the intricate web of logistics Imperium-wide. With the outer worlds taking longer to reach, ships ferrying The Harmony devices needed to depart sooner. It was a breathtaking feat of coordination rivaling the greatest undertakings in history, all shrouded in secrecy. Only an elite few knew of The Harmony's true purpose, most believing it a prophylactic measure right up until the end. Just the Emperor's inner circle and top military brass knew what was truly unfolding. The smooth execution thus far only reinforced Rakeus' growing conviction that The Harmony was providence incarnate.

At last, the fateful hour arrived. At 22:30 Archlon time, all ninety-seven worlds were Harmonized in unison. The Imperial

Council, foremost military commanders, Jesper, the Emperor and a handful of trusted servants convened together in the Council chambers. Through Commander Levitz, the Emperor contacted all relevant personnel on the comm network, commanding final preparations. Three chosen battalions, their officers and other vital members assembled in the hangar bay, poised for action. On Levitz's signal, they reached up and pulled down electronic mufflers resembling bulky winter ear warmers over their heads.

Jesper surveyed the Council Chamber and addressed the Emperor. "All are present, Sire, except Princess Raeka. But I have word she is on her way."

Raeka entered wearing the same headset as the others. "I hope these dampeners work, Zee," she remarked breezily, moving to Zarena's side. Zarena breathed easier at her arrival. They had scarcely interacted for months, and their odd parting at their dinner so long ago left Zarena uncertain if she would even show up.

Levitz conferred with team leaders galaxy-wide over the comms. "We await your command, Sire."

Rakeus took the comm and proclaimed in a booming voice broadcast everywhere, "Friends, what transpires today will be forever remembered. After millennia of turmoil, we now save humanity from itself. The path ahead may be long, with changes great and small, but we will walk it together to shepherd this new universe through the darkness."

Levitz resumed the comm. "Commence final equipment check."

Everyone instinctively touched their dampeners. Jesper personally inspected each one, ensuring all were securely fastened. When he reached Raeka, she smiled. "Thank you Jesper. I hope everything turns out alright for you."

He blinked and regarded her quizzically, his eyes clouded with confusion. "Same to you, Princess," Jesper murmured.

"Okay, activation on my mark," Rakeus announced to Levitz. He inhaled deeply, holding the breath captive between his teeth for a moment, then uttered, "Now."

Levitz relayed the signal and after a moment a thunderous crackle, resembling the roar of a firing mortar, erupted. The sonic pulse was so potent you could feel immense pressure squeezing every inch of your body. For an instant, everyone froze, paralyzed. They couldn't even draw breath. It was as if the device assaulted all their senses simultaneously, waging war on their very beings. Zarena thought for a fleeting moment that perhaps they had miscalculated, and the device would extinguish them all in an instant.

The communication network linked to the Council Chamber's video screens so all present could view feeds from across the universe. They observed transmissions from distant outer worlds, interior realms, and live footage from all over Archlon. It was an astonishing spectacle, unlike anything witnessed before. Displays of people ambling down the street only to halt abruptly, mouths agape in shock. It was as if every soul in the cosmos unanimously decided to stand motionless. Autopilots engaged for all hovering craft, though interstellar travel was scarce. In the days preceding The Harmony, all space flight ceased and the Imperium imposed curfews in major cities so most would be home when The Harmony activated.

The screens brimmed with motionless people as the sonic pulse resonated its discordant tune. It lasted only minutes but felt like teetering on the precipice of eternity, awaiting time's end. The Emperor realized he wasn't actually immobilized and took a step forward. He scanned the faces and a smile blossomed. Relief washed over their faces as beaming smiles stretched from ear to ear. It was working! The Harmony was working!

Just as jubilation brewed, Zarena noticed something amiss. Raeka stood alone, unmoving, her face a blank mask. At first, Zarena thought Rae was concealing her emotions, as she was apt to do. Then she spotted it. Raeka's dampeners dangled around her neck, unfastened. Raeka grinned foolishly at her as Zarena began to scream.

CHAPTER 9
An Era Of Fear

The twin suns of Vergarden cast long shadows across the sprawling estate of House Collette, their light refracting through the crystalline windows of the grand hall. Baron Vergan Collette stood by the massive oak table, his fingers tracing the intricate carvings of ancient battles etched into its surface. His gaze was distant, lost in the tumultuous thoughts that plagued his mind.

"Father, what are we going to do?" The voice of his younger son, Lorian, broke the silence, pulling the Baron back to the present. Lorian's youthful face was etched with concern, his eyes mirroring the same storm that roiled within his father.

Baron Collette sighed, his shoulders heavy with the weight of leadership. "Our people are suffering, Lorian. This madness, this… affliction, it spreads like a wildfire. We need answers, and we need them soon."

Lorian nodded, his expression grave. "Princess Raeka's gave us nothing. Her lack of answers only made me more suspicious. Now it's been months and the Emperor refuses you, one his staunchest allies, even so much as an audience. The Emperor must know something, he has to. Surely, he cannot continue to remain silent while the Imperium crumbles."

The Baron turned to face his son, his eyes filled with a mixture of determination and sorrow. "Emperor Rakeus is a man of many secrets. I've known Rakeus a long time, most of my life. He is one of the better Karmarch emperors but no one in his position can afford too much transparency. I respect he has an entire galaxy to rule, but we deserve better than this. This crisis, whatever the hell it is, is affecting us all. I've heard from some of the other Great Houses. The situation is the same across the entire Imperium."

Lorian responded, "We cannot afford to wait for him to act. We must find a solution on our own."

"And how did you expect us to find a solution to a problem we don't even understand?"

"I don't know," he yielded. "But there must be something we can do."

Vergan sighed, "If we can't get answers we may have to force them. What are the latest reports from Exalon?"

"Things seem better than they do here, but it's hard to tell. There hasn't been much of an effect on industry but that doesn't mean it's safe. There are still reports of unprovoked violence, far above the norm."

Silence hung in the air for a moment until Lorian said, "If we don't figure out what is going on, we'll never be able to cure Romulus."

The mention of his older son, now a prisoner of his own mind, weighed heavily on the Baron's heart. "Your brother… he was brave, and he was strong. To see him reduced to this state is a reminder of how vulnerable we all are."

Lorian's voice was barely a whisper. "Is there any hope for him?"

Baron Collette placed a reassuring hand on his son's shoulder. "Hope is all we have. But honestly, I don't. He seems awake and aware, and you can even speak with him for a while before things turn ugly, but eventually they do. His cell is well appointed but he always ends up destroying anything of value that we put in there. He is filled with so much hate and rage. That's not what I taught you boys. I raised you to be kind and just. I raised you to lead. Whatever is wrong with him, its roots run deep."

A sad, fearful expression crossed Lorian's face. He tried to work up the courage to ask what was on his mind and just as he was about to falter he blurted out, "What do you mean, 'force them' to give us answers."

Vergan raised a hand and shook his head. He drew closer to Lorian and lowered his voice. "Let that lie for now. Rakeus may have some honor in him but his pet viper, Jesper, has eyes everywhere. With all of the suspicions flying around, we have to entertain the possibility that the snake is listening, even here."

The conversation shifted to the planets under their control. Vergarden, with its lush forests and vibrant cities, was the heart of their domain. Exalon, in stark contrast, was a world of industry, its skies dotted smoke stacks and behemoth metallic skyscrapers. Both planets were vital to their survival, yet both were equally vulnerable to the spreading madness.

"We must strengthen our defenses," the Baron declared. "Ensure that our people are protected. We will not be consumed by Chaos, even if Rakeus fiddles while all the worlds burn, like the Origin fable of the Mad Emperor."

Lorian nodded, his resolve hardening. "I'll oversee the preparations, Father. We'll be ready for whatever comes." Vergan looked at his younger son with a mix of pride and sadness. It was a shame to burden one so young with the weight of ruling. Unfortunately for Lorian, he didn't have a choice. He needed his help in the days to come.

Finally, after a long, somber moment Vergen said, "Come with me, son."

The Baron stood up and ushered his son out of the grand hall, out through a side exit, and into an exquisite garden, lush with colorful foliage in bloom. They walked apace for a while in silence until they had moved some distance away from the palace. The Baron stopped and looked around, checking for guards or servants from the corners of his eyes. He took a breath and said, "I mean rebellion, son."

Lorian's eyes opened wide but he remained silent. His father continued, "If Rakeus is hiding something from us, it can only mean one thing: he doesn't know how to contain whatever is going on. If he doesn't know what to do, that means he's weak, vulnerable. There is talk among the other houses, whispers mostly. They are as concerned as we are. If Rakeus fails to show the leadership we need in a time like this, the Houses are willing to draft an order of Impeachment."

"Impeachment?", gasped Lorian. "Against Rakeus? That sounds awfully dangerous."

"It is dangerous," Vergan continued. "The Karmarch fleet is much larger than we could muster together, even with the combined strength of our allies. If he refused to acknowledge the impeachment, it could lead to all out war. Millions could die, and our chances of winning are regrettably low. Still, if we do nothing, millions could die anyway. At least this way we could potentially bring the truth to light."

"You've been planning something," Lorian said astutely. "You've been working on this in secret." He looked at his father incredulously, scared and at a loss for words. His father patted him on the shoulder gently and presented him with a warm, paternal smile. "My boy, you're right to be afraid. We may be entering an era of fear."

After his initial surprise, Lorian probed further, undaunted by the treason they discussed. "Father, House Karmarch is one of our most trusted allies. You said, yourself, that you've known the Emperor for years. You've always respected him. I know that the Karmarch's are not telling us the whole truth, but are you going to wage war on a friend who has helped us so much in the past? I mean, it wasn't long ago that Rakeus sent his own daughter here. Clearly, he was eyeing a possible marriage alliance. When she found me here instead of Rom, she would have known something was up. We might have already lost the element of surprise."

Vergan smiled at his son's cleverness. Perhaps the boy would make a wise ruler yet. "We will do what we must, Lorian, but only what we must. I promise you, I will act rationally. We will only take this course of action if Rakeus leaves us no other choice."

He placed a reassuring hand on his son's shoulder, in an attempt to pacify him. He had already begun to set plans in motion and the time to divulge them all had not yet come. Lorian may be wise beyond his years, but he's still a child Vergan thought ruefully.

As the two men stood in silence, contemplating the uncertain future, a sudden, piercing sound shattered the stillness. A sonic pulse, resonating from every direction, filled the air with an ominous vibration. Afterward, Vergan and his son looked at each other through watery eyes, blinking away the dew of tears. Smiling at each other with amiable, crooked grins, they turned and headed slowly back to the palace, stopping every so often to enjoy the sounds of the birds and admire the bloom of colorful, majestic trees.

CHAPTER 10
I've Never Felt Better

Emerald Selzt's eyes were a majestic emerald green, the inspiration for her name. Willowy and raven-haired, with delicate mocha skin, she could have modeled for the high-end designer shops she passed on her way to work. But it was her eyes that most people noticed. Her serpentine gaze seemed to hypnotize like a jeweled viper mesmerizing its prey. Her father affectionately dubbed her his "Jewel," for her eyes shimmered like flawless emeralds catching the sun's rays on a balmy spring day. Most children with such vibrant irises are born with murky blue or gray eyes that remain nebulous until maturity settles their final hue. But Emerald was born with eyes alight in verdant green flames, a unique chromatic mutation; one in millions, according to doctors. Time never dulled their dazzling brilliance; they sparkled as intensely now as the day she entered the world.

Her parents, Teresa and Willem, had planned to christen her Emira, but upon seeing those haunting emerald eyes peeking from the swaddle, they knew Emerald was the only fitting name. Growing up, she would sometimes catch other children gawking at her on the playground or in class. Usually it didn't bother her, but occasionally their stares stung, making her feel as though something was wrong with her. Her mom would say, "The most special among us always beg the most notice." Then she would tickle Emerald until breathless giggles erased her sadness. Over time, she embraced her singular beauty and came to treasure both her name and the eyes that inspired it.

This morning began like most. Emerald rose early and tidied the spacious flat she shared with her mother in District 7, one of Exalon's most affluent districts.

Exalon, a central system world not far from Archlon, was among the wealthiest planets in the Imperium, famed for its silicon-based computing technologies. Home to leading engineering firms like Raxeon, where Emerald worked, it pioneered developments from farming systems to interstellar travel.

Born on Exalon, Emerald's childhood fascination with machines and computers steered her toward the perfect place to nurture her talents. Though she lived off-world briefly for education, in her heart Exalon was home. Her father had always nurtured her interests in math and science, recognizing her keen intellect needed constant nurturing. She thrived on challenges and knowledge, excelling at every turn. Upon graduating from technology school, Raxeon offered her a mid-level position, an opportunity usually reserved for seasoned employees.

Her father passed the next year, but his pride in her achievements remained a guiding light whenever doubts arose. One lesson from Willem stuck fast: to have others believe in you, first believe in yourself. A well-respected security system designer, he nonetheless cherished time with family over professional advancement. Emerald worked tirelessly, as if repaying the universe for her family's talents. But he never showed any disappointment, only pride in his legacy.

After tidying up, Emerald donned her Raxeon engineer's uniform a sleek grey and black flexsuit and prepared a light breakfast, leaving leftovers for her still-sleeping mother. Raxeon was only blocks away, so today she skipped the hover taxi and walked, savoring the clear skies as the sun crested over the horizon. Exalon's sunrises lacked Eden or Archlon's dazzling hues, but it was still a beautiful world, made more so by this dawn's golden red sky. The streets seemed hushed, even for the early hour, absent of hovercrafts or fellow pedestrians.

Reaching Raxeon's towering city center monolith, she halted for the biometric scanners to confirm her identity and clearance level before entering. Passing security with a brilliant smile, one of the guards nodded to her. "Have a good day, Ms. Seltz." The doors opened and she strode through the foyer to the private elevators whisking her up to the 17th floor engineering department.

Her workstation was piled with diagnostics reports. Pulling on VR goggles, she delved into the digital world, honing in on a corrupted thermal scanner input. For an hour she tinkered, diagnosing the issue as a corroded power supply spewing out errors. Meticulous as always, she still scrutinized every component before concluding repairs. Rotating the lazcuffs into place a third time, she was startled by a tap on her shoulder.

Removing the goggles revealed Jasen Burlet's beaming face, clutching two metal coffee cylinders. His Raxeon garb matched hers, but his stocky build and trimmed beard made him look older than his late twenties. Nicknamed Jazz, his unremarkable features came alive in-person, oozing charisma that attracted ladies less impressed by his virtual selfies.

"I brought Clix coffee! Thought we deserved a treat with all this maintenance work." He handed Emerald a cylinder and set his on the table.

"Just what I need, thanks."

"Still fixing that TES?" he asked, gesturing to her terminal.

"Yep, bad power supply like I thought. But I'm doing a full diagnostic anyway — safety first." She chuckled.

Jazz smiled. "No doubts here." They both laughed. The coffee was delicious today. She took a long sip and set it down.

"Mmm, perfect. Needed a pick-me-up. Staring at circuits too long slowly drives one mad," she joked. "I think that's enough dissecting for one day. We've got a mountain of gear to catalog, so let's split it up for some fun this afternoon."

"Sounds good to me," Jasen said, settling at his station.

Together they formed an unbeatable engineering duo, often given vague instructions and still surpassing expectations. Their comfortable partnership spanned years, back to their prep school days on Rondus when they graduated together. They started at Raxeon in the same department. They lived in the same neighborhood, socialized together, and now had adjoining desks. Emerald kept few close friends, but Jazz was one. They shared a passion for tinkering.

After silently working awhile, Jazz casually asked, "Big plans tonight?"

"I'm cooking dinner for Mom, for all our sakes. Her skills don't match her enthusiasm," she said through a laugh.

Jazz smiled without looking up. "I'm surprising my mom with pastries. Haven't seen her much lately, but she likes when I visit bearing gifts." He chuckled. "There's a great new bakery by Providence. Bringing those cream puffs once means she expects them every time now. More visits means more weight from all the sweets but it's a trade-off."

"That's sweet, in more ways than one!" Emerald laughed. "Nothing fancy for us tonight."

"Well, I'm sure your mom will relish any gruel you make."

"Better than her cooking, for sure."

"Ouch, harsh truths cut deep," Jazz replied, both laughing. Their banter often carried them through tedious work. After a period of comfortable silence, Jazz stretched and rubbed his eyes. "These VR goggles really pinch after a while." Emerald merely grunted, engrossed in a dismantled carbine oscillator. "I think we've done enough gear work for today. Everything can go back into service tomorrow. Just some bad parts, mostly fine though."

Emerald mumbled agreement, still fixed on the oscillator. Sensing he wanted to say more but hesitated, she finally looked up to see him biting his lip pensively.

"Hey, heard anything else about that mystery sickness?" he finally asked.

Worry lines creased her smooth skin. "No, but it's scary stuff."

Jazz nodded. "I know."

"Mom's friend, a District 6 militia desk worker, asked around but got shut down fast. Afterward she wouldn't even discuss it and now she's ghosting her. Weird." A chill ran down Emerald's spine recounting the story.

Jazz looked uneasy himself. "You hear anything new?" she asked.

"No, just more gossip. Rumors a few Raxeon folks disappeared, maybe one from applied sciences. Just gone. But it's probably just gossip..."

He trailed off. Emerald was usually the pragmatic one, but the rumors also concerned her. "What's going on?"

"Well... remember Ryland from school? I talked to him yesterday. He says there are rumors on Rondus too, about this thing, whatever it is."

"Hmm..." Emerald murmured.

"If other planets have the same gossip, this isn't some local flu. With people disappearing, and officials silent, something odd is happening."

Though alarmed, Emerald remained measured. "I'm worried too. The amount of secrecy, whether conspiracy or ignorance, is equally troubling. The threat's unclear. But this could still just be smoke."

"Probably right. I don't buy into this stuff normally. But this feels... more serious, you know?"

"I agree, something strange is happening. Let's agree to keep our ears open and let each other know if we learn more."

"Good idea, but no open calls. We should use that encrypted comm channel from classified projects, just in case."

Emerald laughed. "Normally I'd call that paranoid, but you're right, let's do it."

Her smile eased the tension. She'd pondered these mysteries herself, fearing she would seem crazy if she confided in Jazz. It all resembled those intergalactic spy novels from childhood — likely just wild speculation about nothing. But she couldn't shake the ominous feeling that grave danger lurked in the shadows.

After reviewing the gear, Emerald yawned and stretched. Late afternoon sunlight streamed through the clear polymer windows, blinding without their visors. She spun her chair to avoid the glare as Jazz rubbed his eyes.

"Don't know why I'm so tired. Slept great last night," she remarked.

"Me too, but I feel wiped out. Maybe it's the weather?"

They both froze mid-laugh, recalling their earlier unease about illness. Their paranoia simmered as they forced anxious chuckles, neither admitting their escalating fears over a mysterious, politically silenced affliction. Lately, a malaise plagued the Imperium; a creeping dread sensed by astute minds like Emerald and Jazz that something was deeply wrong. Hard to quantify but undeniable.

"We'll keep watch, but let's face it — something strange happening is unlikely," Jazz finally said. "Superstition connects unrelated dots. We're probably being silly."

"You're probably right," Emerald conceded. "But if there is an Imperium-wide coverup, I'd be curious, wouldn't you?"

"Definitely. But before we go off the deep end, let's gather intel discretely. We're scientists, and good ones. You're maybe this planet's best mechanical mind, truly. Let's approach this logically — facts, multiple angles, no leaps in logic."

"When you're right, you're right," Emerald smiled.

"Right?" Jazz asked.

"Right!" she affirmed.

"Okay then, it's settled. Now, the most pressing issue — I must visit that bakery before I see Mom, or face her wrath."

They laughed, partly at his joke but mostly from frayed nerves over their newfound conspiracy sleuthing. Jazz clutched his side, Emerald wiped tears. A classic moment between them, one Emerald would revisit often later when on the run — sometimes fondly, sometimes sadly, imagining if they'd uncovered the truth sooner, perhaps they could have stopped it together.

As their laughter subsided, Emerald headed out while Jazz prattled on about his mom. Then suddenly, he froze mid-sentence, face slack, eyes glazed as if just injected with morphine. Alarmed, Emerald realized she wasn't breathing. Trying to move felt like wading through hardened amber, and panic started rising in her chest. Then finally, desperately, she inhaled. As oxygen filled her lungs, the fog in her mind cleared. An alien sound emerged, nothing she'd heard before — not an animal or alarm, but the very fabric of the world crying out in magnetic agony.

It continued for lifetimes or mere minutes, she couldn't decide which. Attempting to walk was exhausting, her body forgetting how to function. Eyes watering, tears spilled down her cheeks before she noticed. Initially her thoughts froze, then rebooted. What was going on? None of the likely explanations were comforting. She glimpsed Jazz standing statue-still at his station. Mouth agape, she tried shouting his name, drowned out by the painful buzzing. She staggered toward him until collapsing against his shoulders. Speaking into his face did nothing, he just stared ahead blankly. His muscles seemed oddly relaxed, as if he just emerged from a sauna.

Finally, when Emerald started to worry they may die here, frozen against this unseen force, it ceased. Stumbling forward, she steadied herself and scanned the empty office for answers. Her gaze returned to Jazz's placid face.

"Jazz… you okay? What was that? Jazz?" She repeated his name until some flicker of awareness crossed his features. Eyes fluttering open, he shook his head as if shaking out cobwebs and met her expectant stare.

"Hey Em. That was weird," he said slowly, his voice now curiously light and airy.

Gaping in disbelief, she stammered, "Are you sure you're alright?"

He smiled serenely, a vacant expression in his eyes. "I've never felt better."

CHAPTER 11
I'm Sorry, Kid

Rita erupted into a hacking cough, spewing blood and phlegm from her mouth. She wheezed and gasped desperately for air, eyes glazed and disoriented from the brutal head-butt Lester had dealt her during his rampage.

As she finally caught her breath, she rasped, "They… they aren't going to let you go. They think the disease could spread. If you stay… you'll… you'll vanish without a trace. You must flee. Now. Run!"

Evard moved as if in a dream, his mind foggy as his body operated on instinct alone, pushing himself up to his knees and bracing against the wall to stand. He turned to his mother, still sprawled on the floor, and extended a hand. She clasped it weakly and he hauled her up to sit, then hooked his other hand under her left elbow and tugged her fully upright. They clung to each other, sobbing in gasping breaths. She gazed into his tear-filled eyes and gently wiped his cheeks with the back of her hand.

"It's over, my darling boy. Your father — he's gone," she panted, stealing a mournful glance at Verner's lifeless form. At her words, Evard dissolved into convulsive sobs, inconsolable grief racking his body. She tried to soothe his anguish, resting a feeble hand on his shoulder while clutching her chest with the other. "No, no, my darling. You saved us. He would have slaughtered you too. He thought he'd already finished me off. You protected us, understand?"

She winced at the raw torment etched on his face, an open wound laid bare. She worried this was more than he could endure. He had to pull himself together if they hoped to make it out alive.

"There's nothing left for you here now. Lester murdered the guards, but more will arrive any second. You must flee. Take this," she said, fishing a few loose imperial credits from her pocket. "Don't go home. Just get to a shipping hub and sneak aboard a freighter off-world. It doesn't matter where you end up, only that you get as far away as possible."

Tears streaked Evard's face, blood dripped from the gash on his head, and his injuries made him dizzy. "Mom, I can't leave you. I can barely stand. I need you. Come with me."

As he wrapped an arm around her waist to guide her from the room, approaching footsteps made him freeze. Three security officers stormed in, weapons raised in unison.

"Hands up! Don't move or we shoot!" one bellowed. "Hands where we can see them, now!"

Rita and Evard exchanged a brief, doleful glance before slowly lifting their hands, careful to avoid any sudden moves. One officer remained in the hall, gun trained on them, while the other two entered the blood-splattered room to apprehend them. Surveying the carnage and corpses, one checked for vitals while the other radioed in. "Two bodies. The patient was stabbed in his bed. The apparent killer is down too, no pulse, crushed windpipe by the look of it."

The radioing officer listened to the response, then told his partner, "Cuff them and bring them to interrogation for questioning. Forensics will process the scene shortly. Let's get their statement first."

Rita and Evard shared another somber look. Her eyes radiated a sadness he had never witnessed, as to say I'm so sorry, it's too late. The officer kept his weapon aimed at their faces as his partner wrenched their hands behind their backs and clamped cold metal cuffs around their wrists. Evard yelped at the initial pinch, unaccustomed to the bite of lazcuffs. The officers shoved them roughly from the room without even a chance to bid their loved ones farewell. Evard's last glimpse of his father was a blanket being drawn over the pulpy remains.

They were prodded down the hall leading to reception, arms pinned behind them. Evard took in the rest of the aftermath, bodies concealed by sheets, officers swarming the corridor. From the lobby came a shout, "She's alive! Bring a stretcher!"

Evard was relieved to know the receptionist had somehow survived being shot. *At least someone had been spared,* he thought bitterly. This whole nightmare felt like it had stretched on for eons, though scarcely fifteen minutes had passed since Lester first barged into the infirmary.

The officers prodded Evard and Rita into the same cramped room where Januse and Kento had originally questioned Evard. They unfastened the cuffs, and Evard and Rita instinctively massaged their chafed wrists.

"Sit," an officer commanded brusquely. "Someone will be in shortly to take your statements." He stepped out, shutting the door behind him. Evard went to the window and peeked through the blinds, spotting the officer standing guard outside. His mother sat with her head in her hands, utterly spent.

Evard pulled up a chair beside her, leaning in close so she could hear him whisper. "What do we do now?"

She raised her head, hopelessness shrouding her face like a veil. "We wait. We pray. They know Lester did this. There's enough evidence." Her words spilled out rapidly under her breath. Evard strained to catch it all.

"They'll soon confirm you killed him in self-defense, after he murdered Verner. That's not our concern. Rumors about the illness are breeding panic in the militia. There are whispers that suspected infected people have gone missing. Some believe the militia is killing them off. I don't know if it's factual, but it could be. Folks have vanished. They may presume we're infected too. We must be cautious. Listen close — if we get a chance, we run."

"That can't be true, Mom. This is still the Imperium, even if it is Eden."

"Maybe it's factual, maybe it's not. More likely they just incarcerate the potentially sick until proven otherwise. Either way, it makes no difference. You witnessed what happened to Lester. His rational mind shut off entirely. They're afraid. I don't know what will unfold, but son, our lives here are over, understand me?"

He nodded curtly just as the door opened and a tall, ebony-skinned man in militia attire entered with two officers, one being their escort in cuffs. The militiaman carried himself with a commanding air despite his gangly frame. He flashed a wan smile. Evard realized he was attempting to gain their trust by putting them at ease. *Perhaps Mom was right about the jeopardy they faced,* Evard thought, panic rising within him. He fought to still his mind. If they were probing for any hint of infection, panicking would only rouse suspicion. As the man spoke, Evard slowly inhaled through gritted teeth and exhaled steadily, trying to calm down. He desperately wanted to exchange a look with his mother, but didn't dare give anything away.

"I'm Sergeant Quenter," the man announced. "My condolences for your losses. Today has been extraordinarily traumatic, I'm sure. Please excuse my men's brusque actions earlier. Desperate times call for stringent precautions, as you've witnessed first-hand. We know you've been through the wringer, but first we must learn what transpired."

Evard had lost his father, brother, and potentially his freedom in one morning. He wouldn't be tortured further. "Sergeant Quenter, why are we being interrogated like criminals instead of receiving medical care? My mother is injured, likely concussed. She needs immediate assistance."

Quenter's expression darkened fleetingly, a shadow passing over his face. He adjusted his collar before responding with forced patience. "Of course, but you both appear relatively unharmed. Minor injuries notwithstanding, we'll see to your medical needs shortly. The infirmary is locked down until the threat is confirmed as neutralized. Patients are being relocated."

His wording raised Evard's hackles. He was scrutinizing them for any hint of infection. Evard's mother had been right. "Of course, Sergeant. It's hard to fathom how this happened. I haven't fully processed it all."

"Understandably so," Quenter replied, softening his demeanor. "Let's discuss the incident with your brother and father, from the start."

Evard recounted the morning as calmly as he could manage — the fateful call about his father's accident, his arrival at the infirmary and interview with the now-deceased officers, and Lester's rampage in their father's room, including how Evard had stopped him from killing their mother. Quenter listened intently, jotting notes and nodding along. As Evard finished, Quenter asked, "Did your brother seem in his right mind? Was he acting like himself?"

"No, Sergeant. He seemed totally deranged, like a demon impersonating Lester. I've never seen him remotely act that way before. Whatever that was, it wasn't my brother."

"I see. And when did you first notice this abnormal behavior?"

"This morning," his mother interjected abruptly. She had been silent since Quenter entered but now spoke up. "He was himself yesterday — came home late from work, ate dinner, and went out with friends." Weariness dripped from her voice as Quenter nodded for her to continue.

"He didn't come home, but that wasn't odd. Sometimes he'd stay with a girl. But when he came back around breakfast, I could tell something was already bothering him. He started yelling about how we never loved him as much as his brother, how we didn't want him around — nonsense, all lies." Quenter nodded along sympathetically as if the tragedy was just dawning on him. Rita gave him a tired smile and went on.

"Then he grew violent — flipped the kitchen table, smashed chairs. Vern began shouting and they got into a brawl. Lester pounded him mercilessly, I thought he would kill Vern right there. I grabbed a frying pan and cracked Lester across the head. He collapsed, rolling around in pain. I called for help and he fled before emergency services arrived. I didn't see him again until he came here."

Her words flowed steadily, betraying none of her inner anguish. Quenter regarded her with understanding. "A terrible tragedy indeed. You have my deepest condolences." Rita nodded. "So you see, Sergeant, we know nothing. I've no idea what upset Lester this morning, or why he returned to finish what he started. It's a mystery to us both." Evard nodded along, trying to project earnestness without overdoing it. Quenter seemed to be buying their story — that was promising at least.

Just then, Quenter received a call on his comm. He listened intently, only responding "Understood" before standing abruptly. "A matter requires my attention. I'll return shortly to discharge you to another medical facility for treatment." He hesitated, seeming on the cusp of saying more, but simply repeated, "I am truly sorry," and left the room. The definitive click of the lock bolting echoed behind him.

Rita turned to Evard, raw panic contorting her face. "They just got orders to eliminate us. The official report will say Lester killed us after becoming infected. They won't risk it. They still can't explain what's happening."

"Mom, how do you know?"

"I heard his commander over the comm — my hearing has always been good. I heard the orders. We must escape now."

Evard was reeling in disbelief. "How is this fucking possible? This can't be real..."

"It's happening whether you believe it or not. Disbelief won't help us survive this." She clasped his hands, staring intensely into his eyes. "You are getting out of here, understand me? My last act will be to help you escape. When he returns, likely claiming he's taking us to a medical transport, they'll report we've gone deranged like Lester and shoot us in the hall. Make it seem like we attacked them."

Tears streamed down Evard's cheeks. "No, Mom, please..."

"Shhh… it's alright, baby. You'll get away from here and do as I said — remember? Board a freighter off-world. Anywhere but this goddamned rock." He nodded helplessly through his tears as she dried his eyes with her sleeve. "Promise me, Evard. Swear you'll get off this shithole and make a good life. I'm old and injured. I have little time left, so you'd better fucking promise!"

Despite everything, her snarky tone made him smile. He squeezed her hand tighter. "I'm sorry, Mom. For Dad. For Lester. For everything. I love you."

"I know, baby."

Sergeant Quenter returned abruptly, hands on hips, holding the door open. "Let's go. I'll get you out of here."

Rita and Evard exchanged the briefest glance. Then Evard stepped into the hall, Rita close behind. After a few paces towards their original path, he heard his mother scream, "Now!" He froze momentarily before she shouted "Go!" jolting him into motion.

A gunshot rang out as he sprinted down the corridor. He couldn't resist glancing back to see two figures grappling. When he burst through the double doors into the infirmary wing, he finally turned fully around.

He saw his mother wrestling Quenter for the gun that Lester had brandished earlier. In a split second, the realization struck — Quenter meant to murder them both with Lester's own weapon.

Panicked but nearly free, Evard yelled down the hall, "Hey asshole, leave her be!"

Quenter looked up from his struggle with Rita and, enraged, violently shoved her away before driving his elbow into her chest, knocking the wind from her. She crumpled limply to the floor like a marionette with severed strings.

Evard charged back towards his mother, intent on saving her, but Quenter leveled the gun and fired point-blank into her chest. Her body spasmed from the impact before going still. Evard screamed, the sound ripped from his lungs. He turned to flee but the officers at the hall's far end had drawn their weapons, advancing swiftly.

Quenter shouted furiously behind him, "It didn't have to happen this way!" and fired at the retreating Evard, bullets whizzing past him. Evard pumped his arms, sprinting in a low stance. Just as he rounded the corner, a searing pain tore through his calf as a laz blast grazed his leg. He lost his balance, momentum sending him skidding wildly across the floor until he slammed into the opposite wall. Writhing in agony, he clutched at the wound. Blood gushed over his fingers — he was sure he could no longer stand.

Quenter strode towards him with lethal purpose. Evard looked desperately down the hall and saw the carnage had been cleared. The few remaining officers were lingering when the gunfire drew their attention. Drawing their weapons, they cautiously moved to intercept him. Trapped and doomed, Evard started dragging himself away, leaving a crimson smear in his wake. Quenter's shadow fell over him like the Grim Reaper of legend. Rolling onto his back, Evard gazed up into the sergeant's twisted visage. "Please!" he sobbed. "Don't do this!"

Quenter's expression softened marginally and he met Evard's tearful eyes with a shred of remorse. "I'm sorry, kid. But my duty is to protect everyone." He leveled the gun at Evard's head. Squeezing his eyes shut, Evard waited for oblivion's embrace. He felt suddenly choked, suffocated, as a piercing shriek filled the air. He couldn't breathe for what seemed an eternity. *I'm dead*, he thought. *This must be how it feels.*

He remained still, eyes closed, expecting the end. The atmosphere grew dense, as if heavy clouds saturated the hallway before a downpour. Then he opened his eyes.

The scene was surreal. Sergeant Quenter stood over him, mouth agape and eyes glazed, utterly entranced by the ceaseless screeching din. As if compelled, he slowly lowered his weapon and dropped it to the floor, moving in time to some unheard rhythm. Evard looked back — the other officers also stood inert, arms dangling, with dazed but peaceful expressions that seemed alien on their stern faces.

Unsure what was happening but sensing opportunity, Evard shakily rose, agony searing through his leg. Quenter just gazed at him vacantly, oblivious to the situation. Limping heavily, Evard bent down and retrieved the discarded gun. The officers remained enthralled by the strange pulse resonating through the air. He stood over Quenter, looking into the confusion in his glazed eyes.

Visions of his mother's struggle flashed through Evard's mind. She fought to save him, only to be shot down by this monster. A scream tore from his lungs, raw and despairing. Spittle flew as tears filled his eyes. He kept screaming into Quenter's bewildered face. Rage boiling over, he spat on the dazed man. "Fuck you!" he shouted, angry beyond reason.

Raising the gun, he fired round after round into what remained of Quenter's face. Crazed and splattered with blood, Evard turned to the oblivious officers. He sprayed them with bullets and they crumpled to the floor, their blood pooling around them.

CHAPTER 12

What The Hell Is Going On?

The sun hung low in the sky over the bustling streets of Verenthia, casting long shadows that danced across the cobblestone pathways. Vendors called out to passersby, their voices a blend of mirth and haggling, while children chased each other through the throngs of people. It was a typical day in the heart of the Imperium, where life pulsed with a rhythm all its own.

In the midst of the crowd, Elara stood at her stall, arranging vibrant fruits and vegetables with care. She wiped the sweat from her brow, her heart light as she exchanged smiles with customers. "Fresh produce! Sweet nectarines, ripe tomatoes!" she called, her voice ringing out like a bell.

But as the sun dipped lower, an unusual stillness began to settle over the market. At first she felt a bit faint, as if her blood sugar had precipitously dropped unexpectedly. She tried to steady herself, clear her mind of the cobwebs that had entangled her, when she realized there was a sound ringing from some unknown location. The world itself seemed to vibrate, and she found she could not breathe. It was as if there was an unseen force pushing against her windpipe. A low hum reverberated through the air, growing louder and more intense. It was a sound that seemed to penetrate deep into the bones of everyone present, a sonic pulse that rippled through the square.

She coughed soundlessly into the void of shrieking noise that surrounded her. After a moment it subsided and she stumbled to the ground. Disoriented, she took a few ragged breaths and got herself to her feet, unsteady and confused. As the fog cleared, Elara noticed it first in the way people moved. Slower, as if the world had thickened around them. A man stumbled past her stall, his eyes glazed, and she frowned.

"Hey, are you alright?" He turned to her, blinking slowly as if trying to comprehend her words. "I… am… fine," he replied, each word drawn out a slow drip of molasses. He looked at her with glazed eyes. A crooked smile, like that of a toothless child, beaming from his face.

Elara felt a shiver run down her spine, but the sensation was fleeting. She shrugged it off, attributing it to the heat. Across the square, a group of teenagers were gathered. A few minutes ago their laughter had echoed through the air. Now, they were standing with their arms hanging limply at their sides. Suddenly, as if roused from a stupor, one of them, a tall boy with tousled hair, threw a ball toward his friend. The ball sailed through the air achingly slow, but the friend, caught in his own daze, didn't react. The ball struck him squarely in the face, and he fell backward, landing hard on the ground.

"Hey!" someone shouted, but the urgency in their voice was muted, as if the world had turned down the volume. The fallen boy lay there, staring up at the sky, his expression blank.

Elara's heart raced, and she turned her attention back to her stall. "Is anyone going to help him?" she wondered aloud, but her voice felt distant, swallowed by the thickening atmosphere. Elara's breath caught in her throat as the world around her began to shift. People had frozen mid-motion, their expressions blanking out like a flickering hologram. Everything seemed calm but the calm was deceptive.

Elara turned to another vendor, an elderly man who had always been quick with a joke. "What's happening?" she asked, her voice trembling slightly. He looked at her, his eyes unfocused.

"It's… fine," he replied slowly, as if the words were heavy on his tongue. "We'll be… alright." The world felt surreal, as if they were all trapped in a dream from which they could not awaken.

People stood still, their expressions blank, their memories of the moment slipping away like sand through fingers. Elara felt a strange calm wash over her, as if the chaos surrounding her had been muted. But deep down, a nagging sense of unease remained. What had just happened? Why did everything feel so… different?

The sun continued to dip below the horizon, casting long shadows over the market. The laughter and chatter that had filled the air moments before were now replaced by an eerie stillness. As Elara looked around, she realized that the world had changed, but no one seemed to notice. The boy who had been hit with the ball still lay on the ground, his friends ambling over towards him slowly, no concern evident in their movements.

A hovercar, piloted by a citizen caught in the wave of tranquility, drifted through the square, moving at an agonizingly slow pace. The driver, lost in a trance, failed to notice the gathering crowd. Elara caught it out of the corner of her eye. She yelled, "Watch out!" as the hovercar lurched forward. In the path of the hovercar was a woman pushing a stroller. At the last moment she stumbled back, her eyes wide with shock, but she did not move. The vehicle collided with the stroller, sending it tumbling into the air.

Elara's heart stopped as time seemed to stretch. She watched in horror as the world moved in slow motion—the mother reaching out, the baby's cries echoing in the air, the hovercar's wheels spinning. Then, a sickening thud. The crowd gasped, but their reactions were muted, as if the sound had been muffled by a thick fog. Elara felt her breath catch in her throat, and she stood frozen in place, her mind racing.

As the hovercar driver emerged from the vehicle, his expression vacant, Elara felt a surge of confusion. The world around her seemed to blur, and she could no longer grasp the urgency of the situation. In the square, people began to stir, their movements slow and disjointed. A vendor dropped his basket, the fruits rolling across the ground. He bent down to pick them up, but his movements were clumsy, almost robotic. A woman nearby smiled serenely as she watched the chaos unfold, her eyes devoid of fear or concern.

Elara, panicked and back in control of her facilities, sprinting over towards the accident. People were starting to gather around, standing still and watching, like some sort of spectral onlookers from another dimension. She pushed through the crowd, her heart racing. The mother held the broken body of the child in her arms, silently rocking it back and forth, as if the motion would somehow bring it back to life. Elara rushed over and knelt on the ground, placing one arm on the woman's shoulder. She looked into her eyes, which were distant and devoid of tears. The woman spoke softly, as if in a trance. "She was my darling baby girl", the woman said, almost absently, as if was a broken doll in her arms instead of her flesh and blood child.

Elara spoke gently to the woman, still in shock herself. "I'm so sorry", she cried. "Please, someone get emergency services here, now!" The woman just held the baby, showing little emotions of any kind. It felt like a weight was crushing Elara's chest. No one moved, everyone stood there gathered around the site of the accident, watching with inscrutable eyes.

Just as she was about to scream for help again, she heard another buzzing sound. An aircraft, military by the look of it, seemed to be free falling from the sky. She shielded her eyes to the sun as the craft made its rapid dissent. Screamingly loudly now, she tried to stand and pull the woman cradling the baby with her, away from the falling hovercraft. The craft continued its descent, the onlookers looking up at it with a sense of awe, strangely absent of panic. Finally, Elara realized that they were standing right under the impact zone and she began to run, pushing through the crowd of lemmings that were grazing around the market now. As the craft impacted with the ground its ion engines exploded like a missile, fire and debris engulfing the once peaceful marketplace. Elara's last thought before the conflagration consumed her was, "What the hell is going on?"

CHAPTER 13
I Serve The Imperium

Zarena felt as if a supernova had detonated inside her heart. She had recovered from the effects of the Harmony, the dampeners shielding her against full harmonization. The other test subjects had no recollection of the event, their memories gently wiped clean. Screams stuck in her throat as jubilation erupted around her. The councilors faced the video screens, transfixed by Harmonized people emerging from a hazy stupor, shaking off the fleeting shadows of a forgotten experience. Worlds resumed function, the cured masses oblivious to the plague purged from their blood. Many stood motionless for minutes, then carried on as if nothing peculiar had transpired. This surprised Rakeus—he anticipated more conspicuous changes in behavior. But the multitudes on surveillance seemed much like their pre-Harmonized selves. Though tragic losses lurked beneath the surface, the operation was an unmitigated success, rescuing humanity and the Empire. Smiles blossomed on faces, trepidation dissolving into glee. Only Zarena, sobbing silently, stood apart from the revelry.

Despite all of their best efforts, there were still losses. Commander Levitz chidingly referred to it as the Churn Rate. People who were harmonized while riding in a hovercraft or in unsafe positions they could not recover from. Construction workers in a mine shaft, farmers operating dangerous equipment, fires that burned instead of being put out. The loss of life throughout the Imperium would, for any single world, could be considered catastrophic. Given the complexity of The Harmony operation, some deaths were inevitable. Precautions were taken to minimize the damage but there was only so much order then could instill in the chaos. Levitz, Dorsetta, and Rakeus were discussing the butcher's bill, how many estimated losses there were, and other types of damage. Considering the size and scale of the undertaking, property damage, destruction and death were all within acceptable limits in the initial reports that were coming through. Rakeus et al were starting to realize that as tragic as the losses were on the surface the Harmony was entirely successful. In all probability it was the single most life saving operation in human history. Smiles started to spread across each of their faces, glee and giddiness replacing fear and trepidation. Only Zarena, quietly sobbing, stood out among the revelers. No one else had yet noticed Raeka standing motionless amidst the commotion. She stepped in front of Raeka and faced her. Raeka was smiling an uneven smile, her eyes watery and doughy, like the sad eyes of a herding animal. She grabbed Raeka's hand and patted it gently.

"Oh, Raeka. Are you alright?" asked Zarena.

Raeka seemed for a second like she didn't realize that Zarena was actually speaking to her. Then she said, in her singsong voice, that sounded somehow breezy and carefree, "Hi Zarena, I'm good. I feel wonderful."

"Are you sure, Rae. I… I don't… I don't understand what happened," she stammered.

"I choose this, Zee"

"Why? Why would you do that?"

"The better question Zee, is why would we do this?"

Zarena had nothing to say by way of rebuttal. The time to debate The Harmony was over. Now they had to live with the consequences, as she was painfully learning.

"Don't fret, Zee. This was the right choice. I feel… free. I don't… I don't remember what pain was. Pain and fear, they feel like a distant memory, a long ago dream I woke from centuries ago."

"You… you don't seem like yourself, Rae."

Zarena was surprised at how lucid Raeka seemed. As far as Zarena could tell she was in complete control of her faculties. She was just different. She wasn't the same. Zarena said as much to her.

"Of course, silly. I'll never be the same. You took away my pain. How could I ever be the same again." She giggled a rambunctious giggle, like a parody of the way she used to laugh.

Zarena just stared at her, unsure how to proceed at this moment. She asked, "What do you remember?"

"I remember being me before. I remember being me now. I don't remember The Harmony."

"What about your memories?"

"Memories? Zarena Denamonte, my memories are amazing."

"I don't get what you mean?"

"It's as if you purged my memories of all the bad. The pain, the fear, the death. I know that I had been sad, or scared, I remember what it was like to be that way, but I don't feel it. I can't remember what it felt like to be that way."

The entire time she spoke her voice was even keeled. It sounded like the voice one might hear on a soothing motivational video, or a hypnotist trying to put a patient into a trance. There was a tranquil, almost ethereal quality to it. Zarena supposed it was what all voices would sound like if the people using them were suddenly incapable of anger.

"I have questions, Raeka, so many questions. But first, we need to tell your father."

She approached Rakeus, whose eyes glistened with joyful tears. Clasping his hand gently, she asked, "Are you alright?"

He stared blankly before responding in a lilting tone, "I'm wonderful, Zarena." Rakeus, Dorsetta, Earkham, Cornado, Jesper and Fermonte were standing next to Commander Levitz, reviewing a bevy of reports that were coming in from all Imperium wide surveillance. They were engrossed in the results coming from all sectors of the Imperium. The initial reports seemed to be highly encouraging. They chatted amongst themselves feverishly, like children playing some kinetic game in the schoolyard.

Rakeus then sent Jesper out of the council chambers to personally meet with the battalion commanders stationed in the hangar bay. It was time to begin the preparations for Phase II.

Zarena turned away from the group to find Raeka standing behind her. She held her hand on Zarena's forearm, smiling a beguiling smile that Zarena found to be both fascinating and curious.

"Zee, did I ever tell you how beautiful your eyes are? They are like a field of lavender springs swaying in the afternoon breeze."

Raeka's tranquil demeanor unsettled Zarena. Taking slow, deliberate steps as if on fragile ice, Raeka faced the others. "It's just me, father," she announced.

Realization dawned on their faces. Rakeus erupted in volcanic fury, his face purpling. He bellowed, "What have you done?"

Raeka listened impassively as spittle sprayed her face, his hands flailing like a marionette. She remained relaxed, immune to his explosive wrath. Zarena worried he might strike her, but Raeka showed no reaction. Eventually Rakeus collapsed into ragged sobs, his rage spent. His face withered with new creases and gray hairs. Gasping for breath, he seemed diminished and aged.

"What did you do?" he asked weakly. "I decided that I wanted to know the Emperor's peace. So I took off my dampener. I'm Harmonized." She said this last part with a jubilation in her voice that one might expect to come from a happy child opening their birthday presents. The shock and awe of the situation silenced the room. Rakeus then bellowed, "What the hell did you do, Raeka!" "I did what you did to everyone else. I accepted peace."

"You what?! You *chose* this? But why, why would you do this to yourself, to me?"

"I did nothing. I simply let what you did happen. I can't fathom why all of you wanted to protect yourself. I feel wonderful. You would have, too."

Raeka took his hand gently. "Don't be sad. I wanted this. I'm happy." Her whispered words echoed in the silent chamber.

Thunderstruck, no one knew what to do next. Zarena stepped forward. "I know this is heartbreaking. But given time, I believe I can reverse The Harmony and restore Raeka." Rakeus snapped alert. "I thought you said it couldn't be reversed."

Zarena insisted, "With enough dedication, I know I can de-Harmonize her."

Rakeus stared coldly. "Then you shall never try."

Shocked, Zarena stammered, "I don't understand."

Rakeus said firmly, "We accomplished our mission. A reversal risks that. It is a weapon we must control." He turned to the others. "We must accept the consequences and find comfort in the gift of life." He stormed out, barking orders into his comm. He turned around to look at Raeka, a rueful frown across his face. He turned abruptly and left the room. The leaders exchanged uncertain glances. Kaia escorted Raeka away, urging Zarena to join her.

"Thank you Kaia. I'm perfectly capable of getting myself home. However, if Zarena would like to join me that would be nice."

"Of course, Princess", said Zarena. Zarena waited a moment for Raeka to respond. She had intentionally used her ex officio title to see whether Raeka would respond. Usually she would playfully scold her for her formality. Now, Raeka just smiled and said, "Let's be on our way then."

They walked down the corridors leading out the central government hub where the Council Chambers were located. As they entered the residential district where the royal quarters were, Zarena was acutely aware of the awkward silence between them. Awkward for her at least. Raeka seemed immune to the uncomfortable silence that sat between them and maybe for Raeka it wasn't uncomfortable. She has and will change in many ways, some of those ways harder to predict than others. After enough time had passed Zarena said, "Rae, why wouldn't you tell me this was your plan."

"I did, in a way. I told you in the days to come you may doubt your actions. I also told you not to."

"You did, I remember. At the time I thought you meant something else."

"At the time I did, but I also meant this. I meant everything that was going to happen. You and my father fail to understand the most important thing. I chose this. I may be the only person out of the hundreds of billions of people that got to choose. In a way, it makes this all the more special."

"I suppose you're right. It's strange to me that you seem to still be yourself yet different at the same time."

"There will be a lot of adjustments to this new reality. I'm sure you'll find a way to process it all."

"I suppose processing it has been made easier for you."

"It has, and I have you to thank."

"Raeka, you have to understand something. I'm going to do whatever it takes to reverse this. I'm going to fix you."

"I know you plan to. And you know I won't want you to, but you'll do it anyway. Stopping you seems pointless, so do whatever you think you should do."

They reached the door to Raeka's quarters. It had been a leisurely stroll but Zarena's cheeks were rosy, as if the walk had winded her. There wasn't much she could do or say to sway the new, harmonized Raeka. As she observed when Rakeus had raged at her, she was no longer just incapable of experiencing anger but she also seemed immune to the reception of it. Zarena was fairly sure she hadn't even so much as blinked when Rakeus laid into her. It was as if she heard him, but as a passive observer of events, not as the recipient of his ire. Like shouting into the wind.

"Well Zarena, you've successfully lead me back to the place that I live. I'm sure you would have rather held my hand the whole way like a child but thank you for having the courtesy to not condescend. I'm sure I will be faced with much of that in days to come."

"Of course, Rae."

"Who knows better than you the peace you've brought to the Imperium."

"You do now, it would seem."

Zarena gave her a friendly smile, doing her best to keep the pangs of regret from showing on her face, though she wasn't quite sure it would even matter to Raeka.

"If there is anything you need, anything at all I can help you with, you will let me know, won't you?"

"Indeed, I will. I suspect you will be busy working day and night to try to restore me to my former self. I'd say don't but it won't matter to you, but maybe this will. Tread carefully from here on out. You heard my father. He thinks if you reverse The Harmony you're putting the Imperium back at risk. Now that The Harmony is complete and the Imperium still seems more or less functional things may change. He needs you less today than he did yesterday."

"I don't understand what you're saying."

"Yes, Zee, you do. You just don't want to believe it." With that Raeka moved forward and embraced Zarena in a long hug. "I know you don't want me to, but I'm going to thank you. I'll see you soon, Zarena, won't I?" Then she disappeared into the confines of her quarters.

Zarena slowly made her way back to her own apartment, opening the door with a biometric scan and walking into a darkened room. She took off her vest and the items she was carrying on her and put them on the table nearest the kitchen. It was still dark in the apartment but she turned on a light in the kitchen and fumbled for a tumbler in the cabinet. She grabbed a single malt whiskey that was sitting out on the counter and poured herself a drink.

Standing there, alone in the dark, she took a long gulp then winced a bit as the burning liquid went down the back of her throat. She said out loud, "Lights On". All of the lights throughout the apartment came on at once and Zarena nearly jumped out of her skin.

To her immense fright she realized Jesper sat in her living quarters waiting, a knife in his hand. For a moment, she thought she was dead.

"What the fuck are you doing here?" she bellowed at him. He just raised his right hand and put his extended pointer finger gingerly to his lips, in a shushing gesture.

In his other hand he held a long, slender blade, like a shiv but finely honed and with a lovely pearl handle. He stood up and walked over to where she was standing in the kitchen, slinking a bit as he walked, his finger still on his lips in the universal sign for quiet.

As he approached, much to her surprise, he said, "Why don't you pour me one of those?" He capped off the request with a sly and dangerous smile, chilling her to her very bones.

Terrified, she clumsily searched for another tumbler and poured a swell of whiskey into it. She gently handed him the glass and he motioned with the blade to the dining room table. She walked over and pulled out one of the chairs then sat down, waiting for him to make his next move. He glided over to the table, in that stealthy almost liquid way he always seemed to move. He pulled a chair out and left it angled directly towards Zarena, then sat down and placed his drink on the table. Her fear was palpable but she remained as calm as she could, looking at him expectantly as she waited until he said whatever he had come here to say.

"His Imperial Majesty contacted me privately after The Harmony and explained the situation. He is concerned that your attempts to help Raeka, such as they will be, will put the Imperium at risk. It's a perplexing problem indeed and maybe one that with ample time and resources you could solve. Either way as long as you stay here it's irrelevant. Rakeus will never allow you to discover a way to undo The Harmony. He has ordered me to keep you under surveillance. If I discover any evidence that you are working in secret on a countermeasure then I am to take action. Either you will be Harmonized and join the cult of sheep that now graze over the Imperium or you will be eliminated."

Adrenaline was coursing through Zarena's veins. She had never been so afraid in her life. Terror was gripping her chest and pressing down on her lungs. She thought she was going to suffocate under the weight of her own fear. Jesper saw some of this in her eyes. He said, "If I was going to kill you, Zarena, I would have done so already."

"Then why are you here? Why are you telling me this?"

"Because you cannot stay here on Archlon any longer. Rakeus is becoming suspicious of the leadership. The Harmony has had the unintended consequence of creating paranoia among the un-Harmonized. Sooner or later, he will start to believe you are working on a cure whether you actually do so or not. This may be what triggers his own Sequence and sends the universe into peril but that's a separate matter."

"So why are you warning me then, Jesper? What could you possibly want?"

"What I want is as immaterial as what you want. I'm warning you that if you want to save Raeka, and yourself, you will have to leave here—and soon."

He stood up, raising himself to full height, and as he loomed over her with a subtle jerking motion he slipped the blade he was carrying back into his sleeve. He picked up his drink and downed the whole thing in a single gulp. Placing the tumbler back on the table, he headed towards the front door, moving smoothly like a slithering snake escaping through tall grass. Before he opened the door to leave, Zarena, who began to feel a wave of relief wash over her, stopped him.

"Jesper, thank you for the warning." He gave her a wan smile but said nothing. Gathering up every ounce of courage she possessed she asked, "If you came here to help me, then who do you actually serve?"

He looked at her with an inscrutable expression on his face. It was almost as if he was undergoing The Harmony at that very moment.

"I serve the Imperium," he deadpanned. With that, he opened the door and quietly slipped out leaving Zarena sitting by herself, her heart still beating wildly in her chest.

CHAPTER 14
Who Are You?

Emerald stood in the empty office, watching Jazz out of the corner of her emerald eyes as he prepared to leave for the day. He seemed okay for all intents and purposes but something wasn't quite right. She didn't imagine it, something happened without a doubt. There was a noise and a pressure and the world felt like it was underwater. She remembered not being able to move or even speak for a time, paralyzed like a statue carved from marble. She recalled that Jazz didn't move at all, frozen in place, and she had to work a little to rouse him from whatever borderline catatonic state he had entered. Clearly he was more affected by whatever had happened than she was.

Since the phenomenon had ended, she started to feel more or less normal again, but there was something discernibly wrong with Jazz. Maybe *wrong* wasn't the right way to describe it. *Different*, might be more accurate. He moved around his work station slowly, picking up trash and moving objects around as if he had decided spontaneously now was a good time to tidy up. She kept observing him, watching his every step: the way he moved, the deliberation in his actions. He seemed to be completely oblivious to her concern. He hadn't looked at her directly since she had verified he felt fine. He had then proceeded to flitter around the office, cleaning and organizing, in uncharacteristic silence.

After a while, the questions started to boil up inside of her and she thought she might just scream if they didn't come out. She stood up and walked over to Jazz, interrupting whatever menial task he was attempting in that moment. He stopped and looked at her peaceably, a strange blank expression on his face. It was impossible to tell if this was some sort of joke or he had had a stroke or they had just been brainwashed by some shadow government protocol. She was starting to think it was the latter.

"Jazz, what are you doing?"

"Nothing, Em. Just tidying up my workstation a bit." He spoke more slowly than usual.She looked him over skeptically. If he noticed, he didn't acknowledge it in any way.

"Do you remember what happened before, with that crazy sound? It was like some kind of sonic pulse had been triggered in the building. It was weird."

He stared at her for a long moment. Just when she thought he was going to ignore the question entirely he said in a genteel tone, "What do you mean?"

"A little while ago there was some kind of… I don't know, something. A phenomenon, for lack of a better term. It was like a high pitched buzzing sound, it sounded like it was coming from everywhere all at once. I couldn't even breathe or move for a minute. It lasted for a couple minutes and then, just stopped. Since then, you've been acting strangely. Really strange."

His face had an unflappable expression on it, it was impossible for her to tell if he had even heard what she was asking let alone whether he was going to answer.

Finally, he said, "Sorry, I don't know what you mean. I just remember sitting here, that's all. We finished the diagnostics for the day and now we're getting ready to leave."

She stared at him incredulously, not quite believing this was real. What the hell happened?Jazz collected all of his things and said, "Have a good night, Emerald. I'll see you tomorrow."

Emerald watched in silence as Jazz methodically made his way to the elevators. He shuffled along like he was trying to make his way through a drifting snow bank. He pushed down the elevator button like his limbs were made of jelly then waited for the doors to open. Jazz always liked to complain about how long this elevator took since it was a private elevator that connected the mechanical engineering floor to the main lobby. Today, he just stood in front of the doors with a thousand yard stare, a slightly befuddled and vacant expression on his face. When the doors opened he disappeared inside, Emerald watching him intently. His eyes met hers and he smiled a soft, crooked smile. She managed a weak smile in return and then the doors closed and he descended.

She sat alone at her work station, pondering the events of the day and their implications, not liking the conclusions she was coming to. Emerald supposed it could have been some sort of unique geological event but the duration and consistency of the sound did not remotely fit with any known natural phenomenon. The other, and more likely, option was that it was some kind of targeted sonic warfare. Given the nature of the event itself, it made the most sense that this was a deliberate act and the person or persons responsible had an objective in mind. Emerald rewound back through her memories, reliving the experience in her mind, the pressure, the inability to move, the way the sound echoed, how she felt, how Jazz reacted. She still couldn't ascertain much by way of motive or means but she was becoming steadily convinced that the attack targeted specific neurological systems as the intended outcome.

She had read research that indicated advancements in the manipulation of spectral frequencies could be used in certain types of cognitive therapies. These seemed to be parts of her body that were affected by the *pulse*, as she now began to call it in her mind, all connected to the same regions in the brain. The limbic system and cerebral cortex, most likely the amygdala as well as other areas that played a role in both movement, emotion, and aggression. That didn't seem like a coincidence to her. Certain regions were targeted then, but why, for what reason? Jazz at least still seemed like Jazz, but a version of Jazz that was dreaming and couldn't wake from that dream. It was almost like someone else was controlling him, turning him into an apathetic puppet version of himself.

What changes had there actually been, categorically? Nothing physical, as far as she could tell. He didn't grow horns or sprout wings. He didn't shrink or grow taller, thin out or get heavier. He looked exactly the same apart from radiating a hebetudinous quality he never before possessed. From the limited amount she observed of the effects, they were entirely behavioral. That would be consistent with the brain being the target. He appeared docile and sluggish, his normally vibrant and eccentric personality muted, like a movie playing through stained glass. The images could be seen but all the colors were off. He also seemed to have no memory of the event. All of his 'new' behaviors were consistent with the effects of mood altering drugs, like those to treat anxiety or depression, but greater. Maybe it was a treatment for some type of personality-centered malady. It didn't fully compute but that theory made the most sense so far.

So maybe it was an experimental treatment of some sort? But if that was the case, they were doing it on unwitting participants. If this was some sort of clinical trial, even a double blind test, there had to be some level of consent. No one was told anything about it. It just appeared out of nowhere and Emerald could certainly attest that her permission was not granted. But if it was an act of terrorism or of war what was the motive? What did the damn thing actually accomplish? When it finished there was a period of abeyance, where Jazz seemed to not even register the most mundane external stimuli. It was an eerie sort of repose that he didn't rouse from immediately, as if his mind was rebooting like a computer.

Jazz is acting strange, she was positive the pulse was responsible, and with all the other anecdotal stories about the sickness, it was too much of a coincidence to be nothing.

In order to understand what was going on she needed to observe more. She needed to see Jazz again, and hopefully encounter other people that may have had similar reactions to the pulse. As her mind raced with possibilities and contingencies and plots she remembered she was supposed to have dinner with her mom tonight. She imagined it was highly unlikely her mother was affected by the pulse, but it was too early to rule anything out. She had to be many miles away from the Raxeon building at the time.

She decided to give her mom a call. Curiosity mixed with fear started to overwhelm her sensibilities but she did her best to stay composed.

The line rang a few times and just when she thought it was going to go to a mailbox her mother's voice said, "Hello."

"Hi Mom, it's Emerald. I just wanted to make sure we were still on for dinner tonight." Silence on the other end of the line.

"Mom, are you there?"

More silence and then, "Yes, dear. I'm here."

"Are we still on for dinner tonight?"

"Dinner? Oh, yes, of course we are. I had forgotten." Her mom's voice sounded different, almost meandering as if it had gotten lost and strolled down the wrong back alley.

"Mom, are you OK? You sound kinda funny."

"Of course, dear. I'm fine. Never been better."

"That's great, Mom. I'll see you tonight". Another long pause. "Yes, yes of course you will, dear."

"Okay, Mom, bye bye." And she hung up the line from her end.

Something was wrong. Her mom sounded different. Off in the same way that Jazz had sounded. It was the pulse, Emerald was sure of it. She wasn't there with her mom but from just the voice she could tell some of her symptoms were similar to Jazz. It seems to affect the sounds of their voice for some reason, she thought. Maybe simplifying the mind somehow changed the way a person's voice sounded. Perhaps people's voices were a cacophony of their mood states, their happiness, anger, frustration, worry, contentment, all creating stressors in the way they speak, how their voice sounds to other ears. What if you were to suddenly remove all of those feelings, those subliminal impulses. If you weren't or couldn't feel pain anymore, maybe you would sound different. Both Jazz and Teresa sounded lighter, more buoyant, almost whimsical but also more prosaic, like they couldn't get too excited one way or the other. She made a mental note to investigate this observation further but for now there were more important things to do.

She decided to head home straight away. Then she had a thought that gave her pause; what if she was being watched? Like a rat in a maze that doesn't understand they're in a maze. What if she was expected to act differently? Should she try to emulate the affect and mannerisms of the people around her who were changed? It seemed to Emerald that the world had gone mad, so anything she did other than just sit here and ruminate might be a risk. It was a risk she had to take though. If she was going to survive, or escape and find a way to fix everyone she needed to get more data. The 'how' would come later.

At that moment, a terrifying realization dawned; *why was she okay?* If Jazz and her mother and who knows how many others had their personalities and possibly even their brain structures changed, why did the pulse not affect her in the same way? Was she somehow immune to it? She couldn't think of a reason why her mind had been unaffected by the pulse when other minds, comparable minds, like Jazz, had. *What's so special about me?*

She flipped through her mind like a Rolodex, looking for something that was different about her. Yes, her mind was different than most people. She was widely considered the most brilliant engineer at Raxeon. That didn't quite make sense, Jazz was also exceptionally bright. She filed that away as an incomplete assessment until she had more data. Still, that fact she remained the same when others around her were changed didn't make sense, unless she was anomalous in some other way.

Her train of thought kept leading to dead ends but then something in the back of her mind came to the forefront: *your eyes.* She had known since she was little that she had a unique chromatic aberration that made her eyes an unnaturally bright shade of green. She was named after her eye color after all. Eye color is genetic. She had a genetic mutation. She couldn't draw a correlation scientifically between a mutation that affected eye color and anything that had to do with what she witnessed today. The extent of her own mutation may have only expressed itself as green eyes, what they call phenotype, but what if the mutation's genotype, or code, did more than that. What if it made her divergent in some way, or created some immunity to the pulse that others, without any genetic abnormalities did not have. She'd need far more data to make that conclusion but at least she had a start.

She got up, gathered her things and hurried, without obviously hurrying, to the elevator. She hit the down button and waited nearly a minute for the elevator to come. *Jazz would be so pissed,* she thought, *or at least he would have been before.* The thought made her wince a little bit. Whatever it was, she was committed to helping. She couldn't just go about her life while the people she cared about were turned into some kind of subservient drones. She was going to help them regain what they had lost. The elevator finally arrived and she stepped in, hitting the lobby button.

As the elevator plummeted to the bottom floor, she looked around the small elevator she was enclosed in and a disquieting thought poked through the cloud of her mind's eye. *I'm not safe here, am I?* she said to herself. *Whoever did this most likely did not intend for me to be Immune. I may draw unwanted attention from whoever was behind this.*

Then it clicked, like a key turning in a lock. Secrets, cover ups, people disappearing, rumors of a mysterious illness that causes aggression and rage in the afflicted, a bizarre sonic pulse changing the way people behave, making them more… compliant. A frightening realization began to dawn on her as her mind continued to connect the dots.

"Oh no," she said aloud. "It can't be."

The Imperium, the government, the Houses—they know about this or at least some of them do. They have known probably for a while, long enough to create an inoculation of sorts. It is some kind of sickness and the people that are becoming infected are disappearing, probably local law enforcement killing them or quarantining them away from the public so as not to infect anyone else. The sonic pulse, that's the cure. It somehow reverses whatever the sickness is, or vaccinates against it. But then why would they unleash it on just anyone, or everyone? She had no way to confirm but she had a feeling that many many people were exposed to the pulse. To do what it did the breadth and scope of it would have to have been large. So it was improbable that she and Jazz or anyone specific at Raxeon was the target. For all she knew it could be all of Exalon! But why expose everyone to it, why not just the infected? She saw what happened to Jazz, how he was affected. Why turn people into smiling zombies if you don't have to? Unless you do have to. Unless everyone is actually infected. What if everyone has the sickness already and this was them trying to stop it. A mass vaccination, à la the deafening sonic pulse attack.

"Oh shit. This isn't possible. I'm just being paranoid. This… this couldn't possibly be true."

Emerald felt like her head was spinning. She placed her hands on her face and slowly dragged them towards her chin, stretching and smoothing her skin as she went. She let out a small, defeated sigh. *What the hell do I do?* she thought.

She steadied herself and tried to find solid, rational ground in her mind. First things first, all it is at this point is total conjecture. She didn't have empirical evidence for any of it. Even the pulse, she couldn't be sure that her recollection of events was perfect since it was so disruptive to her mind, most likely by design. She couldn't be sure anything she saw had been real. At least it was a starting place though.

The enormity of this conspiracy would have to be staggering. Did House Collette have any inkling? The Emperor himself? Who was the puppet master pulling these strings, and how far would they go to conceal their secrets? Whoever they were had already crossed a perilous line, activating the pulse during Exalon's languid afternoon. Emerald wondered if District 7 was the sole casualty. Had it claimed other districts, or even blanketed the entire planet? A chorus of unanswered questions crowded her mind as she grappled for clarity.

As Emerald contemplated the terrifying prospect of armageddon, the elevator sang a silvery chime and split open its doors into the lobby. She sealed her eyes for a moment and inhaled deeply. *Don't spiral down paranoia's abyss, Em. It won't unlock any of this mystery. Keep collected, calm, don't attract unwanted attention.*

She strode from the elevator's glossy interior out into the lobby, breezing past the same security guard she had bid good morning mere hours ago. He sat ensconced in his chair behind the polished oak guest desk, his vacant stare fixed on some phantom point in the distance. He barely registered her passing with a cursory nod. Feeling a swell of courage, she approached him and offered a good evening. He seemed suspended in a trance, unresponsive. Then a smile flickered across his features. "Oh, good evening Ms. Seltz. I didn't see you standing there."

The same strange, high-pitched voice emerged from the security guard, echoing the peculiar speech of Jazz and her mother. His face was a mask of detached serenity. She replied, "I'm leaving for the evening. I'll see you tomorrow."

He regarded her with a haunting, mirthless smile that might have seemed sardonic in kinder times. "Have a lovely night, Ms. Seltz. Until the morning."

Emerald turned from Nedd and drifted into the street, resolved to retrace her steps back home along the same path she had trod that morning. An ominous, almost post-apocalyptic hush permeated the avenue, as though the world had been suddenly stripped of humankind and gone mute. As she walked, she scoured her surroundings for any signs of life, anything to intimate people still going about their normal affairs. She wondered if there was a single soul left who was like her, or if she alone had eluded the net. A hovercraft crawled past, bound for unseen coordinates. She could not glimpse the driver and dared not flag them down, unwilling to act out of accordance with everyone else and invite scrutiny.

Emerald arrived home without further interaction, the abnormal absence of activity doing nothing to pacify her foreboding. She placed her hand upon the biometric scanner beside her door, the mechanism recognizing her instantly. She stepped across the threshold, eyes darting about for her mother. Hopefully this stupefied condition didn't endanger basic safety. She set her things down in the chair nearest the door and called out. Her words reverberated through the flat but went unanswered. She summoned her mother once more before proceeding into the kitchen. There she discovered the breakfast she had left that morning spilled in fragments across the floor, shards of the shattered dish strewn about. Panic rising like bile, she shouted again for her mother. Just then, a stirring sounded from the bedroom down the hall. The door creaked open and her mother emerged, moving with the same peculiar, deliberate gait as Jazz.

"Hey, Mom," she forced out, struggling to sound normal. Her mother said nothing until she had joined Emerald in surveying the wreckage. Teresa looked down at the ruined meal and said, "I'm so sorry baby, I was heating up the food but the next thing I knew it was on the floor."

"That's okay, Mom. I'll take care of it."

"No, sweetie, it was my fault. I meant to clean up but I just felt so tired I couldn't keep my eyes open. So I laid down for a nap instead."

Her words spilled out gently, their tranquil cadence mirroring Jazz's manner of speech. Emerald's suspicion was confirmed — her mother had heard the pulse and was now altered like Jazz and Nedd. Terror threatened to override her composure, but she consciously slowed her breathing, focusing on steadying the frantic tempo of her heart. Her mother observed placidly, oblivious to her daughter's inner turmoil.

Every fear kindled by the pulse now blazed to life. *This is no accident*, Emerald affirmed, *but a conspiracy and a far-reaching one at that. I'm likely in jeopardy, and so are Mom and Jazz.* Resolve crystallized within her, girding her nerves for the perilous road ahead.

"Don't worry about it, Mom. I'll take care of the mess. Why don't you go relax on the couch while I start on dinner?" She summoned her most convincing smile and began gathering the shattered plate fragments. Her mom returned a faint smile and drifted over to the couch, settling into vacant-eyed repose.

While her mother sat staring into the middling distance, Emerald retrieved her computer terminal from the bedroom and brought it to the kitchen table. She sat down, interlaced her fingers and cracked her knuckles, like the hackers of old prepping for battle. *Alright, time to get to work*, she steeled herself.

After a while, Emerald rose to begin cooking, periodically checking on the stealth program running in the background as she prepared their meal. Though her expertise was in mechanical engineering, Emerald's interest in the applied sciences ranged far beyond. She possessed an intuitive grasp of the planet's sprawling virtual network, the nexus of communication and repository of knowledge for most citizens. The virtunet linked everything to everything, and if you knew where to search, you could unearth virtually any information. Emerald decided to deploy a covert distress signal of her own design, transmitted via encrypted line so even Imperial agents would be unable to decipher its contents or pinpoint its origin. It was a ghost in the machine, a phantom broadcast. She had helped develop the sophisticated code in her youth as a means of secure communication for people like her. It was how she had planned to contact Jazz before the pulse changed everything.

The program could receive requests from outsiders, granting access only if they passed a series of verification checks. She was trolling the endless data streams for someone, anyone like her who had launched a similar SOS out into the void of the virtunet, hoping another Immune soul had thought to seek out allies. It could take days to fully scan the massive network, and the odds of connecting were slim. Even others who had evaded the effects would need a certain technical prowess to even locate her signal. Still, it was a starting point, and she could continue her daily routine while the program tirelessly cast its net wider.

When the food was ready, she dished it out onto plates. Her mother had drifted off on the couch in the interim, so Emerald went to rouse her for dinner. But just then a chime sounded from the terminal. Perplexed, she rushed over to investigate. Most likely some errant spam snared in the net but she had to be sure. What she discovered left her stunned. It was an encoded transmission.

Emerald quickly employed the cryptographic program to decipher the message and read it, blinking in disbelief:

TRANSMISSION:

::::You aren't losing your mind. There was an event. An assault of sorts on the Imperium's populace. It was done out of compassion, though that may no longer matter. It was enacted on the Emperor's command. The details are complex, but I can explain everything. I am astonished and relieved to have found an Immune person. We are both in grave danger now. This communication must be destroyed upon reading.

Emerald's mind reeled. So she wasn't paranoid or delusional after all. The scope of this was even more ominous than she had feared. She typed a response:

::::What exactly is this "pulse"? Are you Immune too? Who are you?

She anxiously awaited a reply. After a moment, one appeared.

::::The pulse, as you call it, is known as The Harmony. It was a sonic zeta wave devised to alter human behavior, as you guessed. I do not believe I am Immune I was not exposed to The Harmony. I am its creator. My name is Zarena Denamonte.

CHAPTER 15
Nice To Have You Aboard

Evard clutched the stolen hovercraft's controls, wincing as he accelerated over the marshy morass. His breaths were heaving, his hands shaking as he held on to the controls, the salt of his tears beginning to sting his eyes. Before leaving the infirmary, he had hastily grabbed armfuls of bandages, antiseptics and antibiotics. The empty halls echoed eerily as he scavenged for supplies, stepping over the crumpled bodies of the officers he had slain. The officers must have evacuated the building because apart from the bodies of the slain, he didn't encounter another person. With no doctor to guide him, he cleaned the seared laz wound as best he could, swathing his leg in gauze and tape. He gulped down antibiotics and fled into the twilight of the evening. The cauterized wound still throbbed agonizingly, making escape on foot impossible.

As his mind cleared from the fog, he started to appreciate the severity of his predicament. He had no money, nothing on him of value. He had friends that might shelter him for a day or two but he couldn't risk endangering anyone else. He couldn't even risk going home. If there was a manhunt for him that would be the first place they would look. The militia were probably already there, waiting for him. He had nothing and no one. With panic rising in his chest, coupled with the pain in his leg, he started struggling to breathe. Trying to calm himself from hyperventilating, he did the best he could to clear his mind and focus.

His mother's dying words began to echo in his mind: *he must get off-world.* The distant landing port was his only hope of escaping this once-peaceful planet, now plunged into chaos. As the lights of the port shimmered in the distance, he veered off the road, killing the engine and lights. Crouching low in the reedy marsh, obscured from sight, he crept along the perimeter fence. Silently circling to the rear of the mammoth hangar, he slipped through an unlocked door into the cavernous darkness, the pain in his leg searing as he moved.

The empty hangar loomed, metal girders branching overhead like the limbs of ancient trees. Ships were docked on the far side — a few small transports and larger starcruisers. Skulking in shadows, staying alert for any sound, the silence pressed against his ears. His heart thundered as he sneaked toward the ships, ready to flee militia pursuit. He wiped the tears from his damp face. He didn't want anyone he met to see his obvious distress. Yet no alarm was raised, no soldiers arrived. Bewildered but desperate, he limped onward.

A parked forklift offered camouflage to explore the hangar. As he drove between stacks of cargo, his heart jolted — a group of workers lounged on the crates ahead! Flight crew in crisp jumpsuits, cargo loaders in grimy grays — yet oblivious to the wounded stowaway in their midst. Emboldened by their inattention, Evard waved in greeting. Their vacant eyes registered no alarm at his disheveled, bloodstained appearance. Murmuring vague pleasantries, they wandered out of his path.

At the transport ships, Evard's pulse quickened further. *Was escape finally within reach?* A rough-looking cargo loader named Hal greeted him warmly, untroubled by Evard's conspicuous lack of uniform. His offer to help load cargo onto the Exalon-bound cruiser was met with eerie apathy from the zombie-like crew. But Evard's desperation overcame his unease at their bizarre detachment. Donning a borrowed jumpsuit, he returned, welcomed eagerly by the kindly Hal.

"Hello, there," the man said, in a strange sounding but congenial voice.

"Hey there," responded Evard, trying to keep his voice from cracking with nerves.

"Is that the lift we called in for?" the man said, his voice maybe too casual. The man looked at him placidly. He was a large, fleshy man, with skin weathered from prolonged exposure to the sun, with sunken eyes and a goofy smile that threw Evard off for a moment.

He raised an eyebrow quizzically, and said, "So you're a lift driver? I don't recall seeing you around here before." He spoke slowly, as if he had to concentrate on his words before speaking them aloud. Just as Evard thought he might be in trouble, the man flashed him a toothy grin and said, "Of course I have, lad. Of course.""Yea, I heard it over the comm, I was bringing it over for you."

"That's great. Mind giving us a hand here."

"Of course, no problem," said Evard, deciding the best thing to do was to just go with it for the time being. "Whaddya need?"

"Just put those crates over there in the cargo hold of this cruiser."

Evard looked over and the rest of the crew were just sitting there, motionless, on the crates he was supposed to load on the ship. He hesitated for a second then said, "Should everyone move first?"

The crewman who asked him for help turned around, slowly, methodically, almost like a caricature of a person turning around.

"Hey, everyone", he said in an even keeled voice. "You mind moving for our friend here?"

The rest of the crew looked lethargic. *Almost sleepy*, Evard thought. Nonetheless, one by one they slowly began to move out of the way. Evard waited until the last one had moved far enough from the crate then he pulled in and picked up the first pallet, loading them into the cargo hold of the starcrusier one at a time until all of them were on. Once he finished the man who originally asked him for help stopped to thank him.

"I appreciate the help, pal," he said to Evard in a monotone voice. He seemed more alert than the others, more connected to reality or something. Evard had just spent ten minutes moving boxes for this person, who never once commented on the lack of uniform, or the blood and bandages, or any of the other suspicious things about Evard that he feared was going to expose him. He simply seemed happy for the help, as if he was sitting around just waiting for someone to bring a fork lift and didn't care about much else beyond that. Evard couldn't believe his luck since he was staring down the barrel of a gun in that hallway. The strange but fortunate event surrounding his escape gave him the courage to say, "Excuse me, friend, where is this ship going?"

"It's a cruiser but it's mostly carrying supplies and goods to Exalon. A few passengers were scheduled to travel but it seems like all of those tickets were cancelled, so it's just going to be crew and cargo."

"Exalon?" said Evard. "That's a central system planet, isn't it?"

The crewman nodded a slow, deliberate nod that would have been more at home in an animated show than as an earnest gesture by a burly cargo handler. Evard was fairly sure that Exalon was one of the interior worlds, not far from Archlon as he recalled. Some kind of industrial, computerized world, about as far away from Eden as he could get. Sounded like the perfect place to hide from the local Eden militia. Evard, getting increasingly comfortable with the situation, took a shot.

"Yeah, I think I might be scheduled on the crew for this flight." He held his breath for a second, waiting for the other shoe to finally drop.

After a moment of pause, the crewman said, "Oh, good, we could always use another crew member. The flight is scheduled to depart within the hour. Why do you get your stuff together." He pointed off to the corner of the hangar. "Go get changed and cleaned up, and meet back in here in thirty."

Evard couldn't help but break into a big smile. "Sounds good, see you then." He drove the fork lift over to where the crewman had pointed, which seemed to be a locker room of sorts. He walked in and looked around for any other employees but the coast was all clear. Most of the lockers seemed to have locks on them but a few were open. He rummaged through all of the lockers, in search of something he could wear on the flight. In one of the empty lockers he found a blue jumpsuit. It was a little big on him but it would do.

He grabbed it and then went to the showers, stripping off all of his old clothes, making sure to take out all of the medical supplies. He threw all his old clothes away and looked down at the bandage on his leg. There was some discharge on the wound so he gently removed the bandage. The leg had dried blood all around it but he was able to get a good look at the wound, which was about the size of a coin and covered with a large scab, most likely made from the laser itself cauterizing the entrance and exit of the blast. He was going to have a nasty scar and if he didn't heal it right, possibly a limp for the rest of his life, but it didn't look as bad as it could have. He ran the shower and stood underneath, carefully soaping and washing around the wound. Once he had finished washing off, he carefully applied a new set of bandages and then dressed himself in the blue jumpsuit he had pilfered from the locker.

Looking like a new man and feeling a bit like one, too, he returned to the starcruiser and the strange crewman that had welcomed him aboard.

"Thanks for letting me ride along," said Evard honestly. "Of course, I assume you're a newbie so it's good to get some experience. My name is Halbert Jonze but everyone calls me 'Hal'."

Hal extended his hand, slowly, as if it was a retractable ramp of some kind. The rest of the crew lounged around, their faces passive, as if nothing in this particular exchange was of interest to them.

Evard shook Hal's hand and said, "Hi, Hal. I'm Evard, nice to meet you."

Hal smiled as he shook Evard's hand, his grin sitting askance on his worn face, some ragged teeth showing through closed lips. It was an unsettling look but so far Hal had seemed friendly and willing to help Evard out, though out of what he couldn't possibly know.

"Well, Evard, it's nice to have you aboard," Hal said. "The trip to Exalon takes about twenty Imperium standard hours. Should be an easy one."

Evard noticed that Hal spoke with a meter that was both measured and just a beat slower than most people spoke, even in casual conversation. It was off putting at first but he was starting to get used to it. Whatever it was, this man seemed like his only way off-world, best not to hold his strange speaking cadence against him. The rest of the crew still stood around listless, like they were automaton, waiting for a command prompt to react. *This is just getting weirder and weirder*, Evard thought, but not lingering too long on all these questions had been working for him so far. The best thing for now is to get to Exalon and figure out how to start a new life, one away from the ruins his life had become here on Eden.

It's what his mother would have wanted for him. It's what his mother died to ensure. Even if the will to go on was fading and he was starting to fall back into the dark abyss of his own thoughts, he owed his mom this. He resolved right there and then that her sacrifice would not be in vain. He was going to survive and move forward and maybe, one day, find the peace again that he had always lived with but had taken for granted his whole life. He chuckled as a sob got caught in his throat. To think he ever thought his life was boring before today. He was regretful of all that he wasted here on Eden… but that could matter no longer.

In this brave new world, there was not much room for regrets.

If Hal had noticed his emotional turbulence, he didn't react at all. Instead, he walked over, in that slow plodding way people seemed to do now, and rallied the rest of the crew onboard the ship. He motioned for Evard to join them, entering the ship through the cargo hold. Everyone was walking up the ramp single file, like prisoners being herded outdoors for daily exercise. Evard joined the back of the line and made his way onto the ship, entering the large holding bay, where all the cargo that had previously been used as lounges for the crew, was stacked neatly to one side.

Hal moved the crew through the ship, showing them the cabin quarters, the galley where the meals would be served, the lounge where the passengers could mingle during the flight, and the ship deck where the flight crew was sitting, waiting for their orders to depart.

There was a cook in the kitchen, sitting down at one of the tables slowly cutting vegetables, fresh from the fields of Eden. There were two pilots on the ship deck and Hal introduced everyone to Evard. All of the people he met looked at him with that same lack of curiousness that Hal initially did, though they spoke less and stared off into space more. Evard didn't let the idea that the two zombies he just met were going to pilot the tachyon engines to traverse the vast openness of space between here and Exalon bother him… much. *Best not to dwell on the things you can't change*, he reminded himself.

After the awkward introductions, everyone took to their places on the ship, preparing to do whatever task they were hired to perform on such a mission. Without having to transport guests this, ship seemed more like a fancy cargo transport than a starcruiser. At least with a cook on board the food would probably be halfway decent. It seemed weird there would still be a chef on board without guests to feed but the crew needed to eat so Evard supposed that made a kind of sense.

There were several guest cabins and suites on board, as well as the crew quarters. Since the crew was small and there were no fancy guests paying top dollar to have a private room, all the crew were able to bunk in the guest quarters. That should at least make the trip comfortable and give Evard a little time to decompress. His leg still hurt but it was hurting somewhat less now that he wasn't running or crawling on it. He reached into his pocket and found the antibiotics. Fetching a glass of water from the sink in the kitchen he shook out a few pills from the bottle and swallowed them down. They seemed to be helping, but as soon as he landed in Exalon he needed to find more medical supplies.

He wasn't sure what his plan was once they reached Exalon. He could try to hop another ship to yet another distant port of call but Exalon, from everything he heard, seemed as good a place as any to start over. With all the strangeness going on here on Eden, he doubted very much that anyone would be looking for him off-world. Still, he'll need to get a new ID as soon as he could. It was dangerous for him to continue to live as Evard Roost. Whether or not the news made the wires yet, he still murdered three militia officers in cold blood. There had to be security cameras that caught him in the act. It was possible that the Sergeant disabled them before he attempted to murder Evard and his mother, but it still wasn't a risk he was willing to take. Better to start fresh as someone new, somewhere no one would know him, where he could blend in.

His train of thought was interrupted by the sound of the engines humming to life. The parking lock was disengaged and he felt the cruiser float upward. The voice of one of the pilots came over the comm. "This is Captain Vecht. We have been cleared for take off. Everyone please find a seat and buckle in for departure."

The voice sounded like a typical starship captain but had that odd, lithe, airy quality that everyone's voice had seemed to adopt in the past few hours. Hal was walking the halls, in that stutter gait that he had observed back in the hangar. He was checking on everyone, making sure they were secured before take off. Evard was sitting in the kitchen when Hal came in.

"Evard, best find a seat in the lounge. Ship's about to take off."

Evard followed him into the lounge area where the rest of the crew were sitting in their flight seats, buckled in, waiting patiently for the ship to depart. Evard took an empty seat near the back of the room and buckled himself in. Hal walked past him and took a seat in the row in front. He turned around slowly and said, "Time to fly. Say goodbye to Eden."

Evard had never been off-planet before. He was born, lived and, up until today, had expected to die on Eden. He thought about his family and tears welled up in his eyes. There would be no one here to bury them, he realized, and a profound sadness started to grip him. His family was dead, their bodies most likely taken away by the militia. He hoped his uncle would find their bodies and lay them to rest but in his heart he knew better. More likely, any trace of their existence would vanish, like smoke on the wind. The official report would say that they were victims of his brother, a homicidal maniac, who had been killed by an officer during the attacks. Or maybe there would be no report. With all the strange occurrences, it might all just get swept under the rug, as if none of them existed. He had an uncle who lived a few hours from here. Maybe he would be able to retrieve their bodies and give them a proper funeral. It was more likely, however, that the whole incident would be covered up and they would be just another mysterious disappearance. As if their souls floated off with their bodies on the evening breeze.

As the ship rose on a pillar of flame into Eden's darkening skies, Evard grieved that he could never return. That hurt almost as much as everything else that had happened today. His escape honored his mother's sacrifice, though leaving his homeland tore his heart into pieces. He would survive, start fresh, and one day reclaim the peace that he had lost.

Eden dwindled to a glittering orb behind the cruiser, leaving everything he had ever known in the dust. Evard began to weep as he sailed toward his new life.

CHAPTER 16
Yes, I Understand

Hours after Jesper departed her apartment, Zarena still lay wide awake in bed, overcome by a sense of foreboding that clung to her like damp clothes. When she flipped on the light and saw Jesper's sinewy form perched on the couch, she was certain her end had come. Never before had she known such visceral terror as in that moment. Yet it was the conversation that followed which now kept sleep at bay. The revelations left her reeling, and she now faced an impossible dilemma — become a fugitive or possibly a martyr.

She found it hard to believe Rakeus would ever harm her. He'd known her since childhood and had always been kind, especially regarding her friendship with Raeka. She wasn't even sure she believed Jesper. How could she? She had done what had been demanded of her, what was needed. Her triumph could save the lives of billions. Rakeus loved and respected her. She could not imagine a world where he would harm her, especially one in which she did her duty so well. And yet, Jesper's appearance started to cast a shadow of doubt. Somehow, she knew what he said was true, even if it came from a bald-faced liar like him.

She thought back to the fateful day the council decided to greenlight The Harmony. There had been a moment that had fallen out of her mind but she remembered it now. Rakeus had lost his composure and for a split-second she and the other counselors thought he might actually attack them. In that brief moment, she had felt fear. It wasn't much to go on but her instincts usually proved correct. This wasn't the safe haven it once was. Here there be dragons. Her entire belief system was starting to unravel.

Zarena and Raeka had grown up together. Zarena's father was the Imperial Ambassador to the Great Houses. His role was to facilitate cooperation and support between the House Imperiatus and the rest of the Imperium. Growing up, Zarena would sometimes accompany him on his trips, excited to visit these far flung worlds, many of which were so different from where she had grown up on Archlon. As foreign dignitaries, they were treated to all manner of excursions on the myriad of worlds they visited. It instilled in Zarena a love of culture and an appreciation for just how vast and aspirational the human race, and its ambitions, can be. Sometimes they would travel with Rakeus himself on various diplomatic missions, with Raeka accompanying him as Zarena accompanied her father. Zarena and Raeka would play games like hide and seek on board the various ships they traveled in from world to world. As they grew up, they would find ways to separate from the official proceedings and head off to enjoy some personal time on whatever planet they were visiting.

It was during one of these trips that Zarena first witnessed The Sequence, though she didn't realize what she had truly witnessed until later. She and Raeka were visiting a small fishing village on the planet Esper, one of the colony worlds at the edge of the Imperium. Saturated with large salt water seas rife with edible aquatic life, Esper provided almost a third of all fish that was consumed throughout the Imperium. There were exquisite restaurants on Archlon that served fish from Esper, many of them using that fact as a selling point. And like many of the outer worlds, especially colony worlds like Esper, Eden, Laetus, Trilanus, and Dertcis, where most of the agricultural staples and livestock meats were imported from, it was mostly poor, the median income far below the Imperium average. Most of the population worked directly or indirectly for the fishing and farming trades. Villages clustered around the best epicenters for fishing, so Esper was mainly just a minefield of small, mud-soaked towns that reeked of salt and sea.

Craving authentic local culture, Zarena and Raeka slipped away from one of these meetings in disguise with a handful of guards. They ambled through Orelan, renowned for Orelan trout, the sweetest fish in the Imperium. Raeka was keen to see the writhing, wriggling nets heavy with the catch of the day. As they headed towards the docks through the sleepy morning streets, they heard the escalating shouts of fishermen. An older man in traditional garb was berating two younger ones.

The confrontation soon turned violent. Zarena later learned he was a grizzled fishing boat captain, and the others were his crew. As the captain pummeled the men viciously, the sickening crunch of bones pierced the morning air, shaking the girls from their reverie. Their bodyguards surrounded them protectively as the angry captain charged them like an enraged bull, hurling vile curses. The guards swiftly tasered the madman into submission before he could reach the terrified girls.

As time went on, and Zarena learned increasingly about The Sequence, the memory, that image of a haggard old man so seething with rage and violence that he would charge an Imperial envoy, stuck with her. She vowed to help in any way she could, at whatever cost it came with. She realized as she lay awake, sleep as far from her mind as Esper was from her body, that this was the moment that set The Harmony in motion. Though it would take another two decades, it crystallized in her mind on that fateful street on a backwater planet that the Imperium may actually be broken and just maybe she had the tools to fix it. She wondered if her resolve would have been different had she not witnessed the fallout so early on. The point was moot now. The Harmony was done and all the worlds of men now spun a little slower, a little more carefully, a little less thoughtfully. She had orchestrated a fundamental change in the human race and now, scared and alone in her room, she contemplated another.

The thought of Rakeus turning against her chilled her to the bone. Even as a child, she had never feared Rakeus. She always gave him the respect he was due and he showed her kindness in return. As uneasy as Jesper made her feel, it was the Emperor and Council that frightened her more. Her father was gone, but her mother still lived on Archlon. Though they weren't close, leaving her mother forever filled Zarena with sadness. She couldn't endanger her by confiding her plans. Jesper's surveillance made it unsafe to ask anyone for help escaping. If Rakeus was paranoid, detainment could be imminent. She had to believe Jesper's warning. Whether the danger came from Rakeus, the Council, Jesper, or all of them, she was no longer safe here. That much had been made clear.

What do I do next? she agonized. She needed to discreetly flee the planet, but where could she hide beyond Rakeus's iron grasp? Leaving wasn't the problem. As Councilor, she could convincingly claim a need to study The Harmony's impact on industry and agriculture, in case updated technologies were required. The Council would buy this, and it would explain her absence to Rakeus, for a time anyway. If he tried to detain her, she'd deal with that. First, she had to decide where to go.

Zarena had travelled widely, but no particular world inspired her. Backwater colonies lacked the resources she'd need. She could take equipment, but without knowing her needs, picking a remote dead-end like Eden or Dertcis seemed unwise despite their safety. She had to balance personal risk against mission success. If she was sacrificing everything — career, standing, her mother, Raeka — she had to succeed in reversing The Harmony. Her life now depended on healing Raeka, even if Raeka had chosen this herself.

Damn you, Raeka! Why did you do it. To force me to save you? Did you hope that I would throw my life away to undo the good I've done?

Reasons no longer mattered. Fixing what she broke was all that concerned her. She considered finding others who may be Immune. Though unlikely anyone could assist technically, it was more plausible than she'd thought. Certain genetic quirks and neurodivergence tended to confer resistance. Unfortunately, the few cases went unexplored, as The Harmony's success made examining failures seem pointless. Foolishly, she'd focused only on repeating their astounding results rather than probing the anomalies. In hindsight, an unforgivable oversight. Still, enough data existed to look for general markers, a starting point to locate others.

Most neurodivergence didn't prevent Harmonization — dyslexia, dyspraxia, even autism. But some conditions like Asperger's showed reduced effects. Also, non-cognitive mutations sometimes boosted resistance, though the correlations were unclear. Behavior provided the best clues now. The un-Harmonized would stand out. Some might pretend to fit in, but she could spot the tells. The Harmonized ignored those who were different, part of their engineered tranquility.

Those Immune would realize something inexplicable had happened. They'd see loved ones behaving oddly and retain memories of the event itself. Some might be seeking answers online. Perhaps she could locate a few, for shelter or aid, however unlikely. What were the odds any could genuinely help, she mused. Still, it was worth investigating.

Rising from bed, Zarena crossed the dark room and activated her terminal. If anyone unusual was online, their activity could provide leads. She ran spyware used by Imperial security forces to monitor potential terrorist chatter by tracing patterns in the endless static of cyberspace. Normally, this took days or weeks to yield results, but with less traffic since The Harmony, it might suffice.

In minutes, the software uncovered an embedded signal, accessible yet hidden inside the net. Encrypted communication protocols suggested a bespoke system. After cracking the cryptography, she gained access. When prompted, she typed a message asking who was responsible for the SOS. Twenty seconds later, came the response.

SOS: My name is Emerald Seltz, an engineer on Exalon. Something happened. Some kind of sonic pulse struck District 7. In the last five hours, everyone even my mom and my best friend are acting weird. I'm losing it, but looking for answers. If you know what's going on, please contact me.

Zarena gasped in surprise. An Immune person an engineer at the Raxeon Corporation, no less. Exalon was technologically sophisticated and near Archlon.It might be the perfect place to set up shop. Perhaps this Emerald could help. She'd logged on recently, meaning Zarena could reach her before fleeing. She began typing a reply.

TRANSMISSION:

You're not crazy. There was an event — an attack on Imperial citizens, ordered by the Emperor to save humanity. Complicated, but I'll explain. I'm delighted to find someone Immune. If you want to help your loved ones, meet me. We're both in danger now. Destroy this after reading.

Zarena waited anxiously, worried she might scare her off. Curiosity about the inexplicable must be driving her to engage despite the risks. Soon, a response appeared.

What's the pulse? Are you Immune too? Who are you?

Zarena smiled into the darkness. This was promising. She typed quickly.

The pulse is called the Harmony, intended to reprogram human behavior as you guessed. I'm not Immune, at least that I know of. I wasn't Harmonized. I created it. I'm Zarena Denamonte.

A long pause followed. Zarena feared she'd lost her. Finally, text emerged.

Imperial Councilor Zarena Denamonte? You're saying the Imperium attacked its own people, and you created this attack?

Zarena knew she must tread cautiously. She didn't want to alarm Emerald and risk losing this connection through fear. She was lucky Emerald was curious enough to keep engaging despite the dangers. Zarena considered her next message carefully before transmitting.

Yes and no. It's complex. There is a genetic disease that would eventually ensure our extinction. The Emperor tasked me with finding a cure. I devised a solution, but things veered off course.

Patiently, she awaited the reply, which came after several tense minutes.

Can you prove your identity?

Access the Public Data Archives on Archlon. I'll send a sample to verify me.

Rummaging in her drawer for a sharp object, Zarena found a pin and pricked her thumb until a bead of blood surfaced. She pressed the oozing digit to her terminal's scanner, then wiped it clean along with the scanner. After initiating the biometrics app, she uploaded the results via the covert channel.

Here, cross-check this against the Archives.

Likely Emerald was now decoding the DNA and running it against the voluntary identification records to look for a match. Entry was open to everyone, but many officials and professionals registered identities there as safeguard against impersonators. Zarena had enrolled her genome to forestall any potential identity theft. She'd never before had reason to confirm her biometrics, but now gave silent thanks for having the foresight. Soon, a reply appeared.

Why are you telling me this?

It's unsafe for me on Archlon now. I plan to reverse the Harmony but can't do it here. I need help.

What do you need?

I have to leave Archlon very soon. I'll need somewhere to go. And to work.

I can help you. Sending coordinates. Can you make it here securely?

Emerald transmitted location details in Exalon's District 7. Zarena saved them and sat back, pulse racing. This marked a turning point. Accepting this aid set her on a collision course with destiny, for good or ill. The reality of becoming a fugitive sent a chill through her. Steadying herself, she responded. She just hoped that Emerald Seltz was up to the task.

Yes, I should arrive within a week. If not, assume I'm compromised and flee. Understand?

No response came initially. *Damn, I spooked her,* Zarena thought. *I should've been less blunt. What will I do now?* Just as she despaired, the terminal chimed.

Yes, I understand.

CHAPTER 17
How Do We Fix This?

Evard didn't think he was going to be able to sleep given the tragedy of the past day but minutes after his head hit the pillow in Guest Room 5, he drifted off into a deep and dreamless slumber.

The cabin he was in had two full size beds, a couch, two small closets, an adjoining bathroom with a toilet, sink and small shower among other amenities. One of the other crew members was sharing the room with him, a ship steward named Olaver who would have, under different circumstances, been tasked with waiting on the passengers. Instead of serving affluent guests cocktails and hors d'oeuvres in the lounge he was laying in the other bed snoring like a field hand with a broken nose. Evard was oblivious to the noise, his exhaustion plunging him down deep into slumber, his mouth drooling as he made sputtering snores of his own. To someone standing outside of their cabin it may have sounded like a symphony of wood chopping and bird honking, shrill and piercing.

When Evard awoke in the dark he moved about groggily, getting his bearings in a strange place with strange people. He could still hear the labored breaths of Olaver in the bed next to him. Not wanting to disturb his roommate, he crept out of bed slowly and gingerly walked to the bathroom, turning on the light then quickly closing the door behind him.

He stood for a minute looking at his face in the mirror. He barely recognized his own reflection. The face that stared back at him was older and more haggard than he remembered. The events of the past day or so had aged him several years, and just then he felt the throb in his leg from the lazgun wound. He had taken his antibiotics and put them in the medicine cabinet in the bathroom after he picked this room for himself. He opened the cabinet now, took the bottle of pills, opened it, and shook a few out into his hand. He put them in his mouth then filled an empty glass next to the sink with water and swallowed them down in a big, thirsty gulp.

He looked at his leg and realized that it wasn't getting any worse, which was a relief. Still, it had a long way to go before he could consider it healing. The sooner he was able to get proper medical attention the better. He thought to ask if there was a medic aboard the ship but he highly doubted there was. Everything was so surreal now, down to the odd behaviors of the crew. It was like the moment he walked into the infirmary and asked the nurse behind the desk what room his father was in, he entered some sort of parallel universe where the laws of logic and order ceased to exist.

He lived now in a world, and maybe a universe, drenched in madness. The murder, the deaths, the miracle noise that stopped everyone in their tracks, the way people were now acting differently. It was all too much to process. Maybe there would be time to ruminate on just how bizarre a turn his entire world had taken but for now, he needed to just focus on how he was going to quietly slip away once the cruiser docked on Exalon. There would be time later to decide whether it was the world that had gone mad or if it was just him.

He used the toilet, then washed his hands and face, and went back into the dark cabin. He laid down on the bed, staring up at the inky blackness, listening to the gentle whirl of the tachyon drives engaging superliminal speeds through the void of space. The soft humming sound the drives made as their turbines churned was soothing, almost rhythmical, and was lulling Evard back to sleep when a ferocious bump jostled him from near unconsciousness. Olaver seemed to be stirring as well, the force of the jolt brutishly shaking the whole ship awake with its sudden rumbling. Evard stood up and turned on the lights in the cabin.

"What was that," he asked Olaver. Olaver just stared at him a minute, as if he had been awoken from a dreamworld and was unsure if he still was there or not. He didn't say anything, just stared blankly at Evard, who had begun to get dressed.

"Olaver, what was that," Evard repeated and louder. Finally Olaver said, "Don't know, boss. Sounds like we hit something."

"Hit something? In *space*? The odds of hitting random space debris is probably pretty low." He noticed that Olaver seemed totally uninterested in the conversation and had already closed his eyes again, drifting back off to the dreamworld from whence he came. "Fine," said Evard. "I'll go check it out myself."

He opened the door to the cabin and saw that the running lights were on in the hall but not much else. He called out a greeting to see if anyone else was awake but no one answered. Looking both ways down the hallway he headed up towards the lounge, passing the empty kitchen on the way. He peeked his head in the kitchen, no signs of life, so he continued to the lounge. Once he got there, all the lights were turned on and Hal was standing by the entrance to the flight deck, talking to what Evard thought was the one of the piloting team he was introduced to yesterday. They stood there, stiff as statutes, talking in hushed tones. Evard moved over to their position, standing next to Hal and turning his head back and forth to look at both men. Neither of them acknowledged his existence.

"We need to look at the engine then," Hal said. "The odds are something went offline. We won't know until we look."

The other man stood staring at him, mouth slightly agape, eyes a bit out of focus. "You'll have to wake the mechanic," said the pilot. "He should take a look with you."

At this point, Evard injected into the slow moving conversation. "Olaver is the mechanic on the ship. We're bunk mates. I'll go get him."

Evard ran back to his cabin and found Olaver sleeping again, snoring and wheezing away in whatever dreamworld he was in. Evard began to lightly, then more forcefully, shake him awake. Not ready to be roused to action, Olaver tried turning over and away Evard, who was becoming more frustrated with each passing second.

Evard turned on the lights and said firmly,"Get up, Olaver! There's an emergency!" Finally his eyes fluttered awake like the wings of a hummingbird and he sat up with a breathy cough.

"Alright, I'm awake," he said groggily. Slowly and methodically, in the way that everyone Evard met now acted, he swung his feet off his bed and rose to them, stretching his arms and neck as he stood. Then he walked past Evard and out the door of the cabin towards the lounge.

Evard wasn't sure what the problem was but given the strange, lethargic state of the crew he thought maybe he should be part of this. Heading down the hall after Olaver he joined him and Hal and the co-pilot in the lounge. They were talking to themselves, and it struck Evard that maybe something serious was wrong but you wouldn't know it from observing them. You had to listen to what they were saying.

"...the thruster on the 1KS turbine isn't turning. That's what the diagnostics report says." Then a long pause. "Someone will need to go to the engine room and pull the thruster up to check." Another long pause, which in reality was probably not as long as Evard was imagining but given the circumstances felt excruciating.

No one volunteered.he three men just looking around at each other, lights on but nobody home. Evard, nervous that whatever was going on would get more serious without immediate action, said, "I can help. If someone accompanies me to the engine room and shows me where the thruster is."

A few heartbeats passed and Evard thought his offer of assistance was going to be ignored. Finally, Hal said, "Sure thing, new guy. Olaver can help fix it. Why don't we all go back to the engine room and take a look."

Evard thought at least Hal was being reasonable. The other two seemed to have frozen in the face of an emergency response. Still, the way that all three men seemed so calm, like they had no worries or fear or anxiety at all was starting to concern Evard. It was unusual and more than a little disquieting. Hal and Olaver headed towards the engine room with Evard in tow. Evard didn't know much about starship mechanics but he did know a bit of hovercrafts, having rebuilt a few hover drives in his day. He doubted that knowledge would make him valuable in this scenario but he felt like these guys needed a leader to make sure the task was performed. In the long road ahead he would come to see himself as a true leader, but in this moment, it came as a surprise to him. In fact, though he didn't realize it, this was the first moment of his life he ever had felt like one.

The trio entered the rear starboard engine room and the lights all came on at once, bright sterile lights casting a white hazy pall over all the churning machinery. The room hummed with the vibrations of the engines, though Evard expected engine systems this large to be louder. He said as much to Hal who replied that the engine rooms were equipped with sound dampeners for the comfort of the guests. There were turbines that moved using counter magnetic balances and they were suspended over an open hole in the floor that had a guard rail around it. Everything seemed to be moving and Evard wasn't even sure what the problem was. He asked Hal to explain.

"See this engine, this one here? It draws power from this turbine *here* that uses electromagnetism to generate static which is converted to fuel for the engine. The main thruster here isn't turning on, probably because there is not enough power coming from the turbine." Evard waited for him to elaborate but Hal just stood looking at the system. Olaver also stood, just looking around with almost a passive disinterest.

"Well, we just need to see what's blocking the thruster and get it to kick on so that it can feed power to the starboard engine." Sounded simple enough but Evard wasn't comforted.

"What happens if we can't fix it?" he asked.

Hal just kept looking at the floating turbine, but eventually said, "If we don't fix it, the engine will most likely drain all the existing power and could stall out. If that happens we could still fly with the port side engine but most likely won't be able to engage the tachyon drive."

"What does that mean?"

Hal turned to him and gave Evard that toothy, sly grin that everyone seemed to be giving him since he got to the landing port. "It means that we won't be able to achieve superluminal speeds."

Evard, not understanding exactly what the ramifications of that would be, asked, "Alright, and what does that mean?"

"It means that this trip will take a long time to make. Maybe too long."

"Too long?"

Hal looked Evard directly in the eyes and said in his peculiar cadence, "We only have enough rations for a short trip. If we lose this engine we will most likely run out of food before we can make it to the nearest planet or outpost." The situation was starting to come into focus now.

"So, you're saying we'd be stuck out here in the void. We could die?"

"Yes," said Hal, in a completely neutral, unburden tone.

"Could we send out an SOS, could we be rescued?"

"Maybe, but that would be taking a chance. We're in the dead center of the plotted course, in the smack dab middle of nul-space. The turbine also provides power to the ship's other systems. If this one goes down and we try to fly on the other we may lose communications. Lights, refrigeration, climate control —all that — could go on the fritz. That will shorten how much time we can float out here."

Evard was now the one to just stare, unblinkingly at his compatriot. "What happens if the climate control goes?"

Hal looked at Evard, with a placard smile. "We have an emergency power system but if that fails we would freeze to death in the vacuum of space." He said it with no jest or irony in his voice, as if he was just mildly stating the answer to a benign question, like how much salt to put in a soup recipe. Abject panic started spreading through Evard's body, like a fire consuming a dry piece of wood.

Hal continued on with the doomspeak ignoring Evard's re-action. "Even if someone could be dispatched it would be difficult to pinpoint our exact location. Then they would have to haul us in. Not something we want to leave up to chance."

Evard thought about it and it seemed like the path ahead was crystal clear. "We just have to fix it then."

Hal smiled in agreement, continuing this entire 'no worries' persona that everyone seemed to have now. "So, again, how do we fix this?"

Hal slowly lifted his index finger and pointed right at Olaver, who seemed totally oblivious to the entire conversation, almost as if he was falling back to sleep on his feet. "Olaver here can fix it."

No one moved after Hal finished speaking. Evard was about to start screaming out of sheer frustration. Why the fuck is no one worried about stalling out in the middle of nowhere, potentially running out of power and freezing or starving to death in the darkness of space? It felt like something that should at least be a priority. Evard realized that everyone seemed to be moving through an invisible field of molasses and since this required a sense of urgency, it was going to have to come from him.

"Okay then Olaver, guess what? You've been selected to save all of our lives, who would have thought it? Certainly not me," he said with a wry smile. "I will be playing the part of your lovely assistant! Let's go!"

Olaver sluggishly started moving again, apparently taking no umbrage at the commands being barked at him by some newbie, who was in truth a stowaway. He started to get the tools from the mechanical closet, getting everything set up for the maintenance.

Evard turned to Hal and said, "What does he need to do exactly, so I can make sure he does it."

Hal, flashing him that unsettling hangdog grin said plainly, "He needs to turn off this turbine, pull it out, inspect it, and put it back then jump start it."

Something dawned on Evard. "So we need to turn the engine off to repair. What if we can't turn it back on?"

"Same thing that happens if we let it burn out." Hal's leering grin was becoming more ominous.

We are going to do this, thought Evard with a certain amount of gumption. *I know I can do this. I'll get this sloth of a man moving and fixing the ship so we don't die stranded out here in nulspace and then I can get off this infernal flying insane asylum and away from these sleepy human mannequins and get down to the business of surviving.*

He never thought before this whole ordeal that he'd actually relish the thought of fleeing for his life, but it seemed preferable to dying a violent death in the hallway of a hospital, or freezing to death in the emptiness of space. Hal looked on, standing behind Evard who was helping Olaver select the proper tools for the job from the closet. He waited a few minutes then left the repairs in their capable hands.

The two men worked in silence for a while, Olaver pointing and nodding towards things he needed Evard to fetch. They first had to turn the starboard engine system off, which required both a main line shut off and a temporary disablement of the emergency back up system. It could only be performed with two people, as both a safety measure and as a design necessity. The entire system was suspended on a hydraulic lift that was powered by magnetic suspenders that first required deactivation. Both the primary engine key and the secondary key had to be turned synchronously from disparate panels in order to engage the engine lock mechanism. They had to attempt this several times as Evard was finding it difficult to align the timing with Olaver, who didn't seem particularly concerned about turning his key in sync with Evard. After fumbling through a few tries, they were able to activate the mechanism successfully.

"Glad we got it that time," mused Olaver. "Another miss and the system would have locked us out for a bit."

Evard glared incredulously at his partner, "What?"

"Yeah, it's a fail safe to prevent authorized access," Oliver said in that slow lyrical way everyone was now speaking in.

Evard just shook his head in amazement. "That was probably something you should have mentioned."

"Yeah," was all that Olaver said in response.

Once the engine was off, Evard thought the best course of action was to fix the problem as expeditiously as possible, which he mentioned to Olaver, who merely grunted affirmatives in return. Evard radioed Hal on a comm to let them know the engine had been powered down. Hal then instructed the pilots to put the port engine in neutral so they didn't burn out and the ship shook, like it was brushing off the clamps of a dry dock and then a sort of popping sound could be heard. The ship began to drift, slowly, aimlessly.

Hal called back over the comm, "We don't want to stay this way for long. Try to be quick."

Evard looked at the face of the space cadet working in silence next to him, then replied sheepishly, "We'll try."

Watching Olaver methodically repair the turbine, Evard realized he had no idea what he was looking at. Starcruiser engines were a far cry from hovercrafts, differentiated by the sheer number of integrated systems alone. Olaver opened the turbine and found that one of the magnetized plugs had been negatively charged and needed repair.

"We can either replace the plug or recharge it," said Olaver looking into Evard's face expectantly. Evard wasn't sure what the difference was so he asked.

"No difference, unless the plug has a short."

"What happens if the plug has a short?"

"The system could catch fire."

"How long would it take to replace?"

Olaver seemed to be contemplating this with what would have been, under different circumstances, a comical face. Eventually he said, "If we don't hit a snag, probably an hour, maybe more."

Evard wasn't sure if they had that much time so he asked, "How long if we recharge the plug?" Again Olaver seemed to consider it but the answer came faster this time.

"About ten minutes."

He didn't want to make a decision without as much information as he could get so he called Hal back. "Hal, the problem is a bad plug. We can replace it but it'll take at least an hour. If we recharge it it'll take ten minutes but there's a chance it could short."

It took a few beats for Hal to respond. "Do it right. Replace the plug."

"Do we have that kind of time?"

Hal responded right away, as if he anticipated this question in advance, which frankly surprised Evard. "The risk is about the same either way. If the plug shorts and it starts a fire we'll die a lot quicker than floating dead out in the middle of nowhere."

Evard was surprised at how reasonable and dispassionate Hal sounded. When he started to think about it himself he realized that Hal was definitely right. He was panicking so much over the idea of freezing to death that he was contemplating taking the risk of blowing the ship up. *No good choices and all that.* Still, he was being reckless. Hal and Olaver and the rest may seem like versions of real people with the sound muted but they were making decisions rationally. He was oddly impressed with this whole bizarre situation.

"Alright then, Olaver will replace it. Fingers crossed this works."

"No need for luck, it either works or it doesn't."

Brutal honesty is a tool sharp at both ends, Evard mused. He watched with great interest as Olaver meticulously removed the part and replaced it with a new part. Worrying about how much time they had before system failure Evard felt like a millennium had passed by time Olaver had finished replacing the part. In truth, only about forty minutes had passed. He had never witnessed a more punctilious effort in all of his life. Olaver handled the replacement with total aplomb, no sense of urgency but absolutely no jitters or hiccups. He just worked, steadily, the whole time until finished.

All of this was both pleasantly surprising and somewhat perplexing. No one seemed to care about what happened. In fact, no one seemed to care about anything. Yet when faced with a task that needed executing, he'd never seen someone work more efficiently. It was almost sublimely efficient. It was as if the only concern Olaver had was the work, no distractions.

Amazing, he thought to himself, and a smile braided on a face that had been full of consternation just a minute ago. Maybe he could get used to living in whatever brave new world that seemed to awaken, as if from a deep slumber, during that dire moment back in the hallway of the infirmary. Everything, everywhere, seemed different but not necessarily *bad* different. Just not the same anymore. It was like the universe decided to trade urgency for thoughtfulness and though that seemed reductive, even to Evard, it also seemed appropriate.

He picked up the comm and said to Hal, "Good news, the repair is done." He looked at Olaver and said, "Is it time to fire it up?"

Olaver nodded and Evard confirmed it to Hal with excitement in his voice. Olaver motioned for Evard to take a few steps back and then, like magic, the magnetic field began to engage and the engines hummed to life. The ship shuddered again as the engines came back on and they both nearly stumbled. Once they caught their footing they could feel the ship begin to move again through space. *Phew, another crisis averted,* thought Evard, sarcastically.

Olaver looked at Evard and stated plainly, "Looks like we're good." Then he turned around and ambled out of the starboard engine room, going nowhere in particular.

Evard sighed and put his hand to face, rubbing the bleariness out of his eyes. *I can't believe this is my life now,* he thought, sardonically. Walking out of the room he meandered back to the front of the ship where he was intercepted by Hal.

"Nice job, rookie," Hal smiled, grinning that crooked and irascible grin again. "For a minute there, I thought there would be more trouble. Tell me, why did you volunteer to help?"

"Well, it seemed like it was a serious situation and, um, I was worried that we needed a little motivation, I guess?"

"Why would we need motivation?," said Hal, his voice losing for a moment that singsong quality that everyone's voice seemed to have lately. Evard wasn't sure how to answer in a polite way. Whatever eccentricities people had started displaying these days, no one seemed to be aware of it but him. He thought for a second then decided to answer honestly.

"Everyone seems to be acting, I don't know how to put it… strange, I guess. I didn't want to die out here. I thought maybe my help could prevent that?" he said, the last part more like a question than a definitive statement. Then Hal did something Evard remembered the rest of his days. He laughed. A weird, deep laugh, filled with mirth and more than a little joy.

After the laughing subsided he said, still flashing that patent grin of his, "Well, my boy, you did good. Not sure why you thought we needed help but it seems we needed it today."

Evard thought about it for a moment. Then, against his better judgment, said, "Did you?"

Hal stopped, his body relaxed as if he had just stepped out of a warm bath. "Does it matter? The problem was solved."

"You weren't worried we would fail?" Evard said, pressing the issue forward.

"Fail?" said Hal, and a genuinely perplexed expression crept around his normally serene, soft eyes. "Why would I be worried we would fail?"

Evard was poised to give a response but Hal just put his hand on his shoulder and patted him, stopping him in his tracks.

"My friend," he said. "What is a *worry* anyway? I don't even know what the word means anymore." As he said this last part a foreign shadow of doubt crossed his face, a shocking contrast to the normally benign expression he'd been wearing since they met. It was as if he had caught a remnant of a dream, something alien yet familiar but then in the briefest flash it had dissipated, gone as quick as it came. He shook his head and let out another chuckle. "You're a hard man to understand, Evard."

Evard laughed in spite of himself. Maybe it was hard to understand him. He lived with so much pain now, while everyone else walked around as if all of their burdens had been lifted. He gave Hal a reticent smile, mumbled goodnight, and started back to his cabin.

As he walked away, Hal said from behind him, "We'll be landing on Exalon in about nine hours. Barring any more mechanical troubles, it should be smooth sailing until then. I'm sure it'll be tiring for you to start your new life on a strange world. Get some rest."

Evard turned around when Hal said that last part, but he had already started shuffling away. It was surprising how astute the observation was given how simple minded everyone seemed to be on this ship. Either way, it was true: the countdown to new beginnings had begun.

Evard made his way back to his room where Olaver was already fast asleep and snoring. Evard crashed on his bed and was asleep moments after his head hit the pillow. The rest of the crew woke hours later but Evard slept like the dead so they let him rest. His sleep was deep and dreamless and when he inevitably opened his eyes he was finally on Exalon.

CHAPTER 18
One Way Or The Other

A half-baked plan had coalesced in Zarena Denamonte's mind. It wasn't particularly inspired but she reckoned it might be the safest gamble. If she tried to slip off Archlon in the dead of night by catching a covert ride off-world, her absence would be noted before she could afford it to be. Instead, she intended to simply notify the council that she wanted to study the effects of The Harmony with living, Harmonized test subjects. This would mean she planned to observe how The Harmony had transformed daily life across the Imperium.

She requested a diplomatic shuttle, one that would ferry her on a contrived "tour" of the Imperium, visiting several planets with diverse cultures, social customs and industries as a means to observe a relevant cross-section of Imperial life. The trip would be staged under the guise of research. The Harmony had catalyzed such a seismic shift in human behavior that enumerating the sheer number of changes to society was impossible, and cataloging the variations was imperative to comprehending how the landscape of the Imperium had changed.

Zarena had prepared an argument that rendered her reasons for departure plausible should they be scrutinized. Under normal circumstances, the rationale behind this excursion wouldn't even be questioned since observational research of this nature was to be expected. However, there was a catch — Zarena would insist on going herself.

As the architect of the entire Harmony project, it made sense for her to lead the research team, but given the situation Jesper had explained, a sudden departure from Archlon could arouse the Emperor's suspicions. If he was as paranoid as she'd been led to believe, he might institute travel restrictions on Council members under the pretense of assessing whether further threats had been unleashed in The Harmony's wake. Attempting to detain key players on Archlon is what she would do if she were him. It mattered little now; it was a risk she had to take. It seemed safer than the alternatives.

She was working at her terminal, drafting a terse missive about the variables The Harmony may have introduced and her intent to study them. She dispatched it to the Council and separately to Rakeus himself, steeling herself for a potential collision.

Within the hour, most of the Councilors had replied that it seemed a reasonable and even imperative course of study and wished her well, expecting periodic updates. No response had come yet from Rakeus. She began to grow anxious, fretting that he was livid about her mission and was at that very moment in his throne room deciding whether decapitation or firing squad was the optimal solution to the Zarena problem. Or perhaps something more subtle, like poison or an "accidental" drowning. As her mind raced with morbid possibilities, a message came through the terminal. It was from Jesper. Her heart almost burst from her chest. It said:

REPLY::::

Madame Denamonte. Emperor Rakeus of the Great House Karmarch, seventh of his line, noble protector of the Imperium, and faithful servant of all humanity, requests your presence in the Imperial throne room posthaste to discuss the matter you've brought to the Council's attention.

Sincerely,

Jesper Manderlay

A chill scurried up her spine. She couldn't discern whether the fact Jesper had responded was a threat or signal. She felt after her last encounter with Jesper, he might not be as inclined to escort her to her demise so soon after explicitly instructing her to secretly undertake this mission.

Still, nothing could be taken for granted. If Rakeus had an inkling of her plans, she might not leave the throne room alive. She wondered if it wouldn't be safer to just flee now, walk out the door and make a run for it, but getting caught would guarantee a death sentence. This option presented the least risk, as far she could predict. A summons from the Emperor was not to be taken lightly, and if Rakeus was becoming more erratic, it would be prudent not to keep him waiting. She stood from her terminal, inhaled deeply and closed her eyes. The wheel of fate had already spun; all that remained was to see where it landed.

She tidied herself and headed to the Imperial court. Even by Archlon's standards, the Mark was vast, and it was a long trek on foot to reach the capital's interior, but Zarena opted against using a transport. She needed to keep a clear head for her encounter with Rakeus. He was probably having Jesper surveil her now, she thought with discomfort. The Harmony was supposed to herald peace, but perhaps that was never achievable without the entire populace enthralled. *Maybe it was a mistake to leave everyone imprisoned in their own minds,* she mused. She batted the thoughts away. All this introspection was only making her more nervous, and she didn't want Rakeus to detect even a whiff of fear, lest it entice him to pounce on her like prey.

After a lengthy walk, she entered the inner sanctum and proceeded to the throne room. Normally there were guards posted outside when the Emperor was in chambers, but as she approached, all she saw was the lone, looming figure of Jesper standing before the entranceway. He made no motion at all until she was in full view, at which point he greeted her with a thin smile and slight curtsy. She returned a smile and nod as she approached him. He regarded her evenly, betraying no hint they were co-conspirators in a plot to reverse The Harmony.

"Nice to see you again, Madame Denamonte."

"Likewise, Lord Mandalay."

She stood before the large gilded steel doors leading into the throne room, patiently returning Jesper's smile as she waited for him to make the next move. He gestured to unseen servants, and the doors swung open before them. Bowing his head slightly, he said, "The Emperor awaits you, Madame. He wanted to ask you a few questions before your *important* journey of scientific discovery commences."

Jesper's subtext was obvious to Zarena — Rakeus needed to believe this was important, otherwise there would be trouble. She had to finesse her way past him if she wanted to depart the Mark with his blessing. She gave him a subtle nod in reply and followed him inside.

After passing through a small antechamber, they entered the expansive throne room with its soaring cathedral ceilings buttressed by ornately carved stone pillars and sculpted supports, royal banners draping along the side walls, and marble floors with a long velvet runner extending from the door to the throne. The design emulated pre-Imperial Origin church architecture, the throne elevated on an altar resembling a church transept, with several steps of the chancel separating the throne from the farthest point supplicants could approach in the nave.

The Karmarchian throne was an actual seat of iron, gilded with gold leaf and adorned with a relief sculpture on the back depicting a hawk and dove encircling each other as if dancing, its plush purple satin cushion beckoning. There before Zarena, lounging casually on the throne with his body angled to the side and legs crossed, was Emperor Rakeus. He greeted her with a congenial smile as she approached, then rose from his perch and descended the steps until they were face-to-face. She bowed formally. "Your Majesty, how may I be of service?"

Rakeus returned a slight nod. Placing both hands on her shoulders, he said, "Zarena, thank you for seeing me on short notice." His smile was jovial, as if this was a reunion between Zarena and a beloved uncle.

She smiled brightly, taking care not to betray any unease. "Of course, Your Majesty."

He turned to Jesper. "Zarena and I have some matters to discuss. Please ensure we are not disturbed."

Jesper spread his hands in deference and leaned forward in a sinuous pose that might have seemed insolent without his earnest expression. He glided back through the main doors, his footsteps barely whispering on the marble floor, the solid thud of the closing doors echoing in his wake.

Rakeus faced Zarena again. "How are you, my dear?"

"Well, Your Majesty. As well as can be now that our decades of work have finally borne fruit."

Rakeus chuckled. "Quite right, Zarena, quite right. Come, let's chat about this trip you're planning. Tell me, what do you hope to accomplish?"

Zarena smiled with her eyes and mouth, taking pains to keep the mood convivial, as if conversing with a treasured confidante rather than a deadly emperor. "I don't think it would be overstating matters, Your Majesty, to say the galaxy has been transformed into something entirely new."

Rakeus watched her expectantly, an avuncular expression on his face. Zarena continued, perhaps too casually, "Of course, we understood how a person would be different afterward, but there was no way to predict what society will become. We need to study the interactions."

"The interactions?"

"Yes, how people relate to each other now. How they engage with the world. We must observe how society has changed, chronicle these changes, and try to chart a course for our new society."

"Why is this important, in your view?"

She had prepared an answer but her mind drew a blank standing before him. His face seemed to cloud with impatience, real or imagined. Finally she decided to improvise. No time for timidity with the universe at stake. *Fortune favors the bold*, she reminded herself before launching into an unrehearsed diatribe.

"We may need to alter how we govern, where we devote Imperial resources, how we tackle problems. We must understand what those changes are. For instance, we should consider whether each planet requires a standing militia, or at least a reduced force. Based on our testing data, we anticipate The Harmony essentially eliminated criminal tendencies. The Harmonized appear to have lost the baser urges that typically motivate crimes. It's reasonable to expect violent offenses will plummet, surely, but does this hold for all misdeeds? Will crooked financiers stop embezzling? Will white-collar crime disappear now that material desires are muted? Will the poor stop stealing to survive, potentially starving? Is money even necessary anymore?"

Rakeus interjected, "Will people truly cease coveting possessions, Zarena?"

"I don't know, Sire", she said, sincerely. "Most psychology indicates our desire for fine things stems from the need for comfort and validation, sometimes emotional voids, or at least substituting emotions. If people no longer feel empty, they may not need to fill that void with merchandise."

Rakeus listened intently, enthralled and concerned by her speculations in equal measure. She had to drive the point home.

"For example, Terrupan has a thriving metal industry. Terrupan alloy rivals Archlonian vermacite despite being cheaper and easier to mine, because it's less durable. The wealthy favor vermacite for its unparalleled strength. But if you no longer feel fear or anxiety, would that still matter? There is scant difference between the metals, so would people continue paying a premium for vermacite if perceptions of safety and status no longer motivated purchases? What purpose does vermacite serve now? What about Terrupan alloy? Why not revert to using common irons and steels?"

"So this concerns the metal industry?" Rakeus asked skeptically, unsure of her aim.

"That's one of a million examples, Sire. If people have lost their penchant for luxury, excess, and decadence, entire industries may be obsolete now. Will anyone still care about buying couture or jewelry? How will that affect gem and precious stone mining? What of entertainment and recreation? If people can't experience sadness or melancholy, do they need to self-medicate with substances? Will they want to watch movies tapping into emotions they barely remember from before? It would be like viewing a film in a foreign language without subtitles — recognizing you once felt sorrow or jealousy or anger but unable to recall how. Why make movies now, who would watch them? Other pleasure industries, like prostitution, will likely wither away. And then..."

She halted mid-sentence, an unsettling realization dawning. "That raises a bigger evolutionary question."

Rakeus listened eagerly. "What evolutionary question?"

"Sire, procreation could become an issue. Specifically intimacy."

Rakeus guffawed in surprise. "Sex? Sex will be problematic now?"

Zarena sighed heavily, bracing herself as much as Rakeus for these revelations. "Sire, research shows anxiety, aggression, sadness, frustration and sometimes fear play a role in our sex drives and experiences. We don't yet know if desire will decline after The Harmony, but it could. Over generations, that could lead to a catastrophic dwindling of the human population."

He barked incredulously, "Are you saying The Harmony ruined people's sex lives? Doesn't that seem a bit absurd?"

"Sire, we eliminated their pain. We can't fathom the implications."

The space between them now felt saturated with air heavier than concrete. They paused to process everything said, perspectives realigning. Rakeus spoke first.

"So you're saying we removed the capacity for pleasure and desire along with pain, and we'll still perish anyway?"

Zarena spoke slowly, leaving no room for misunderstanding. "I'm saying, Sire, we saved the galaxy. That came at great cost, one we knew would be steep and agreed to pay. Now we must tally what that cost actually was."

She had him on the line, she could tell. His demeanor shifted from friendly to skeptical to worried within minutes. She could imagine the gears of his mind clicking into place around her conjectures. Her case was made.

"Zarena," Rakeus said almost paternally, "this seems to be an important mission. Why did we not foresee any of this?"

"How could we, Sire?"

He shook his head ruefully. "We knew the risks. It was either this or oblivion."

Zarena returned his mournful look. "What choice did we have?"

"None, Zarena. None at all." Rakeus' smile was taut as he bit his lip. "Please send regular reports. Any useful intelligence to aid our governance should come immediately."

Zarena bowed formally, sensing the meeting was over and Rakeus would sanction her departure. As she turned to leave, Rakeus called her name. She pivoted to face him.

"Zarena, it was lovely to see you, as always. I hope your trip is enjoyable and fruitful. Will you visit Raeka before departing?"

Zarena hadn't expected him to mention Raeka. The question caught her off guard, but she quickly composed herself. "Yes, I plan to. We usually say goodbye in person before trips."

"I imagine nothing about this farewell would be usual," he said sternly, goosebumps rising on her arms. Before she could panic, he waved goodbye and retreated to his throne, stretching out his legs.

"Please send the next delegation in when ready," Rakeus said absently.

As Zarena neared the doors, they began to open. She saw high-ranking military members waiting with Jesper.

"The Emperor will see you now," Jesper told them with a serpentine bow. They proceeded inside as Zarena exited, murmuring "Afternoon, Councilor" as they passed.

Jesper waited for her. Once the doors closed he said, "Best wishes for a fruitful and productive trip, Councilor. It sounds like an important mission." His gaze seemed to bore into the back of her skull as he spoke.

She met his eyes evenly. "I trust it will be, one way or the other."

She headed for the transport station, feeling Jesper's eyes on her until she was out of sight. Now that the unpleasant business with Rakeus was finished, Zarena had somewhere she needed to be

CHAPTER 19
All The Best Parts Of Me

About twenty minutes after leaving Emperor Rakeus' throne room, Zarena was rapping on the door to Princess Raeka's private quarters. After a few knocks Raeka answered, her face a peculiar mask of tranquility that rendered it both angelic and eerie. She wore a sublime yet askance grin, dressed in formal attire.

"Welcome, Zee. I wondered if you'd come to say goodbye."

"You knew I was leaving?"

"Yes, Father forwarded your message to the Council." Raeka's voice was unhurried and pleasant. Before Zarena could reply, she said, "Please excuse my lapse in manners. Come in."

Raeka led Zarena through the circular foyer with its statuary and plush chairs, down a hallway to a sitting room. The space was decorated in ancient style with marble sculptures, long velvet couches, thin white walls adorned with original paintings and garlands evoking buttresses. A large video screen loomed for media viewing, a small bar with vermacite stools adjacent to the couches, an array of food on the counter.

"Can I offer you something?" asked Raeka congenially.

"Sure, Rae, I'm famished actually."

The women sat at the bar, nibbling olives, cubes of cheese, crackers with apricot spread, and cured meats. Zarena crammed olives into her mouth as if they were going extinct and she needed to ingest her fill before then. Raeka laughed, amused by the spectacle.

"What?" Zarena asked through stuffed cheeks.

"Nothing, I've always enjoyed watching you eat. When hungry, you descend like a vulture."

Raeka beamed so brightly it seemed beams of light might burst forth. She chuckled airily, but her tone was grave. Zarena returned an uneasy smile.

"So," Raeka said, breaking the silence, "what's the real reason for this trip, Zee?"

"Research, of course. Learning The Harmony's impacts on the Imperium. Documenting societal changes to better govern."

"Of course," Raeka said, no longer smiling but regarding her tranquilly.

"I noticed you inspecting my face. Does The Harmony's effect disturb you?"

"Your face is the same, Rae. Your expressions have changed. That will take adjustment."

"I enjoy smiling now, frequently. All Harmonized probably do. The beauty of it, I suppose."

Zarena studied her carefully, unsure if she was being sarcastic, not even entirely sure she could still be sarcastic.

"What, that answer did not please you, Councilor Denamonte?" chucked Raeka. The chuckle was light but the tone was surprisingly serious. Zarena didn't want to upset Raeka, but then again, she wasn't sure that she actually could, even if she was trying to. Zarena didn't answer, just looked on as Raeka gazed in her eyes, eyes that were both the same and different looking.

Zarena finally mustered up the courage and said, "Is it really still you?"

"Yes, Zee. It's still me. All the best parts of me."

"What do you mean, exactly?"

"I feel great. I feel happy and when I'm not feeling happy I feel content or satisfied. I don't worry much any more. I see the truth of the world. You think that because those that were Harmonized talk slower, move slower, grin wider, that we are somehow less than you, with all of your pent up rage and frustration and fear. We are not. When your sense of urgency has been removed, you tend not to move as fast. You tend to smile more, even if your smile is a little goofier. Sure, you could probably beat me in a foot race if you were so inclined, but why would that even matter anymore? One person being better than another, what could matter any less?"

Zarena listened, stunned by both the truth and bitterness of Raeka's words. Raeka continued.

"There was a time in human history where we actually noticed, cared about and then used pejorative terms to describe the differences in peoples' skin colors. Can you fathom a world where the shading of your skin mattered to other people? It's a relic so long forgotten in our history that we forget our race was borne to ignorance and suffering and pain. In the future you created, Zarena, one day people will look back into the past and say, 'do you remember when people used to hurt, used to suffer' and we'll say that as academics, recounting facts. Of course, in the future no one will know what it's like to suffer, just as we don't know what it would be like to judge the color of someone's skin. 'Suffering' won't mean anything, it'll just be a word, like 'Hate' was and is just a word.

"You asked if I am still really me. I'm all the lightest parts of me. I remember what pain and anger and hate were. I know there were times when I felt them, I can recall how the weight of those feelings pushed down on me, suffocating me with their poison. I just don't remember how it feels any more. I have the memories of pain without the experience of it. I'd say that is the best of all possible worlds. You didn't break me, Zarena. You fixed me and I am so happy you did."

Raeka's cheeks began to glisten with tears of gratitude. She took Zarena's hand and clasped it in both of hers. "You see, Zee. This is what I wanted. This is what I've always wanted. This is what everyone should have. I don't know what sadness feels like anymore but if I did, I would be feeling it for you right now."

Zarena asked, "Why would you feel sad for me?"

"Because you created this peace and haven't shared in it. Because you think you've made a mistake, because of me. You think less of me now and you want to fix me for your own selfishness. So I can be who you would like me to be, not who I would like me to be."

There was no malice behind Raeka's words. She said it as casually as someone ordering ice cream from a street vendor in Kadzer. Zarena's eyes began to swell with tears of sadness. Raeka took her sleeve and patted the tears away. She leaned in and embraced Zarena, the two of them sobbing and hugging each other tight, one of them so happy and the other so sad. Finally they broke their embrace and wiped their faces with the sleeves of their shirts.

"I'm sorry for judging you. I'm sorry about everything." Zarena cleared her throat with a small cough and said a little more abruptly than she intended, "I need to prepare for my flight."

She stood up and smoothed out the wrinkles in her clothes. Raeka just sat on the bar stool, patiently watching Zarena as she prepared to depart.

"My ship leaves for Exalon in a few hours. That's the first stop on our trip. I need to get myself ready and over to the landing port."

Raeka just kept watching her, in her serene way, not making any indication that she realized Zarena was trying to escape this now awkward situation. Raeka finally relented and stood up to walk Zarena out. They walked back to the main entrance to Raeka's quarters in silence, Zarena turning to embrace Raeka as she reached the doors. They held it each for a long moment, both of them squeezing the other into near asphyxiation.

"Do you really need to do this, Zee?" said Raeka. The way her voice warbled for just a second, it almost sounded like a plea.

"I do", Zarena said solemnly.

"Of course. Please come find me as soon as you're back."

"You're the first person I plan to see."

Raeka leaned up on her tiptoes and kissed the taller woman on the mouth. "I love you, Zee. I will be awaiting your return."

"I love you too, Rae. I'll see you soon. I promise."

With that Zarena walked away from Raeka's door as fast as she could, putting her back to her so she couldn't see the tears in her eyes.

CHAPTER 20
Meeting Of The Minds

merald was expecting Zarena Denamonte very soon and she was absolutely terrified. The tumultuous events of the past few days had been a surreal maelstrom, culminating with her possibly aiding and abetting a rogue Councilor who created a super weapon that transformed the whole galaxy into grinning shells of their former selves. Now this Councilor wanted to reverse the damage against the orders of the Emperor.

Emerald gulped hard. Her role in this scheme may well end with her death. She had to account for that grim possibility. Wandering the ruins of her old life, unaffected and acting differently than the placid populace, could provoke unwanted scrutiny. Nevertheless, conspiring with Councilor Denamonte seemed decidedly more perilous. Curing a malady already intended as a cure? She had a feeling her troubles were just beginning.

Emerald spent time since contacting Zarena observing the shuffling masses in District 7. The old adage held true — the more things changed, the more they remained exactly the same. The people still ambled about their lives, however big or small. Offices still teemed with employees, streets still had occasional traffic, people still shopped and strolled. Superficially similar to before this "Harmony", but the post-Harmony world rendered these mundane tasks vastly different. People walked slower, smiled more - the smiles were the most unsettling part to Emerald. Most spent free time navel-gazing, never complaining, not a single argument to be heard. Just placid pod people shuffling about their lives, while she, the outsider, moved among them undetected.

That was the strangest thing — no one noticed she was different. Her failure to blend in went entirely unnoticed by the affected populace. Being Immune, or whatever it was that she was, felt more curse than blessing. *They all seemed like self-herding sheep putzing around the farm*, she thought. None she met recalled the horrible pulse of The Harmony. All acted as if their new behaviors were normal. She probed her mother about painful, scary, or sad memories. Her mother recalled them in perfect detail, but spoke of sadness like a virgin speaking of sex — understanding the concept abstractly, but not from experience.

Emerald had mixed feelings about it all. The wisdom and beauty of this peaceful world was apparent, yet it seems this peace was not a choice. It was imposed by a powerful few through furtive means requiring immense planning and subterfuge. *This peace was a poisoned pill*, she reckoned. Zarena had promised explanations. She claimed a blood-borne plague would eventually extinguish humanity, and The Harmony was the cure. *Could any plague really require something so heinous and fascist as a countermeasure?* It seemed insane, like a fever dream. She hoped Zarena could lend some logic to the madness. She doubted anything could make sense of this, but she clung to hope.

When Emerald was young, her parents gave her a doll with emerald eyes. She loved the doll, Sally Green, and took it everywhere. She and the doll were Team Green, and they would lecture Emerald's other toys about saving the world from evil. Afterward, she would dismiss the motionless toys with a wave and go off adventuring with Sally — playing doctor and healing sick toys, or pretending to fly around the galaxy helping others like the storied Heronauts of her bedtime tales. She and Sally would make the world better.

As she dressed for her rendezvous with Zarena, she looked at her bed where Sally still sat, worse for wear but sporting those bright green eyes. "I told you Team Green would save the world, Sally," she said. "I never expected this, but Heronauts must answer the call." She smiled grimly.

She stole a final glance at Sally and walked out, passing her placidly video-watching mother.

"Bye Mom," she said, voice tinged with bitterness.

Her mother looked up with a perfect, doting smile. "Bye honey," she replied.

Emerald left the flat, the creepily grinning people shuffling past her downtown. At the deserted Raxeon warehouse, she used her handprint to open the door. Inside the mostly empty space were racks of irrigation compressor parts, carburetors, and more — Raxeon had tendrils throughout Exalon's mechanical industries.

We can use this stuff, she thought. She had chosen this place for its lack of guards and cameras. The rear workshop where she had worked before would have tools. No one cared where she was anymore. Other divisions barely remembered to send their broken items to her. She suspected they couldn't camp here indefinitely, but it was a good start for whatever work she and Zarena would undertake. Chances were they would need to construct a device, and this was the most discreet site she had access to.

Zarena was to arrive at 0900. At 0850, Emerald waited anxiously. By 1030, with no sign of the Councilor, panic swelled within her. Zarena had said if she didn't come, it likely meant she had been caught, and Emerald would need to flee for her safety. The prospect of escaping imperial agents filled her with fear.

"This is it," she whispered. As Zarena advised, she had acknowledged the need to flee but hadn't sincerely prepared. The realization she was in over her head started to make her dizzy.

She closed her eyes, breathing slowly to calm her racing pulse. Her mind turned over the situation. She hadn't packed anything or put her affairs in order, and had no idea where to go. What about her mother? Could she come too? Would it be safe? As she considered leaving, the buzzer sounded. On the camera was a tall, slender woman in plain clothes and a hat. Emerald's heart leapt — it was Zarena!

She sprinted to the door and enabled the intercom. "Hello," she said nervously.

"Hello," came the reply. "I'm looking for Emerald Seltz?"

Emerald unlocked the door and Zarena slipped inside. Doffing her disguise, Zarena's eyes bored into Emerald's astonished face.

"Hello. You must be Emerald. I'm Zarena. It's a pleasure to meet you."

Flustered, Emerald stammered, "Y-yes, I'm Emerald. Nice to meet you."

Hello," said Zarena. "You must be Emerald. I'm Zarena. It is a pleasure to meet you."

Emerald was still settling herself from the previous panic. She quickly composed herself and said with a slight crack in her voice, "It's nice to meet you, Madame Denamonte."

"Please, call me Zarena."

"Of course, nice to meet you, Zarena," she said, still a bit stupefied from the reality of it all.

"I can see why your parents named you Emerald. Your eyes are the most beautiful green I've ever seen."

Emerald blushed from head to toe and all she could manage was a pathetic sounding "thank you" in response.

"Well," said Zarena. "I'm sure you have a million questions. Is there a place we can talk?"

Emerald led Zarena back through the warehouse to the workshop she had spent nearly two hours waiting in. They both took a seat around a large table, Zarena putting down her sun visor and hat whilst unbuttoning her coat that she threw around the back of the chair.

Emerald was nervous and it was apparently stamped all over her face because Zarena said, "Listen, Emerald. Don't be frightened. We are on the same team." She tried to put Emerald at ease with her friendly demeanor. "I would be lying if I said associating with me was safe but I can assure you that you're safe from me." She gave Emerald a congenial smile and light pat on the hand that Emerald was using to clutch the table for dear life.

Emerald tried to calm herself. Meeting new people always rattled her. Most found her shy or arrogant, but truly, she was simply never fully at ease beyond her inner circle. She thought of her mother and Jazz to steel her resolve.

"I'm sure you have questions. Shall we talk?" Emerald led Zarena to the workshop where they sat at a table. Noting Emerald's obvious anxiety, Zarena said kindly, "Listen, don't be afraid. We're on the same side." She reassured Emerald of her safety.

"I understand," said Emerald.

"I'm sorry, Madame… ah, Zarena. I'm trying to stay calm but all of this," she waved her hand around the room, "sitting here with you, about to discuss this grand plan to save the universe— it's daunting."

"Of course it is," smiled Zarena. Then she said, just a tad patronizingly, "But Emerald, I've already saved the universe. What you and I are going to do, is free it."

CHAPTER 21
Peace Is A Choice

The conversation Emerald and Zarena had over the next two hours oscillated between casual palaver and serious government conspiracy talk. Zarena filled Emerald in on everything that happened from the discovery of The Sequence to unleashing The Harmony. Zarena did an admirable job of allaying Emerald's fears and answering her questions. Zarena found it refreshing to talk to another scientific mind. Emerald had a more applied science background but her grasp of the key concepts involved in The Harmony were impressive. She was a special talent and Zarena thought that she had been supremely lucky to have found her. Considering that they needed to make a physical device which seemed to be the green-eyed girl's field of expertise and Zarena had already shed her technical staff Emerald, it would seem, made a highly valuable asset. Beyond all the practical reasons, she liked her as well.

They also spoke about personal matters, their friends and family, a bit of what their lives had been like. Zarena told her about Raeka, struggling to keep just how despondent she felt about it out of her voice. After a while, Emerald started becoming comfortable with the rogue Councilor and as their talk became more conspiratorial, they started to form the beginnings of a bond. Trust was not something easily earned with either of them but the circumstances they faced and the secrets that they shared hastened their alliance.

Emerald spoke ruefully of Jazz, what happened during The Harmony, and how things were with Jazz and her mother now.

"He was so full of charisma. All day long he would make jokes about the people we work with, the strangers he'd met, basically everyone. He was like a force of nature. Now he's… I don't know… not the same any more."

"I understand how you feel. The apathy was an unintended consequence. It seems like you can't remove all the friction without decreasing motivation. The things we don't know until we know them, I guess," Zarena said, with an almost wistful smile.

"So the Sequence couldn't be genetically eliminated?" asked Emerald.

"It's so pervasive that even through genetic manipulation, the mutation just reoccurs somewhere else. It can't be scrubbed. Believe me, we tried. The best minds in the Imperium worked on the project. We truly had no other way to stop it," she bemoaned. Her emotions started to boil to the surface. "I wish there had been but I am starting to realize how foolish I've been. I thought I was so clever. Turns out the one thing that never dawned on me was losing Raeka. Had it even crossed my mind earlier, maybe all of this would have been different."

"So, she's very special to you, I take it?"

"She's my best friend. I love her. I don't really have anyone else. Everyone who ever deigned to care about me, I sacrificed for the sake of my political aspirations. Being the daughter of a well respected diplomat provided opportunities not available to others. I did everything I could to take hold of that advantage. I left everyone behind, except for Rae."

Zarena tried to hold back just how much pain she was in but Emerald could see right through it. "I understand, Zarena. I've never really been able to make friends. My mind always seems to work in a way that makes people, I don't know, I guess feel uncomfortable. Most people think I'm weird or a snob, but not Jazz. He liked me for all the reasons I like me, and no one had ever done that before. It was refreshing but also, it was comforting, like a warm blanket."

"Well, hopefully we can save our warm blankets", said Zarena in an encouraging tone. Emerald nodded in agreement but something seemed to be nagging at her, an uncertainty.

"You agree, don't you?" Zarena asked.

"I do, but I'm wondering something else". Zarena watched as Emerald braced herself for a big reveal, as if she needed to muster up courage in order to say it aloud.

"What if The Harmony really *is* peace? I mean, as much as I miss the way Jazz and my mom and the people in my life were, I have to admit they all seem…" She paused searching for the right word. "… content, I suppose? Maybe this is actually the best thing for them. Maybe this is what they would have wanted."

"Rae presented me with the same argument before I left Archlon. She said that I had fixed her, that if I tried to reverse her condition I would only be doing it for me. She said that 'suffering' would just be a word with no real meaning in the future. I've been thinking about that the entire way here."

Zarena took a beat to compose her thoughts. She had been wrestling with this very question since she walked away from Raeka's quarters at the Mark. Raeka had very plainly stated she wanted to stay this way. It made Zarena's desire to restore her to her former self feel self-serving.

"I think it comes down to choice, Emerald," she said plainly. "We didn't give people a choice."

"Raeka had a choice, Zarena. You said so yourself. She planned it and purposefully took off her dampeners. She may be the only Harmonized person in the galaxy that actually got to choose."

This was hard for Zarena to hear because it meant that maybe Raeka was living with pain she didn't want to deal with anymore. How could Zarena not have seen it? She always seemed so together, so prepared for anything. Zarena felt more confused than she ever could remember being before. She felt a creeping doubt begin to niggle at her mind. It was not too late to abort the plan, continue on with the fake mission and return to Archlon with data as she had told everyone she intended to do.

As if Emerald was reading her mind, she said, "It's not too late to back out of this. Maybe, the universe is better off. It could be debated endlessly whether forcing this 'peace' upon the galaxy was morally right but that point is moot now. The question we're faced with today is whether or not going backwards is best? I don't know, honestly."

The two women sat in silence, contemplating the enormous scope of the quandary they found themselves in.

Zarena turned to Emerald. "What about your friend Jazz? Do you think he's better off?"

Emerald thought long and hard about her answer. Finally, and with some measure of trepidation she said, "Honestly, no, I don't think he is. He loved life. Happiness and even sadness. I think if he could choose between a simple, carefree life and a complicated life with highs and lows, I think he would choose the latter. You can't appreciate the highs without the lows." She seemed lost in her own thicket of doubts. Hesitantly she finished, "I can't be sure though. I've never lived without fear and anxiety. I don't think anyone ever has, until now."

Her words were sincere and tinged with melancholy. The two women mused contemplatively, thinking of all the things they lost and what they would have to gain.

In the end it was Emerald who said, "I'm not sure if it matters whether people are better off Harmonized or not."

Zarena had been surprised by Emerald's candor from the moment they met and she continued to be.

Emerald added, "It's done."

"Yes. It is done," sighed Zarena.

"It seems like engineering this solution was quite a feat, and I have to say I'm impressed," Emerald said, pensively trailing off at the end of the sentence. "But," she continued, "Was this really the only thing that could have been done? Did any of you ask yourselves if there was another way?"

"We did, Emerald, we did ask ourselves that. Rakeus wanted the Imperium to survive. He felt, all of us involved felt, that the Imperium provides safety for the galaxy. If it became destabilized because of The Sequence, the suffering would be too great. It would ensure a violent end for us all."

Zarena didn't even attempt to hide the sadness in her voice. Unlike Raeka, she could still feel pain and, at this very moment, it was suffocating her.

"You mentioned that The Sequence was, in your view, something like a kill switch. As if evolution had decided on our extinction."

"Yes, that's how I see it. The other Councilors, too."

"And the Emperor?"

"Rakeus was more concerned with defeating The Sequence than the 'why's' of it all. He saw it as an obstacle, I don't think he saw a metaphor in it. In retrospect, that always seems to be the way with those in power."

"What do you think makes us truly human, Zarena? Is it our genes? Do you believe our DNA writes our destiny?"

"I do, in part, of course. I also don't think that's the whole story."

"Is the rest of the story our ability to make choices? Throughout human history wars have been fought, entire civilizations torn asunder for the freedom of choice. Is it better to take that away so that we can survive? Is survival the cost of slavery?"

"Slavery? Look, Emerald, humans already were slaves. Slaves to their worst instincts and The Sequence proves that. The desire to destroy has always been in our blood, long before evolution cursed us."

"Does that make it any better?" asked Emerald, clearly vexed.

Zarena was startled by the bluntness of Emerald's words. with more than a hint of fatalism, she said, "I don't know anymore. I don't know what matters. All I know is that I lost my best friend trying to save everyone else." She closed her eyes for a second while the pain washed over her like a cresting wave. "But I can't make a decision that could affect hundreds of billions of lives to save one person."

"How do you know you'd only be saving one?"

"I don't get what you mean."

"Jazz wouldn't want this for himself, not if he could see how it turned out. My mother wouldn't want this either. he only way to know for sure would have been to ask them before you Harmonized them. That's the problem, Zarena. If The Harmony had been a choice, we wouldn't be here, discussing treason in an abandoned warehouse," Emerald said, dripping with a kind of invective sarcasm. "But you, the Council and the Emperor, took that choice from every living person across almost a hundred worlds. Don't get me wrong, I'm impressed with how you were able to pull this off from a logistical standpoint, but that makes it even worse. You went very far out of your way to take away the choice of every person alive."

"Emerald, think of the lives we saved. The men, the women, and especially the children, that were saved from gruesome deaths. I've seen people who have had their mutation triggered. It can turn into the stuff of nightmares. Sometimes, to protect people from themselves, duplicity is needed."

This was beginning to exasperate Zarena. She didn't like having to defend her actions to a stranger. "In the interior when children are born, they are given immunizations, the parents don't know what's in them..."

"I do..." Emerald interrupted.

Zarena gave her a frustrated look. "Well, most people don't, but we give them to children anyway and the children have no memory of it. They now have this resistance against illness and they don't know anything about it. When they grow up and find out, they usually are grateful. How is this any different?"

"Their parents know they are getting it. They make the choice and can choose not to. Sure, certain freedoms could be restricted if they refuse but no one is holding them down against their will or secretly dosing them in their evening tea. Whether the choice is right, or wrong, they get to choose."

"But that's what we'd be doing, Emerald!" Zarena said, exasperated. "We already Harmonized the whole fucking galaxy. For all the people who wouldn't choose it, so many of them would, and we'd be taking their choice away, again!"

Zarena was a raging sea of emotion and teetering between viewpoints was driving her slowly insane. *This is what is going to trigger my own Sequence*, she thought to herself. *This is what's going to drive my own body to kill itself.*

"Not if we gave them the choice back, Zarena."

Zarena blinked at her, perplexed. "What does that even mean?"

"What we are talking about here, the fundamental problem, is similar to your original problem. It's not necessarily if we should — right now it's simply, *can we?* We don't have the means to take their choice away because you and I haven't figured out how to reverse it. The first step would be to engineer a reversal. Then we can decide how to implement it. Did you expect, as you decided to make this journey into exile, to only de-Harmonize Princess Raeka or were you thinking we could do more than just free one person?"

Zarena didn't respond, she listened to Emerald intently. "If, and that's a big if, we can figure out a way to de-Harmonize everyone," continued Emerald, "then maybe we can liberate entire populations all at once. Then, we give them the information. We make everything we know about The Sequence public, inform everyone what peril the human race faces, and let them decide whether or not they want to be Harmonized."

"What if we shot for something even more modest? Small groups, maybe somewhere in the colonies where the Imperium might not notice us. Liberate batches of people and those that want to can opt to be re-Harmonized, the rest can be free to live their lives in whatever way they want, but it would be *their choice*," said Zarena.

"Isn't the problem that the Emperor will crush us as soon as he gets word of what were doing? We'd need some protection.

You said that all the Great Houses were Harmonized with the rest of the population", protested Emerald.

"Yes, they were"

"What if we found a small House, one with a decent size military force, on the outskirts of the Imperium. If we de-Harmonized them, we could explain the situation and..."

"...if they didn't execute us immediately..."

Emerald gasped at Zarena's comment, and she could feel her terror rising again, but she pushed onward. "If we could get their support then maybe they would give us the cover we need to do this in secret. As you suggested, they may be furious that the Emperor didn't include them in the list of those slated to be un-Harmonized. If we can get past that, they may be able to protect us from outside interference. Then we could give the people under their control that choice. They could be the ones to give it to them."

Emerald shrugged at the last part. This was a political quagmire and their plan to gain allies might backfire. Still, this seemed the best way forward. The gears in Zarena's mind began to churn, the basic tenants of a plan beginning to form with clicks so loud they were almost audible.

"Esper," said Zarena flatly. She chuckled bemusedly and Emerald gave her a sideways glance, worrying that the stress may have finally broken Zarena's mind. "House Carchel controls Esper. The Baron Andros Carchel is a young man, his father passed away about two years ago. Esper is a fishing colony, their Orlen trout is a particular delicacy," she said with a smirk that Emerald didn't understand. "There are probably less than a billion people on the entire planet, which is larger in land mass than either Archlon or Exalon; one of the smallest populations in all of the Imperium. Per capita by acre, maybe the smallest. Andros, Raeka, and I played together as children, so we have a good history. It's also the start of The Harmony," she said with a bitter laugh.

She told Emerald the story of the fishing captain from her youth and how it had set her on the path that led to The Harmony. Emerald listened with equal parts fascination and horror.

She finished the story by saying, "It would probably be the best chance we have of liberating a Great House and not being immediately beheaded. That said, if we do this, we could be starting a war that may not end in our lifetime. It could spell the end of Karmarch as House Imperiatus and millions, even billions, could die in the bloodshed. We would be starting to unravel the first threads of peace, the peace we now have, thanks to The Harmony."

"Peace is a choice," said Emerald. "In your heart, you understand that now, I can tell."

Zarena lowered her head and rubbed her temples in a clockwise motion. "Yes," she finally said. "It is a choice. So is violence…"

"But not death," said Emerald. "We don't choose to die, if we're very lucky all we can ever hope to choose is the manner of our death. We'd also be giving that choice back to the peoples of Esper."

Zarena didn't say anything so Emerald continued. "Don't you think they want it? To choose the type of peace they can have or to choose the type of peace they can make. Rakeus stole their lives, Zarena. You stole their lives and you're starting to regret that now. You said yourself, The Harmony could lead to all kinds of future problems, not the least of which is a rapidly declining birth rate. In the end, when we are called home to the halls of our ancestors, don't you think it would be best to go there knowing you gave at least some people the freedom to choose their own path?"

Zarena had heard enough to know what choice she was going to make. This stranger with the piercing green eyes was right. She owed the peoples of the universe the choice to end on their own terms. Emerald, who had been inspecting her face closely, could tell she had made her own kind of peace with the choice.

"So, what do we do now?"

"We find others who are Immune, others like you. We recruit their help, maybe we can find a few with skills that we can use. After that, we engineer a way to reverse The Harmony. If we can't, none of this matters anyhow."

"Alright, but how are we going to find anyone to help us? You said there were maybe a few hundred thousand Immune throughout the whole of the Imperium. That would be like finding a needle in a haystack the size of the Raxeon building."

"I don't know," sighed Zarena, "but there has to be at least one of The Immune out there that can help us."

CHAPTER 22
What Do You Want From Me?

Exalon was a bustling hub of the Imperium. Large corporations, factories, silicon plants, nanotechnology research centers; it's home to some of the biggest manufacturers of technology based products in the Imperium. Billions of people, all living together, almost like the hive of rats huddling for warmth in the sewers below.

Evard landed in what was called District 7, one of the twelve Districts on the continent of Aluxa, and the most densely populated region of the planet. The Districts were each like a sprawling metropolis in their own right.

He had never seen anything like it.

There were skyscrapers that tickled the clouds, taller than anything he had ever seen on Eden. There were concrete roads and metal structures, living units that connected together in an endless line of steel and stone, stretching as far as the horizon. It was a mechanized world, with tram lines, and hovercraft highways, and energy plants. From the street level, looking west towards the setting sun on the horizon you could see nothing but a concrete and metal jungle with buildings blotting out the sun as it fell on it's daily descent below the horizon.

The weather was mild but cool, slightly colder than it had been on Eden, and he wasn't wearing a jacket so he shivered a bit in the fading rays of sunshine.

He had said his goodbyes to Hal and Olaver and the rest of the crew. Once they landed, Hal had let on that he suspected when they first met that Evard was running from some trouble. Evard didn't know what to say but Hal had just patted him on the shoulder dismissively and said that "we all have a past." Evard had admitted Hal was right and he was just trying to find a way off-world.

He didn't know anybody and didn't have a plan, he was just trying to get off of Eden any way he could. Hal had looked him up and down for a moment, reached into his pocket, and had given him some Imperium credits. Then he had told him about a shelter for indigent citizens "down a ways in District 7." It was a place he could find a bed and a warm meal until he figured out how to get on his feet again. Then Hal had given him a hug, a firm embrace, with a hard pat on the back. Evard had sheepishly taken the credits and thanked him profusely, to which Hal had just given him that serene, if somewhat goofy, grin of his.

Now Evard was standing on a street corner a few blocks down from the landing port, still wearing his stolen blue crewman jumper that was a few sizes too big for him. If he was going to blend in, he would need a change of clothes.

With his hands in his pockets, he walked down the thoroughfare connecting into the heart of District 7. The wound in his leg was throbbing a bit but the antibiotics were doing their job. It was better today than it had been on the flight here. As he walked he began to pass rows of two and three story buildings, with doors out front advertising different goods and services by their brands. He wasn't familiar with any of the names he'd seen on the signs.

Eden wasn't exactly a cultural hub and a lot of high end off-world brands never made their way out to the colonies. The backwater planets on the edge of the Imperium don't quite match the typical customer demographics for premium products. As a result, he didn't want to blow the credits Hal gave him on a designer outfit that he probably wouldn't like anyhow. He walked a bit and finally came across a storefront whose brand he was familiar with: Agi Kent. Agi Kent was a clothing line that was popular on Eden, all of their threads made from organic plant based materials. The clothes were usually cheap and durable, if lacking in fashion. He decided to go inside and have a look.

The store had a small front window and entrance but once Evard walked inside, he was impressed with the amount of floor space. The store showroom extended in width after a few paces and reached farther back than he could see from where he entered. It was lined wall to ceiling with various items of clothing. He'd never been inside a store this large before. You could probably fit all of the stores in his home settlement into this one gigantic clothing store.

He scanned the aisle for whatever might pass as the discount rack, which he found much further in. He pulled a long sleeve olive green organic-fiber shirt from the rack and found the matching pants in his size. He was pretty certain it would fit, and it didn't look half bad, so he paid the young girl at the register in the credits Hal had given him. She was dressed in a posh white and gray pantsuit, her hair and makeup done nicely; nicer than he remembered seeing on any of the girls back home. She had her hair braided in rows and partially pulled into a bun. Her skin was smooth like silk and the color of mocha. She giggled at him a bit behind her soft gold eyes. His face became warm as he blushed, a wave of scarlet blooming on his cheeks and forehead.

He paid for the clothes (luckily there were some leftover credits) and hightailed it out of the store as quickly as possible. *It's going to be hard to fit in here*, he thought. The thought began to sour some of the relief he felt when he had finally gotten off the cruiser. Part of him had been expecting a squad of local militia waiting in the hangar to apprehend him upon arrival. Once he realized that no one here was looking for him, or even *at* him for that matter, he began to feel an almost jittery excitement at the prospect of starting over in a new place.

He had a chance to be something here that he could never have been back on Eden. Looking around at the wealth and luxury made him feel a little envious at first but then it began to motivate him. He had a chance to do remarkable things if he could find the right break. But now, running like a shy boy in the schoolyard from a pretty sales clerk at a second rate clothing store made him feel embarrassed. He started to realize he didn't really belong here and the longer he hung around out in the open, the more obvious that was going to be.

He started walking in the direction of the shelter and after a few blocks, he ducked down what looked like an abandoned alley. He scanned around to make sure no one was watching him, then quickly disrobed, tossed the crew uniform into a nearby garbage compactor, then quickly put on his new shirt and pants. Once he was changed, he strolled out of the alley as casually as he could and continued down the street, heading in the direction that Hal told him. He was counting blocks and reading street signs along the way to make sure he didn't get lost. *With so many intersecting streets, it would be easy to get turned around,* he thought.

He looked at the facade of every building and read every sign he saw on the lookout for the District 7 Wellness and Public Outreach Center.

There were WPOC locations on Eden too, so he more or less knew what he was looking for, but everything just looked and felt so different here he started to get paranoid that he had already passed it. That's when he saw a sign hanging from a street light that said District 7 WPO Center for Disadvantaged Persons. He started to jog a bit, even though his leg hurt, in a hurry to get out of the chill that had begun creeping into the air as he walked.

While he ran with a slight limp amongst the crowd of people, all slowly shuffling along down the road without any real sense of urgency, he saw two women across the street walking at a natural pace. Both of them were pretty, like the girl in the shop, one of them a little older than him with mid length chestnut hair, wearing what looked like an official government uniform. The other was about his age, slim and tall, with eyes so green he thought they were glowing from across the street. He stopped running for a second to get a better look at the two women. They seemed different than the rest of the pedestrians ambling down the streets of District 7. They stopped walking once they noticed him and stared back, a look of clear surprise on both their faces.

After an instant, the green eyed girl whispered something to the regal looking one who immediately nodded. They started walking in step in his direction, as if they were planning on ramming right into him on approach. He started to panic. *They're agents*, he thought to himself. *They were looking for me. They're going to arrest me right here, on the street, or worse.* He thought about the last moments he spent with his mother and remembered how much worse it could be. His fight or flight mode kicked in and he immediately turned and started sprinting down the block when he ducked down another alley. It was dusk and the natural light of the sun began to give way to the artificial light of the street lamps and neon signs. There were still large crowds of people, plodding along like grazing cattle, so he felt confident he had lost them in the crowd.

He peaked around the corner, looking back down the street in the direction he came from. He saw people everywhere but he no longer spotted the two women. He waited another moment, his eyes searching every face until he was satisfied he had shaken them. Several minutes passed and he began to feel confident enough they were gone and maybe he had imagined it all. He had been through an exceedingly difficult few days and that was bound to make him paranoid.

He slipped out of the alley and started walking towards the shelter. His eyes scanned the crowd as he kept his head down. His heart was racing but he walked slowly, keeping pace with the shambling crowds of people heading in the same direction.

When he got to the doors of the shelter, he looked both ways to see if he was still being followed, then opened the door and ducked in.

There was a small reception area near the main entrance, with two hallways on either side, heading down towards the kitchens and dormitories. Behind the reception desk was a pair of open double doors and he could see that there were rows of tables inside, filled with people eating a hot meal.

He walked up to the receptionist and said, "Hello, I'm looking for a warm meal please. Maybe a place to stay for a few days."

The receptionist was a middle aged woman, with dark hair that had streaks of grey in it, tied up tight on her head like a bun. She was dressed like the nurses from the infirmary he had escaped on Eden. The sight of the uniform brought a flood of sad and violent memories crashing through his mind, like a cresting wave on a beach. He had to catch his breath, and he took a big gulp of air to calm himself.

The attendant said in the slow drawl that all people seemed to have these days, "Of course, my dear. Here, this is the sign-in form. The mess hall is behind me, feel free to go there and eat."

"Thank you," Evard said, still a little uneasy.

The attendant continued. "Food is available until 9pm, but snacks and fruit will be available after the kitchen closes. After you eat, you can head down that hall right there." She motioned to the long hallway on his left. "There is another reception desk down there and they can help you get set up with lodging. There are still several beds available but you may want to go register as soon as you can to make sure you get one."

He smiled at her wistfully and thanked her for her assistance. He figured he would need a bed tonight but his stomach had started to rumble so he thought it best to go into the mess hall and eat. Still paranoid from the bizarre encounter he had out on the streets, he looked around the mess hall for any signs of recognition that might mean danger. All he saw were hungry people who were struggling under the boot of a highly industrialized machine designed to disadvantage them. That's what his brother and his father would have thought anyway. *In truth, this is just how life goes sometimes,* he thought bitterly. *At least they are safe here tonight.* Which is more than could be said for him.

He expected most of them to look old and sickly but there was a fair amount of young folk like him, as well as couples, and families with small children. People from all levels of society, huddled around a bowl of soup, with no where else to go.

I'm one of them now, he thought dejectedly.

A few days ago he had a family, friends, an easy job; a decent life. Now he was a refugee, eating at a soup kitchen a hundred million miles away from the furthest he'd ever been from home. He was now, for the first time in his whole life, all alone.

He staggered up to the serving counter, observing how the line worked by watching the people standing in front of him. He took a tray, a plate, and some utensils off a nearby table and waited in line as he approached the various serving stations. The spread was impressive for a soup kitchen. There was an array of diverse foods from various places around the Imperium. He took a piece of bread and some beef stew that smelled surprisingly good, along with some fresh fruit.

The servers were kindly looking people, with patient, smiling faces, but the people here, like everywhere he went, still seemed like they were wading through flowing amber—like they had been secretly replaced by androids or possessed by spirits. He chuckled to himself, *maybe this was what was going on everywhere. People are possessed.* He smiled a mischievous smile and sat down at the end of a long table, far enough away from the other diners but not so far away that it would draw attention.

He devoured the bread and stew ravenously. Ripping off a chunk of bread, he wiped it around the rim of the bowl, sopping up all the stew juices. He had eaten a little on the starcruiser but it still felt like he hadn't eaten in weeks. He couldn't tell whether or not the stew really was delicious or if he was simply starving but either way he lapped it up quickly and leaned back, his belly satisfied for the first time in a while. After having scarfed down the stew and bread, he picked gently at the fruit. There was an apple, what he thought were slices of mango, and a small bunch of grapes. He ate the fruit in silence, occasionally washing down the food with sips of water. He took out the bottle with the pilfered antibiotics, shook a few out, then washed them down with a swig of water.

Even though he was sitting in the middle of a giant cafeteria surrounded by people he let his mind drift a bit, his thoughts settling for the first time since he left Eden. He felt aimless, like a feather drifting on a strong summer breeze. *I guess I can do anything I like*, he thought to himself. *I need to find work, maybe something where they don't need to know my identity*, he mused. *There has to be somethi--*

He stopped short in the middle of his thought. He had gotten lost in his reverie and hadn't noticed he was being approached by two strangers. He sat there, a look of incredulity on his face, not sure whether to fight or run. Somehow, they'd found him. Standing on the opposite side of the table were the two women from the street who seemed to recognize him. He was about to scream for help when the older woman put a finger to her lips in a shushing gesture. Then she said evenly, "It's okay. We're not here to hurt you. We'd just like to ask you a few questions."

Evard noticed that the timber of her voice was different than the other people he had encountered since the hallway of the infirmary back on Eden. It didn't have the lithe singsong quality that everyone now seems to sport. It sounded heavier, filled with stress, as if it was weighed down by bags of sand. She also spoke faster than Hal and Olaver—and everyone else he'd encountered. He was scared but also intrigued.

The woman with the chestnut hair gestured to the table as if to say 'can we sit?' He nodded awkwardly and both women sat down on the bench across from him.

They both were smiling pleasantly but their smiles were different somehow. More like the regular smiles that were common for people a few days ago, before some strange noise drove everyone insane. They were absent the conspicuously toothy grins he'd seen recently on the faces of every passerby.

Once they sat down, the woman who was doing the talking said, "Hello. I'm Zarena and this Emerald. What's your name?"

"I'm E-E-Evard," he stammered. "H-h-ow can I help you?"

It felt like the nervousness was oozing out of his every pore. Both women seemed to notice he was nervous and the one with the piercing green eyes threw a sideways glance at the other, as if they were acknowledging some hidden secret. The woman who had just introduced herself as Zarena continued on.

"Evard, it's nice to meet you. We noticed you on the street. I'm sorry if we startled you, it's just we noticed you were acting differently than everyone else: you were running." She smiled an amused smile as if that observation in and of itself was silly. "What I mean to say is that, well, to be blunt you were acting differently than the rest of the people on the streets. We have been looking for someone, ah, I guess you can say, acting "normal"?"   Evard stared at Zarena blankly, as if all the thoughts he was about to have just fell out of his head. He rubbed his eyes to make sure he wasn't somehow hallucinating.

"Uh huh, I've, uh, yeah, I had noticed something." He stuttered, still nervous.

"Well," continued Zarena. "It seems like you were immune to it. Just like my friend here." Zarena gestured to Emerald, who had up until this point been sitting quietly next to her.

Evard looked over at Emerald and when their eyes met he almost jumped out of his skin. Her eyes were unlike anything he'd ever seen. It was almost as if they were giving off a neon glow of their own. The way those piercing eyes illuminated her angelic face made his heart flutter for a second. He looked into her eyes just a moment too long then looked away bashfully, cheeks flushed with crimson. If this made the girl with the green eyes uncomfortable she gave no indication. Instead she said, somewhat rigidly, "I understand this seems strange. But it's true. You seem to have been unaffected by The Harmony…"

"…the what?" interrupted Evard, with a look of puzzlement on his face.

"Yes, that's what it's called," said the girl with the green eyes, who then paused for a second before saying in a diffident tone, "apparently." It was a…" she hesitated for a moment then said "…a biological attack, I guess you could say? The target was everyone. Everyone on every world. There's a lot to discuss about it but this isn't the place for it." She looked around to see if anyone was paying an unusual amount of attention to them but everyone seemed to be eating their food in sullen silence, eyes on the table or each other.

She then continued in a cautious, conspiratorial tone. "Zarena and I are trying to help by engineering a way to reverse the effects. We need help. There aren't many people like us who are Immune. We were just about to go to the Raxeon building to widen our search pool when we saw you acting normally on the street. That's what gave you away. You were acting like a person might act before all this, so we followed you. We didn't want to spook you so we waited until you were finished eating to approach you."

The girl with the piercing green eyes, who went by the name Emerald (Evard almost chuckled at how on the nose the name was), was speaking in a very direct manner that took him more than a little by surprise. He was trying to listen to her words, which he realized were important, instead of being hypnotized by her eyes, which he was having trouble resisting. He'd never seen such a strikingly beautiful girl in all his life. Both of them were. He thought to himself as he studied their perfect bone structure that this must be what it's like living on one of the interior worlds. Everyone was so beautiful and glamorous. It made the mud stained villages of Eden look like a pauper's den in comparison. He blushed again, this time in embarrassment. He must look like a total rube to them. Still, they sought him out so he figured he would go along with it, for now.

"So, you want to, what? Recruit me?" He asked skeptically.

"In a word, yes," said Zarena. "That's exactly what we want."

"So you're not… ah, you weren't, looking for me then? You didn't know who I was when you saw me. You just noticed that I was running?" He laughed out loud at that last part. They both looked at him and nodded in sync with each other.

"Why would we be looking for you?" Emerald asked, inquisitively.

Evard thought for a moment. These two strangers seemed nice enough but also slightly deranged, like maybe certifiably crazy. That could present its own dangers but whatever they wanted from him they didn't seem to know anything about what happened on Eden. *Why would they?* he thought. Having now been to Exalon he couldn't imagine anyone here actually caring a whit about something that happened out on the edge of the galaxy. Eden mind as well be a thousand galaxies away from the bright center of the universe that made up the interior worlds. He had to face certain realities: he was stranded on a foreign world with nothing more than a few credits in his pocket, nowhere to go, nowhere to even start, staying in a halfway house, and now two women wanted to recruit him for some secret weapons project. It sounded insane but he was starting to think that going with them was his best option. At least for the time being, until he could figure out a solid game plan.

"OK," he said, ignoring the question. "What do you want from me?"

Zarena answered. "We'd like you to come with us. We have a workshop not far from here. We'll explain everything once we get there. Less eyes and ears on us. Once we explain, you can decide whether or not you'd like to help us. We're not going to lie, there is danger in helping us. But given where you are and how you reacted when you saw us you're obviously in your own precarious situation. Maybe we can help each other out."

Evard took a long moment to contemplate the choice before him. He could stay here, where it's safe, but then he'd be floating along without a rudder. No plan, no prospects, no one to help him. Or he can follow these two insane strangers that accosted him on the street and followed him into a shelter rambling about some doomsday weapon. They already warned him if he agreed to help them there could be danger but, as they rightly deduced, he was in a fair amount of danger himself. Maybe if he allied with these two they could help the whole situation on Eden go away.

The one with the chestnut hair was dressed like a diplomat. Her clothing was regal, similar to the garb that members of the Royal Houses wore. He remembered going to a parade with his family as a kid and seeing members of House Colette there, dressed like this Zarena woman was now. A question finally dawned on him, maybe a risky one to ask but he went ahead anyway. "Who, exactly, are you two?"

Emerald answered first. "I'm Emerald Seltz, an engineer at Raxeon. I'm here because I am Immune. Like you. This is Zarena, Zarena Denamonte."

Zarena Denamonte. He had heard the name before somewhere but he couldn't quite place it. Sensing his puzzlement Zarena interjected.

"I'm a member of the Imperial counsel. I'm also the architect of The Harmony. I'm the one who designed it."

"You did what?! Are you fucking joking?"

CHAPTER 23

Welcome To The Resistance

An uneasy hush permeated the cluttered workshop in the musty Raxeon warehouse. Zarena and Emerald had just spent an arduous hour explaining every intricate detail of their predicament to a flabbergasted Evard, who could only gawk and throw in an occasional head shake. After the exhaustive explanation, the women allowed the fresh-faced farm boy time to digest the scope of their circumstances. They waited patiently as he struggled to come to terms with the jarring reality. Just when they thought his mind might shatter completely, he erupted at them in a vitriolic torrent.

They weathered his outburst with patience. Zarena realized Emerald's reaction was far more poised and astute than one could reasonably expect. She had already deduced several key pieces of information before even connecting with Zarena. Evard's reaction aligned more with what one would anticipate when dropping earth-shattering news on the unsuspecting masses. They offered him warm, sympathetic smiles, allowing his tirade to run its course until his rage simmered down.

"...I mean... I mean it's fucking nuts. Y-y-you, you're a supervillain, a fucking supervillain!" he shouted, jabbing an accusatory finger at Zarena. "I mean... I mean this is crazy. This is unconscionable. This is madness and tyranny! *You're a tyrant!*" he bellowed, his voice quaking with ire and dismay.

Eventually, when his tempest of emotions began to subside, he tilted his head back, gazing at the ceiling as tears welled in his eyes. He slumped back in his chair, dropping his face into his hands, propped up on his knees, and began to softly sob.

Zarena shot Emerald an anxious glance, silently asking, *what should we do here?* She knew the truth could be hard to swallow but had underestimated how devastated he would be. They considered comforting him but thought better of it. After a minute of hiccuping sobs, he collected himself, and met their gaze, his reddened, irritated eyes displaying his anguish.

With a resigned sigh barely above a whisper, he finally said, "Well, I guess I should be grateful. You saved my life."

Zarena and Emerald made no attempt to hide their puzzlement. Zarena responded, "Well, yes, we did in a way. That was the whole point."

"No, not like that," Evard croaked, still awash with emotions. "I don't mean it as some stupid metaphor. You literally saved my life."

He divulged the details of his harrowing experience — how his brother had snapped (he now grasped why), how Lester had slain their father and nearly killed him and their mother. How his mother was then murdered by the sergeant trying to contain the chaos. How Evard lay bleeding and pleading for his life in the infirmary hallway, seconds from execution, when an eerie sound transformed everyone but him into pacifist zombies. He described fleeing off-world, the altered behavior of all he encountered, his help repairing the starcruiser, and their spotting him on the streets of District 7.

After baring his soul, he sighed, "I feel like I'm still back there, in that hallway, begging for my life. I feel like some part of me will always be in that hallway. But I'm alive. This *Harmony* went off the instant before the sergeant pulled the trigger. A few seconds later and I'd be dead."

Zarena listened to his chilling account with the patient dignity befitting her stature. She solemnly shook her head saying, "How awful that something so heinous happened to you." Her face radiated genuine compassion, bridging the gap between them. "There were whispers, rumors really, of militias taking matters into their own hands. Fear of The Sequence had spread through local and planetary governments, though they didn't grasp what it was. Many secretly dubbed it a 'rage flu'."

Evard just listened mutely, profound sorrow etched on his face.

Zarena continued, "This fear-mongering has bred much harm. It drove our haste to ready The Harmony, to halt the slaughter squads using it as pretext to murder innocents."

Emerald, who had listened fretfully, finally interjected, "So that's why you fled from us? You thought we were after you for the sergeant's murder?"

Evard nodded, speaking through clenched teeth and quivering lips. "Yes", he spat in a quaking voice. "I thought people would pursue me. For the killings. It wasn't just the sergeant, I killed the other officers too after they, you know, stopped coming after me." His breathing grew labored as he struggled to restrain his emotions. "T-t-t-they… killed my, m-my Mom! They killed my *mom*!" he shrieked.

As he spoke a torrent of tears streamed down his ruddy cheeks like waterfalls. His wails were banshee shrieks saturated with anguish. He surrendered all pretenses and gave himself over to the flood — anger, rage, and torment gushing through him.

This time Emerald and Zarena went to him, Zarena gripping his shoulder firmly as if to hold his roiling emotions in place. Emerald pulled her chair close, embracing him and gently kneading his other shoulder in soothing motions. He continued to blubber, dripping snot onto Emerald's sleeve. If it bothered her she didn't show it, she just held him as he cried himself out. It was an agonizing scene and Zarena felt her own emotions churn. This young man was saved by The Harmony — not in some abstract, metaphorical way. He was literally snatched from the jaws of an imminently violent death. She felt a kernel of hope blossom in her heart. She had done some good after all.

Eventually, Evard emptied out his vast well of despair. Wiping the tear streaks from his cheeks, he coughed up some phlegm and swallowed it back. Standing to grab a rag, he blew his nose with a loud honk. Zarena watched this display with vaguely morbid fascination. The honking was almost comical and Emerald let slip a small giggle, which she struggled but failed to suppress. Evard noticed and for a moment they feared anger, but instead he began to laugh, which then dissolved into coughing fits. Emerald went over, patting his back to help clear the phlegm and ease the coughing.

With the intensity passed, the three regarded each other with uncertainty, unsure of the next move. Eventually, Zarena suggested they sit back down. Pulling up chairs, they settled around the table again. No one quite knew what to say after such a raw moment. Just as Zarena moved to restart discussion, Evard interjected.

"Thank you, um, Emerald—and you also," he offered, glancing at Zarena. "Thanks for, well… just thanks." His eyes had already cleared. It seemed he had wrung every last drop of sorrow from his very marrow. Gazing at them evenly, he continued, "Listen, thanks, okay. I needed to tell someone. To grieve. Thank you for letting me."

No one spoke so he went on. "This thing you did saved me and I'm grateful. Incredibly grateful. Look, I've seen this Sequence thing first hand. I've seen the horror of it." His eyes flitted to Emerald, her phosphorescent green eyes warmly returning his gaze. "I doubt you've witnessed it up close like I have. It's the most terrifying thing imaginable. My brother, Lester, he was a good man. A good brother. He cared for me, for our family. The way he changed, it was like he became someone else—dark, sadistic; a madman from a horror vid. Whatever good was in him before, it was just gone. A ruthless killer had taken his place."

He shuddered at the chilling memories. Deciding to cut to the chase, he declared, "Look, you wanted my help so you've got it. I'm in. Let's fix the universe."

"Really?" Zarena asked. "Are you sure you're up for this?"

"I know it's risky. If old man Rakeus comes after us we're likely dead. Plus, the local militia will do anything to bury this." A vengeful spark flickered in his eyes for a moment then vanished.

"But honestly, I've got nowhere else to go. I've lost everything. What more can I lose?"

Zarena contemplated this as she gently patted his hand. "Well then, Evard Roost, welcome to the Resistance."

CHAPTER 24
We'll Start With You

"Ahhhh!!" Zarena yelled, crumpling a sheet of calculations and pitching it across the workshop. "This is impossible!"

"Just breathe," Emerald soothed. She watched Evard gleefully careening around the warehouse on the forklift, ostensibly moving materials but mostly just having fun. "We're stuck, I know. But there must be an answer. We just need to calm down and think it through."

"Emerald, you have one of the sharpest minds I've encountered—with you on the original team we could have accomplished more in less time. But I used to have a whole team: scientists, neurologists, psychologists, spectrum engineers, acoustic experts; every resource the Imperium could provide, all at my disposal." She flopped down into a chair with an exasperated sigh. "I don't see how this is possible. We're nowhere close to starting. What was I thinking?"

Emerald smiled at the praise but frowned at the despair. Zarena looked to her almost pleadingly, searching for any glimmer of hope.

"You're right, we're at a disadvantage," Emerald conceded. "But I wouldn't say it's hopeless yet."

Zarena waited expectantly for her to explain how it wasn't a totally futile endeavor.

Emerald watched Evard zipping around with abandon. "You haven't realized yet, but you have something now you didn't before," she remarked, swiveling to face Zarena sharply. "Something essential. You have us. Myself and Evard. You have two Immune people to study. You don't need us to lend you our skills, you need us so you can figure out what makes us immune. That could be the key to solving the puzzle." Slowly, like a setting sun, realization dawned on Zarena. *We've never had Immune to test before*, she thought. *Maybe we could...*

As if reading her mind, Emerald continued. "We could run tests on us. Discover what makes us different. That may provide a starting point. Determining what enables immunity could help unravel how to undo The Harmony's effects. Just studying Evard and me likely isn't enough - the factors could be different for each of us. But by compiling the results, we may identify a common variable to target."

Zarena mulled this over carefully, scenarios flying through her mind in rapid succession. After some contemplation, it was as if a light bulb switched on. Emerald thought she could almost see the thought bubble materializing above her head.

"We need more Immune — as many as possible for a healthy sample size. Studying a sampling of Immune is the key. The answer must lie in whatever protects them from the effects. Unfortunately, just you two isn't sufficient, as you said. Even if we isolated your specific immunities, the causes are likely distinct. We'd need to synthesize the factors to formulate a universal inoculation. Hopefully with enough samples we can find some commonality we can leverage."

Lost in strategizing, Zarena muttered half to herself the beginning tenets of a plan.

Emerald interrupted her train of thought. "But how will we find more Immune? Stumbling on Evard and I was largely luck. We could scour the Imperium for years and never locate another."

"That part is more simple," Zarena grinned broadly. "Once we crack what specifically makes you and Evard Immune, we can engineer a system to identify other Immune hidden in the populations—a lure of sorts. It may not be that difficult. Many are probably concealed among society or literally in hiding, fearing discovery. We may be able to flush them out." She cautioned against getting ahead of themselves but seemed invigorated by the possibilities.

"Alright, now we're getting somewhere," Emerald agreed enthusiastically.

Over the next few days, Zarena and Emerald toiled in the workshop, sketching plans for an anti-Harmony prototype. Evard manned security and supplies, monitoring the exterior cameras for any suspicious activity and making food and supply runs. Zarena had given him a stack of credits to pay cash at different places each time. They also tasked him with menial labor like driving the forklift to retrieve spare parts from the towering shelves. Evard bunked in the warehouse, sleeping on a dingy old cot. Zarena did the same. Emerald would leave late each night to check on her mother, usually returning in the morning with fresh food and drinks — the coffee was especially welcome to Evard. It reminded him of home.

After a few days, they had hashed out some concepts but nothing solid yet. It was clear they lacked materials to attempt even a rudimentary prototype, but that wasn't the real issue. The underlying math still eluded them. Zarena began having doubts this plan would work at all. Their original research never indicated The Harmony could be undone once inoculated. Maybe there truly was no way.

Zarena began gathering an array of devices — a spectral analyzer, medical kit, stethoscope, and other assorted equipment, cobbling together a makeshift spectral wave analyzer. She directed Emerald to a terminal to code an algorithm while she spliced components together and connected wires into various hubs, fashioning a headset-like contraption. She worked furiously until Emerald asked if she needed assistance.

"No, I'm almost done," Zarena assured her, wholly engrossed in splicing wires for the jury-rigged device that resembled a hybrid defibrillator with drone remote control.

"Evard, can you come here a minute?" she called out. She looked at Emerald. "We'll start with you," she told Emerald. "Sit and try to stay completely relaxed." She hastily affixed sensors to Emerald's wrists, arm, temples, forehead and neck. Emerald waited patiently until she had finished.

"What exactly are you doing?" Emerald inquired politely.

"This is a makeshift spectral wave analyzer. I'm going to scan your brain first, then test Evard's. Seems a reasonable starting point."

"I suppose so," Emerald chuckled. The work had begun.

CHAPTER 25
This Requires A Delicate Touch

Rakeus sat alone in his private chambers, the muted morning light filtering through the windows, casting long shadows that danced across the floor. His mind was a whirlpool of thoughts, each one pulling him deeper.

He seemed almost asleep, his eyes half-closed, when a sharp rap at the door jolted him back to the present. Rakeus turned, his voice booming through the room, "Come in!"

The door creaked open, and in slunk Jesper, dressed impeccably in courtly attire that seemed to absorb the dim light. Despite the early summons, he betrayed no hint of annoyance, his demeanor as smooth as silk. "How may I assist you, Your Majesty?" he purred, his voice dripping with obsequiousness.

Rakeus motioned for him to enter, and the two men settled into cushioned chairs separated by a small table. Jesper crossed his legs with the grace of a dancer and regarded the Emperor with a placid expression, waiting patiently for him to speak.

In a gravelly voice that seemed to echo from the depths of his being, Rakeus rumbled, "Where is she?"

Jesper leaned forward slightly, his eyes narrowing with interest. "Still on Exalon, it seems. She's made a few friends," he replied, his voice calm and measured.

Rakeus raised his eyebrows, a silent prompt for Jesper to continue.

"Yes," Jesper elaborated. "An engineer of considerable talent, arguably one of the best in the Imperium." He paused, allowing the weight of his words to sink in before continuing. "They're accompanied by a rather conspicuous young fugitive from the colonies. Reports have him sprinting down the main avenue in District 7, apparently fleeing some legal troubles back on Eden."

"Legal troubles?" Rakeus inquired, his interest piqued.

Jesper nodded, his expression one of practiced neutrality. "It seems his brother had The Sequence triggered and went on a rampage, slaying their father. The local sergeant botched containment and ended up dead. The young man apparently escaped off-world—no travel logs, but intelligence confirms he fled on a starcruiser bound for Exalon."

"Sprinting, you say?" Rakeus mused, a hint of curiosity in his voice.

"Yes, Your Eminence. The report indicates behavior atypical of the Harmonized," Jesper replied in his usual even tone.

"He was on Eden during The Harmony activation?" Rakeus asked, leaning forward slightly.

"He was. Departed the morning after. Seems he may have exploited it to escape," Jesper confirmed.

"So there are some Immune," Rakeus coughed, a dry sound that echoed in the quiet room. "That was expected. And now he's with her?"

"Indeed, sire," Jesper replied smoothly.

"She's piecing it together. An engineer, some rabble-rousing Immune. I should have heeded you, Jesper. We never should have let her leave," Rakeus admitted, a rare moment of vulnerability in his voice.

"As you say, Your Grace. But this way is much tidier. She's made no attempt to contact other Councilors since arriving on Exalon. We control all intelligence now. None who matter will know, and the rest..." Jesper made a dismissive gesture, his lips curling into a thin, sanguine grin that reminded Rakeus of a snake's jaw unhinging before striking.

"Very well. Do we have their location?" Rakeus asked, his voice regaining its authoritative edge.

"An abandoned Raxeon warehouse in District 7. The engineer had access credentials through her job," Jesper replied, his tone confident.

"Where is this intel coming…" Rakeus began, but Jesper raised his hand mid-sentence and shook his head. If anyone else in the entire Imperium dared to act so brazenly in the Emperor's presence, they would be executed on the spot. Instead, Rakeus just grimaced. "It's handled, Sire. It's best not to trouble yourself with the details," Jesper assured him.

Rakeus grunted in frustration, then continued, "How long until you can get a team in position? Even now, I'd rather avoid witnesses."

"A team is en route and keeping it quiet. They should be in position soon," Jesper replied, his voice smooth as ever.

"This requires a delicate touch, Jesper. You understand, yes?" Rakeus emphasized, his eyes locking onto Jesper's.

Jesper rose before being dismissed, much to Rakeus' annoyance. "Of course, Your Eminence. Is there any other way?" he purred smoothly, his voice a velvet promise.

Rakeus waved him off with a flick of his hand, his patience wearing thin. Jesper slunk out almost soundlessly, sending a chill through Rakeus. *He moves like a prowling tiger*, Rakeus thought, a shiver running down his spine. He put his hand to his mouth as he let out a gaping yawn, then walked out of the sitting room back to his bedchamber and closed the door, the weight of the morning's revelations settling heavily upon him.

CHAPTER 26

Whatever You Think Is Best

"Good Morning," Emerald chirped as she breezed through the warehouse doors, toting coffee and pastries from home. "I hope everyone slept well!" She lugged a bulging bag over her shoulder and plopped it down with a thud on the workshop table as she entered.

Evard was sawing logs on a decrepit old cot tucked away in the corner, as was his habit. The mattress had certainly seen better days and was most likely infested with critters, but he figured it beat snoozing on the cold, hard floor. Zarena was crashing in the workshop, head and arms sprawled across the table in what looked to be an extremely uncomfortable position. It was her usual way of catching some shuteye after burning the midnight oil analyzing data late into the night. When Emerald had bid her goodnight long after sunset, she was still glued to the terminal, scrutinizing the results she collected on Emerald and Evard.

Emerald breezed into the room, rousing the bleary-eyed duo from their slumber as they stirred awake with yawns.

"You two really should stay at my place. At this rate you'll keel over from exhaustion," Emerald chided in a cheerful tone. She was feeling more hopeful about their chances after their recent breakthroughs.

Zarena unfurled her limbs in a luxurious stretch, rolling her neck to work out the kinks from snoozing at the table.

"I don't know, Emerald. Staying at your place would endanger your mum, you, and us. But you raise a fair point — we shouldn't linger here on Exalon much longer," Zarena replied.

Evard had just shuffled in, hair disheveled and eyes glazed from a restless night's sleep. All he caught was something about leaving Exalon. He and Emerald exchanged a look and in unison. "What?"

Zarena stood, shaking the pins and needles from her legs as she elaborated. "Yes, it's safest if we move on. My extended stay is already suspicious. I wasn't even sure Rakeus would permit me to visit Exalon, let alone make a side trip here." She began to pace, limbering up for the day ahead. "By my planned itinerary, I should've departed the planet days ago. The longer we remain, the greater the danger for all of us."

Zarena tilted her head towards a wide-eyed Evard. "Now we have Evard in tow. It's likely any unusual events around the time of The Harmony will be forgotten. Highly doubtful anyone from Eden is tracking the aftermath. Still, the Imperium may be interested in developments immediately following The Harmony. We could be on someone's radar. Either way, the risk multiplies each day we stay."

"You mean it's time to skip town again? I just got here!" Evard exclaimed, exasperated.

Concern crept over Emerald's face like a shadow. "Really?"

"Yes," Zarena stated flatly.

"Yes?", Emerald parroted again.

"I'm sorry, but leaving is safest. We have no playbook — from here on out, we'll be riding on instinct alone," Zarena reasoned.

Emerald had been mulling something over since the conversation began and finally mustered the courage to voice her thoughts aloud. "Could we take them with us?"

Zarena walked over and gave Emerald's shoulder a supportive squeeze before responding gently, "I wish we could, Emerald.

But I don't believe it's safe for us or for them. If we're caught, it likely means execution for me at least. You and Evard would probably become lab experiments, or left to rot away in some dark cell. Anyone with us would face the same fate."

Emerald's eyes brimmed with sadness as the gravity of her situation came crashing down. "Honestly, Rakeus would probably just have them killed on the spot," Zarena added, more nonchalantly than the others felt comfortable with. She gave Emerald's shoulder another pat and clasped both hands on her arms.

"If we leave them be, it's unlikely Rakeus or Jesper will give them a second thought. They're Harmonized, so they'll pose no threat in their minds." She injected as much confidence into her voice as she could muster, hoping to reassure Emerald this was the wisest course.

"Who's Jesper?" Evard asked.

The hairs on the back of Zarena's neck prickled at the question. "The Emperor's attack dog. If Rakeus unleashes him, we'll wish we were dead long before he's done with us." She grimaced, trying to banish thoughts of the sinister Jesper from her mind. His motives remained a mystery — tipping her off about Rakeus, enabling her escape from Archlon, practically pushing her to help Raeka. Yet Jesper could never be trusted. He was simply too dangerous.

Emerald and Evard exchanged anxious glances, reading the fear in each other's eyes.

"So, what are our chances of actually surviving if the most lethal people in the Imperium are hunting us down?" Evard asked apprehensively.

Zarena gave a noncommittal shrug. "We don't know if they're even looking yet. Unlikely they've connected many dots beyond their suspicions about me. But we must assume we're being watched, if not actively hunted. The stakes are too high. Rakeus would execute us all in a heartbeat rather than allow a cure for The Harmony to be created. He sees it as the ultimate threat to his new peaceful Empire."

Sensing the others' unease, Zarena longed to quell their fears yet refused to sugarcoat the truth. "Look, Rakeus is a better man than he seems. I've known him most of my life. His pursuit of power does drive him, of course, but he's far more just and fair than any of his predecessor's were. He wants to maintain control but he does genuinely care about his people. These decisions didn't come easily to him."

Childhood memories of Rakeus flooded back - he had been like an uncle, always so kind and attentive towards her despite his vast responsibility.

"My relationship with him and his daughter Raeka could potentially spare me the worst punishment, but Rakeus has always placed the Empire's needs above personal ties. If we're discovered, we'll likely be doomed. I don't mean to frighten you, but it's important you both grasp the severity of this."

Evard gave a casual shrug despite his obvious dread. "Every moment I've been alive since The Harmony has been a bonus. I should've died back on Eden. Whatever happens now, happens."

"Alright then, it's settled. We'll start planning our exit," Zarena declared.

"Is it wise to abruptly flee Exalon before finishing the detection device?" Emerald corrected. Zarena smirked at her fastidiousness.

Emerald continued. "Should we remain until we can at least get a prototype operational? You're closing in on identifying the common thread among the immune, aren't you?"

"Not exactly. Unfortunately, I lack the equipment to pinpoint why either of you are Immune. But I may have uncovered something useful. I observed distinct variations in your neural alpha wave patterns — obviously different from the Harmonized, but more intriguingly, not matching fully un-Harmonized individuals either."

Emerald quirked an eyebrow. "Hmm, fascinating."

"It could be," Zarena agreed. "I scanned my own brain waves and found they don't match either of yours, curiously enough.

I was wearing a dampening device during The Harmony, so the sonic zeta waves never reached my brain."

"What does that mean, exactly?" Evard asked, thoroughly engaged despite his limited grasp.

"It suggests The Harmony actually did alter those who are Immune, just not in any observable way. In some cases there may be mild effects, like your acquaintance Hal—Harmonized but incompletely. That's a special case, though. For you two, no visible Harmonization occurred, yet your brains still underwent subtle changes in your neural wiring."

Evard blinked rapidly, as if banishing a speck of dust from his eye. "Ah, so that means..."

"In short, not total resistance. Likely minuscule tweaks to electrical impulses along neural pathways, but sparing behavioral centers. As you said, you're essentially unchanged. The variance between my readings and yours is slight, statistically insignificant. But it could be just enough to detect immunity versus those Harmonized."

Comprehension dawned on Evard's face. "So we act and think the same as before, but our brains are a bit different now?"

"Precisely," Zarena confirmed, pleased by Evard's eureka moment. "We can leverage these subtle distinctions to potentially identify others like you." The trio's mood lifted at this glimmer of hope.

Emerald considered the implications, then frowned. "Wouldn't you need to hook people up to a device? Random testing doesn't seem feasible."

"I have an idea about that. The Harmony utilized echo location techniques, enabling planet-wide Harmonization with just a few devices. We didn't require return pings, but we could employ a sonar ping to detect minds with divergent signals from the Harmonized."

Evard's eyes widened. "Whoa, really? You'd use sonar to find Immune people?"

"Somewhat — it would be integrated into the device. The positive is it could actually work. The negative is limited range — we couldn't blanket Exalon and locate all Immunes. I'm unsure of max distance, but maybe a few kilometers at most."

"Still seems workable, potentially," Emerald mused. "We'd deploy it in dense areas to maximize our chances."

"Precisely. The range is restricting but it's feasible. Now we just need to construct it."

"Sounds like you have the gist of it," Emerald remarked. "With your breakthrough, I can help model the logistics. Shouldn't be overly complicated now."

"I'd agree, except for our limited materials and unfinished specifications. We likely can't obtain the ideal components. That will add time, and could cause the readings to be less accurate."

Emerald tapped her chin contemplatively. "Well, it depends. I still work for Raxeon — they have warehouses, storage rooms, and facilities all over the place. If we list the parts, we could cross-reference their inventory. The snag is it's behind security protocols. To avoid triggering alerts, I'll need the mainframe terminal at Raxeon HQ."

Zarena nodded approvingly. "Excellent idea. Let's compile the parts beyond what we already have, with some alternates just in case."

The duo diligently discussed each component's function and the optimal substitutes.

"...So we'll require a virunet access chip to ping the GPS, Raxeon produces two modular models, but one draws more power..."

"...I think sheer Vermacite works best for the casing. We could hollow out a proton drone's capacitor, see if that provides enough space for the nanocircuitry..."

Before long they had a plausible parts list that seemed viable from an engineering perspective. Evard observed the two volleying ideas back and forth, feeding off each other's frenetic energy. Though he grasped little of the technical jargon, he could tell they were onto something big. Finally they produced a complete list of primary and backup parts.

"It's still mid-morning. I'll head out now and stop at Raxeon HQ. Once I run the search, I'll map the component locations and report back," Emerald stated decisively. "Accessing the system under my credentials could raise flags overnight, but I can at least find the parts, if not acquire them yet."

"Understood. Do your best, then return immediately. We need to gather supplies and depart this rock ASAP," Zarena replied.

Emerald held her gaze for a moment as unspoken thoughts passed between them. "If we succeed, we'll come back for them. As soon as we can undo the programming. I promise," Zarena assured gently.

Emerald sighed, "I know. Still doesn't make leaving any easier."

"You should go home first, say your goodbyes and pack. Tell your mum you're away on business, whatever you think best."

Emerald nodded and headed off, flashing Evard a sweet smile as she left. Time was the enemy now.

CHAPTER 27
It's One Little Girl

On the 17th floor, Jazz sat mellow as could be, diligently working away with nary a glance up from his terminal. He had steadily typed since arriving that morning, only rising to use the restroom.

Emerald suddenly materialized through the private elevator doors and breezed over. Seeing his cheery wave when he saw her approach, for a fleeting moment she forgot everything that had transpired. It was just Jazz and Em, like old times, and all felt right in the world. Then reality snapped back like an overstretched rubber band.

Jazz flashed a Harmonized smile before re-immersing himself in work, seeming intent on concentrating despite the disruption. Emerald approached and gave his back an affectionate pat. He peered up with a grin. "Hey Em. Was wondering where you've been off to."

She smiled as warmly as she could while holding back the tears welling behind her eyes. "Yeah, sorry Jazz. Working on a special project."

He ducked his head, returning focus to the terminal. She watched him for a minute, realizing how much he'd changed. Usually he'd be bouncing off the walls, cracking jokes and filling any empty space with his boundless exuberance. Now he seemed engrossed in work, something she couldn't ever remember witnessing in all their years together. He was capable of seriousness and brilliance, but always blended fun into everything. This new Jazz was all work, no play.

She settled at her desk across from him and linked her comm to the terminal, uploading the component list to the inventory search. Approximately ten minutes remained as the engine ran, so she sat quietly scanning her surroundings.

Though she'd worked alongside Jazz here for years, it already seemed a relic of her old life. Raxeon was slowly transforming into a vestige of the past. She wasn't Emerald the Engineer anymore, but Emerald the Freedom Fighter. Each Harmonized person she passed reminded her of the countless minds she hoped to liberate if her mission succeeded. Beyond her mum and Jazz, this went so much deeper, impacting all humanity across the Imperium's great expanse. Despite the enormity of it all, in her mind's eye it always wore a familiar face - Jazz had become the embodiment of the Harmony's oppression. Not just him, but everyone like him, everywhere. This wasn't only for Jazz, but for all those muted voices.

She logged onto the security server, where all surveillance throughout the entire Raxeon footprint was accessible. She used her clearance codes to gain access but then ran a script that offloaded the data directly to her own comm. That way, even if someone thought it was suspicious she was accessing high level security data no one would be able to see what she was actually looking at, which provided some measure of protection to her and the group.

The first thing she looked at was the warehouse, checking the perimeter video feeds. She had deactivated the interior feeds to provide them with privacy but she flipped them on to take a look.

The video monitors showed Zarena working in the workshop, toiling away at deciphering all the data she had collected over the past few days. Evard was in the warehouse, lounging around on his cot, taking a little bit of downtime for himself. *Poor Evard*, she thought. *He's been through so much.* She felt bad for him. His plight had been the roughest but he still managed to smile 1and add a little levity to the darkness of their mission. She watched him lazily scratch his head and yawn and a smile formed on her lips. *He is a nice guy — and very cute*, she thought, immediately blushing.

A security alert flashed as the search completed. Minimizing the results, she pulled up the alert—an identified Imperial agent had just approached the front desk downstairs. Heart hammering, she pulled up the lobby feed.

A squad of armed agents stood at attention by the desk while one conferred with the attendant. The attendant departed while the team moved toward the private elevator leading directly to the seventeenth floor. *Oh shit! They're coming for me!* Thinking fast, she checked the warehouse cameras. To her horror, another tactical team, geared up in black with weapons drawn, was converging on the front and rear entrances. She hastily typed a message to Zarena.

THEY FOUND US. RUN

Just as it sent, the feeds simultaneously went dark — the agents had cut her security access. With a sinking dread Emerald realized that the agents had terminated her access to the entire Raxeon security system. She turned off the comm and disable the locator so they couldn't use it to track her. *They know what I'm doing*, she realized with in a panic.

She had already compiled all the location data for the parts that Zarena needed. *Time to run*, she thought.

There were four separate ways off the seventeenth floor: the private elevator she typically used, another elevator for the general public that stopped at every level, and a back stairway that led both up and down. Without the video feed she wasn't sure whether or not the agents were using the public elevator but she didn't want to take the chance they had. From the footage she saw before she was disconnected, it seemed like a team of about five operators, all carrying laz weapons and body armor, were in the lobby. Hopefully they had underestimated her resourcefulness and only sent a single team to apprehend her. If they had a team covering all the exits she was as good as dead.

Zarena and Evard may already be dead, Emerald thought. *I may be the Imperium's last hope.* She pocketed her comm and dropped to the floor, crawling around the back of her workstation as she heard the elevators open. Besides Jazz, there were only a few other people on the floor, most of them working at stations on the other side of the large engineering offices. Crawling on her hands and knees, she started to move in the direction of the stairwell.

The stairwell was on the opposite side of the offices from the elevators and there were rows of workstations, with half wall cubicles forming aisles and providing her ground cover at the moment. She did her best to stay low, crawling down the aisle that offered the most direct path to the stairwell doors. Suddenly, she heard a voice speak and stopped dead in her tracks.

"Excuse me Sir," an agent said. He was talking to Jazz!

"Yes, how can I help?" Even under duress, his tone remained calm, almost robotic.

"We're looking for Emerald Seltz. She works with you, correct?"

"Yes, that's her station there." *Dammit Jazz, don't lead them to me!* More footsteps fanned out, searching.

"This is her desk?" The lead agent sounded annoyed.

"Yes."

"We were informed she was here today. Where is she?"

"She was just here. I believe she went to the bathroom." *Clever Jazz! He must suspect something's amiss.*

"How long ago?"

"A few minutes, maybe."

"Where are the restrooms?"

"Down that hall."

She heard footsteps recede toward the restrooms by the express elevator. This was her chance to move. She scrambled on hands and knees, crawling swiftly but silently. They'd soon realize she wasn't there.

A loud bang echoed from the hallway. The agents were kicking in the restroom doors. "It's all clear, she's not here," a voice reported over comms.

"Why did you say she went to the restroom?" the lead agent growled.

"She got up and walked that way. I assumed that was her destination."

"She may have taken an elevator. Grab someone and check the lobby! I'll radio surveillance - search this floor!"

After crawling for what felt like an eternity, Emerald finally reached the door to the stairwell. *If there are agents in the stairwell, I'm dead. They'll know where I am. I'll have to make a break for it.*

Heart pounding, she stopped crawling before the door to catch her breath. One of the agents off to her left was closing in, she could hear him walking down the aisle, the sounds of his rubber-soled boots making a gentle clicking sound as he stepped. Another few seconds and she would be found.

She closed her eyes and braced herself, clenching her hands into a fist. *This is the end, it's all over now.* She was about to move when a voice came over the comm again.

"We're checking her terminal — she tapped building security! Stop!" The footsteps halted. Staying hidden, she listened intently.

"She knew we were coming. Dammit! The target must've taken the public elevator. You two, with me! Ground units, cover the exits. Secure the stairwell!" Boots stormed toward the elevator.

Static, then, "Where's my visuals? Get surveillance online, now!" The voice was livid. "Sir, should we pull back and regroup?"

"Pull back? It's one little girl, you imbecile! If you can't handle her solo, I'll shoot you myself!"

"Copy that."

"FIND HER! FIND HER NOW!"

She heard the footfalls moving away from her toward the elevators. She hadn't taken a breath while listening to the conversation between the agents. Her lungs began to hurt so she let out a small gasp. *Can't forget to breathe!* Then once she heard the elevator doors close she opened the door to the stairwell, stood up and started to run.

CHAPTER 28
An Old Friend Of Yours

Evard lounged on his cot, absently scratching his head as he let out a long, raspy yawn. He was weary, his nerves frayed, but still he felt a wave of relief wash over him. He was starting to believe he could leave his past buried in the sand. The crucial mission he was on seemed like the most vital endeavor in human history, and fate had somehow chosen him, a simple farm boy from the frontier, to help rescue the universe. Pretty unbelievable when you pause to ponder it, which he was now doing for the first time.

Zarena and Emerald were both wonderful. Wise and kind, they seemed to genuinely care about his well-being. He could hear Zarena tinkering in the shop, the sound of metal clanking occasionally as she fine-tuned her devices. Emerald had embarked on an errand to her old workplace. Evard disliked any of them separating, fretting about Emerald's safety whenever she departed the warehouse, but without the components Zarena required, they were stuck in limbo.

He rose and stretched his arms, stifling another yawn as he did. His hair was disheveled and his eyes bleary, but otherwise he felt good. Emerald had brought more medicine for his leg, which was now nearly healed, aside from occasional twinges of pain when he overexerted it. He seemed to have developed a faint, almost imperceptible limp, hard for an onlooker to notice but something he was acutely aware of. *I'll probably have it forever*, he mused. Oh well, it's far better than being a discarded corpse in a hallway, body disposed of in a crematorium or landfill. It was a memento of the trauma he endured and the fact that each new day was a blessing. He ambled through the warehouse, leaning on the doorframe leading into the workshop.

"What's happening?" he mumbled.

"Not much, just fine-tuning the analyzer," Zarena replied.

"Why? Is it broken?"

"No, just trying to get the most accurate readings possible. Emerald still at Raxeon?"

"Yeah, I reckon she is. She's been gone a while. I expect she'll be back before long."

Zarena glanced up from the worktable with a yawn muffled behind her hand. "I could use one decent night's rest," she lamented.

"Why don't you take the cot tonight?" Evard offered. "I can sleep on the table or throw some blankets on the floor. It's not too cold in here and I've slept in far worse spots."

"I've still got loads to accomplish, but yeah, maybe. Thanks for the offer."

Evard pushed off from the doorframe and pulled up a chair at the table. "How long d'you think we'll be here?"

"Well, I suppose it depends how long it takes to gather everything on the list, but ideally just a few days more."

The table shuddered. Zarena's comm, which had slid across the table teetering half off the edge, was buzzing. She looked puzzled and asked Evard, "Could you slide that to me?"

He passed the comm gently and she grabbed it, flipping it over. Her eyes said it all. Evard noticed and asked, "What's the matter?" as his throat tightened.

She angled the comm screen toward him. A terse message from Emerald read:

"THEY FOUND US. RUN."

"Fuck!" Evard exclaimed. "What do we do now?" Zarena, ignoring his panic and keeping a level head, pulled up the terminal and logged into the security feed using Emerald's access codes.

Outside, a small team of commandos, or "agents" as Rakeus styled them, stood before the building wielding laz weapons in a pre-assault stance. Zarena toggled through the feeds and saw another team poised in the back alley near the rear exit.

"Damn," she whispered, then turned to Evard. "We're surrounded by Imperial agents armed to the teeth."

"What do we do, Zarena?" Evard was on the verge of a breakdown.

Zarena looked at him calmly and said, "We've little choice. Surrender means certain death. Our only chance is to fight back."

"How can we fight them?"

"I prepared for this. Stay here."

Zarena rushed to a cabinet and started removing glass beakers filled with a mysterious substance, wrapped in cloth. She unwrapped them and removed the lids, then found a long-stemmed lighter in a drawer, giving it to Evard while pocketing another.

"We ignite the liquid and screw the cap on quickly," she instructed. She lit her lighter, lowering it into a beaker. The surface caught fire but the liquid below remained clear, feeding the flames above. She screwed on the lid and passed it to Evard.

"Throw it hard enough to shatter on impact. It'll detonate. Might even torch this place down, but it could provide our only escape."

Evard gulped a deep breath, gently rolling the beaker while watching the fire expand, the glass warming. "I heard burning alive is horrible."

"Then be careful with that thing."

Zarena had prepared five incendiary bombs, lighting each before capping them. "Do you think Emerald's alright?" Evard asked.

"Can't say, but odds are she's better off than us. Listen, Evard. Any second they'll burst in shooting. We'll hide by the door and throw these once they're close enough."

Evard was panting with adrenaline and fear but his mind was clear. He nodded to Zarena so that she knew he understood. He held the beaker in his hand, the warmth starting to become a burning sensation the longer they waited. Zarena positioned herself on the left side of the workshop door as he positioned himself on the right. They both held the flaming beakers in their hands, waiting for the moment to use them when a loud crashing sound, like thunder, rattled the workshop. The agents had battered down both the front and rear doors and had entered the warehouse, weapons drawn and scanning for signs of life.

The team spread out with brutal efficiency. Zarena had transferred the security feed from the terminal to her comm and watched as the leader of each squad gave silent commands through a series of hand signals, the agents moving outward in a fan formation. The team coming through the front door separated, two agents moving through the warehouse and the remainder moved through the aisles searching for them between the storage racks. The rear team moved into the warehouse more slowly then the front team, as if preparing for an intercept, anticipating that the targets may try to escape out the back when flushed out by the advancing squad.

Evard held his breath, squeezing the beaker hard but not hard enough to break it, waiting for Zarena's signal. She watched as the teams slowly advanced, looking through every corner of the warehouse. As the teams converged together both squad leaders realized there was only one place they could be: the workshop. The teams were now in close proximity. This was the moment.

"When I say go, you throw the bomb through the door directly at the agents and immediately head out the back door, staying as low as you can," advised Zarena. "I'll be right behind you."

Evard, nodded, his heart in his throat. He steadied himself and waited for her signal. A few seconds ticked by as Evard watched Zarena intently, her eyes on the surveillance feed. Just as he thought the anticipation was going to drive him insane, Zarena looked at him and said in a soft voice, "Go".

Evard launched his bomb into the clustered agents. It detonated in a fiery blast, immolating them in shards of glass and gouts of flame. Their agonized wails pierced the air as the inferno consumed them. Chaos erupted as survivors scattered. Evard sprinted for the back exit as planned, looking back to ensure Zarena followed. He saw her in the doorway hurling bombs at the agents, each explosion engulfing them in licking flames.

Most were ablaze, screaming until their seared lungs failed, incinerated in their suits. The rest fled the raging fire lest they suffer the same fate. With her arsenal depleted, Zarena ran after Evard, laz bolts whizzing past as they neared the smashed exit. She gasped as a beam grazed her shoulder, stumbling from the wound. It began to swell and mottle but the pain was worse than the actual damage. She grabbed her neck reflexively and felt the cauterized skin as she lurched forward. More shots sizzled by, burning holes in the walls around them, narrowly missing their bodies.

Suddenly, loud knocking reverberated through the inferno as the sprinklers activated, dowsing the conflagration in fire-retardant foam. The surviving agents fired blindly into the blanket of white as Evard and Zarena spilled through the shattered door into the alley. Evard leapt up and went to Zarena, still prone on the ground. She was injured but they had to flee. He helped her stand, bracing against the building wall for support.

"We must go now, some are still alive." Zarena urged, through heaving breaths. "They'll be on us in moments."

Evard grabbed her hand and they ran towards the alley's end, Zarena pulled along at full tilt. Abruptly he skidded to a halt, nearly toppling them both. Blocking their escape stood another team, armed and wearing protective goggles. They aimed their guns directly at the pair.

After a tense moment, the broad-shouldered leader, wearing a black leather hat and yellow shooting glasses, lowered his weapon. "It's them. Stand down," he ordered.

Bewildered, Evard and Zarena froze in their vulnerable position. Behind them, the warehouse team charged into the alley, weapons raised. With lightning speed, the mercenary leader thrust Evard and Zarena backwards. They sprawled to the ground as he spun and shouted, "Open fire!" His squad ruthlessly gunned down the advancing agents.

Stunned, Evard helped Zarena up as they were surrounded. The big man asked his team to check the warehouse, then turned to them.

"Greetings, Councilor Denamonte, Evard Roost. I'm Jaxxon Rill and these are friends of mine. We're here to rescue you from the evil Imperium and help you escape this industrial hellhole." He flashed a roguish grin at Zarena. He was a big man, muscular and strikingly handsome with strawberry blond hair and sky-blue eyes. His face was weathered stubbled, as if he'd seen his share of living.

She returned a smile. "Much thanks to you, Mr. Rill, and your team. But why save us? How did you even know we were here?"

"Please, call me Jax," he replied in an unplaceable accent. He scanned the alley warily. "We gotta go. Take them to the safe-house," he told his squad.

When one of the men grabbed Zarena's arm, she yanked it back defiantly. "I'm not going anywhere until you explain who sent you!"

Amusement glinted in Jaxxon's stern eyes. "An old friend of yours. Madame Kaia Dorsetta."

CHAPTER 29
The Time For Cover Has Passed

Two days prior, Imperial Councilor Kaia Dorsetta waited patiently on a bench amidst the splendid sculptures in Kadzer's Promenade D'Arten Les Arts gardens. She wore a plain grey robe, its rippling hemline sweeping her ankles, and a headscarf obscuring her face. Having shed her Councilor vestments, she resembled a religious mendicant who was congregating furtively in the secular capital's shadows.

She had slipped out of the citadel unrecognized and avoided main thoroughfares, yet she did so, anxious with fear. She could sense the danger she was now in. Still, to disregard the meeting invited greater jeopardy. These days, any clandestine meeting imperiled any official, particularly Councilors. She surveyed escape routes should things go awry.

A stranger in similar garb approached noiselessly from behind like a stalking alley cat. Kaia startled at his sudden appearance beside her, stifling a yelp when she recognized her awaited visitor. Jesper wore a black cloak and tunic, face hidden by a hood and dark goggles. He scanned their surroundings, ensuring no undue attention.

"Greetings, Madame," he purred, voice like oil. "Please accept my apologies for such secrecy, but we've much to discuss and it's best done outside Imperial walls."

Kaia acknowledged him warily, growing more unsettled. Lingering here was risky enough without Jesper's presence compounding her unease. She wanted this meeting over swiftly. "Who could object to a covert rendezvous outside the citadel with the Emperor's attack dog?" she replied, affecting confidence.

Jesper smiled congenially at her attempted barb.

"How may I assist you, Lord Manderlay?" Kaia asked crisply, unable to keep irritation from her tone. He pulled up his goggles. She avoided his mesmeric gaze. Staring into Jesper's eyes was its own peril. His russet irises seemed to smolder with dying embers. The effect could be profoundly unnerving.

He paused before responding, scanning their surroundings again. Then, in velvet tones, he confessed, "I need your help, Kaia."

Surprised and more than a little confused, Kaia decided to meet his eyes directly, wondering if he jested.

He continued methodically, voice low. "Not I, per se, but Madame Denamonte requires your aid urgently. She's in grave trouble, I fear."

Concern rose in Kaia at the mention of Zarena. She must be desperate if Jesper was intervening on her behalf. "What's happened?" she asked, feigning casualness.

"She is attempting to reverse The Harmony in an attempt to restore the princess to her former self. Rakeus has dispatched agents to eliminate her."

Kaia sighed bitterly. "I worried she might try something foolish like that. Her attachment to Raeka will be the death of us all," she lamented.

"Indeed, Madame Councilor, yet she desperately needs assistance now," Jesper pressed. Kaia considered this carefully. Some angle eluded her, but if Zarena was truly imperiled, she must at least listen. "Very well. What's her situation?"

"Her travels were mere misdirection, as many suspected. She is on Exalon presently, aided by two Immune allies constructing a device to undo The Harmony. She's hiding out in an abandoned Raxeon warehouse. Rakeus sent a team to eliminate them."

"This is serious," Kaia muttered. "But what could I possibly do to help?" She added pointedly, "And even if I was able to, why would I?"

Jesper's smoldering stare burned her face. She worried for a brief moment if she might catch fire. He ignored her last question. "I would ask you to discreetly send an Exalon team to intervene, given your contacts there. Ideally one of your un-Harmonized squads. Utmost discretion is imperative."

"And her companions?"

"Extract them if possible, but she is the priority." His thin lips curled into an unsettling smile. Kaia said nothing, mind racing. Jesper watched her keenly, a viper eyeing prey.

I'm at risk here, she realized, *and not just from Rakeus*. She understood crossing Jesper was unwise. In all her years serving the emperor, only Jesper instilled fear in her. Not an overwhelming dread, but ample wariness. Officially a mere steward, he was Rakeus's covert enforcer, manipulating events while secretly crushing dissent. The Council harbored grave concerns about his fealty to Rakeus, suspecting he would readily sacrifice them on the emperor's whim. Why then would Jesper now betray him? She pushed aside the thought, summoning her nerve.

"Rakeus will execute me if he discovers this."

"Yes. He may kill you anyway, if that sways you," Jesper stated matter-of-factly.

Stunned speechless, Kaia squirmed. "Surely you jest."

"I assure you, I am quite serious. Rakeus has become paranoid, reclusive. The Harmony and the princess have taken their toll. I fear his sanity is unraveling." He paused for just a moment, then said, "Perhaps this will trigger his Sequence."

Kaia held his stare as he elaborated. His explanation did bear scrutiny. Killing Zarena could push Rakeus over the edge. And if he was unstable, the Council represented unfinished business. With compliance guaranteed, what need had he for diplomacy? They had all become expendable, save Rakeus himself.

"Would he truly go that far?" she asked resignedly. She thought back to the hallway, when Rakeus dispatched the triggered guard that attacked them. He seemed calm in the face of danger but his viciousness scared her. It hadn't been the first time either.

"I hope not, Kaia, though of late I find hope does more harm than good."

"So, if I help — and from what you're saying I don't really have much of a choice — will there be cover for me?"

"No, the time for cover has passed," Jesper said, dismissively. "Zarena Denamonte must get off of Exalon. Your people should move her to one of the colonies, somewhere where the Imperium has less presence. Once she's safe I would book immediate passage off-world if I were you. Perhaps you may even consider joining her."

"Perhaps I shall. And the other Councilors?"

Jesper shrugged with indifference. "I cannot say. Maybe Rakeus lets you all play act your former glory at the citadel. Perhaps public executions await. Anything between is possible as well." He smiled mirthlessly, clearly indifferent to their fates.

Kaia said nothing in response. She felt nauseous and a little dizzy.

"Listen," said Jesper, throwing her a lifeline. "Do this, and I will help you when the time comes. Do you understand?"

"Yes. I understand."

"Excellent. Now, your comm, please."

Kaia retrieved her comm as Jesper produced his own. "I'm transmitting the data for your extraction team. Make sure they receive it. When Zarena is secured, we will meet again to discuss your personal 'arrangements'." Jesper rose and slipped away wordlessly into the gardens.

Kaia watched him slither off like a serpent before gazing skyward. *May mercy yet forgive us for our follies*, she prayed silently. Steeling herself, she focused on the task at hand. She had a rescue to coordinate.

CHAPTER 30
Time To Run Again

Emerald burst through the door, terror and dread overwhelming her like a punch to the gut. She slipped as she entered the stairwell on the seventeenth floor of the Raxeon building, desperate to evade the pack of agents sent to apprehend her. Her feet skidded and she halted abruptly when she slammed into the railing lining the concrete steps from first floor to rooftop, the unyielding metal railing smarting as she smashed forcefully into it.

Pausing only a moment to gather herself, she realized she wasn't sure which way to flee, up or down. Down was the obvious choice and the only safe exit from the building, but she had overheard the lead agent send an order for one of them to sweep the stairwell. She also heard them request video surveillance. Every floor of the building was blanketed by watchful cameras but the roof was surprisingly sparse, with only one pointed at the rooftop door itself. If she hurried, she might be able to reach the roof before they spotted her on the feeds.

She wasn't sure what to do and time was running out to decide.

If she went up, she'd probably evade detection longer, but would have no way to escape the building. If she went down, she would likely be seen, even if she tried exiting on another floor, unless she avoided the agent currently heading up the steps. It was risky, but Emerald's rapid calculation was that there was no escaping the building while the agents scoured it. Her best chance, however slim, was to hide on the roof and hope she had fooled them into thinking she had already fled before they reached the engineering level. This split-second evaluation flashed through her mind and once the decision was made she sprinted, legs pumping as fast as they could, up the stairs toward the rooftop.

Emerald panted as she bounded up the steps two at a time. There were thirty-six floors to the monolithic Raxeon building including the mechanical levels. She worked about halfway between the summit and base, so either path meant covering substantial distance. At any moment the agents could be monitoring the video feeds, spotting her frantic ascent. She couldn't risk even a brief respite, faint echoes of pursuit reverberating up from below. If it was an agent, they were likely moving slower, meticulously checking each recess and cranny.

She kept climbing, trying to regulate her breath so the sounds of her escape were muffled. Her hurried footfalls rang too loudly on the hard concrete and the echoing footsteps below seemed to be gaining pace. Her muscles started to burn as if injected with acid and when she reached the twenty-sixth floor landing, she had to pause for a moment to gulp in air. She wheezed in and out as quietly as possible, straining to listen to the echoing footsteps. They suddenly ceased and she wondered if it had just been an employee traversing floors but the stairwell was seldom used. As abruptly as they stopped, they resumed and so did she, not daring to take any more time than absolutely necessary to reach the sanctuary of the rooftop.

She thought her lungs might burst when she finally reached the top floor. She risked a quick glance over the railing and saw an endless open shaft boxed in by the railings. No one else appeared to be in the stairwell so she allowed herself a second of relief before cautiously pushing open the rooftop door. The biting wind stung her cheeks, leaving them raw and chapped.

Once on the roof, the midday sun blazing, she instinctively shielded her eyes. With labored breath and still bracing the door open, she eased it closed, trying to gently nestle it back into the frame without any noise. There was a faint click as the latch engaged. She started taking in deep breaths, her sides knotted from the grueling ascent.

Need more cardio, she mused, half joking and half serious. She scanned the flat, open rooftop for somewhere to hide. The roof was bare, with clear views of District 7 below, offering little concealment. There were a few bulky air conditioning units, large enough to hide behind when crouching, and a small utility shed, about three meters square with a padlocked door and a biometric panel by the handle. She didn't dare try the door, as it would surely trigger alarms. Instead, she sprinted for the shed, darting out of sight of the lone security camera, shoes pattering on the hard rooftop.

Reaching the back wall of the shed, she collapsed against it to catch her breath. She waited in silence, the only sound her ragged breathing that had begun to slow to normal.

She finally steadied her nerves and stretched her cramping muscles. In front of her was a ten meter expanse to the roof's edge and the cityscape beyond. As she waited anxiously for the door to open, she gazed out over the cloudless sky and saw, far in the distance, wispy tendrils of inky smoke rising above downtown. She knew without doubt it was the warehouse. Zarena and Evard were dead. She choked back a sob as the reality of her own likely demise slammed into her. *I guess we tried*, she thought mournfully. *The odds were always against us.*

She slumped back against the shed, closing her eyes and coming to terms with her predicament. *I could think of better places to die than here*, she mused grimly, *though people rarely get to choose how they meet their end.* This was it, and Emerald was ready for her final stand.

She expected only one agent to come through the rooftop door. *They will be armed and armored but I won't surrender without a fight*, she resolved. She tensed, poised for battle once her hiding spot was discovered. Just then, the door creaked open. Emerald held her breath, which she had finally gotten under control, and listened for the sound of footsteps.

She thought of her mother, how she would never see her again, never be able to help her recover from The Harmony. Jazz flashed through her mind too, the Jazz she had always known, and the new Jazz who milled around the office like a grazing cow. She'd never be able to help him either. They both would be stranded in this liminal space their minds now occupied forever. Tears started to well in her eyes and fear pushed her adrenaline into overdrive.

She could hear the agent moving slowly, his steps barely audible over the sound of the wind breezing past her. He seemed to be moving away from her. She looked around the roof to see if there was anything she could use as a weapon but found nothing suitable. *Fists it is then*, she said to herself. If she could take them by surprise and land one good punch, she might be able to disarm them and take the weapon herself. Then she could try to shoot her way out of the building, if it came to that, which it was looking like it might.

After a minute or two the sound of footsteps started to draw nearer. It sounded like the agent was at the door of the utility shed. They tried the door and it didn't open. Then she heard them speaking over the comm.

"I'm on the roof. Stairwell was clear. Over."

She couldn't hear the person on the other end but there was a short silence as they spoke to the agent pursuing her.

"Yes, I'm at the doors of a utility shed on the roof. What did the video feeds show?"

Another pause then, "Well she couldn't have just vanished." More static and then, "I guess it's possible she made it out the front door before we got to engineering. The door to the closet on the roof is locked. Can you check the logs to see if she accessed the panel to gain entrance?"

More silence mixed with static and the gusts of winds. Suddenly she heard a change in the voice of the agent.

"What? I can't believe...Yes, sir. Yes, I'm on my way."

Emerald could hear muffled sounds from the other end of the conversation, most likely as the person on that side was yelling loudly. *They escaped*, she thought. *How could they possibly have escaped?* She was starting to grasp on to a glimmer of hope. She continued to listen, her adrenaline pumping acid through her veins. She couldn't hear anything so she hunkered down and braced for a battle.

As the seconds ticked by she waited on the edge of the precipice, ready to fight for her life on the top of the place she worked at for so long. *I worked here, now I'm going to die here*, she thought. *There's a sad sort of poetry to that.* She dug her nails into her fist and waited.

Nothing came, no sound of footsteps as the wind picked up. Just then she heard the faint slamming of the exit door leading back down to the stairwell.

She waited what felt like hours, but was in reality a minute or so, to make sure she wasn't being tricked out of her hiding spot. Finally, she peered around the shed and confirmed she was alone on the desolate rooftop. The biting wind howled past, stinging her skin. Convinced it was clear, she decided to risk approaching the exit. Clutching her comm, she felt it vibrate with an alert. A message flashed from an unknown sender.

ARE YOU SAFE?

She studied it warily. A trap to reveal her location?

WHO IS THIS

A FRIEND

She waited, hoping for clarification. Finally she took a chance.

I AM SAFE

GOOD. WE NEED TO LEAVE. MEET FOR SOME STEW

Meet for some stew? A code, but at first its meaning eluded her. Then she remembered meeting Evard at the downtown District 7 soup kitchen. He was eating stew.

ON MY WAY

The channel went dead. *They escaped*, she realized with relief. *Waiting at the shelter.* After taking a steadying breath, she steeled herself. Time to run again.

CHAPTER 31
The Only Help I Can Offer

Kaia Dorsetta sat passively on a bench in the Promenade D'Arten Les Arts, dressed in her street urchin disguise, waiting apprehensively for the axe to fall. She had received word from her team of mercenaries on Exalon that they had successfully extracted Zarena Denamonte and were preparing to smuggle her off-world. It seemed the immediate threat to Zarena had passed, though Kaia knew she was far from safe. *She's on her own now*, Kaia thought ruefully. *I did my part, just in time it seems.*

She realized with unease that Jesper was uncharacteristically late. Never a good sign. His tardiness left her deeply unsettled but she had come too far to turn back now. *No point worrying, what's done is done*, she brooded.

Kadzer was known to tourists as the Sunlight City, rays typically sparkling and dancing through the endless metallic surfaces found throughout its grand monuments. But today storm clouds shrouded the sun, drifting menacingly over the city, cloaking it in dreary shadow.

The overcast sky mirrored the weary malaise that had settled over Kaia since her last meeting here with Jesper. *I might as well have made a deal with the gangsters, probably would have been safer*, she thought bleakly. Jesper was playing some Byzantine game she couldn't decipher. Not knowing his true agenda made allying with him even more perilous. *No going back now, she thought. Hopefully, I can get off Archlon before Rakeus publicly executes me, maybe right here in these very gardens.*

Before she could spiral further, Jesper appeared and sat beside her on the bench. Also dressed as before, he had approached noiselessly. After sitting down in silence, he turned to her and pleasantly said, "Thank you, Madame Dorsetta. You have done the Imperium a great service."

"I'm sure Rakeus won't see it that way," Kaia replied guardedly, a bitter edge to her voice.

"I'm sure he won't, but the best servants do what is needed, not what is commanded," Jesper lectured gently, as if explaining basics to a child.

"I suppose," Kaia said. "Didn't seem like you gave me much choice last time we met."

"There was no alternative, Kaia," Jesper said, malice creeping into his affable tone.

Kaia shifted uncomfortably on the bench, gazing skyward, wishing to be anywhere but here. "So, how do you plan to get me to safety?"

"There is no safe place for you, Kaia. Nor Zarena Denamonte, I fear. Things will get much worse before they get better," he mused. "Whatever 'better' ends up looking like." He flashed his sly, vicious grin and Kaia pretended not to notice. She pressed on impatiently.

"Our deal was you'd help me escape Archlon."

Jesper just watched her silently, an amused hunter tracking his prey. His mouth creased as if tasting something bitter. In a blur, his hand darted out and flicked across her throat, the blade slicing through skin and sinew with the ease of a hot knife through warm butter. It was so fast she barely felt it, thinking at first he was swatting an insect.

She started choking as blood spurted in a crimson-colored geyser from her neck. Eyes wide with fear, she pressed both hands to her throat, futilely trying to stem the wound despite her fading strength. Jesper moved fluidly behind her in one swift motion. Grabbing her head with his left hand, he wrenched it back, then swatted away her feeble attempt to staunch the bleeding.

Leaning in, breath warm as a summer breeze, he whispered in her ear, "I never said I would help you flee Archlon. I simply promised I would help you when the time came. That time has come, and this is the only help I can offer a traitor."

He held her twitching body still with his right hand clamped on her shoulder. The other hand kept her head pulled back, blood flowing freely. Once she stopped moving, he let go and pulled out a handkerchief, popular on pre-Imperial Origin but now an antique curiosity he fancied. He casually wiped the blood from his hands and tucked it back into one of his many hidden pockets.

Glancing around the empty gardens, just as he had arranged, he sauntered away casually as if out for an evening stroll.

Emperor Rakeus VII sat on his gilded throne in the ornate throne room of the ancient Kra Markhan citadel. He was expecting an arrival and drummed his fingers impatiently on the armrest, trying not to show his agitation. The longer he waited, the more vexed he became.

Just as his thoughts turned to sinister punishments for his servants, there was a knock at the towering doors. He shouted, voice echoing off the rafters, "Come in!"

The doors groaned open and Jesper slide in, moving with subtle vigor.

"It is done?"

"Yes, Your Majesty."

"So many traitors in our midst, Jesper. Who would've thought noble Kaia Dorsetta would commit treason by aiding Zarena Denamonte of all people! I thought they disliked each other."

"Well, sire, I don't think Madame Dorsetta aided her out of fondness. More out of, shall we say, similar ideology?"

Rakeus barked a harsh laugh. "I suppose treason makes for strange bedfellows! Where will they find her?"

"The Promenade in Kadzer, Your Majesty. I thought handling it off palace grounds would be cleaner."

"Yes, agreed. Well done."

Jesper bowed deeply before Rakeus, using the ancient gesture of obeisance. Maintaining eye contact, he said, "As you command, My Lord."

"What do we know about Zarena?"

"Still gathering intelligence, Your Majesty. We know Kaia sent trusted mercenaries from her old political days, already on Exalon, so the extraction was smooth. Zarena was found in an abandoned Raxeon warehouse downtown with the young man immune to the Harmony. There was a fire during the raid, likely Zarena creating a diversion, and they escaped. Then the mercs intercepted and eliminated the agents."

"Dammit!" Rakeus raged, eyes blazing. "How did Kaia know?"

"She and Zarena were in contact and her team was preparing to escort her off Exalon. Our agents happened across them at the wrong time."

Jesper waited stoically for Rakeus to vent his anger but instead he smiled.

"I must hand it to Zarena," he mused. "She was a great asset and now a formidable adversary."

Lost in thought, Rakeus murmured, "Jesper?"

"Yes, sire?"

"I don't want her to suffer. No cruelty."

Jesper looked mildly surprised but it quickly vanished. "Of course, sire." He bowed again.

"Do we know if she's left Exalon?"

"We lost her after the mercs intervened but should have her location soon. She'll be planning to leave, certainly to a colony world."

"Of course. You don't seem concerned about this failure."

"I'm not, sire. Best to have stopped her on Exalon but there may be unintended benefits."

Rakeus raised an eyebrow inquisitively. "Such as?"

"She's gathering Immunes, presumably for her anti-Harmony research. We don't know how many there are or how to find them. Perhaps..." Jesper trailed off leadingly.

"Perhaps what, Jesper?"

"Perhaps it's best to let her gather as many as she can find. They threaten our peace. Once she has a colony, we can eliminate them in one stroke." His words hung in the air expectantly.

"Interesting plan. Dangerous, but interesting."

"You flatter me, sire. I leave it to your wisdom."

Rakeus gazed off contemplatively, weighing the options. Jesper waited, standing motionless as a statue, watching Rakeus' face cycle through the motions of deep thought. Finally Rakeus chuckled, a sly grin touching his lips.

"Very well, Jesper. Monitor her closely, I want to know everything. But let her be for now. We must stop her before she succeeds, however."

"I don't anticipate that being an issue, Your Majesty. She seems far from a solution presently."

"When the time comes, I want all of her research, whatever she discovers. That knowledge is the greatest threat we face and must be controlled. We will be the ones to decide how to use it."

"Excellent, your majesty. I will watch and wait."

Rakeus flicked his hand dismissively but as Jesper turned to leave he called out, "Remember, when the time comes, no suffering. She deserves a peaceful end."

Jesper bowed, head lowered to hide his devilish grin, the smile of one who has sealed a dark bargain.

He glided from the throne room, leaving Rakeus alone on his throne.

CHAPTER 32

Better Luck Next Time

The safe house was a dusty, decrepit apartment on the outskirts of the city.

Jaxxon Rill reclined in a fraying armchair, pulling a rolled smoke absently from his jacket. He pinched it near the end and retrieved a small black rectangular device that traders referred to as a merc hand. The contraband gadget had several illicit but useful functions for gaining access to wherever needed for the job.

He turned the device, clicked a button, and a small blue flame jetted out. He lit his smoke and returned the merc hand to his pocket. Rolling the cigarette between his fingers, he exhaled a billowing white cloud as Zarena watched, fascinated. Given the cost of exporting from the colonies most people smoked cheap plant leaf tobacco. It was a pastime of the working class. With her privileged upbringing, she'd had little chance to indulge in such things.

Jaxxon seemed unconcerned about another run-in with the agents. Zarena and Evard had been waiting anxiously for hours. They'd contacted Emerald and miraculously, she'd slipped away from the agents at the Raxeon building. With the other teams diverted to pursue Zarena, Emerald had escaped into the city. They left coordinates at the soup kitchen, and now Emerald was en route to the safe house while they awaited her arrival. Jaxxon lounged casually, but the others were on edge.

"Mr. Rill, shouldn't we go get Emerald ourselves instead of waiting here?" Zarena asked.

"Nope," he replied simply.

"You're certain?"

"Yep."

"You're a man of few words, I see."

"Yep."

Frustrated, Zarena stood and went to Evard, who sat pensively on an old bench in the dingy kitchen. Two mercs were playing cards at a table, smoking as they passed time. Their weapons lay nearby, safeties off. One of the mercs, Whurr Takern, looked leathered beyond his years, as if he'd spent most of them fishing the bogs of Esper. Dressed like a frontier cowboy, he wore a long black coat over a loose red shirt secured with a bandolier of laz cartridges. Like Jaxxon, he rolled his smoke between his fingers, periodically tapping ashes into a chipped mug.

Across from Whurr sat a woman called Ayr. Zarena had no idea how old she might be. Dressed head-to-toe in skintight green armor made of some flexible polymer, she boasted it could stop a direct laz shot. Twin pistols rode her hips, with a laz rifle slung across her back, now propped against the table as she eyed her cards. She and Whurr traded occasional barbs amid chuckles as they ignored Zarena and Evard on the bench.

Zarena clasped Evard's hand tenderly. "Are you alright?"

"I guess so," Evard said pensively. "We're alive and safe, at least." His smile was bittersweet as he glanced at the mercs. "Better than being burned alive like those agents." He looked away, pained.

"We didn't have a choice. They would've killed us."

"I know. I'm grateful you saved my life," Evard said, trailing off. Zarena watched him maternally until he added, "I've just seen too much violence already."

"I know you have. I know," she said, patting his hand before letting it go. They sat in silence, observing the card game.

The other mercs milled about, peering out windows for threats.

"Once Emerald arrives, they'll take us off-world somewhere safer than here," Zarena whispered. She tried to smile encouragingly, but the mood was too heavy. Rising, she left Evard watching the card game and returned to the main room, sitting across from Jaxxon.

Lost in thought, he stared absently out a grimy window. His team bustled around on various tasks while he sat motionless except for the occasional blink.

Zarena's comm vibrated. She pulled it out and read the encrypted message:

ITS OVER FOR NOW. GET TO WORK.

Goosebumps prickled her neck. Jesper. Was he giving her space or planning something worse? Either way, she refused to cower anymore.

"Fuck it," she muttered, typing a reply:

STARTING ASAP. BETTER LUCK NEXT TIME.

If Jesper wanted to play games, so be it. The time for fear had passed. The Emperor, the man she knew since childhood, her father's closest friend, had tried to assassinate her for defying his orders. The battle standards may not be waving over the gun ships of the Imperium as yet, but make no mistake, they were at war. For whatever reason Jesper and Rakeus suspended hostilities, it didn't matter. The day would come when Jesper would strike at them again, she was sure of it. She also started to feel confident that it wouldn't happen until she made her next move.It was a stalemate, for now at least. *I'm proving harder to kill than they expected*, she mused darkly. But it didn't matter, she'd find a way to survive regardless. She would save Raeka, whatever came next.

Another message arrived — an image of a winking face. *That smug bastard.* Shaking her head angrily, she put her comm away.

Suddenly everyone drew weapons as the door opened. Realizing it must be Emerald, Zarena rushed over and threw it wide. Emerald looked haggard but unharmed. They stood looking at each other a moment, then Zarena lunged forward and fiercely embraced her, laughing and crying simultaneously. Though they had only just met, a bond had already formed. Zarena was overwhelmed with relief to see her friend alive.

They clung together until Jaxxon's voice boomed, "Get inside!"

Laughing nervously, they hurried in and slammed the door. Bewildered, Emerald scanned the room before Evard pushed past the mercs and stopped before her, beaming with joy. She hugged him as fiercely as Zarena had embraced her, saying "Thank goodness you're alright."

Zarena joined their heartfelt reunion, the three wrapping arms around each other, finally reunited after the chaos. Jaxxon strode up and clapped Zarena's shoulder. "Well, well, the gang's all here after all," he said with a wry smirk.

Emerald looked at Zarena pleadingly. "What's happening, Zee?"

Zarena quickly explained how the mercenaries had saved them. Emerald glanced around warily. "I've never met a mercenary before. They're about what I expected."

"That they are," Zarena agreed. She looked at Jaxxon decisively. "It's time. We're going to Fasmouth, to see Andros Carchel."

Without responding, Jaxxon twirled his finger in the air. The mercs began gathering their gear to depart.

The small starskipper fleeing Exalon entered orbit above the aqueous world of Esper.

The landmasses were mostly comprised of large archipelagos scattered throughout the vast azure oceans of the modest colony planet. The seas of Esper teemed with more life than almost all the rest of the Imperium combined. The various aquatic species constituted ninety-six percent of life on the planet, despite its diverse rainforest and mountain ecosystems.

The continent in the center of the archipelago was known as Ornast, home of Fasmouth, the large city-state that had served as the seat of House Carchel for a millennia. Fasmouth was nestled along the craggy shoreline of the northern coast of the continent. It bordered a seemingly endless ocean known as the Great Sea. Beyond the shore were lush jade forests and green plains that stretched across to the other end of Ornast, providing real estate for farming and the excavation of materials. The Great Sea was the most expansive of the oceans on Esper, and also the most treacherous. Its center was almost impassable by sea vessel as perpetual storms and aqueous tornadoes raged day and night. The shallows around the edges of the Great Sea however teemed with valuable, edible life. The fishing industry comprised most of the commerce of Esper, as their bounty of the sea was transported to all corners of the Imperium.

House Carchel originally rose to power over a thousand years ago on the backs of the fishing trade. Emmetz Carchel was a wealthy fish-steward from a small village on Ornast who, over time, was able to leverage his burgeoning fortune and status to negotiate an arrangement with the Imperial Council on fishing exports to the interior worlds. As a result, he was able to successfully lobby the Council to become a member of the Great Houses and Esper was his charge.

As with all of the Great Houses, the House Charter bequeaths a line of succession that allows the power and titles to pass down from heir to heir in perpetuity. As a result, Emmetz's descendants have served as the stewards of Esper since that time and over the centuries, have proven themselves quite adept at both cultivating and preserving the immense ecological treasures hidden below the waves.

Zarena explained all of this to her companions as the starskipper descended through the oxygen-rich atmosphere on its way towards Fasmouth. As they hurtled towards the continent of Ornast, several of the other island-continents could be seen along with the vast bodies of water that separated them.

After getting briefed on the history of Esper, Evard said, "Yeah, I've heard Esper was basically an aquatic version of Eden. House Collette was fairly well-liked but from what I gather House Carchel is even more beloved. Fair rulers and all that."

"It's true, Carchel is one of the most well-liked Houses in the Imperium despite the fact that they are among the smallest. Andros' father was a good man, I remember him always being so kind whenever I came to visit with my father or Raeka." She smiled ruefully, and both her companions knew what she was thinking.

Emerald asked, "So what's the plan? We just show up as if we were some kind of emissaries and you just drop on an unsuspecting Baron Carchel everything we need?" "I assumed we'd use more tact but yes, something like that."

Zarena looked out the port windows towards the ground below as the ship began its final descent towards Fasmouth. Evard broke the silence with a question that was also on Emerald's mind.

"So, are you gonna tell us what happened with the Baron or are we going to just have to guess?" He said it in a serious tone but when Zarena looked over at him, he had a sly fox-like grin on his face.

She sighed. "Okay, a little over a decade ago, when I was still entrenched in my academic career, I spent a little time on Esper, researching various native species..."

"Okay, we get it, you're a scientist. Fast forward to what happened with Andros," Evard said, with a laugh.

Zarena smiled weakly. "I spent some time here. Andros and I were friends as kids; He, Raeka, and I. Over time it became a little something more. Andros and I got close, he was still the heir to the Baron then, and his father was pressuring him to find a spouse. He worked very carefully to groom Andros for his role as the Baron one day. Andros and I were young, thought we might be in love, and he proposed. I said yes. Things were good for a bit."

She looked out the window, her thoughts drifting into the murky ether of the past, imagining how things might have been different for everyone if she had decided to stay.

Eventually she said, "My political career was taking off. Rakeus and I were close and he trusted me, at least back then. He had great affection for my father and he saw potential in me and I knew I was on the fast track to becoming the youngest Councilor in

Imperium history. I wanted that. I craved it. But to be a Councillor I needed to spend most of my time either traveling or on Archlon, where I had grown up. I couldn't move to Esper and Andros, as the future lord of Esper, couldn't leave. So I ended it. He was hurt. We both were. I've only seen him a few times in the decade since, mostly at Imperium functions, the Great Convening, where the all Houses meet to discuss legislation, places like that. Never alone."

She signed again, and stretched her arms over her head. "When his dad died I sent my condolences. He responded with a thank you, nothing more. I guess some wounds run too deep. That's why coming here is a risk. He won't be happy to see me. He'll be less happy to find out I was at the center of an Imperium wide conspiracy to subjugate the human race." She started to rub her temples, as if this whole talk was giving her a migraine.

"He loved me once though. He would never hurt me. He may not even be capable of it, given that he and his people were Harmonized. So that's why we're here." Zarena rubbed her temples and then continued. "He won't hurt us but I don't know if he will help us either. I guess we'll find out soon."

The ship continued to drop and Jaxxon entered the small traveling cabin the trio was sitting in. He let them know that they were landing in a small landing port a few clicks outside of Fasmouth.

"Are you planning on letting this Baron know you're coming, or are you just going to surprise him?" Jaxxon asked, with a grin.

Zarena was feeling anxious the closer they got to landing on Esper. "I think maybe a surprise visit is best."

"Whatever you say, Madame," said Jaxxon, and he disappeared from the cabin door.

"That guy seems like a jerk," said Evard, dismissively.

"All mercs are. That's the gig. Most of them are Imperial militia rejects or deserters. So they go wherever they can find work for a soldier's skill set. Most of it's on the seedy side."

"I've never met a mercenary before", said Emerald. "They're, exactly what you're picturing", Zarena said with a smile.

"That they are," said Zarena. "This one though thinks he's a bit of a comedian, which makes him a tad more insufferable than most. I wonder where Kaia found him."

Jaxxon Rill appeared back in the doorway, seemingly appearing out of thin air. He smiled wide, as if he was enjoying himself far too much. "Sorry Councilor, my ears were ringing," he said with a sardonic wink.

The cabin they were sitting in wasn't large but he barreled his way in anyway, sitting down next to Evard who had to move over to make room for him before he was squished. He shimmied in his seat a bit, banging his elbows into a hapless Evard as he did so, before leaning back and taking off his hat. The party looked at him as if to say, 'can I help you?' but before anyone had a chance to speak he answered their question.

"I *am* a bit of a comedian, thank you very much. Don't often deal with important government types so you'll excuse any lack of decorum, I hope." He still smiled that big shit eating smile, not unintentionally goofy like The Harmony smile, but sarcastic and brazen. "As for how Madame Dorsetta came upon our services, well that's an easy one. She's my aunt."

Zarena's jaw dropped so fast that Jaxxon started belly laughing at the reaction. He laughed some more before saying, "I was an orphan. I grew up in a home on Celeon. Not all that far from here actually, as the ships fly. Ended up my parents were killed in a hover accident and I had no other family. My dad, well, he was a bit of a rogue, I guess you could say."

"Seems like the apple didn't fall far from the tree", snipped Zarena.

Jaxxon chuckled heartily again. "No, in my case it didn't. Didn't stop my mum from loving him, I hear. Anyway, turns out my mum had left her family years ago to follow my dad on his 'adventures' across the stars and her family disowned her. Her father was a rich diplomat that served the Karmarchs on Archlon. She was the daughter of his second wife. His first had died years before and he had a daughter from his first marriage. His name was Owane Dorsetta and his oldest daughter's name was Kaia. She's my mum's half sister."

He leaned back in the chair, looking out the port window past the three of them as he continued. "When I was twelve, my aunt came to see me. Said she didn't know about me but when she found out, she came to make it right. She took me in for a few years, at the start of her political career. I got in some law trouble and I didn't want to reflect poorly on her and her ambitions so I left at eighteen. She supported me financially for years until I made my own way."

"And Kaia had no problem with you being a merc?"

"Not at all. She thought the Imperium needed people like me to help those who couldn't help themselves. Sure we took their money but the ones that couldn't pay, well we worked out other deals. Never turned away a person I thought I could help. Some of them made us quite a bit of money too, which keeps my crew happy." He spoke with a slight twang in his voice, as if he had spent his whole life on the frontiers, wrangling livestock.

"I can't believe Kaia thought you being a merc was a good idea. I can't believe I didn't know she had a nephew. I've known her for well over a decade."

"I bet a lot of things about Kaia Dorsetta would surprise you," he said bemusedly, as if he was in on some secret knowledge the rest of them could only guess at. "Anyway, she called me about this job, told me that it was high priority."

"I guess that explains why you and your people aren't Harmonized. She must have helped you."

"That she did. Told me the whole story. She sent those dampener things for me and the crew in secret. Gave us all the details. We wore them for hours before that blasted thing went off." He looked Zarena in the eye. "You really the evil mastermind behind that asinine plan? It's been bad for business, you know."

Zarena ignored his question and said, "Did she tell you how she knew where we were or what we were doing?"

"She did. I don't think she was supposed to either. After she sent me the data sheet on your location, background on you, all that stuff she called me on an encrypted line. She seemed a bit stressed honestly. Said that the Emperor's royal ass wiper, Jesper, had asked her to intervene. That Rakeus had ordered you captured. She was nervous about the whole thing."

He took a moment and looked around, all of their faces stunned as they recovered from the shock. He noticed that Zarena seemed the most deeply disturbed. Her face was dark and her eyebrows had narrowed.

"That not sit right with you?" Jaxxon asked.

"Jesper," she said, as if the name itself was a curse. "He's playing some sort of game and I have no idea what it is and that scares the shit out of me."

Jaxxon looked at her with a mix of real kindness and a touch of concern in his voice. "I only know him by reputation but what I've heard about him would make your skin crawl."

"If Jesper is involved, Kaia is not safe. Where is she?"

"She told me after the extraction she was going into hiding off-world. Said Rakeus was turning against the Council and she wasn't safe on Archlon."

"Any idea where she was going?"

"Said she was going dark. Would contact me when she was safe."

Everyone sat in silence. Then Jaxxon said, in a softer voice than he had used before, "You really think Rakeus would hurt her?"

"If you had asked me that question a month ago, I would have said there was no way he would… but now?" She shrugged wearily. "I think the squad of death agents he sent to kill me suggests otherwise."

"And this Jesper, you think he's dangerous?" asked Jaxxon, a hint of nervousness entering his voice.

"I think if Jesper asked her to do this then he is up to something—and I can't even fathom what. Whatever it is though, we're all expendable. We are incredibly grateful to you and your people for saving our lives but I'm afraid you're now in danger, too. Jesper has somehow been tracking everyone involved. He'll know she used you and he'll know how to find you. You may end up finding a death squad at your door one of these days. Can't imagine he is going to leave any loose ends by time this is finished, Mr. Rill."

Zarena thought it was best to be blunt. Despite his gruffness she was beginning to like Jaxxon and his ragtag crew. She didn't want them to end up collateral damage.

"Well fuck," Jaxxon said, exasperated. "I had a feeling there was gonna be trouble here. I just hope she made it safely off Archlon."

The ship bounced a bit as they prepared to land. Everyone held on to something to brace for the turbulence. The ship shuddered as it hovered over the landing pad, vibrating like a live wire as it gently touched down. Everyone breathed a small sigh of relief that they had made it to Esper without any further trouble.

Jaxxon stood up and stumbled his way out of the cabin. He turned around and addressed the group.

"Looks like we're here. Time to move. You have a Baron to see." The roguish grin had returned to his face. "Oh, and please. Call me Jax," he said, with a mock bow, then disappeared down the hallway.

Zarena looked at Evard and Emerald, who seemed shell shocked by the entire thing. "Alright. I guess it's time. Let's hope Andros doesn't kill us on sight." She stopped for a second, then said, "Well he's Harmonized. Maybe he'll just imprison us and then forget and let us starve to death." She meant this as a joke to lighten the atmosphere but no one was in the mood for humor today.

Zarena got up and left Emerald and Evard staring at each other, a look of terror on both of their faces.

CHAPTER 33

Are You Surprised?

The small landing pad was enveloped by a verdant forest, the trees cloaked in dark emerald leaves peppered with bursts of fiery orange, crimson and sunburst yellow. A winding road led from the landing port through a series of fishing hamlets on the approach to the imposing citadel of Fasmouth.

Jax had arranged transport into the stronghold, his team remaining with the ship now docked in a temporary space lot. He told Zarena he would join her in Fasmouth, intent on preparing any direct aggression from Andros. Zarena considered any actual hostility unlikely but Jax was still wary. Though Jax wished to bring some of his crew for support, Zarena dissuaded him and he reluctantly conceded, voicing his displeasure in that unrefined way of his.

Their open-aired hover tram afforded little shelter beyond an awning overhead. The day was bright but not sweltering, a gentle sea breeze wisping inland along the coast. The road into Fasmouth was paved in timeworn bricks, leading into the first fishing settlement. The muted villagers shuffled listlessly along, moving without purpose like so many in this post-Harmony era. Emerald wondered how The Harmony had impacted the fishing trade. To the east, the boundless ocean swelled into the horizon, a vast expanse of sapphire as far as the eye could see. There were a few vessels gliding in and out of the ports. It had been a long time since she had seen such an unfathomable mass of water. This aquatic world had always been far beyond her urban sensibilities. The ships coming and going was evidence that fishing was still prolific here, though to what extent production had declined was uncertain. Less catch, less exports, less wealth. The people of Esper, shuffling along oblivious to these new travelers, likely faced an imminent crisis alongside all Great Houses as The Harmony heralded sagging economies across the Imperium.

The villages appeared impoverished, the structures simple affairs of brick, timber, clay, and straw thatch, many in states of disrepair. The villagers had a certain earthiness about them, calloused hands and plain garb weathered by lifetimes steeped in the sea's bounty. The main thoroughfare turned from brick to dirt as the citadel of Fasmouth loomed ahead. Despite what one might expect after seeing the villages, the stronghold was surprising formidable in scale, a sprawling walled fortress spanning kilometers in every direction. Its ramparts were forged from earthen bricks muted in tone, even the larger edifices and towers bearing a crumbling, reclaimed-by-nature aesthetic. Like an ancient abandoned castle being slowly consumed by the encroaching forest, this mammoth structure appeared like the echoes of a once-glorious civilization now lost to the ravages of time.

Battlements and watchtowers crested the stronghold at intervals, vantage points Emerald imagined would showcase breathtaking views of the azure ocean and muddy fishing villages below. As they drew closer, an ominous silence descended, as if the winds themselves quieted in deference to Fasmouth's might.

A shiver of apprehension rippled through their group, and try as she might to appear calm, Zarena could not conceal her concern. Emerald glanced at Evard, anxiety already etched on his face, fearing he may bolt from the tram outright and flee to the forest, never to be seen again. Since meeting Zarena, events had unfolded at a dizzying speed. It was easy to forget the freshness of Evard's loss that set his odyssey in motion. But he had proven resilient thus far, though uncertainty still plagued him.

The fortress entrance was a colossal iron gate, immense metal bars weathered by centuries of ocean storms yet still standing resolute. Emerald imagined this gate had welcomed guests since the days of Emmetz Carchel. Indeed, much of Fasmouth was likely unchanged from that age, a quiet society frozen in time. Its sheer scale and antiquity rendered it unexpectedly impressive. The winding road up to the gates snaked between craggy outcrops, finally cresting the hilltop perch where Fasmouth kept watch over land and sea. The ominous quiet persisted as their tram approached the gates which soundlessly opened.

A handful of guards were positioned on each side of the gate, moving forward at their arrival. One raised his hand to halt their progress, stepping forth to address the new arrivals. Zarena spoke first, her tone strained but steady as she conveyed their purpose here and requested an audience with the Baron. The guard's placid demeanor following her appeal was benign, thanks to The Harmony's influence. With a congenial nod, he promised to inform the Baron and waved them through.

As the gates groaned open, Emerald tensed. Despite everything, it was still difficult not to envision a violent outcome. She pictured Jax ruthlessly gunning down guards to clear their escape while Zarena seized control of the tram, spiriting them away from the spaceport as she and Evard cowered in terror. But none of these imagined horrors came to pass. The guard's comm link crackled and he relayed that the Baron welcomed Councilor Denamonte and would receive her in his throne room. With that, he directed two guards to escort them, who swiftly reappeared riding a hover skiff. Their tram lurched back to life, trailing the skiff into Fasmouth's inner sanctum.

The sprawling stronghold consisted of barracks, courtyards, training grounds, and a residential quarter with endless rows of stone and timber dwellings. While far humbler than Kra Markhan, these homes appeared opulent next to the fishing villages. Soldiers drilled in the streets alongside servants scurrying on errands. Fishmongers, captains, sailors and merchants seemed to dwell inside Fasmouth's walls. Food stalls and shops selling local wares and off-world goods flanked the thoroughfare. In one square, an open fish market displayed the day's catch on ice blocks in a bustling bazaar.

Strangest of all were the oblong chapel structures peppered throughout the keep, their slender spiraling towers and enormous bells evoking temples of worship incongruous with this secular age. Emerald wondered if they venerated some ocean deity as they passed one such sanctuary. Centuries ago on Origin, myriad belief systems converged on revering a singular humanistic god, with superficial differences in their beliefs sparking wars over the cracks between their creeds. Space travel eroded those original religions until a secular worldview took root in the Imperium. Though remnants survived in secret, public displays of religiosity were rare. Yet these temples suggested that open devotion was still thriving in Fasmouth.

Their small caravan soon approached the inner keep, a mountain rising above the lower fortress. Most Great Houses flaunted opulent strongholds of shimmering metals or elaborate stone or marble work. The Keep of Fasmouth was an unconventional throwback. While other Houses modernized, Fasmouth remained a relic from antiquity. Colossal russet bricks weathered by centuries of storms comprised the facade of this earthen titan. It resembled a medieval castle, four towering ramparts anchoring each corner of the box-shaped inner keep. While modest by the modern standards of most industrial planets, they still loomed tall over the stronghold, ancient bastions to bygone era.

A mammoth staircase ascended towards arched wooden doors, bound in iron and braced by metal joints. Emerald had never seen anything so archaic yet formidable. Their escort halted at the base of the steps and motioned for them to continue. As the doors slowly creaked open, the stony walls around them echoed the groan of the grinding wood. They stepped into a cavernous hall lit by candles and adorned with tapestries depicting epic naval battles and harvest scenes. Many were beautiful depictions of Esper's oceans. The inner walls were concrete, smoothed down by time. Dark stains marred the upper reaches, most likely from candle smoke or torches used in the past.

Passing through the antechamber, they entered an expansive hall supported by buttressed columns. Far across the empty expanse, upon a raised dais, sat an ornately carved wooden throne known as the Sea Throne. The intricate patterns and criss-crossed tridents carved into its frame evoked a seat fit for an ocean deity's undersea kingdom.

The company was led partway through the cavernous throne room, halting several meters in as the guards raised their hands to signal they should advance no further. One guard proclaimed in a booming voice muted somewhat by the deliberate slowness of his speech, "Your Majesty, Madame Denamonte and her associates have arrived. They seek an audience with you."

Sitting on the throne was a man, Emerald guessed likely in his mid-thirties. He appeared athletic, the sinewy muscles of his arms apparent even from afar. His olive skin and raven hair, grown out slightly and tousled about his head in a windswept manner, framed a chiseled face. He wore a cobalt and gold tunic with his arms bare, his legs clad in leather breeches and ankle-high sandals. Emerald was momentarily mesmerized. *So this is Andros Carchel*, she thought. He was striking, the type of man who frequently starred in the midnight fantasies of the lovelorn. She considered what Zarena had confided about their past romance. It would be difficult to let go of a man so attractive, Emerald conceded to herself with some embarrassment.

As the guard presented them, Andros Carchel arose, striding towards them more briskly than Emerald anticipated. Something is amiss here, she thought with unease. Andros approached with swift, purposeful steps, waving the guards aside dismissively. He stood before them, mere feet away, and bowed stiffly to Zarena at the front of the group. His expression was taut, not angry but calm, while his amber eyes blazed with what Emerald suspected was fury. *What is happening?* Suddenly it struck her like a lightning bolt splitting a tree. *It can't be*, she thought frantically, *could it?* She stared at Andros' handsome but hardened face, no trace of the tranquility that glossed across the visage of every other person.

Oh no, this is bad. We should never have come.

They were trapped now. All she could hope was that Zarena could find a way out of this mess.

Andros inclined formally, the gesture devoid of the Harmonized's natural geniality.

"Welcome to Fasmouth," he declared, his voice resonating with authority. "It's nice to see you again, Madame Denamonte, and friends," he added, gesturing dismissively to the rest of them.

He spoke with an accent Emerald couldn't quite place, his words clipped as if he was restraining himself. Nothing in his mannerisms or speech suggested he was among the pacified. If Zarena was startled, she didn't show it. Instead, she returned his bow and replied evenly, "Baron Carchel, thank you for welcoming us on such short notice."

Andros stared at her wordlessly, his gaze piercing. Emerald sensed the tension escalating all around her. She noticed Jax had subtly moved his hand to rest on the weapon at his hip.

Finally, Andros uttered accusingly, "I'm surprised to see you here, Zee. Have you come to finish the job?"

Zarena, ever the politician, answered smoothly, "I don't know what you mean, My Lord."

"I'm not your 'Lord", Zee. You abandoned that path long ago."

"My apologies for offending you, Baron," Zarena demurred diplomatically, maintaining her poise despite the circumstances.

Disregarding her attempt to pacify him, he continued sharply, "Are you surprised, Zarena?"

"Surprised by what, Baron Carchel?"

"Did you expect to find me a slobbering idiot? A fool like the rest? I'm sure you would have delighted in seeing my face frozen with that accursed empty grin."

He signaled the guards who closed in around Emerald's group. "I presume you came to complete your treachery, anticipating I had been neutered like the rest of these slack-jawed dullards." He addressed the guards, "Train your weapons on them. If the mercenary," he indicated Jax, "makes any sudden moves, shoot him in the torso then in the head."

Then to Zarena he clarified, sardonically, "I've learned one must be explicit nowadays. Robbed of their inner violence, they tend to bungle combat directives."

Everyone stood stock-still. Jax's hand remained poised at his hip, a gun aimed point-blank at his head and chest, so he kept perfectly still.

Finally, Zarena interjected firmly, "Baron Carchel, I implore you to listen a moment. I'm not here to incite conflict or endanger you or anyone under your authority. I've come seeking your assistance."

Andros paused, considering her plea. He scrutinized her intently, the fury fading from his face but his eyes still hard and unrelenting.

"When have you ever required my help, Councilor Denamonte?" he asked accusingly.

"Many times, Baron Carchel," she replied, her voice tinged with regret. "Now is the first occasion I've found the courage to ask directly. I would not have come if there was any other recourse. I understand your anger, Baron. You can execute us where we stand, or permit me to speak plainly with you. I promise to answer any questions you have."

He regarded her warily but not without a glimmer of compassion. He didn't respond right away, appraising her and her ragtag group pensively before speaking.

"Zarena, I know Rakeus has cast you out. I could display your corpse in the town square and he would send tribute in thanks. You knew you had no refuge here. You may have assumed I was... altered, like the rest of my people, and perhaps thought you could manipulate me as a result. So I wonder, what is so vital that you would come begging my assistance?"

Zarena said nothing, staring resolutely into the distance beyond Andros. Emerald prayed this was deliberate strategy rather than hesitation, as Andros did not seem a man to be trifled with.

At last, Andros conceded, "I know Rakeus has disavowed you, though I don't yet understand why. I presume the answer relates to your visit here. Rakeus will pay for what he's done, to my people and my home." A vengeful glint sparked in his eye as he spoke this vow. He continued flippantly, with a wave of his hand, "Perhaps you hold information that will prove useful to me."

His demeanor had shifted from fury to calculation, as if contemplating a range of possibilities.

Eventually, he declared, "Zarena, you and I will continue this discussion privately. Guards, please escort our guests to the dining hall. Provide them refreshments and any comforts needed. They've traveled far to see us and must be weary."

The guards nodded deferentially and motioned for Emerald, Evard, and Jax to follow them to the eastern corner of the room, leaving Zarena alone with Andros. As they departed, Emerald overheard Andros state, "You have one chance to convince me, Zarena. For everyone's sake, I hope you prove able."

On the verge of hyperventilating but trying not to attract notice, Emerald walked alongside Evard, who appeared as pallid as a specter. She reached for his hand as they were shepherded down a small corridor into an expansive dining area. He squeezed her hand firmly, attempting a wan smile as they shuffled along.

Jax strode ahead, clearly vigilant yet more composed than either of them. They seated themselves at the far end of a long table of ornately carved wood and precious stones. As they settled in, the two guards assumed stations behind them, gazes fixed vacantly into the distance. A servant emerged from a side door wearing black robes over a pristine white frock. He offered them a platter of bread and cheese and filled their glasses with crisp water from a pitcher before placing it on the table. Then he exited without a word, leaving them to eat, drink, and contemplate the day's alarming turn of events.

"I hope Zarena will be alright," Evard said worriedly.

"She'll be fine, kid. Tough as nails, that one," Jax reassured confidently, easing their concerns.

"What do we do now?" Emerald asked quietly.

Jax regarded her solemnly. "We sit. We wait. We hope for the best."

"And if the best isn't possible?" Emerald whispered, her voice quavering.

"Well then, darling, you'd better stick close to me and pray for a miracle."

CHAPTER 34
The Hospitality of Fasmouth

Andros escorted Zarena into a windowless chamber illuminated by electric lights. An ornate chandelier dripped crystals over a table and chairs, contrasting the room's modernity with the medieval grandeur of the main hall.

Though Zarena hadn't been here in many years, memories flooded back to her of the time she spent at Fasmouth.

Alone now, Andros pulled out a chair for her while circling to the other side of the table. His fury had abated but not entirely. Some still simmered below the surface.

"Baron Carchel," she said formally. "I know you're mad. At me, at Rakeus, at all of this. I didn't come here to start trouble but I also didn't come here to be threatened. You've made your point in the throne room. You could kill us on a whim, if you wanted. You didn't kill us though. You know I can help you achieve your ends. I also know you can help me achieve mine. On this matter, our goals are the same. So please, stop scaring my companions and let's cut the bullshit. We have a lot to discuss."

Zarena braced for his temper to flare but Andros just sat calmly, regarding her with no small measure of consternation. His gaze was uncomfortable, but the peril in it had passed.

"You're right, Zee. If I had really wanted to kill you, you never would have made it inside the keep but now you know I mean business. So let's talk business."

"Do you remember what I told you, all those years ago, about The Sequence?"

"Of course I remember. It was one of your reasons for leaving."

"I found a cure. That's what this is. It's what you see on the smiling faces of all of your subjects. It's the cure for The Sequence. Its code name is The Harmony."

Andros didn't respond, he just looked at her intently.

"Alright, Baron Andros, the..."

He interrupted her. "You can call me Andros, Zee. The time for posturing is over."

"Andros, I'll tell you everything. The whole truth. It will be upsetting to you, and you may be inclined to murder us afterward, but before I begin, know one thing, and believe that it is the truth: myself, and the people traveling with me, we are the only ones that are capable of fixing it. No one else. In an Imperium of half a trillion people, we are the only hope to restore humanity to… well, I guess you could say back to itself. You can be an instrumental part of that but to achieve this goal you and I will need to trust each other, like we once did. Do you understand?"

"Yes, I understand. Now, tell me," he said with no small amount of irritation in his voice. Zarena unfurled everything. Her research, Rakeus' edicts, The Harmony's deployment, Raeka, Jesper, her escape to Exalon, Emerald and Evard, the firefight, Jaxxon's band of merry mercs, and of course, their reason for coming here.

Andros listened, his face an unreadable mask. He neither interrupted nor asked questions, simply absorbing her epic chronicle.

"My plan was to come here after I had developed the de-programming device. I was going to liberate you and then tell you this story. You've surprised us when we realized you were not Harmonized. It's quite incredible. Are you Immune?"

"Rakeus will try to kill us all," he mused, as if he was speaking only to himself, blatantly ignoring her question. "We will need to strike first."

"Strike first?"

"Of course, Zee. We are at war. You must understand that."

"Yes, of course I do. That fact was plainly clear once I had to burn Imperial agents alive in order to escape with my life."

"Then you understand we can not wait for Rakeus to strike first. He will come here, with his armies. But.." he trailed off, as if lost in thought.

"But what, Andros?"

"Jesper. What you told me about Jesper concerns me greatly. There is something you need to know. It will not be pleasant for you to hear."

"What is that?"

"Kaia Dorsetta is dead."

Zarena's eyes went wide as tea saucers. She shook her head vigorously.

"No, no that can't be. She saved us just a few days ago. Jaxxon said she was leaving Archlon and heading to a safe place. We're supposed to contact her soon."

"I'm sorry, Zarena. It's true. I have someone inside the Mark. A mole that I've used for many years to keep tabs on Rakeus. Fortunately for us, he was among the small group that you didn't Harmonize. After everything you and Rakeus did, he was eager to help.

Andros looked away, almost as if lost in reverie. "I always thought he'd do something like this one day, bend the Imperium to his whim. His ancestors were savages. The Karmarchs have been a danger to the peace of Esper for centuries. You clearly kept your Harmony plans secret enough that my informant wasn't privy to any of it beforehand, kudos for that, but they did send a secret report recently. The body of Kaia Dorsetta was found on a bench in the Promenade D'Arten Les Arts three days ago. She was dressed as a street beggar and her throat was slit. The official report was she was working on diplomatic relations with some of the organized criminal elements of Kadzer when the negotiations went south and she was killed. Rakeus is using this as a purge of all organized crime, not that crime is much of an issue any more."

Zarena felt tears welling up in her eyes. She was never friends with Kaia Dorsetta but she always respected and trusted her. Kaia put her life in the crosshairs in order to save her and she was murdered for it. Zarena's face became flush with anger.

She spat out a single word, seething with hatred. "Jesper."

"Yes, given what you've told me, Jesper was most likely behind her murder."

"I'm going to have to tell Jax, the merc I'm traveling with. She was his only family."

"There will be time for grief later. I don't quite understand what Jesper is playing at here. He tells you to escape Archlon then he sends a hit squad to kill you but not before he asks Kaia Dorsetta to send a group of mercenaries to save you and bring you here. Then he kills Kaia? Why all the theater?"

Zarena thoughts for a moment. "He wants me to succeed but he doesn't want Rakeus to know. He's following Rakeus' orders to kill me but he's sending us help in secret. He probably killed Kaia because she was a loose end."

"But why? Why does he want you to succeed? What could be in it for him?"

"I don't know. He more or less told me on Archlon when he was waiting for me in my quarters that he wanted me to help Raeka. When I asked him why he said 'because he served the Imperium.'"

"Hmm, I can't imagine Jesper cares about anyone other than himself but his loyalty to Rakeus is legendary. I find it hard to believe he's betraying him, even now," said Andros. "Maybe the secret is, he's not."

"What do you mean?"

"Almost nothing is known about Jesper. He showed up one day and hasn't left Rakeus' side since. I've heard some of the things he's done for the Emperor. They would give you nightmares. I once tried to look into his past but all records of him have been purged from the Imperial databases. It's like he's a specter, he doesn't exist. The only thing I could find on him was a small tidbit, no more than a rumor so who knows if it's actually true, but my sources told me that somehow Rakeus saved his life when he was young and the reason for his vicious brand of loyalty was repayment for the life debt he owed. Like I said, who knows if it's actually true."

"I guess it doesn't really matter. Jesper, regardless of what he has done to help us get here, is our enemy. He wields too much power for a steward, and Rakeus allows it. The emperor is the only member of the Imperial court who seems not to fear him. We all must be very careful."

"I agree. But our concerns stretch far beyond just Jesper. It's the whole Imperium, Zarena. Whatever your role, Rakeus wanted this peace for his own ends, not as a cure but for control. He didn't inform the people, just forced it upon us. Maybe you meant well, but Rakeus had darker intentions — to subjugate us utterly. With the Great Houses subdued, none can oppose him."

Zarena had considered Rakeus' motivations before, but hearing Andros voice them aloud gave them new weight. The Harmony was never meant as a weapon, not by her, but in the wrong hands something so capable of reshaping a human mind was destined for abuse. She had not considered handing it to Rakeus as putting it in the wrong hands, but now she seriously questioned that.

"I still find it hard to accept, foolish as that sounds now."

"He sent assassins after you, Zee! A Councilor of the Imperium. He murdered Kaia, another Councilor, painting her a conspirator. The others will soon follow. He dismantles the Imperium's democratic pillars, cementing his total dominion." Andros leaned forward, his voice ominous. "None but us."

"I didn't come to Esper to fight a war, Andros. I came to use your resources to build the device. To free Raeka and give people a choice."

"No, Zee, you didn't. I know how much you love Raeka, but you're not doing this for her any longer. Rakeus will return, not with daggers in the dark but armadas burning the sky. Now you are here, he will come for you and House Carchel, with blood and vengeance. We must answer in kind."

Zarena felt a profound sadness at the turn of events. She wasn't even sure what she wanted anymore. Sounding a bit defeated she said, "What are your plans, Andros?"

"My plans," he said with a laugh. It was a mirthless laugh but still the first sign of humor he had displayed since she got here. He had changed so much in the intervening years since their engagement but his laugh reminded Zarena of the man he was in his youth. "My plans are now simple. Your arrival, despite my reservations, has proven a stroke of luck. I will spend all my vast resources to aid your efforts to build the device. Once my people are freed, we will ready for war. House Carchel will battle House Imperiatus and destroy Rakeus utterly. Then we give the Imperium a choice — remain Harmonized or be liberated."

"And who will become the new House Imperiatus if you defeat the Karmarchs? House Carchel, I presume?" She smiled softly at him, careful not to antagonize him again but adamant her point be made. "You are using this as a play for power," she said gently.

"No, Zarena. I seek to free the Imperium from tyranny, forever. Our decline owes less to The Sequence and more to complacency. Rakeus was so fixated on our blood he forgot our souls. He allowed this degeneration, the erosion of values, and of our collective cultures. Lust and greed had turned this empire into a prison for its people long before this. The time to resist has finally come. You will give us the means for victory. I will give you the path to redemption."

Zarena knew the truth in his words, even if she was suspicious of his motives. Andros had clearly been planning retaliation and now that he knew everything his goals were finally in reach.

"When do you think Rakeus will strike?" she asked. "Maybe soon. Maybe after he learns we've completed the device. Completing your mission may be in Rakeus' interest. He may want the technology for himself. Or he may just destroy it. It's hard to predict his next move so we must act quickly if we are to survive. He has far more un-Harmonized troops than we do at present from what you've told me. He could take us by force easily if he were to attack now. Our first priority must be completing the device."

"It's not that easy, Andros. I told you, I need to study more of the Immune. Perhaps I could start with you?" she said, with a raise of her eyebrow.

He laughed again, this time with more warmth. "I don't think I am Immune. I was off-world, on a rendezvous with a lover of mine. We parked a cruiser on the edge of the Carpexus Cascade and watched the lights for days while we drank plum wine and enjoyed each others, ah… company." He grinned the same grin a lion might have before pouncing on a gazelle.

"I thought he had set up a ruse to keep the Great Houses on-planet during The Harmony?"

"Oh, we received the order. But when have I ever listened to Rakeus? It was fortunate for us I didn't."

"Wait, so is your lover also unaffected?"

"Yes, and so is her twin brother. Interestingly though, he was on Esper when the minds of my people were turned to mush."

A smile beamed across Zarena's face. "So he's Immune?"

"He must be. Maybe Twila is, too. I will make sure to introduce you."

"Are they the only ones?"

"As far as I have been able to tell. It is a start at least."

"We should get to work soon. We have no time to waste."

"That's the Zarena I remember. I will prepare accommodations for you and your companions. A lab will be set up here in the inner keep. I will procure any tech you may need and offer my people as test subjects. Is there anything else you require?"

"Well now that you ask, yes, I could use something to eat. It's been a long day and I'm hungry."

"Of course, you may join your friends in the dining hall." He stood up and as if that was a signal a porter came through the door. "Please bring Madame Denamonte to her traveling companions and provide her with food and drink. We will need rooms for each of them here in the keep."

He walked over to Zarena and put a hand on her shoulder. "Please, follow Dorne here. He will take care of any needs you may have."

She stood and followed the porter and, as she reached the door, she turned around and looked at Andros. "Thank you Andros. I am truly sorry we had to meet again under these circumstances."

"As am I, former Councilor Denamonte. You may remember a saying we have here on Esper. 'The sea doesn't always give us what we want, but it can always give us what we need.'"

With that, Zarena left Baron Carchel, relieved to e finally be safe, worried about the dangers to come.

Zarena was ushered into the dining hall where Evard, Jax, and Emerald were sitting at a table while picking at a charcuterie plate and looking anxious. Emerald's head popped up, her eyes searching as she heard the door open. As Zarena walked in, Emerald jumped out of her seat and ran over to her, hugging her tightly, clearly relieved that Zarena was okay. Zarena just patted her on the back and smiled, touched that she felt so close to these people, people she barely knew. They were all in the crucible together now and camaraderie made that easier to handle.

"Are you okay?" Emerald asked her.

"Yes, I'm fine, Emerald, thank you," Zarena responded, gently. "Are all of you alright?"

Jax and Evard were sitting there quietly. Evard looked a bit worse for wear, trying to hold it all together. When he had fled Eden with little more than his life, he never expected to end up in the middle of a galactic conflict whose outcome would decide the fate of the human race. He was coping as could be expected but Andros had scared him truly and he still had yet to recover from escaping the warehouse on Exalon alive. The recent past for Evard had been a blur of fear and tragedy and running. He barely had time to process one event to the next and the stress was beginning to show on his young face. He tried to be brave, for the rest of them. He didn't want to hold them back from their important work. He stood up and ran over to where Emerald and Zarena were standing and, giving Zarena a big smile, he put his arm on her shoulder in a sign of comfort. Zarena grabbed him and gave him a big hug. She turned to face them both and said, "I'm so sorry about this. Baron Carchel and I have come to an understanding. We're safe here, for now."

She smiled as warmly as she could at both of them. She put her hand on each of their shoulders. "Andros is a proud man, a strong man, and he's angry. But he is also a good man. The danger from this point forward will not be from Andros. We need his help. Only he can protect us now."

"Sheesh, Zee, can't you sugar coat this crap for us, just for once?" said Evard with a smile and a nervous laugh.

"We understand, Zarena. Thank you for smoothing everything over. We're with you. We trust you," said Emerald, taking on a different tact.

Zarena looked at Emerald as her eyes began to mist over. It was incredible to her that these people put their faith in her, after everything she had done. She looked over at Jax who was still sitting at the table, watching the proceedings with a cautious grin. Their eyes met for a moment and Zarena smiled. Jax, still wearing his old leather hat, tipped the brim to her in kind.

"Is there anything to eat, I'm starving".

"Yeah, there is, and it's pretty good," Evard proclaimed with enthusiasm. They all sat around the table and snacked in silence, porters coming and going, bringing in plates o food. Many were local delicacies — beef stew, sweetened vegetables, grain bread, honey, cheese, and of course, fish.

Evard was inhaling a piece of thin white fish, gobbling up it greedily, licking his fingers after each bit. "This is delicious," he mumbled, through a mouthful of food.

Fruit wines and grain alcohols were served and the party continued to eat, and talk, and attempt a few laughs — as much as they were able to under the circumstances.

Zarena kept stealing glances at Jax, who was entirely enthralled by the food and drink, and said little in the way of conversation. She had to tell him about his aunt and she didn't want to wait longer but their minds had finally been put at ease. She figured she could risk a bit more time, at least until after the feast was over.

As the feast ended, nearly two hours since Zarena had returned from her private meeting with the Baron, Baron Carchel himself entered the room. He was flanked by a retinue of guards and two individuals, dressed in brown hooded robes. They looked like peasants in comparison to Andros himself. They wore leather sandals on their feet and a golden sash around their waists. As they entered the room, the two strangers removed their hoods. Their skin was as pale as snowfall on a mountain top. Both of them had hair as black as the night, cropped closely, almost like a cap that was fitted around their skulls. They both had deep brown eyes, and smiled as in unison as they removed their hoods at the guest seated around the table.

"My friends," Andros proclaimed. "I apologize for getting off on the wrong foot. It seems like we will be great allies in the battle yet to come. I hope you've enjoyed the hospitality of Fasmouth and found the food and drink to your liking."

He stepped forward, as did the cloaked figures behind him. Zarena thought that they were beautiful, in a very austere way. Their features were not soft but angular and sharp. They looked like ancient statues carved from a slab of marble. He gestured to them to come forward. They took their places next to him, hands folded together encircled in their flowing robes.

Zarena knew what they were immediately. The robes, the sash, the haircut — they were members of the Esperlin. The Esperlin was a quasi-religious sect that was native to Esper. Pre-dating the Imperium, their order claimed to be descendants of the First Settlers, passing traditions of the old ways down from generation to generation.

They respected nature, the sea and the earth and the sky and believed that an unseen and unquantifiable energy bound the elements together to create life. They revered the planet itself, referring to it as Gaia. Gaia was worshipped as an earth goddess by a people long since lost to history. They used the term out of respect for the ancient wisdom, which they parsed out to the people like missionaries.

Instead of living their lives in isolation, like many of the ancient sects, secreting away their knowledge and wisdom, the Esperlin lived among the people. No abbeys or monasteries or priories, they lived in ordinary homes though usually in rural areas where they could spend time outdoors. Many had families, jobs, and contributed to the community in ways simply beyond teaching and preaching their ancient words. Esperlin were fully integrated members of Esper's society, working and living side by side with the rest of the fishers and farmers. Many of them were fishermen themselves, relishing working on the water and liberating the sea of its many treasures. Others were farmers, growing fruits and vegetables on the plains of Ornast and other island-continents; some were ranchers, herding livestock.

Whatever profession they chose to endeavor in was always connected to the land. They were a peaceful, gentle group, congregating in their homes, toiling away in their studies in whatever free time they could spare. Their robes were ceremonial, made from natural fibers and pigments; a symbol of their devotion to the natural order.

Zarena had met many of them during her time on Esper and always found them pleasant. Still, it was strange for Esperlin to associate with royalty. Most of them steered well clear of galactic politics and though they always had a good relationship with House Carchel, it was rare for any member of their order to associate with the Baron or his family. They weren't ascetics by any means but it was certainly surprising to Zarena that one of them was Andros' lover.

"I would like to introduce my companion, Twila Everfield, and her brother, Therus", said Andros to his guest. They both bowed when introduced and Zarena rose to greet them.

"Pleased to make your acquaintance," she said.

"We are pleased to make yours, Madame Denamonte," responded Twila. Her voice was light and sweet, like the fragrance of flowers on a morning breeze. Her eyes were almond shaped with long well-tended lashes. Zarena smiled, a wry smile at home on the face of someone who was meeting their ex-lover's new lover for the first time. She nodded warmly in response, in a manner that did not belie the thoughts running through her head. Twila's brother also greeted the travelers.

"It is nice to meet you and your companions", said Therus, his voice soft and gentle. "We have not seen many off-worlders here on Esper for some time".

Zarena flashed him her best Councilor smile, courteous but not smug. "It's been a while since I've been to Esper. I believe this is the first trip for my companions." Zarena turned towards them as she spoke. "These are my friends, Evard Roost, Emerald Seltz and Jaxxon Rill".

Each of them stood in turn and nodded. "Nice to meet you both," said Evard.

Emerald bowed formally and Jaxxon tipped his hat, as he usually did upon greeting strangers.

"You are Esperlin, I see," Zarena said to them. "It's been a while since I've been in the company of a member of your order."

They both bowed graciously, as if they had been given a great honor. "There are not as many of us as there used to be," lamented Twila. "The ways of machines and metal hold great allure for the young. Still, we are highly active here on Ornast. We also enjoy meeting outlanders when the opportunity arises."

Andros interceded, stepping off to the side between Twila and Zarena. "I've brought Twila and Therus up to speed, Zarena. They are willing to help in whatever way they can."

"If you are familiar with the Esperlin, Madame Denamonte, then you know we do not favor technology. This Harmony is a blessing to the soil and the seas in many ways. Yet, we feel that the Imperium has greatly wrong our people, as well as the peoples through the galaxy. We hope to aid you in undoing this great wrong. We offer assistance in any way we can," said Therus to Zarena.

"Thank you. help is most welcome."

Andros went over to the table, took a glass, and poured himself some wine. He held the glass up high. "A toast. To new alliances. May the earth forgive us our many wrongs and the wrongs yet to come."

Everyone nodded in appraisal. Twila moved to Andros' side and gave him a kiss on the cheek. "Yes, my love. May we all find the victories we seek, together."

CHAPTER 35
Bathe In Their Blood

The weeks marched onward at the grand stone keep of Fasmouth. Andros had commissioned an elaborate laboratory to be constructed within the inner keep's thick walls, where Zarena and Emerald could immerse themselves in their vital work. Their motley group was given luxurious quarters inside the ancient fortress, each with their own spacious chamber furnished with opulent tapestries and succulent meals delivered promptly to the laboratory, dining hall, or their private rooms depending on where they happened to be. Andros had extended an invitation for Jaxxon's battle-hardened mercenaries to reside in Fasmouth's quaint seaside village, preparing comfortable apartments and provisions for the warriors.

Jax had informed his team of all that had transpired, offering them the chance to depart and seek fortune or safety elsewhere. But each stalwart fighter chose to remain and stand ready for the looming battle. Their sleek starship was relocated from the windswept cliffs outside Fasmouth to a secure hangar nestled inside the fortress walls.

Zarena would glimpse the mercenaries from time to time as they honed their combat skills, some taking to the waves in fishing skiffs, while others drilled with the local militia.

The peculiar twins, Twila and Therus, proved invaluable in the laboratory, permitting Zarena to meticulously scan their entire physiologies with the sophisticated equipment Andros had acquired. Vastly superior to her humble tools in the Exalon warehouse, Zarena could finally gather comprehensive data from Emerald and Evard as well. She had a fully-outfitted laboratory on par with her former research facilities. Whatever reservations she held about the Baron, Andros was unquestionably devoted to their shared cause.

While the initial tensions of their arrival had faded, an ominous dread still clung to them, permeating the ancient keep. The looming specter of war against the Imperium, even hindered by the Harmony, was a terrifying prospect. As bold as Andros acted, even he feared the devastation of a full-scale Imperial invasion. If the Emperor brought his fearsome fleets and endless legions to bear on House Carchel's forces before they could be liberated, there was little hope of victory. The fate of his entire planet teetered, the stakes immeasurably higher still. Esper boasted only a modest army by the standards of most Great Houses. The Imperial forces vastly outnumbered them, with several elite battalions of their finest warriors spared The Harmony's reach, granting the Imperium a formidable advantage in any ground campaign.

Andros had been feverishly preparing his military since returning from the Cascade anomaly to find his planet subtly altered by an invisible force. Despite his outward confidence, their only hope was to free his soldiers before open war erupted. Andros demanded constant progress reports, hovering around the laboratory like a watchful griffin. He was desperate for even a glimmer of breakthrough. Their entire gambit relied on producing a functioning device, a prospect Zarena still could not guarantee. The frenetic pace of research continued as they awaited the Empire's inevitable reprisal.

Personal dynamics within the group also gradually shifted. Evard and Emerald had grown closer, and Zarena suspected their deepening friendship was blossoming into something more. Zarena and Jaxxon had bonded in the wake of Kaia's shocking murder. That first night in Fasmouth, after their tense confrontation with Andros and meeting the peculiar twins, Zarena paid a late visit to Jaxxon's chamber.

Knocking softly on his door, Zarena stood anxiously in the hallway outside. Jaxxon, who had just begun to unwind, answered clad only in his undergarments with a pistol in hand.

"Oh, it's you. What do you need?"

"I need to talk to you, Jax," Zarena said solemnly.

"Alright, give me a minute." He closed the door and returned shortly, fully dressed with his weapon stowed away. Waving her inside, Zarena entered the spacious room.

Vaulted ceilings towered overhead, peaked above an ornate canopied bed anchored by towering oaken posts. The walls were an eclectic mix of smooth metallic panels bordered with carved wood and plaster. A couch, table with high-backed chairs, antique dressers and other furnishings, were sprinkled throughout the ample space. Far more luxurious than their recent lodgings, modern amenities like charging stations and virtual terminals hinted at the hidden technological advancements seamlessly merged into the antiquated grandeur. Despite the ancient aesthetic, in some ways it felt like a lavish hotel one might find on Archlon itself.

Zarena settled into one of the carved chairs as Jaxxon sat across from her, minus his signature hat, which he had flung like a disc onto the foot of the bed. His bare head made him seem oddly vulnerable, not fully himself. Zarena watched him intently, steeling herself to deliver the devastating news.

"It was good of Andros to let your team stay down in the village. He's been quite generous since threatening to kill us all."

"It's been a long day, Zarena. Let's make this quick."

"Of course. It's just… I don't know how to say this, but Andros told me something earlier that you need to know."

"Alright then, what is it?"

"It won't be easy to hear. It's about Kaia, Jax. She's dead. Her body was found on Archlon."

"What? No, she got away, she was leaving the planet…"

"She never made it off-world. She was murdered the day after she sent you to rescue us."

Jaxxon sat motionless, staring blankly as if the words had snatched away the world he knew and left him adrift in an empty void. Nearly a full minute passed before he stood abruptly, moving on autopilot.

He strode to the large dresser in the corner and punched through it with a thunderous clap, his fist connecting with the lacquered wood like a meteor crashing through a frozen lake. The dresser exploded in a hail of shattered timber with a deafening crack. Jaxxon shook his battered hand, wincing in pain.

He gripped his throbbing fist and sat heavily on the bed, tears welling in his eyes. His body began to tremble as he struggled to restrain the roiling anger and anguish inside him, attempting to erect a dam against the rising flood. His face flushed crimson, neck veins bulging.

Just as Zarena feared his head might erupt, he unleashed a primal scream, a wounded lion's death roar. The chilling cry froze Zarena in her seat. She watched helplessly as he gasped ragged, sputtering breaths. It took what felt like an eternity for him to regain a semblance of control. Zarena went over and squeezed his shoulder comfortingly. He placed his own quivering hand over hers, letting the other dangle limply.

After a long moment he rose and shuffled past Zarena to the door. Opening it wide, he said gruffly, "Thank you for telling me. Please leave."

She passed by silently as he held the door. Continuing down the dim hallway to her own chamber, she didn't look back until his anguished voice called out, "Zee, who was it?"

She turned to face him. "Jesper, on Rakeus' orders."

"Andros is right, you know? We are at war now. You better be ready for that, Councilor. There's no going back." He spoke with eerie calm, as if his raw outpouring had now purged all emotion. His eyes narrowed to slits and a chill slithered down Zarena's spine.

"Before this is over, I'm going to bathe in their blood."

With that, he slammed the heavy door, leaving Zarena alone in the shadowy hall wondering how much more suffering awaited them all.

CHAPTER 36

A Light In The Dark

They spent nearly two months cloistered in Fasmouth Keep and the vital research continued unabated day and night. Everyone had adjusted to life on Esper. Emerald and Evard enjoyed occasional jaunts down to the picturesque fishing villages to observe the ships hauling in their daily catch, sampling exotic local delicacies. Jaxxon spent many hours carousing and training with his battle-hardened crew, though the choppy open sea did not agree with his iron constitution. He preferred to keep his feet planted firmly on solid ground when possible. Zarena devoted endless days immersed in the makeshift laboratory, poring over schematics and tinkering with the ingenious devices Emerald helped assemble.

One day after an especially late night Zarena called all of them together, as if she was the Emperor summoning her own Council. Andros, Twila, Therus, Emerald, Evard, and Jax all sat around an oak table that was set up in the sterile lab, their inquiring gazes fixed on one another as they wondered what awaited them.

Zarena strode in last, a leather folder clutched in her grasp. She took her seat at the head of the table and powered up her terminal. Surveying their expectant faces, she finally uttered, "I may have found something important."

She opened the folder and began rifling through stacks of notes and intricate sketches. She retrieved her comm device, connecting it to the terminal. A flickering hologram materialized above the table, projecting the ghostly image of a human brain. Different regions began to illuminate sporadically, as if testing their own neural pathways.

"This is a comprehensive cranial scan of Evard's mind," she explained, looking at him with a gentle smile. Evard appeared on the verge of fainting at the sight of his own mind laid bare. "The lights showcase the various sectors activated during our battery of tests, thanks to the state-of-the-art equipment provided by Baron Carchel," Zarena added, with an appreciative nod toward Andros.

"Now observe Emerald's brain."

Another spectral brain blinked into view alongside Evard's.

"Though the size and shape may vary slightly, look closer," she instructed, tapping the terminal screen. In eerie synchrony, the two minds began to light up in a dazzling neon display, utterly in tune with one another down to the last neuron.

"Fascinating, isn't it? The so-called 'Immunity' doesn't completely prevent The Harmony from altering the brain, as we discovered on Exalon. I assumed no behavioral shifts occurred, but that's not exactly true. The Harmony synchronized the neural patterns of the Immune, forging identical brain pathways."

She paused to let this revelation sink in. Evard was the first to find his voice. "What exactly does that mean? Our thoughts are identical now?"

"No," Zarena chuckled nervously. "You don't have the same thoughts or experiences, Evard. You're matching brain waves, but still retaining unique cognizance," she clarified, patiently. "It means… well, I believe I've found the key to reversing The Harmony."

Rapturous applause and cheers erupted around the table. Andros shot to his feet, bellowing "This is phenomenal news!"

Zarena allowed herself a brief moment to bask in their elation. This breakthrough had seemed impossible not long ago, but thanks to fate's intervention, here they were on the cusp.

"You're brilliant, Zee! I can scarcely believe it - you did it!" Evard exclaimed joyously.

Zarena noticed the twins exchange a cryptic look. Twila was regarding her like a ravenous lioness eyeing prey after months of subsisting on roots and shrubs. "Is that the full truth, Zarena Denamonte?" she purred in her melodic voice. All eyes swiveled towards the mesmerizing woman.

"What more is there, my love?" Andros asked. She tipped her head toward Zarena, tacitly urging her to elaborate.

"Well, as I mentioned, the Immune have similarly configured brains, just like the Harmonized," Zarena continued. "Both differ from minds never exposed to The Harmony, like mine, Andros, Jax and Twila's."

Emerald interjected, "What about Therus?"

"That's the puzzle, I'm uncertain he truly is immune."

Their faces knotted in confusion as she manipulated the terminal again. "This was Therus' brain when I first scanned it." His brain appeared beside the others, regions flashing in perfect sync.

"But this is his most recent scan."

The other images winked out, replaced by two versions of Therus' brain. The illuminated sections were no longer coordinated. Shocked silence descended on the room.

"Now compare with Evard and Emerald's recent scans." Two more brains popped up, identical to their earlier counterparts.

"As you can see, Therus' initial scan matches the other immune brains. But his newest scan..." She dismissed Evard and Emerald's images, calling up her own brain and Andros'. "Is starting to more closely resemble our un-Harmonized minds. It's as if Therus is losing his Immunity. His mind is reverting to its pre-Harmony state.""What's happening?" Emerald whispered, bewildered.

"I believe Therus only had a partial immunity," Zarena revealed. "I think…" she paused for a moment before continuing. "That his brain patterns were, I guess you could say, shielded by a psychic link with Twila."

Jaws dropped in unison. Emerald gawked at her, eyes wide and unblinking. They gaped wordlessly at the flickering holograms, struggling to process this bombshell. Evard shattered the stunned silence.

"You mean Twila and Therus have extraordinary twin abilities? That's incredible!"

Twila smirked at Zarena, who returned a knowing smile. "It's not necessarily twin powers, although their bond likely intensified it. We don't know what factors make someone Immune, but there is compelling evidence to suspect that there is a genetic component at work, a mutation of some sort. It's why I think Emerald was Immune, her eyes are a singularly unique genetic mutation. I can't prove it yet, but the mutation may have protected her."

Emerald, blushed at being called out, her emerald eyes blazing like wildfire.

"I think there are other factors as well. I still don't know everything I need to; it could take years to unravel all of the data." Zarena took a deep breath and continued. "After reviewing Twila's brain patterns, I was unable to tell if she would be Immune or not, but looking at a DNA sample she provided, she has a genetic mutation. One that doesn't express itself in any way but something she carries. I think she is Immune."

The eyes of the assembled just stared at her blankly, so she continued.

"Fraternal twins are born from separate embryos. One can have a mutation the other does not. After checking, Therus doesn't have any mutations. I think, somehow, Therus's mind created a connection to Twila's. That is what protected him."

Evard and Jax said in unison, as if they had rehearsed it beforehand, "I don't get it."

"The Harmony didn't just sync your brains, it interlinked them, like plugging into a shared neural network," Zarena answered, authoritatively. "As a result, I believe all Immune can achieve a form of telepathy. And it goes beyond communication."

She grabbed some papers from her folder, leafing through them eagerly. "I suspect you may even be able to influence changes through the connection. That's how Twila shielded Therus from The

Harmony. Once Therus was triggered, as The Harmony activated, his fragmented brain waves transmitted across an unfathomable distance and connected with hers, an Immune. It seems this connection persisted until completion, normalizing his brain as The Harmony sought to alter it.”

The room was filled with a stunned silence. It was Evard who broke through the static as he exclaimed a little too loudly, “What the *fuck* does that mean?”

Andros burst into hearty laughter punctuated by coughing fits. “You can’t be serious? Psychic abilities?” He chuckled in disbelief, shaking his head.

Jax finally weighed in. “You pulling our legs here? This is for real?”

“Yes, I think so, as surreal as that may seem,” Zarena stated, plainly. She flashed a languid smile. “Furthermore, I believe these connections will endure even after we reverse The Harmony.”

Emerald blurted out, “Can Evard read my thoughts?” She flushed crimson.

Jax guffawed, as Evard turned even redder.

“No, I don’t think so. I suspect you can regulate the link, Emerald. With practice, you should be able to filter what’s transmitted. At least I believe so, this is a new science. What we don’t know far outweighs what we do.”

“So you broadcast selectively, like using a comm device,” Emerald concluded. “Can you also sever a connection, if you wanted to?”

“Probably,” Zarena answered with an uneasy laugh.

“So how did Therus tap into Twila’s brain waves?” Andros asked.

Twila smirked at Evard. “It must be our extraordinary twin powers.”

Everyone looked to Zarena, who just shrugged ambiguously. “Perhaps. No one else has yet to demonstrate these abilities, at least that we are aware of. Therus didn’t do it on purpose, certainly.

This was an accident. Maybe his mind instinctively reached out and grabbed a piece of his sister's when threatened. Maybe, like an emotional anchor, the link shot out to the person he was closest too, and since he may have only been partially Harmonized, and she was…"

"But if Twila wasn't exposed to the Harmony," Emerald interjected, "then how was she able to transmit back through the link?"

"At this point who knows, but I don't think she was transmitting. I think Therus was pulling, from her. Still, I don't understand how Twila was able to shield him. This is all so surprising. We'd need more time to unravel this, far more time than we have. It's something we have to get to the bottom of, but the point is, it's real."

No one said anything, each face looking at the others in a shared moment of disbelief, as if a madness had gripped them all at the same time. Zarena broke the silence, elaborating on her theory.

"I think there are other factors at play, like I said. It's possible something they encountered, a substance or a chemical, might have contributed. Honestly, I don't know, and I don't like not knowing.

"Does it matter? You said you could reverse what you did. Wasn't that the goal?" enquired Jax. "It may matter at some point, and if we all survive this perhaps we'll have the time to figure it out. But yes, for now, the takeaway is that we can start the real work."

"So you've created a new species — people with connected minds," Andros said with curiosity and concern in his voice. "Can any of them do this?"

"Yes, in fact, they should probably try to see if they can. I don't know how you'd go about that, it may just start happening on its own. I should also note that the Harmonized should be able to create psychic links with each other as well, though I don't think it's likely they will. It seems like the initial contact requires an emotional anchor that the Harmonized wouldn't necessarily possess."

"The universe after The Harmony won't be the same old universe. It will be one where thoughts can be shared. Is that accurate?" Andros asked, gently.

"Yes, I suppose so. There's no returning to our former reality. The Harmony irreversibly altered that."

It was Emerald who finally voiced the critical question. "What about The Sequence? Would reversing The Harmony eliminate the threat?"

Zarena sighed heavily. "I don't know. The Sequence may still affect the de-Harmonized. It's too early to predict. The Sequence is genetic. The Harmony affects things like neural connections and cognitive faculties. There's no guarantee at this point that deactivating the effects of The Harmony would prevent future calamities."

Andros spoke resolutely. "It seems the one certainty is that we can free people now, make them messy and unique again. Must we know more than that?"

Jax concurred. "Andros is right. Whatever else comes, Rakeus will have us in his crosshairs. No one is going to escape this war. If we want to live, we need fighters with all their marbles intact."

"He's right," Evard agreed. "Even if we figure everything out, the Emperor will still kill us all at some point."

"I agree, we can't turn back now," Emerald asserted. "Rakeus could arrive tomorrow or next year. Either way, we must finish the device. What do we need, Zarena?"

Zarena handed Andros a sheet detailing required components. He, Emerald, and Twila scrutinized it intently. "If we gather these materials   Emerald and I can assemble the device in a few days' time. Then we'll commence human trials."

"What's the effective range?" Emerald inquired.

"We can adjust it, but at maximum, approximately a kilometer or less. We'll need to gather people together for mass inoculations."

Andros looked at Zarena and gestured to the component list. "I'll secure these immediately. We haven't a second to waste."

CHAPTER 37
Wait, Where Are You?

After the meeting Evard was walking along a corridor back to his room. All of his new friends were busy trying to prepare for the coming storm, toiling away in a lab or training their combat skills for battle.

He wasn't sure where he fit into the mix.

Sure, Zarena needed him for her research but he wasn't sure he offered the people he now lived with any more than that. Zarena and Emerald were brilliant, so much smarter than he was. They were making a device that was going to change the course of human history.

Andros was powerful, his military preparing to go to war with the Emperor. The twins seemed clever and mysterious and without them, Zarena might never have figured out how to even make the anti-Harmony device. Jax and his team of mercenaries were skilled fighters. Jax was more clever than he appeared and he couldn't imagine many people getting the upper hand on him in a fight.

I have nothing to offer them, he thought to himself.

He opened the door to his chambers and collapsed on the bed, feeling overwhelmed and exhausted. As he lay there in the empty silence of the keep blanketed in his own thoughts he heard a voice, clear as day, echo inside his head.

That's not true, Ev, it said. He sat bolt upright, all the color draining out of his face. He looked around the room and didn't see anything.

What the hell? he thought.

Don't be scared. It's me, Evard. It's Emerald.

Emerald? You're in my head? What the…I heard you. Like you're hearing me. You must have been thinking about me, said the voice of Emerald, that only he could hear.

After a moment she finished, *well, I was thinking about you. I guess Zarena was right, if we try to connect, we can. It wasn't that hard. I'm scared, Em. This is freaky*, he thought back to her.

Wait where you are, the disembodied voice of Emerald said inside his mind.

He did as the voice asked, sitting there on the bed and half wondering if all the trauma and stress had actually made him go crazy. A few minutes passed and he sat there, still as a statue, until there was a soft knock at the door.

He stood up robotically, as if he was being controlled by a remote and walked to the door. When he opened it, there stood Emerald. They came to Fasmouth with very few personal possessions so Andros had furnished them with various amenities, such as new clothing and grooming products. She was wearing the type of clothing a wealthy woman on Esper would be seen in.

It was a gold and brown tunic with a medium length skirt, with high strappy sandals. Her dark hair was beautifully braided in a complex pattern that must have taken quite a long time to do. She looked lovely and he couldn't help but think it.

She blushed as his thought reached her. She walked past him into the room.

"Sorry, I couldn't help it," he said aloud, as he now blushed a shade of scarlet, closing the door behind them.

"Its okay. Neither of us can fully control it yet. I noticed that when you think of me you push some of those thoughts across our… our connection. I don't get all of it, just bits and pieces, but I get enough," she said with a kind smile.

Evard started to stammer, his heart beating so fast he thought he might faint.

"Don't be nervous," she said. "We're connected now. Maybe it's so strong because we were connected before we even knew about this." She took his hands, led him over to his bed, and sat down. He sat next to her, trying his best not to show how nervous he was and failing.

"Look, Em. I… I… um, look I'm nervous so, so just wait a second."

He closed his eyes and took in a deep breath. She watched him patiently as he slowly began to calm himself, breathing in and out rhythmically while he kept his eyes closed.

Suddenly she heard a voice in her head.

I'm going to try it like this, he spoke aloud inside her head.

She closed her eyes too, holding his hand while they communicated through the link that connected their minds.

I'm not good enough for you, Em. You could do anything you want, be anything you want. I know you love your friend, Jazz, and I know you miss him. I know you miss your mother. I'm sorry that I'm the one you're stuck with here, he said telepathically.

His body became very still as his mind continued to speak to her. She could feel his hand and hear his voice but being connected so deeply in the moment she could also feel his sadness, the endless abyss of despair that swam below his casual, goofy exterior.

She also felt something else. Something so warm and bright she had never experienced anything like it before. It was his love. His love for her. She could feel his love for her from its source, pure and raw and wondrous. She was overwhelmed by it, as she began to silently cry through closed eyes.

I'm not what you deserve and I'm sorry for that. But if the Emperor sends his army to kill us tomorrow I just want you to know. I lo…

Before his thought finished in her mind she flung herself forward and kissed him, full on the lips. He hadn't expected that, even with their minds connected, and his eyes flew up in surprise. She pulled her face away from his and said out loud, "I love you, too."

She could sense his feelings through the connection. Despite all the pain he carried, she could tell he was thinking that he was the luckiest guy in the whole galaxy.

Her emotions began to boil over, and suddenly he could feel her emotions too, her surprise and her joy and her love. The connection deepened and it became as if their bodies merged along with their minds, as if they were no longer themselves but part of a greater whole they shared together. For the first time in a long time they both felt at peace.

CHAPTER 38
The Law Of Parlay

Jesper was standing outside the throne room of Emperor Rakeus VII, Lord of House Karmarch, the House Imperiatus, Emperor of the Known Universe.

He had a coin in his pocket, a rare heirloom that he had pilfered from his father when he was a more reckless youth. It had a sigil on one side and a stern visage on the other. Its value was considerable but money was not the reason Jesper had clung to it for so long. He kept it as a token of fortune. A reminder of the chaos that was the true sovereign of the galaxy.

He held it between his fingers as he waited. It helped purge his mind of distractions. On occasion he would flip it, as a game of chance, allowing it to decide the outcomes of certain endeavors. He felt the weight of it in his hands, revolving it over and over between his fingers. He flung it up in the air with his left hand and snatched it out of the air with his right as swift as a viper striking. He slid the coin back into his pocket without seeing which side was up.

The doors parted and Commander Levitz strode out alone, his military cap nestled under his left arm. He saw Jesper standing there and uttered stiffly, "Good day, sir."

Jesper gazed at Levitz with a placid smile and replied, "Good day, Commander."

Levitz would have sworn there was menace in those eyes, that Jesper was appraising him like a butcher appraises a lamb selected for slaughter. Jesper always filled him with unease. Rakeus permitted his petty threats, like some leashed attack hound, so Levitz found it was best to just shun him when feasible.

Levitz could never comprehend why the Emperor's personal attendant wielded more authority throughout the Imperium than anyone. He thought it made Rakeus appear weak, bestowing so much command to a man who never served a day in a military uniform. He knew next to nothing about Jesper except for the only thing he needed to know; he was an animal who could never be trusted. Levitz didn't like to linger on it. The notion that Jesper may be manipulating Rakeus' actions disturbed him, and these were dangerous times.

He hastily purged all traces of Jesper from his thoughts. As irrational as it might seem to anyone else, Levitz sometimes wondered if Jesper could literally decipher his mind. The idea filled him with disquiet and though he would never admit it, a bit of dread.

Detecting his colleague's discomfort, Jesper flashed a predatory grin at Levitz for his own amusement. He reveled in making the worms squirm. He bowed formally then sauntered inside the throne room, the doors sealing behind him as if by sorcery, abandoning Levitz standing there just watching him depart.

"Good day, sire," he said pleasantly.

"Levitz has been briefed. He's assembling his forces."

"That's auspicious news, Your Majesty", said Jesper.

"Do you still think you can retrieve their device?"

"The situation has become more complicated. Andros is preparing for an invasion."

"Before it was a matter of controlling this technology. Things have changed now. Do you believe their claims are even possible?"

"Sire, before the Harmony this would be deemed a fantasy. Now it's harder to say. Zarena believes it, and whatever else she might be, she's a pragmatist. If this is real, sire, we would be foolish to ignore the implications."

Rakeus thought for a moment, his chin resting on his reclining fist. He seemed a bit distracted to Jesper. Maybe 'weary' was the best way to describe it. He broke off his train of thought with a grunt. "If it's true, we need it."

"Your Majesty, would it not be better to simply destroy it, along with the rest of them?"

"It would be easier, but I'm not sure it would be better. We wanted to keep this deprogramming tech safe, out of the hands of others. If we had to sacrifice it, then it would have been an acceptable, though undesirable, loss. But now we know it does so much more than that, if we are to believe Zarena. This isn't just a liberation, it's an evolution. I don't have to tell you, of all people, what type of peril this could be. If we are going to retain our grip on the Imperium we must be the arbiters of this power."

"If we destroy it then no one will have it," said Jesper flatly.

Rakeus looked him in the eyes. "Then we will not have it. This power may come in handy. If we could control who this power was given to it would strengthen our grip on the Imperium. We could have agents communicating with each other without the use of comms or devices. They may even be able to speak to each other across planets. No one could stop us. It would be the end of any resistance to House Karmarch."

Jesper's eyes didn't waver from the Emperor's. He spoke his next words slowly and calmly. "The Harmony ensured we had an ironclad grip on the Imperium, Your Majesty. Rebellions like the one Zarena and Andros are planning could be settled by force within a day. Think of the message it would send. Even if by some chance other Great Houses had un-Harmonized members who wanted to try what Carchel is doing, this would silence them all. The Harmony will keep the Houses in line, and crushing Carchel will ensure that."

"I want the fucking technology! roared Rakeus. He had stood up, his face red with anger, his posture menacing. He pointed a finger at Jesper. He was breathing heavily, seething with rage. "You've never disappointed me before, boy," he spat. "Now would not be the time to start."

Jesper bowed deeply. "My apologies, sire. I understand we must get the technology for ourselves. I did not mean to distress you."

His words were as sweet as drips of nectar harvested from a honeycomb. It had a soothing effect on Rakeus. *I must tread carefully*, Jesper thought to himself.

Rakeus sat back down, the outburst over. He spread his hands out as he asked, "Well?"

"The device will be in the keep at Fasmouth. It will be guarded day and night. The bulk of the forces have been assembled outside the gates. To retrieve it without destroying it would be a nearly impossible task, however there might be something we can do."

"And what would that be?"

Jesper spoke smoothly but with just a touch less confidence then he usually exuded, as if the idea had only now occurred to him out of duress and had not secretly been his goal all along.

"We parlay."

"Parlay? That's your best plan?"

"We assemble the fleet. We bring the planet-killers: the proton bombs, the sky-to-surface missiles, the fusion weapons. Everything. Let them know we intend to obliterate them, turn Esper into space dust. We can do it, of course. They know we can do it. So we prey on their fear."

Rakeus was now listening intently, leaning forward on his throne in anticipation.

"We stay in orbit over Esper," Jesper continued. "We tell them we want to negotiate a peace. We invoke the law of parlay. I will take a shuttle down to the planet with a small but elite force."

"You want to do this yourself?"

"Yes, sire. I believe I can be adequately persuasive. I will meet with Zarena and Andros to convince them to show me the device. Once I have a location, I will extract it and bring it back here. Then we can proceed to annihilate them."

"How would you extract it? You'll be surrounded by an army."

"Leave that to me, sire."

"Fine, but they'll never let you land. Andros would sooner shoot you out of the sky then allow you to land on that muddy dirtball of his."

"I think I have a solution for that, sire."

Rakeus raised his eyebrow curiously. "You do? It must be quite a solution."

"It is, Your Majesty. It will require your permission however, and that may not be something you're eager to grant."

Rakeus looked at him, intrigued. "What is it you need?"

"Princess Raeka, sire. I need to bring Raeka."

CHAPTER 39
It's Time To Wake Up

ndros sat on the Sea Throne, looking at all the faces assembled before him. Zarena, Emerald, Jax, Evard, and the twins were among those present. Andros had also summoned his man-at-arms, a warmaster named Zedyn Trill.

Zedyn was tall and lean, with a muscular build, short brown hair, and dark eyes. His features were lean and angular, as if they were cut from hard stone. He was dressed in an officer's uniform. Trill was among the Harmonized. He wore the telltale expression on his face, the serene and almost goofy smile, the softness in the eyes. He had only a vague understanding, as most Harmonized do, that they are somehow different from others. Regardless, he knew his duty to the Baron full well and volunteered himself as test subject.

Prior to The Harmony, Trill was responsible for commanding the army of Esper. If all went to plan, he would be again.

He stood as still as a statue, waiting for Andros to speak, a crooked smile on his face.

"Friends," began Andros from his throne. "The time for war is upon us. My mole inside the Mark has informed us that Rakeus is sending a battalion of ships to annihilate us. They will be here within two days."

A silence fell over the room, no one daring to speak. Andros continued.

"Commander Levitz, that witless buffoon, will be in charge. We should meet them in the neutral space above the atmosphere of Esper. We will also need ground troops stationed around Fasmouth in case they launch a ground assault."

Everyone's eyes were on him and he laid out the plan for battle.

"This is not the only news. We have word that Rakeus will attempt to parlay."

Emerald looked around in confusion. She didn't know what that meant but she didn't want to ask a question in the meeting with the Baron. However, Andros explained without her asking.

"The right of parlay is an ancient custom, one that has been honored since the dawn of the Imperium. When it is called, a truce begins. All hostilities cease and shelter is given to the enemy while the heads of state attempt to negotiate a truce. It has been many a year since the last time a parlay was called in a conflict. I find it very curious."

It was Zarena who spoke up. "Curious how?"

Andros titled his head to the side and looked off to the distance, as if unsure what to say next. "Jesper, is coming. He will be their ambassador."

Zarena and Andros locked eyes, a quiet understanding passing between them. Jaxxon's face pinch up in a display of restrained anger but he kept silent. Emerald and Evard had both heard enough about Jesper to be frightened. They looked at each other as Emerald grabbed a hold of Evard's hands.

"Jesper Mandarlay has played a curious role in all of this," said Andros. "He was the one that encouraged Zarena to leave Archlon so she could discover the cure in the first place. We have come to believe that he was the one who asked the late Councilor Kaia Dorsetta to send Mr. Rill's team of mercenaries to save Zarena and her companions on Exalon. We also believe he was the one who ordered the agents to kill Zarena and is responsible for the death of Madame Dorsetta."

Zedyn Trill was doing his best to understand the situation. He asked in a voice that sounded lighter than air to the people around him, "What does that mean, my lord?"

"It means we have no idea what we are dealing with. Jesper is going to request a parlay once he reaches our space. He will ask for safe passage to Fasmouth so he may palaver with us under the pretenses of finding a truce. I can't believe that will be the aim, however."

"We can't let him!" barked Jax. He looked around at the surprised faces around him and said. "With respect, Baron Carchel. He is a mad man. He is a danger to you. Letting him land would be a mistake."

"I agree," said Andros, ignoring the outburst. "There is more. Our contact went silent a day ago. I fear that Jesper may have gotten to them. But before he did they sent one last communication. Jesper met with the Emperor before departing. He requested permission to bring something with him, something secret. We don't know what it is but we believe he intends to bring this secret with him to Esper."

"It could be a weapon," said Emerald, practically. "He may be trying to destroy the anti-Harmony device."

"Maybe, but I don't know," said Zarena. Emerald whipped around to look at her. She hadn't expected Zarena to disagree. No one knew better than Zarena how dangerous letting Jesper waltz into Fasmouth could be.

Zarena ignored the eyes on her. "It's not a coincidence that Rakeus is sending his fleet now, after we've been sitting ducks here for months. He must know we have the device ready. He must also expect that we would use it to liberate our forces in order to fight more effectively. That evens the playing field a bit. Jesper isn't coming to destroy the device. I think he's coming to see it. For whatever reason, something in the back of my mind has been saying since I left Archlon that Jesper wants the device. Maybe for Rakeus, maybe for himself. I have no idea what he could want with it. But my instincts tell me he won't destroy it unless we force him to."

"It's hard to say what forces are at play here," Andros mused. "We all must realize the stakes we are dealing with. If we refuse they will attempt to destroy the planet. Even with our full armada at the ready they still may be able to do so. As dangerous as it is to allow Jesper to come here, it might buy us time to figure out the broader plan. We can always use Jesper as a hostage if we need to."

Jaxxon chimed in again. "I'm not sure the Emperor will back down, regardless of who we have on the ground here. Given what we know about the new power this device can grant, it makes the most sense that they would want that power for themselves. It would benefit the Emperor in the future."

"That leads us to the last concern of mine. How does he know we have the device? As Zarena said, it's not a coincidence his forces are coming now, not before. But how do they know we have it?"

"There must be a spy in our midst, My Lord," Trill volunteered, a bit too cheerfully.

"I've thought of that," said Andros dismissively. "Nothing has gone on here at Fasmouth since Zarena and company arrived that I do not know about." He smiled at Evard and Emerald in a knowing way that made them both shift uncomfortably on their feet. "All communications off-world have been monitored. Our efforts are not infallible but I think it may be something else."

No one volunteered any ideas. Andros waited patiently, expecting someone to speak but no one did. He was about to move on when Emerald said, "nanotechnology."

"I'm sorry?" enquired Andros. "How would nanotech be used for surveillance? It would need to be implanted. No one from the Imperium has been to Esper in ages."

Emerald gulped. She wasn't sure but she was hoping she was right. She continued on.

"When I was at Raxeon, they had recently received a large contract with the Imperium, on behalf of the Emperor for development of specific nanotech. This was long before The Harmony, mind you. I didn't work on the project, the nano technicians were the ones that worked on the engineering but it was codenamed 'whispers'. I can't be sure but I believe it may have been surveillance tech."

"You never thought to mention this until now?" asked Andros, with obvious frustration in his voice.

"No, sir. It was a long time ago. I had forgotten all about it until now."

Andros just shook his head in dismay.

Emerald continued. "Even if we had developed a special nano spy device for Rakeus, it can't just materialize out of thin air. It would have to be implanted. Somewhere. Like the Baron said, it's unlikely any agents infiltrated the keep, especially after the Baron realized what was going on. Security seems as tight as a drum around here."

Andros laughed. "That it is, Ms. Seltz. Still, is it possible they found a way to get it here?"

"Given the top secret nature of the project, it must do some things way beyond the scope. I can't imagine exactly how, but yes, I believe it might be possible."

"Well then, we will stay vigilant. After this meeting is adjourned, we will take extra precautions when discussing this situation. None of you are to talk about it amongst yourselves from now on. I will set up a safe room, free from detection, and further discussions will occur there. That settles that matter. Now, for the moment we've all been waiting for…" Andros gestured to Commander Trill, who stepped forward. He stopped in front of the steps to the throne and stood at attention.

Two guards came out of the hallway that led to the lab, gently carrying the device that Zarena and Emerald had completed. This device would come to be known as the Chaos Device. It was circular, made from onyx vermacite, which was pitch black in color. It was about half a meter long, and half a meter tall. It had a panel on it with a keypad and a small screen. They placed it gingerly on the ground behind Commander Trill as the others made space for them.

Once it was placed on the ground they backed away, Zarena walking forward to initiate the activation sequence. She fiddled with the keypad for a bit as the others watched with bated breath. Suddenly, a whirring sound started emanating from the device. Zarena stood up and turned to Andros.

"It is set for a one meter range. Please have the Commander Trill stand next to the device. Everyone else move back. It will begin in one minute".

The device began to make a humming sound, low at first, like the distant rumble of thunder. The top of the device began to slowly open, a metal arm extending from underneath with a shiny orb at the top. The orb had receptors that looked like small metal panels that followed the curve of the orb in parallel. As the arm extended from inside the casing the orb started spinning. It spun faster and faster, until the arm had fully extended a half a meter above the casing. The orb was spinning so fast that it created the optical illusion it wasn't moving at all. A sound, like a thrum of electrified metal, started amping up. The airspace around the device started vibrating. Zedyn Trill looked like a blur to those outside the affected area. It was as if reality was bending inside the field emitted by the device, spinning the atoms of the air as fast as the whirl of the transmitter itself.

Everyone outside the affected area was enthralled by the unfolding events. Though they were out of range of the device each of them could feel a slight flush of nausea at the sight. For a full minute, Commander Trill sat there motionless, reality bending around him. It seemed like an eternity to those watching. Suddenly, the device began to slow. The field around the device began to warble then dissipate. Finally, the device clicked off, the metal arm retracting back into the chamber as the hum faded away. Trill continued to just stand there, unmoving.

Once the device had completely stopped, Zarena walked over and faced him head on. His eyes were open and his mouth was agape, a small bit of drool dripping from his mouth. She took a small flashlight out of her pocket and shone it directly in his eyes. His pupils were dilated and they showed no signs of responding to the stimuli. She thought that his mind might have broken, that overwriting The Harmony had somehow shut down the functional centers of his brain.

He began coughing, his eyes snapping back into focus, like his whole body was rebooted from an emergency shutoff. He shook his head, like he was trying to shake the ringing out of his ear. He turned around quickly, looking around at everyone assembled. His face had a look of confusion and had taken on a slightly haggard appearance. His brow was pinched with concern. "Ah, ahem, what just happened?" His voice sounded normal but raspy, the sloppy smile on his face from minutes ago was gone. He stretched his neck from side to side.

Andros approached him cautiously.

"How are you feeling, Commander?"

"I feel just fine, sire," he said in a loud, crisp voice. "A little disoriented."

"Take your time, Commander."

"I'll feel okay, sire. I feel Iike myself." As he said the words, he bent over with nausea and vomited bile onto the ground. He coughed as he wiped the discharge away from his mouth. He straightened himself up.

"Deepest apologies, my lord," he said in an embarrassed tone.

Andros stepped back and motioned for Zarena to do the same. He motioned to a guard off to his left, who brought him a long wooden stick. he guard handed the stick to the soldier, who grasped it tightly and clicked the bottom of it on the floor in a type of acknowledgement. "Never mind all that, Commander," said Andros. "Please, perform a weapons drill for us."

Commander Zedyn Trill took the stick in both hands and began to twirl it, spinning it between each arm, then around behind his back, occasionally tapping the floor as he did so. It was a furious display of speed and coordination that would have taken him years to perfect. After a flurry of thrusts and lunges, he stood at attention, pounding the floor with the heel of the stick to signal that the drill was done.

"Wow," said Zarena. "That was very impressive."

"What do you remember from the past few months, Commander?

"Apologies, sire. I'm not sure I understand?"

"Do you feel any different right now than you did yesterday?"

"No, sire. I don't know how to describe it." He stopped for a minute and contemplated. "I do feel… maybe heavier today? That's not quite the right word." His brow furrowed as he struggled to explain.

"Take your time," reassured Andros. "Try to describe it for us as best you can."

"This morning I vaguely remember feeling calm. Lighter, somehow. More at ease. Now, I feel a little nervous, sire. I don't really remember the last time I felt nervous."

Andros patted the young man on the shoulder. "Good work, Commander. Please report to Madame Denamonte after the meeting is adjourned. She will be conducting some follow up tests."

Commander Trill abruptly stood at attention and saluted Andros. He then stepped aside, waiting for the meeting to conclude. Andros spread his arms towards the congregation. "My friends, we have done it."

A cheer erupted from the small group. It felt like a collective sigh of relief. Zarena bowed to Andros and he returned the gesture. Twila slid over to Andros' side, slipping an arm around his waist and kissing him on the cheek. Therus stood there like a statue but a broad smile streaked across his face. Zarena and Jax nodded to each other, Jax throwing in a wink that Zarena wasn't quite sure was purely celebratory. Emerald and Evard, who had been holding hands through the deprogramming demonstration turned to each other and kissed on the lips. They made eye contact with Zarena afterward and she flashed them a wink and a grin, as Emerald squeezed Evard's hand and put her head on his shoulder. Andros gestured to a servant to come and clean the vomit off of the floor.

After a bit of happy celebration, Jaxxon asked Andros, "Baron Carchel, now that the test was successful what is the plan?"

"In a perfect universe, Mr. Rill, we would have time to properly test this device. We are dealing with a new science here. Despite being the progenitor of that science, I'm not sure even Madame Denamonte knows what to expect in the long term. There could be side effects and other such complications. Unfortunately, we do not have the luxury of time to find out. The Imperium will be upon us soon. Our reports say that their ships have already entered the FTL tunnels between here and Archlon."

Commander Trill was getting up to speed. He said, "We should immediately use the device on all personnel slated for orbital deployment."

"Yes, Commander. We need to prepare our ships for intercept," agreed Andros.

"Furthermore," continued Trill, "We will still need to prepare our troops for a possible ground assault. We don't want the enemy to surprise us on the surface when our troops are still under The Harmony's influence." Trill's voice seemed tinged with sadness. "Their minds are very peaceful now. I know what that is like. Unfortunately for them, war is ugly. They need to remember that. The time has come for them to remember. Like most things in life, peace is short lived."

Evard blurted out the question that everyone was trying to restrain themselves from asking. "Commander Trill? Are you happy you were de-Harmonized?"

Trill looked at Evard more kindly than any of them expected given the unintentional rudeness of the question. "Son, The Harmony was every bit as peaceful as you've been told it is. Unfortunately for us, we don't live in a universe that's meant for peace."

He squeezed his hands together, almost like he was squeezing juice out of a fruit. He turned his palms around and looked at them inquisitively. "Being Harmonized is like living in a dream. It's a beautiful dream but a part of you knows that it's not real. Now is the time for reality. It's time for us to wake up."

CHAPTER 40

The Universe Is A Dangerous Place

The dimly lit chamber thrummed with an unsettling energy, the air thick with the metallic scent of blood and the faint hum of machinery. Shadows danced across the walls, flickering like the last gasps of a dying star. Jesper stood at the center of the room, a figure cloaked in darkness, his silhouette sharp and menacing against the cold, sterile backdrop.

Suspended from the ceiling by his ankles, the spy dangled helplessly, his body swaying slightly with the movement of the air. Jesper had taken great care in his preparations, ensuring that the man was strung up just so—his arms bound tightly, the pressure on his joints a constant reminder of his vulnerability. The spy's face was pale, a sheen of sweat glistening on his brow, but his eyes burned with a defiance that Jesper found both amusing and encouraging. Everyone has their breaking point, after all.

Jesper approached, his footsteps silent as he moved closer. He wore a surgical mask, the only hint of his true intentions hidden beneath its sterile facade. In one hand, he held a sleek instrument, its blade glinting ominously in the low light. The spy's breath quickened, a staccato rhythm of fear that echoed in the chamber.

"Do you know why you're here?" Jesper asked, his voice smooth and cold, like the steel of his weapon. He patted the man's forehead with his open palm, gently, the way a pet owner might pet a dog.

Leaning down, he spoke in a casual tone, as if he was speaking to a friend over brunch. "Carchel is a traitorous mutt. I've allowed you to send your communiques up until now, but feeding them information is no longer useful to me." Jesper looked at the blade in his hand and turned it over slowly, as if performing a careful inspection.

"It's regrettable that he ever involved you. I truly wished for a different outcome. If only we had Harmonized you, instead of placing our trust in one so easily bought. Alas, there are now things I need to know. I'm sure you understand."

The hanging man spat defiantly, a thin stream of saliva that landed on Jesper's boot. "I'll never tell you anything," he hissed, his voice hoarse but resolute.

Jesper chuckled, a low, menacing sound that reverberated off the walls. "Ah, but that's where you're mistaken." He leaned in closer, the blade gliding effortlessly across the spy's skin, tracing a seeping line of crimson that blossomed like a dark flower. "You see, I have a talent for persuasion. To be fair, it's not my only talent, but it is the one you will be acquainted with today."

With each precise incision, Jesper revealed his expertise, a cruel artist crafting a masterpiece of agony. The spy writhed in his suspended state, gasping at the pain as his nerve endings exploded.

Jesper remained focused, his movements deliberate and unhurried. His expression was blank and unreadable. He did not seem to take pleasure in the process, he was simply a craftsman committed to a trade.

"Let's start with something simple," Jesper said, his voice a whisper now, intimate and chilling. "Why did Carchel ask you to spy on the Imperium?"

The spy's eyes widened, the defiance faltering as the pain intensified. "I won't…"

Jesper pressed the blade deeper, eliciting a strangled cry. "You will. And if you don't, I'll make sure you wish you had."

Minutes stretched into an eternity as Jesper continued his work, the spy's body becoming a canvas of suffering. Each revelation was met with a new torment, a twisted game of cat and mouse where Jesper held all the cards.

Finally, the man began to speak through ragged breaths, spurting out words in short clips, the pain of speaking evident in the rasping sound of his voice. Afterward, the confession hung heavy in the air. Jesper paused, a satisfied smile creeping across his stoic face. He had what he needed.

"Good," he said, stepping back to admire his handiwork. The spy hung limply, his spirit broken, the fire in his eyes extinguished. Jesper's gaze hardened as he prepared to burn another thread in the tapestry. The spy was a mere pawn in a dangerous game, depths of which he couldn't possibly fathom, nothing more.

Jesper smiled ruefully, as if all the pain he caused had made him sad. He placed another hand on the man's face, cradling it gently with what could almost pass as compassion. "Unfortunately for you, the universe is a dangerous place, with so many routinely crushed under its boot."

With a swift motion, he severed the bindings, allowing the spy to crumple to the ground like discarded refuse. Jesper turned away, the thrill of the hunt was over, it was time to get back to work. In this world of shadows and secrets, he was the predator, and the Empire would remain safe, at least for another day.

As he exited the chamber, the door slid shut behind him with a finality that echoed through the silence, leaving the broken spy to bleed out in the darkness, a reminder that even in this new dawn, betrayal will not be tolerated.

CHAPTER 41
Dangling Threads of Fate

The Imperial cruiser, The Dawn Sky, illustrious flagship of the Imperium, had engaged its hyperdrive and was sailing smoothly through the shimmering FTL tunnel. When it emerged from hyperspace, they would be orbiting above Esper, a bleak little orb on the far side of the galaxy from where they had departed on Archlon.

Flanking The Dawn Sky was an armada of ships—bulky starships with devastating beam cannons, and nimble space fighters with searing laz weapons designed for close-range firefights. Three lumbering transports also accompanied them, each ferrying the un-Harmonized Battalions. The full might of the Imperium had converged on this inconsequential speck at the fringes of the known universe.

Overkill, mused Jesper. *But sometimes it's best to bare your fangs early.*

He was impressed by the Baron's gall. Carchel was no lily-livered lord of the formerly Great Houses. He had backbone. Since he had avoided the Harmony, their game remained fascinating. Jesper allowed certain intelligence to filter back to Carchel, so he would grasp the scale of the forces amassed against him. However, Jesper kept certain surprises up his sleeve.

He thought about the interrogation with Carchel's spy. *The man took a bit to break but in the end I got what was needed.* He always did. His other sources confirmed the spy's admissions were likely factual. Carchel had no inkling of what to make of his arrival.

The path ahead was clear, Jesper mused. *Well, mostly clear.*

He chuckled to himself. Rakeus had covertly ordered the assassination of the remaining Councilors. Earham had squealed like a stuck pig when stabbed in the gut. Elias had soiled himself while being garroted in his bedchamber. Only Artis had evaded death. Always more cunning than he let on, Artis grew suspicious of the Emperor's motives early on. After Kaia's corpse was discovered, he paid mercenaries to smuggle him from the Mark. Now he was hiding in some safehouse in Kadzer before being shuffled to parts unknown.

It would be child's play to tie off that loose end, Jesper thought.

Though no fool, Artis was no mastermind either. Once Jesper turned his focus to the hunt, he would uncover the man's location within a day. Nowhere in the Imperium would remain safe for him. Jesper relished the notion that Artis might begin to feel secure, convinced he had truly escaped. He had not. The Councilors had all beenRakeus' sheep, even Kaia at times. Only Zarena consistently displayed any true autonomy. The events of recent months had proven that beyond any doubt.

Jesper reclined in a private lounge, resting his elbow on the velvet couch arm as he snacked on fruit slices cut with a hidden pocket knife.

I don't expect a warm welcome on Esper, he mused. *No matter, they will agree to my offer once they comprehend it.* A sly grin split his lips. *We shall see,* he thought. His mind turned over the intricacies of his machinations, scrutinizing every angle. A knock at the door disturbed his ruminations.

"Jesper," sang a lovely voice. "You wanted to see me."

"Come in, please," he said courteously.

The door swept open and in glided Raeka Karmarch, Princess and heir to the Imperial throne of House Karmarch. The same vacuous smile she wore after The Harmony still clung to her face—

the smile that had sent Zarena into hysterics. *A smile that toppled an Empire*, he thought with wonderment.

She was adorned regally, wearing the thin silver crown studded with gems she had worn on her last diplomatic mission when Zarena awaited her arrival. A lustrous gold dress trimmed in silver draped her frame, and a brooch emblazoned with the crest of House Karmarch was pinned to her lapel.

She looks every inch the Empress, Jesper mused.

Still smiling dreamily, she settled into a chair opposite him. He leaned forward gently.

"Thank you for coming, Princess."

"Please Jesper, I've asked you not to call me that in private," she said, slow and even.

"Of course, Raeka. My apologies."

Though still wearing the placid Harmonized smile, she responded more astutely than he expected. "I'm sure that won't be your last apology. Quite a mess you've made here."

Unfazed, Jesper said conspiratorially, "Yes, it is, Raeka. We've nearly reached the climax of our game. Are you ready?"

"I am ready."

"Are you certain? Once we make landfall on Esper, there's no turning back."

"I am certain," she declared, steel behind her languid words.

"Good," he said, reclining once more. "Zarena will be surprised, I imagine."

"I know. I look forward to seeing her."

"After she frees your mind, you may feel anger toward her. But it would be wise to remember the dire lengths she went for you. She was willing to die. She almost did, repeatedly. Her love for you has shaken the universe itself." Jesper spoke with earnest conviction. He meant every word, devoid of irony or sarcasm.

In her Harmonized state, Raeka found herself highly attuned to empathy. She could now tell if he was lying. It was a gift he desired with envy, despite his own uncanny abilities. He was not lying. Raeka just kept smiling serenely.

After a time, she murmured, "When this ends, I will try to remember that."

Raeka and Jesper sat in prolonged silence. He plucked a slice of fruit from his lap and held it up. She gave a small nod and accepted it from his hand. After eating, she pinned him with an unnervingly direct stare. "Why do you care about Zarena?" she asked.

"I don't," he stated plainly. "It's not Zarena I'm concerned with. I only care about one thing, Raeka. One person."

"I know."

She rose and gave a formal curtsey which he acknowledged by bowing his head. As the door closed behind her, leaving Jesper to contemplate the events ahead, she glided away down the hall.

The armada emerged from the FTL tunnel, scattering ships across the endless void as they slowed over expansive distances. The ocean world of Esper loomed ahead, cerulean pinpoint in a sea of stars. Nested in orbit, the modest fleet of Carchel awaited, larger than expected for such a remote planet but still outmatched by the Emperor's imposing navy. Blood would flow freely once battle commenced. Jesper remained undaunted, simply eager to reach the surface before hostilities erupted.

As the fleet neared the Baron's blockade, the Carchel command ship hailed them.

"This is Commander Trill of House Carchel. State your purpose."

On the bridge of The Dawn Sky, Jesper gazed at the Carchel ships hovering around Esper like hornets guarding their nest. He tapped the comm, opening the channel.

"This is Jesper Manderlay, Servant of the One True Emperor and Appointed Imperial Ambassador. I've come to parley with Baron Andros Carchel about a matter of utmost importance."

Trill's wary voice replied, "You've brought quite an armada just for a chat, Ambassador."

Jesper smiled. He liked this Trill already. "Indeed, Commander. My orders are to obliterate you and your world for harboring Imperial fugitives and contraband. But I've convinced the Emperor to authorize negotiations instead. I seek safe passage to Fasmouth Keep and an audience with the Baron and Councilor Zarena Denamonte. A small protective contingent will accompany me planetside. Once concluded, we will depart and you will remain unmolested, pending the outcome."

A pause. "We will allow you to land, Ambassador, but you must submit to scans and come alone."

"Very well, no guards," Jesper conceded smoothly. "But I will require a single companion."

"Alone or no agreement."

Jesper smirked. "You drive a hard bargain, Commander. But I must insist on a guest. I assure you, the Baron and Councilor will be most pleased to see her. Shall we proceed, or would you prefer we skip the pleasantries and commence hostilities?"

A tense silence, then, "Who is this guest?"

"Why, Princess Raeka, of course."

Stunned silence greeted this revelation. Jesper wondered if the channel had been cut when Zarena's clipped tones sounded.

"Jesper. This is Zarena Denamonte."

"Madame Denamonte! My apologies, you're no longer a Councilor. Still, your reputation demands respect. Greetings."

Zarena's icy response left no doubt of her sentiments. "Raeka is with you, Jesper?"

"Yes, Madame."

"Let me speak with her."

Jesper grinned a wolfish grin, you could hear it in his words. "By all means. Here she is."

That was her cue. Raeka moved slowly toward the comm station. "Hello, Zarena," she said softly.

"Raeka? Is it truly you?"

"Yes, it's me."

"Prove it. Tell me something only we would know."

Raeka pondered, then spoke slowly. "The night before The Harmony. I told you not to blame yourself, remember?"

A shocked pause. "It is you, Rae..."

Jesper interjected. "As you can hear, the Princess is indeed with me. She will be accompanying me planetside, if your Baron consents."

"Wait, what—"

"All will become clear, I assure you. First grant us safe passage to Fasmouth."

Another silence, then Trill responded. "You have safe passage, Ambassador—you and the Princess. We'll transmit coordinates shortly."

"Splendid," Jesper said warmly. "I look forward to our visit."

He closed the channel and turned to Raeka. "Ready?"

She nodded. "Yes."

"Then let us be off."

CHAPTER 42
A Sign of Good Faith

Jesper's sleek starship glided into the familiar landing port outside of Fasmouth where Zarena had touched down what felt like eons ago. The Baron had dispatched a squadron to intercept them upon arrival.

The stern-faced Carchel guards, freshly restored to their former glories, scanned for any contraband that could pose a threat. Jesper looked at their scorned faces and smiled, for he knew what that meant: the scans showed nothing amiss. The hover tram whisked them along the coast, past the quaint fishing villages and up the craggy path to the imposing gates of the great keep. Heavily armed sentries flanked the route inside Fasmouth to the inner stronghold.

Once inside, Jesper guided Raeka's delicate hand as they ascended the weathered steps, flanked by a phalanx of militia whose wary eyes stalked their every movement. The towering doors creaked open and they were briskly escorted into the cavernous throne room.

Andros and Zarena stood sentinel before the throne, encircled by a ring of mail-clad guards. Jax lingered off to the side, coiled tight as a spring. Emerald and Evard had humbly asked permission to attend. They hovered apprehensively behind Jax, as if he could shield them from the sinister ploy Jesper had surely devised.

All eyes bored into Jesper and Raeka as they crossed the endless throne room at a measured pace. Zarena couldn't peel her eyes from Raeka, who glided forward serenely, ignoring the sea of prying eyes as if she were alone in a moonlit meadow. They halted several paces before the Baron. Jesper and Raeka bowed with courtly grace.

"Greetings, Baron Carchel. It has been too long."

"Greetings, Ambassadors," Andros replied dryly.

"It's unfortunate to reunite under such troubling circumstances. We have much to discuss and time, I fear, is scarce. Might we retire to somewhere more private?"

Andros, thinly disguising his distaste, responded as cordially as he could muster. "Yes, we have a meeting room just down the hall."

"Excellent," said Jesper.

Before anyone could react, Zarena interjected. "Hi Rae. It's wonderful to see you."

Raeka turned to Zarena, her face alight with a radiant smile. "It's wonderful to see you, too, Zee. I've missed you these long months."

"There will be ample time for catching up afterwards," Andros cut in brusquely. "First, say what you've come here to say."

Jax was boring into Jesper with a molten glare, barely bottling his all-consuming fury. Jesper noticed him out of the corner of his eye. Andros motioned for them to proceed to the meeting room, but Jesper suddenly slid the other way, so swiftly all the guards instantly trained their weapons on him. Andros waved them down. Jesper approached Jax and stood toe to toe. He peeked around Jaxxon's imposing frame to see a petrified Emerald and Evard.

"You must be Emerald Seltz. Lovely to finally meet you. Your eyes are truly mesmerizing." He bowed with courtly flair, disarming her unease. He turned to Evard. "And you are Evard Roost. I'm deeply sorry for your recent losses." He bowed solemnly.

Then he regarded Jaxxon, who was oozing vitriol. "You must be Jaxxon Rill," Jesper remarked casually.

Jaxxon said nothing, just continued his smoldering glare, his hand hovering near his holster.

Andros saw the situation escalating. "Please, this way Ambassadors."

Ignoring him, Jesper met Jax's fiery stare. "I understand Kaia Dorsetta was your aunt." Jax stiffened at her name. He was about to grab his gun when Jesper said gently, "Whatever you've heard, I am truly sorry."

"You killed her!" Jax spat. His face had begun to turn red as an apple.

"Yes, and many more besides," Jesper replied evenly, regarding Jax like an opponent in a gentleman's duel. Jax's face contorted in fury.

Jesper spoke calmly, with a touch of empathy, as if he was a caring father consoling his child. "I know you crave vengeance. There will be justice in time. But for now, the needs of the Imperium transcend you and I."

He stepped back and bowed deeply again, as if to an Emperor. He regarded Emerald and Evard, frozen like statues, their faces bloodless. "A sincere pleasure to meet you all." He turned briskly. "Princess, let us accompany the Baron."

Raeka just kept smiling benevolently. If she noticed Zarena's penetrating stare, she didn't show it. The four of them proceeded down the hall.

Andros led them to the same chamber where he and Zarena had brokered their own armistice months ago. "Please, sit. I'll have some refreshments sent in."

They settled in, Zarena and Andros on one side, their esteemed guests on the opposite. A pitcher of ale and a lavish charcuterie board arrived. Andros sampled a morsel then sipped his ale, signaling the fare was safe.

Jesper raised his glass. "May we together find the peace our times require."

Raeka raised her own glass, then Andros and Zarena cautiously followed suit. They drank the solemn toast.

Andros dove right in. "It's hard to envision peace with your armada looming overhead, Lord Manderlay."

"I understand your unease. Please, call me Jesper."

Andros eyed him silently for a moment. "You arrive with enough power to raze an entire system. You insist on this face-to-face. You bring the Imperial Princess. I cannot fathom your aim..."

Zarena erupted impatiently, "Just tell us why you're here!"

Jesper just smiled placidly. "What do you mean?"

"We're all friends here, Jesper," she said, with malice in her voice. "So why help me just to try to kill me later? Why have Kaia aid me only to then kill her? Why..."

"Zarena," Jesper silenced her with a commanding tone she'd never heard. She stopped short, startled. "You have many questions. I won't answer them all. I've come to discuss three critical matters. Two involve secrets I will share."

Andros and Zarena exchanged puzzled glances as Raeka sat smiling vaguely.

"Very well. These secrets better be worthwhile."

Jesper nodded in acquiescence. "The first secret — you must be wondering how I've tracked you so closely. It probably seemed like I was almost in your mind." He chuckled uncomfortably. "In a way, I was."

Zarena looked incredulous. "You were in my head?"

"Not precisely. But I've been privy to your conversations and actions since you left Archlon. Before you departed, I implanted nanotechnology in you that you ingested. Interestingly, it was created by Raxeon — Emerald's employer — though without her knowledge. The groundwork was laid years ago. The Emperor wanted to crush enemy espionage, to control the flow of all information. He paid fortunes to develop this theoretical tech. What Raxeon created exceeds expectations. The nanobots integrate with your DNA, syncing your physiology to a network. We can pinpoint your location, monitor vitals, and occasionally overhear your conversations remotely. So in a way, I was inside your head."

Andros and Zarena's jaws almost dropped all the way to the table. They couldn't hide the look of sheer surprise on their faces. Jesper enjoyed watching it settle over them, the reality that he has known everything they have known since the beginning. When the tension had reached its summit he slipped his hand into his pocket. He pulled out a small wooden box and slid it across the table to Zarena.

Confused, she opened it up to find two small black capsules that looked like pill casings for medication. "What is this?" she asked.

"It's an antidote for what ails you. You should take them with two glasses of water. Take the first pill, drink the water, and wait eight hours. Once eight hours have passed, take the second pill with water as well. It will permanently deactivate the secret spy in your body and the Imperium will no longer be able to follow your every move."

"But, but, w-why?" she stammered? "Why? Tell me! Why give this to me now?"

"We'll get there," he said. "For now, accept this as a sign of good faith."

"Wait just a minute, you slimy warlock. How did you even get that into me? When did you implant a nano device into my body? "Jesper looked over at Raeka, who continued to smile, and said, "That would best be explained later." He settled a bit in his chair before continuing.

"Wow," said Andros, having trouble hiding his astonishment. The implications here were staggering. "So you have known everything the whole time?"

"Yes and no. The tech is still imperfect. I was always able to track Zarena but I couldn't always get a clear sound recording. We couldn't hear everything. Though certainly we heard enough."

"How can I trust that this is what you say it is?" asked Zarena holding the box with the pills in her hand.

"What else would it be? If I meant to harm you, I would have killed you long ago, Zarena. I have given you the deactivation device. You are free to do with the pills as you wish."

Zarena looked at Andros, who was just staring at her confusedly, offering no counsel. She raised her eyebrows and said, "Alright then", swallowing the first pill and downing it with a mug of ale. After drinking the first whole one down, she asked Jesper, "Is ale okay?"

"All the better," he grinned.

She poured herself another mug and drank that all the way down as well. She wiped some of it from her mouth with the back of her hand. "Okay then. Done."

Jesper was openly amused. He didn't even attempt to conceal his good humor.

"So, you used top secret cutting edge technology in order to keep tabs on me. Very close tabs," summarized Zarena. "I'm impressed, Jesper. I knew you were devious but that is a truly deceitful move and an impressive one. I can only imagine how much blood you spilled for this kind of intrusion."

He shrugged lightly and made a face as if to say, *eh*. "Now then, the second piece of information I wish to share with you is one of the best kept secrets in the entire Imperium. Rakeus is my father."

"Get the fuck out of here!" shouted Andros.

Zarena burst out with an unintentional laugh. "Jesper," she giggled. "Really? You expect us to believe that?" Zarena looked at Raeka, who was now looking directly at her. "Rae, this can't be true? Right?"

"It is true, Zarena," Raeka said, slowly. "But I was surprised when he told me he planned on telling you."

Zarena was floored. Everything she thought she knew about Rakeus and Raeka and Jesper was upended in a moment. The shock was almost too much for her to handle. She stood up and began to pace back and forth behind Andros, like a lunatic raving in the moonlight of their cell.

"How?", she finally asked. "How is any of this possible?"

"When Rakeus was a young man he enjoyed shall we say, certain *sport*, at a particular brothel outside of Kadzer. This was before his father died, before he was Emperor, before he married Raeka's mother. There was a young courtesan there whose company he enjoyed the most. After a visit from him she found herself with child. She couldn't raise the boy herself so she sent him to an orphanage to be raised by strangers, but not before she sent word to the father in secret about the child.

"The child lived there until he was twelve. Then one day, a man from Kra Markhan came to visit. He took the boy out of the orphanage and set him up with foster parents who took care of him until he was sixteen. It was never explained to the boy why this had happened. Then one day, after his sixteenth birthday, a man came to visit the boy in secret. He wasn't just any man. He had just become the Emperor of the Known Universe. He told the boy who he really was. The boy was instructed to never ever tell a single soul. If he did that, if he kept that secret from everyone, he could join the Emperor's service, as his personal steward. His right hand.

"First, the boy was sent for an education. For years he trained on far away worlds. Trained in the art of combat, of diplomacy, of keeping secrets. He learned that influence was the true power of the universe. He learned how he could use this power to achieve great things. This continued and eventually this boy became dangerous. Very dangerous."

There was a glint in his eye that sent chills running down the spines of Andros and Zarena, for they both knew the truth of those words.

"Finally the boy returned a man. He began his service to the Emperor, as promised. But he had learned much about the universe during his education. The Emperor told him that his sole duty was to serve the Imperium. He was right and the boy believed him. He realized he could use his skills to help shape the destinies of people all over the galaxy. But the Emperor had made a mistake. You see, the Emperor had come to believe that he and the Imperium were one and the same. He never considered that an emperor's job was not to be the empire itself, but simply to serve it. It was beyond him to understand his own legacy was to keep the Imperium together so that his heirs may truly serve the people, instead of fretting over their own petty power. "So," he continued. "The man did everything the Emperor told him to do. He lied, he manipulated. He hurt people. He bathed the walls of clandestine lairs in blood. He pulled the strings of the Imperium behind the veil, helping the Emperor shape the universe in the process. He did everything that the Emperor had ever asked and as a result, he became respected, by some, and feared by most. The man did everything he was ever asked to do. Everything but one thing. He told someone who he really was. One person. Only one person, ever, before today. He told his sister."

He turned to Raeka who was smiling her Harmony smile. She grinned at Zarena. "It's true, Zee. When Jesper told me at first, I didn't believe him. Then I secretly had his story investigated. It was true."

"This *can't* be true," said Zarena, in utter bewilderment. The room fell silent. Zarena didn't know what to say next.

"OK, even if this is true, why didn't you tell me, Rae?"

"Because it wasn't my secret to tell. It was dangerous for anyone to know. You have only recently discovered what my father really is. I, on the other hand, have always known."

"Why are you telling us this now? It doesn't make any sense!" exclaimed Andros. "You come here with your *sister* to tell us this dark family secret while your armada hovers above us ready to blow us all to cinders!"

"Now for the last thing to discuss: a truth," said Jesper. "The Emperor wants your reversal device. He wants to use it as a weapon. The psychic connection that it creates among the Immune who are reverted back to their default states is very valuable. Imagine what an Emperor who is trying to control everything could do with something like that."

"So he sent you here to do what? Kill us all and steal it?"

"Yes", said Jesper.

Andros and Zarena began to panic. Andros stood up and guards came in, swarming into the room from just outside the door.

Jesper just sat patiently as the guards created a perimeter around them. They had their weapons drawn and pointed right at Jesper's head. Zarena also stood up, standing behind the guards and Andros, watching the event unfold.

"That's not what I'm going to do," Jesper said calmly. "Though I am pleased you were prepared for that. It would have been foolish of you not to be."

"We were prepared alright, you monster," spat Zarena. "We expected this to be a trap. There is more going on behind the scenes than even you may guess at. Nothing you can do here now will end with you stealing the device for that tyrant."

Jesper scanned around the room, taking in the guards and their guns. He looked at Andros. "Perhaps. Perhaps you could stop me. Perhaps not. Either way it makes little difference. I'm not here to kill you or to steal what's yours. I've come here to ask for your help." He turned to Raeka and said, "We both have."

Andros and Zarena had their hackles up. They were prepared for anything. Jesper and Raeka continued to sit there, as if nothing at all was happening around them. Jesper moved slowly, placing his hands on the table palms down. He made a motion with his eyebrows, suggesting that there was no danger here.

Zarena wasn't so sure she believed him.

"Fine," Andros said. "We will hear you out. The guards, however, will remain in position, for our protection. I'm sure you understand."

Jesper nodded politely. "Please, sit. Let's finish this conversation before one of your guards gets an itchy trigger finger."

Andros and Zarena sat back down with more than a little trepidation. Jesper on the other hand seemed as calm as a man enjoying a cup of tea with friends.

"Rakeus wants me to find a way to sneak the device back onto my flagship then he plans on murdering you and all of your people in a fiery halestorm."

"And how exactly did he expect you to accomplish that?"

Jesper mused for a moment. "I don't know. I just told him I had it handled. After a lifetime of following his orders without fail, he trusted me that I could." He thought for a moment. "I probably could, too. I have at least three possible ideas in mind."

The guards began to tense up, waiting for Andros to give them the sign to fire. Andros just remained calm and said. "Enough. If you don't want to steal it, what do you want?"

"Isn't it obvious, Baron? I want you to use the device on the princess."

Everyone was stunned into silence. Zarena reflexively looked at Raeka, who was looking at her pleasantly, as if they were discussing what to wear to a formal Imperial banquet. "Is this true, Rae? You want us to de-Harmonized you?"

Raeka didn't respond right away. She just smiled and sat there as if she hadn't heard Zarena's question. When Zarena had started to think she hadn't, Raeka spoke.

"I do now. I didn't before. This life is so… so peaceful. I've never been happier. But the difference between me and everyone else is that I know what happened. The peace is so warm. So serene. You think it's been there forever. It colors your every thought until you believe this is who you always were. But I remember what happened. What you and my father did. I know this peace is false. Still, I would choose to stay this way forever, if I could."

Zarena looked at her wistfully, tears beginning to well up in her eyes. "Why can't you, Rae? If you are truly happy maybe you should."

"I can't, Zarena. I can't rule, not like this. I never wanted to rule but now I will need to. Someone must succeed my father."

"So you're doing this so you can become the next Emperor, even though you never wanted that?"

Raeka thought hard on the question. It was difficult for her to articulate herself these days, such as she was. She took the time to put all the words together correctly.

"Yes, Zarena. I fear that is not something you can understand. You have only ever concerned yourself with what you could do, with what was possible. I love that about you, I always have. Maybe all of this was necessary. It probably was, but not the way that we did it. We lied to the universe, to protect ourselves. No more lies for us, Zarena."

Zarena felt like a dagger had pierced her heart. It felt as if she had been slapped right in the face.

"I know this is upsetting to you, though I do not remember how being upset feels. I just know that I have felt it before. It's easy to allow fate's threads to dangle when you don't feel pain any more. But Jesper has convinced me. My father's rule must come to an end, one way or the other. Afterwards, the Imperium will need a Karmarch to guide it."

Andros said, in almost a whisper, "So that's it."

"Yes," replied Jesper. "That is it. Rakeus wants me to steal your device and kill you all. If you help us, then I will help you survive. You will use your, what do you call it? Your *chaos device*, let's call it. Seems like an appropriate name, considering you plan to plunge the universe back into chaos. You will use this device to restore Princess Raeka to her former self. Then you will allow us safe passage back to our ship. In return, I will help you survive the war that is brewing above your heads. Meanwhile, I am happy to continue to leave the device in your care."

Andros said angrily, "So you want us to liberate the princess and then you'll turn your ships around and just go home?"

"No," said Jesper. "Perhaps I wasn't clear. Rakeus is intent on attacking regardless of the outcome. You will liberate the princess and in return, I will instruct you on how to keep your lives."

CHAPTER 43

The Time For War

Over an hour passed while Andros and Zarena met with Jesper and the Princess behind the imposing oak doors. When the doors finally creaked open, the foursome strode out purposefully, an unspoken understanding passing between them like a secret.

As they marched back to the cavernous throne room, their footsteps echoing off the cold stone walls, Jesper halted them.

"Baron," he said in a grave tone. "We must swiftly contact your Commander Trill and instruct him on the battle plans. He will require time to prepare your troops. Meanwhile, please have Zarena uphold her end of the pact."

"Fear not," assured Zarena, her voice steely with determination. "I have awaited this moment for far too long."

Jesper's tight smile did not reach his eyes as he nodded. He pivoted to address Andros. "Can you retrieve the secret weapon you mentioned? It may prove useful should the ground offensive become protracted." Then he added for good measure, "The naughty Carchels hiding illegal contraband and right beneath their very seat of power…"

"I shall retrieve the device myself, Twila will accompany me," affirmed Andros, ignoring Jesper's barb.

"Just ensure you do not accidentally trigger it and obliterate us all," Zarena said, acidly.

"Everything will be fine," Andros replied with false bravado.

"It is time to act," declared Jesper, decisively with a nod.

Andros regarded Raeka and then Zarena. "This is the moment you have desired. Who could have foreseen it would be Jesper delivering it?"

"I will escort her from here. When it is finished, we will find you," Zarena said with quiet authority. She nodded to Jesper, who gestured for Raeka to accompany her. Zarena led Raeka down the dimly lit stone corridors to the laboratory, their footfalls echoing in the silence between them. She retrieved the chaos device from its secure containment chest and hauled it to the center of the room, muscles straining under its substantial weight.

"Please stand here," she directed, indicating a spot on the floor near the imposing device. Zarena began configuring the machine to administer a single, concentrated dose. It had required extensive modifications to prime it for a lone target after they had spent days un-Harmonizing House Carchel's army.

Once prepared, she stepped away. "The room is shielded. I must exit before the device activates. Remain still. It is painless, I assure you. A full dose takes approximately one minute."

Raeka's smile was serene as she nodded in acquiescence. Zarena headed for the heavy door but paused as she pulled it open. "Are you certain this is what you want?"

"It is not a matter of desire, Zee, but necessity," Raeka replied calmly.

Zarena dipped her head ruefully and stepped outside, securing the door behind her. The machine whirred to life, its central arm spinning at blinding speed as it had when they had freed Trill. Zarena scrutinized the procedure unfolding before Raeka, who stood as motionless as a statue. When it was finished and the device powered down, Zarena re-entered the room.

Raeka remained frozen, as if entranced. Then, like Trill, she began shaking her head vigorously, casting off the last clinging cobwebs of Harmony's influence.

In a breathless voice she exclaimed, "That was far more intense than I anticipated! I must sit down a moment."

Zarena hurriedly brought a chair over and Raeka collapsed into it, clearly drained by the ordeal. Zarena pulled up another chair to sit nearby as Rae recovered from the taxing process. They sat wordlessly as Raeka's mind re-knit itself, her thoughts crystallizing once more.

After some minutes passed Zarena asked gently, "Are you well, Rae?"

Raeka's gaze was penetrating, her eyes narrowed and hard. "Yes, I am fine now. It is like waking from a peaceful dream. You can recall the tranquility, yet cannot grasp it any longer. The peace vanishes when the dream ends."

Zarena felt a swell of emotions rising to overwhelm her. She leapt up and rushed forward, grasping Raeka fiercely as she too rose to meet her embrace. They clung to each other as tears spilled down both their cheeks. They hugged with such fervor it left them breathless. Raeka pulled back, laughing so hard it dissolved into coughing. Zarena laughed through her tears, wiping her eyes. They collapsed back into their chairs, emotionally and physically spent.

"I missed you desperately," confessed Zarena.

"I know, Zee. And I you, in my own way. I can only now remember the full depth of it, with my mind unshackled."

"I am sorry, Rae. So deeply sorry, for everything. I know you said it was not my doing, but it was. I never should have..." She broke down sobbing, covering her face in shame.

Raeka gently squeezed her shoulder. "No, Zee. You bear no blame. You did as commanded, believing it righteous. The Emperor himself charged you. Had I wished to stop it, I would have spoken up. There was no turning away from the course we were on. You fulfilled your duty as Chief Scientist and Imperial Councilor."

"No, Rae, I failed completely. The Harmony should never have been created, that power should never have been given to Rakeus," lamented Zarena.

"Come now, Zee. The Sequence still endangers all humanity. You halted it the only way possible. And now," she smiled tenderly, "you have unlocked something wondrous. The Harmony saved mankind, by subjugating it, so you could uncover the means to truly heal us. The chaos device does not just restore wholeness, but connects us too. You have unified humankind, into the single radiant entity we were meant to be."

Zarena felt the heavy weight inside her lift away. She had completed her mission after all. Whatever came next, she had saved her dearest friend.

"Rae, this cannot wait. I must know."

"Jesper," Raeka interjected. "Yes, I'm sure you have many questions. But first, how are you handling Andros? He seems cozy with his new partner. She's a Esperlin, how exotic." Raeka smiled a rosy smile as the words touched her lips. "Andros is more or less the same," Zarena replied. "Twila is quite lovely, actually. It was a long time ago, Rae, and much has happened since," she said, impatient to return the conversation back to more pertinent matters.

"So, Jesper," the name hanging in the air like the scent of pungent cheese. "Why did you never tell me? All those years, all those conversations about him, yet you never trusted me with the truth?" "I only learned recently, just before The Harmony plan was approved by the Councilor. Jesper was worried about the Emperor's designs, what The Harmony could mean. He came to me one night and confessed everything. He wanted me to know, before it all changed."

"I see. So you didn't say anything to keep me safe. And I never imagined your father capable of such cruelty. There is something else..."

"The nanotech," finished Raeka. "Yes. You wonder how it entered your body? It was in the whiskey you drank the night Jesper waited for you in your quarters." Zarena looked at her for a moment, puzzled. "But Jesper also had a glass, if I recall."

"Yes, but it was already coded to your DNA. It had no effect on him. He had asked me to dose you myself during our dinner together that final night. Jesper vowed he would use it to aid you. He said the coming tempest could divide the Imperium. I tasked him with protecting you, for me. But I couldn't do that to you, Zee. I didn't want to taint our last real night together. So he did it his way."

Zarena regarded her, anguish etched on her face.

"I know this pains you. But I did it out of love, as you created The Harmony to secretly help others," implored Raeka. "Our lies, our little omissions — they stem from love. My love for you surpasses all others."

Zarena managed a sad smile.

"I had resolved to undergo Harmonization long before that night," continued Raeka. "No one else knew — not you, Jesper, my father. I knew if things worsened I could not shield you, once changed. I allowed Jesper to deceive you, and in the end are we not better for it?"

Zarena returned an icy stare, one that Raeka didn't acknowledge. "I understand. All of this betrayal and scheming still hurts, deeply. I'm sorry I didn't see another way. But as ranking members of the Imperium, our duties don't always align with our desires," finished Raeka.

"My love for you ran so deep, Rae. It still does. But all of this would have been better if you told me."

"Perhaps, perhaps not. I fear we would all have been in more danger."

"More danger than this?" exclaimed Zarena. "We're about to be bombarded into oblivion by your father."

Raeka looked at Zarena patiently, as if she expected these objections. "You were always going to end up here, Zee. It didn't matter what I did."

Raeka rose and went to Zarena, grasping her hand and drawing her up. They stood facing one another, Zarena towering over Raeka, their eyes brimming with a lifetime of love, joy, and sorrow. Raeka stretched up on her toes and kissed Zarena passionately, their hearts spilling over like an overflowing river. They clung together, suspending themselves in this one perfect moment before fate would inevitably turn against them once more.

Raeka pulled back slowly, licking the lingering taste of their kiss from her lips. "I have always loved you, Zee. I always will. Perhaps one day we can live in a universe where love is still possible. I hope beyond hope. But as Jesper and Andros said, war has come. There will be no peace, not for some time."

"And I love you, Rae. I have, I do, I will, forever. I will do whatever you believe is right."

"Then what is needed now, my darling Zee, is to clear your mind of love and feelings. Now is the time for war."

CHAPTER 44
We're All Going To Die

By the time Zarena and the newly restored Raeka made it to the War Room, the meeting was already well under way. Everyone was there — from Andros and the twins, to Zarena's team of Emerald, Evard and Jax. Jaxxon's mercenary team was also there, along with a host of other military personnel that Zarena didn't recognize, all of them recently restored by the chaos device and ready for battle.

There was a giant holographic screen behind Jesper, with a positional overlay of all the ships above the planet as well as screens showing various fortification efforts around Fasmouth.

All of the local villages had been abandoned and their occupants, the good peoples of the fishing villages, were bunkered inside the walls to keep them safe from the burning and pillaging that would likely occur during a ground assault.

Jesper and Andros were in the middle of talking to Commander Trill, who was still stationed on the Carchel flagship, The Draconis, at the center of the fleet in orbit.

"...that will only ensure annihilation," said Jesper. "Only these ships carry planet-killers." He highlighted them in red on the screen. "The explosions from the neutrino arsenal will cause shockwaves that will disrupt the fleet but even so, you're still woefully outnumbered."

He pointed to the project with his finger and highlighted a series of ships in yellow.

"These are the transports carrying the ground assault teams. Going after the atomics is necessary but that will leave little firepower to disrupt their deployments. There may be disarray once the fighting begins that could be advantageous, but we will need to assume most of these ships will make it to the planet."

He looked at Andros, who could do little to hide the concern on his face. "Unfortunately, Baron, you don't have adequate anti-craft weaponry to stop them before they land. There isn't even a PGen field around the keep. We will have to expect a ground attack."

Andros then took command. He spoke to the entire audience, as well as the ships in orbit.

"We have moved all the civilians inside of Fasmouth. They will need to land their transports outside of the city, near the landing port and make their way over rocky terrain to the keep. We can funnel them here," he said, as he pointed to a map of the route from the landing port to the gates. "This will allow us to repel them for a while. Our troops are un-Harmonized, so they will fight better than any of the Harmonized Imperium soldiers, but we will be outnumbered probably two to — " "Three," interrupted Jesper "You'll be outnumbered *three* to one."

Andros continued, grimly but determined. "Those odds aren't favorable but we have the high ground and our un-Harmonized teams will fight much harder than the Emperor's. Still," he said, as he looked over the screen. "The chance of victory is stacked against us unless we can win the battle above. That's where you come in Commander Trill."

As Trill discussed the strategy for engaging the Imperial warships in orbit, Zarena caught Emerald out of the corner of her eye. It looked like she was concentrating on something, something that was taking all of her attention. She then noticed that Evard, who was standing next to her had the same look of consternation on his face. She realized in that moment that they were communicating telepathically. Zarena strode over to them quietly and slipped in between them. Startled, they both looked at her wide-eyed. She gave them a stern, frustrated look.

"Something on your minds?"

"Ah, no, no, it's nothing Zee," stuttered Emerald.

Evard blurted, "No it's not Em. It's something. You need to tell her."

"Tell me what?" asked Zarena.

Emerald sighed. "It's stupid. It'll never work. We're just trying to think of ways we can help."

"No idea is stupid at this point, Em. We're fighting for our lives. Jesper is right, we're outgunned here. There's a chance..." she drifted off before finishing her thought.

"I know, Zarena. I know we could die." Emerald's face pinched together like she had just sucked on a lemon. "Fine. No idea is stupid, right? Well, I had an idea."

Before she could explain, Evard blurted it out with an enthusiasm he could barely contain.

"We call for help!" he shouted, a little louder than he expected. A few of the officers in the room turned around and gave him an odd look.

"Help? Who could possibly help us?" asked Zarena. "I'm sorry, but we're all alone."

"No Zee. We're not. Ask the twins. Ask any of these officers here! Our ability to mindsnap. That's what Ev and I are calling it — when we connect telepathically. *Mindsnap.*" She coughed awkwardly to clear her throat. "Anyway, Evard and I are getting quite good with mindsnapping. We've connected with other Immune. Dozens of them. All over the galaxy..." She paused.

Zarena just glared at her, not saying a word.

"Don't be mad, Zee. Please," implored Emerald.

"I'm not mad, I just thought you would have mentioned it."

"Sorry, it's been so hectic and you've been busy. Anyway, we've connected with other Immune. Evard and I. Also, Therus. He has done it too."

"Get to the point, Em. Please." Zarena said, with a hint of frustration in her voice.

"Alright. Well... we've mindsnapped with lots of Immune, all over the Imperium. They were completely confused, like we were, about what had been going on. I mean, Zee, it's crazy. Most of them thought they were going crazy. Some of them thought they had died and this was a weird sort of afterlife with..." She could tell from the look on her face that Zarena didn't have time for details. "They want to help, Zee. We explained everything to them, the ones we connected with so far at least. The Harmony, the chaos device, the war — everything. We let them prod our thoughts. They want to fight. Some of them have been connecting with each other. Forming groups, trying to rally. It's like a whole army of Immune. They are trying to come here to help us. They want to save the chaos device, so we can free the people they care about."

Emerald abruptly stopped talking. Everyone in the room was looking at her and listening to her conversation with Zarena. She flushed with embarrassment.

No one said a word, everyone just stared at them for a moment.

Jesper smiled and said, "Miss Seltz. That is a brilliant idea. If any of your new Immune friends can get here before the fighting is done maybe more ships can turn the tide."

Andros looked at Twila. "Is this true, my love?"

Twilia smiled that sly and seductive smile that Zarena had seen her flash many times since they first met. "According to Therus, yes, it is possible, my love, but not likely. They are all scattered to the stars. Many of them are scared. I do not think we can rely on this."

Emerald stood up as straight as she could. She drew in a breath and spoke in a loud, commanding voice that seemed completely foreign coming out of her mouth.

"I know it's a long shot, but I think it's worth trying. Evard and I will try to recruit as many of the Immune as we can. Therus, if you can help us, we would appreciate it."

Therus bowed to her with a subtle smile. Inside her mind she heard him say 'yes, of course, Ms. Seltz. As my sister said, it may be a fool's errand but I will do whatever I can to aid you.'

Everyone noticed Emerald had gone quiet for a second as she was listening to Therus. When she snapped out of it, she said, "Therus is in." She grabbed Evard's hand and squeezed it tightly. "We'll start right away."

"It's settled then," Andros declared. "Our Immune allies will try to recruit others. We can't count on anything but it can't hurt."

As Andros continued the meeting, Evard tapped Zarena on the shoulder, a strange look on his face. "Can I talk to you for a second?"

"Sure, what's going on?"

"When I escaped Eden, before I met you and Emerald on Exalon, I had stowed away on a private starcruiser."

"I remember you telling us."

"The crew boss was nice. He helped me a lot. He was Harmonized, except, well except he wasn't fully." Zarena recalled Evard explaining this before back on Exalon. She waited for him to get to his point patiently. "He wasn't like us, you know, he wasn't normal but he wasn't full on Harmonized either. It's like it didn't fully take or something."

"Yes, I remember you telling me. I've thought about that. I think some of the Harmonized had some Immune characteristics but not enough to protect them, similar to the situation with Therus. They may act differently to us but also differently from the Harmonized."

"Yes, exactly. That's it. He wasn't entirely like us, but he was, I don't know, more of himself I guess then every other Harmonized person I met. Anyway, I talked to him, with my mind. Kinda."

"You what?"

"Yeah, it's weird right? I can't talk to him all the time. The mindsnap is fuzzy. Like he's speaking with marbles in his mouth or something. But I *can* talk to him, even if it doesn't always work. That's crazy, right?"

Zarena thought about this. It was an interesting development. "Maybe not, Ev. His brain may rest somewhere between a brain like mine and a brain like yours. Maybe it's similar enough to yours you can mindsnap him sometimes, but he's still enough like the rest of the Harmonized that it's a bad connection? I honestly don't know. This whole thing turned out much different than I expected". She sighed. This wasn't what she had imagined at all.

Evard looked around at all the people assembled. "I know Zee. Look around. No one expected this. Well maybe Rakeus. And Jesper," he said, throwing a furtive glance at Jesper, who was still talking to Andros and the rest of the officers. "The whole galaxy is different now. Maybe we should stop worrying about why and start worrying about how we are going to fix it."

"You're right. Anyway, I'm glad you could connect with your friend. I know he helped you." Evard was lost in thought for a moment, reliving his escape from Eden.

Emerald came up alongside him and gripped his hand. "When this is all over, if we survive the battle, promise me we can use the chaos device on Hal and Olaver and all the rest of them. They deserve to be free too."

"Of course, Ev. We are going to use it on everyone. Everyone who wants it. I promise."

As they spoke the briefing was coming to an end.

"Everyone is clear on the plan," said Andros to the room and the entire fleet. "I know we have never faced a threat like this, but bravery is in our blood. We have sailed the perilous seas for generations. We can handle one battle with the Emperor of the Known Universe.

"I want to thank you all for everything you have given and everything you have yet to give. I promise you, stick to the plan and we will win the day." He spoke over the silent, staring faces of all those assembled, his words echoing over the comms of dozens of ships about to engage in a celestial blood bath above. He looked sad, sadder than Zarena had ever seen him, but also resolute. He stood tall, his voice never wavering. This was the man she remembered. The man she had once loved a lifetime ago.

Andros fell silent for a moment. He looked his men in the eyes and a small smile began to touch his lips. Seeing the courage in the faces around him started to refill his own vigor. This was the time and he was ready. He spoke so loud, it was almost a scream.

"We will win this fucking fight! We will win! Be brave, fight hard, and remember, if I am killed, the stars as my witness, I will come back like a ghoul from a gravestone and haunt each and every one of you until you pray for death!"

The whole room erupted in a burst of laughter and applause. Andros grabbed Twila and kissed her deeply as the officers around them cheered. He pulled away, and continued in the same uplifting tone, "This is our planet! This is our home! We will send Rakeus and his armies into the void! We will free the universe of tyranny!"

As the cheers continued, Zarena caught the eye of Jax. He had spent most of the briefing off to the corner, watching Jesper with a stare that dripped with all the venom of a rattlesnake. He was standing behind the officers, near all of his merc buddies and he was looking Zarena's way. When their eyes met, he walked over and stood next to her. As the cheering continued he leaned in close and whispered something in her ear. Then he smiled and tilted his hat with his hand, before walking back to his crew.

Emerald, who had been watching the two of them, leaned over to Zarena with a mischievous grin on her face. "What was that about?" she smirked.

Zarena returned the look, a hint of sadness and fear behind her eyes.

"He said 'We're all going to die'."

"Oh. I thought, ah, I thought it was something else."

"It's just his way," Zarena said with a small laugh. "I guess we're all kind of nervous."

"Zarena? I heard what Evard asked you about his friends on the starcruiser. I want to ask you something too."

"Sure, Emerald. What is it?"

"If something happens to me, if I don't make it, promise me that one day you'll go back to Exalon and you'll free my mother and Jazz."

"I promise you, Emerald. If I survive this then I will find your mom and your friend and set them free."

"Thanks, Zee. I just… I just don't want to forget them, you know? I miss them."

Zarena looked over at Raeka, who was standing off to the side of the hologram screen behind where Jesper, Andros and the rest of the team were assembling. Raeka could feel her looking over and caught her eye. She smiled the loveliest of smiles back at Zarena who grinned and nodded to her in turn. Then Raeka went back to watching the briefing close. "I know. I miss people, too.""Everyone", Andros boomed. "We are a *go* in twenty minutes' time. Say what you need to say to each other and then get ready. The war begins now."

CHAPTER 45
The Skies Are Burning

The void of space was silent as the ships hovered in place above the planet of Esper. The Baron's forces were positioned in a phalanx formation, the smaller fighter crafts creating a perimeter around the larger weapon ships. Commander Trill stood upon the bridge of the capital ship, The Draconis. The Draconis floated in space, nestled among the armada of ships creating a barrier between the Imperial fleet and the planet itself.

From the command bridge on The Draconis, Trill could see the sheer size of the Imperial armada, silhouetted by an ocean of stars behind them. The bridge was a hexagonal room, with a captain's chair in the center and various terminal stations lining the walls. At the front of the room was a holoscreen with various intelligence data and live feeds broadcasting from the bow of the ship. The screen was filled with the giant starcruisers, battleships, and smaller fighters of the Imperial fleet. Their fleet had roughly the same composition as the Carchel fleet, only much, much larger.

It was cool on the bridge but Commander Trill felt damp, a bead of sweat dripping down his forehead. It was as if he was standing on the rocky shores below Fasmouth, the salt spray slicking his brow. He was awaiting the command from the Baron, steeling himself for the conflict to come. He'd never faced an enemy force of this magnitude before. As long as he had been the Warmaster of House Carchel, his men had mostly served to keep the peace, most of them militia recruited from the small muddy villages that littered the land masses of Esper.

The time for them all to prove their worth had come.

There was a small hiss of static and the Baron's voices echoed over the comms.

"Commander Trill. The time is upon us. Begin the assault and stick to the plan. Good luck and may fortune favor our efforts."

The comm went silent. There were several crewmen on the bridge stationed at various terminals. They all swiveled their chairs towards Trill, awaiting his order. He moved to the front of the bridge, standing between two of the weapon terminals manned by officers of the Draconis.

"Bring up the intel that Jesper provided us," he said. The crewman to his right, Crewman Rathbone clicked a few buttons on the terminal and the data appeared. "Overlay with current positions."

"Yes, sir," said the Crewman Rathbone.

He addressed the crew team and connected the comm so all the Carchel ships could hear him. "OK, the schematics should be visible on all of your command screens. As we discussed the ships in yellow are the ones carrying the neutrino weaponry. These are planet killers. Repeat, these are planet killers. If they are allowed a chance to fire from orbit, the surface will be reduced to ashes. The battle will be over. All of our homes, all of our lives, will be lost. Whatever happens those ships must be destroyed first.

"The fleet will focus all firepower on the targets. Once all, I repeat all, targets have been eliminated, all ships will focus on the transport carriers. We need to destroy as many of them as we can so that our forces on the planet stand a chance of repelling a ground assault." He took a deep breath. "We cannot fail. The fate of our planet and the dignity of our House, everything our people have built over a millennia, are put on the line today. You're not just fighting for me, or his lordship the Baron, you are fighting for your very lives, the lives of your families, and the lives of your friends. Today we make our stand.

"The first volley begins on my mark."

The bridge was as silent as the space around them, the only sound the light thrumming of their spatial stasis engines. Trill faced the holoscreen and closed his eyes.

"FIRE!"

Every ship in the Carchel fleet began a relentless volley of photon blasts, speeding through the negative space between the Carchel and Imperial fleets. As the first blasts connected, the planetary weapon ship at the front of the Imperial fleet began to take heavy fire. The ship began to set adrift, the stasis drives damaged as more fire rained across the void from the Baron's fleet.

The Imperium was clearly taken by surprise as several volleys blasted their way through the metal hulls of the lead Imperial vessels before the first return shots had even begun.

Trill screamed, "Again! Fire! Destroy those weapons!"

The blasts continued as the first weapon ship exploded, the vacuum of space absorbing the blast like smoke trapped in a jar. As the first Imperial weapon ship exploded, shockwaves began to emanate from the hull as the pressure created by the exploding weapons shook the ship apart. The shockwaves started rippling through the Imperial fleet as pandemonium ensued.

"Keep firing!"One by one, the Imperial targets exploded, scattering the ships in their vicinity, spreading the opponent fleet outward as they escaped the exploding dreadnoughts.

Trill looked at the screen. Almost all of the initial targets were neutralized.

"Keep firing! Keep firing!" "Sir," said a crewman, sitting at the navigation terminal. "The enemy is engaging us ship to ship."

"We have incoming!" The Imperial ships began to move forward, in a chain formation, bee-lining directly towards the heart of the Carchel fleet.

"Sir, they are coming straight at us. I think they are planning on suicide bombing our fighters."

Trill looked at the data report on the screen. "Oh no," he whispered, before shouting, "Fighters, form a blockade, they are heading straight at us!"

The small craft fighters engaged their engines and rushed to the forward position of the phalanx, firing at the ships torpedoing towards them.

"Stop them before they ram through our line!"

The Imperial fighters zipped forward, a line of ships trailing behind them, blasting the blockading ships with heavy fire. Fighters started exploding, falling out of space like pebbles dropping from the roof of a building. Several of them spun downward, losing flight controls, as they plummeted towards the atmosphere below. Many of the falling ships were heavily damaged and, upon hitting the oxygen rich atmosphere, burst into giant balls of flame.

"Cruisers, move into position! We're dropping fighters like flies!" yelled Trill. He watched as the cruisers with their mid-range weapons moved forward, positioning behind the blockade of fighter ships. He turned to the nav crewman. "Move The Draconis out of the line of contact. Bring us to the rear of the fleet."

The stasis engines began to hum as The Draconis lurched backward, zipping past the fleet as the balance of their ships rushed forward to join the fray. The firefight continued, as the line of fighters began to close on the blockade. A hail of fire sprayed across the blockaded line, as Esper fighters continued to drop out of orbit.

"Sir, the carriers are descending. They are making a run to the planet."

"All teams stay on those heavy weapon ships; we didn't get them all."

"Sir, the enemy is reforming their lines. They are creating a defensive perimeter around the remaining dreads."

"Shit. We need to get to them." Trill spoke to the fleet again. "Cruisers, rush the Imperial line until you can get a clear shot at the heavy weapon. They still have enough firepower to do some serious damage to the surface."

The cruisers started blasting forward, as if they were shot out of cannons. Several sped past The Draconis, jumping into the heart of the fight. Laser blasts whizzed past them as the sky was alight with laz fire. The Imperial dreadnoughts dropped below the battle line, turning their nose towards the planet.

"Sir, they are about to launch an orbit deep strike. What are your orders?"

"All available fighters from squadron beta, pull off the blockade and hard line after those weapon ships."

As a handful of fighters broke off from the pummeled vanguard, the dreadnoughts prepared to drop their first load of orbit-to-surface gravity bombs. They moved slowly along their trajectory but once they hit the atmosphere they dropped like lead balloons, capable of incinerating entire cities on impact. Of the three remaining dreads left, the first locked their systems onto Fasmouth and fired a giant arrow-shaped missile, the size of a small fighter, that zipped towards the Esperian skies as it locked onto its target.

Trill began to panic. If that missile makes it to impact? All of Fasmouth would be obliterated in an instant. He activated the comms and screamed, "Get those missiles! Shoot them out of orbit!" The smattering of fighters that had broken off to engage increased speed as they barreled towards the dreads.

One of the pilots came over the comm. "Sir, this is Squad Leader Farson. I will pursue the deployed bogey. The rest of the team will make haste to those dreads before the next payload drops."

Squad Leader Farson spun the fighter into a dovetail and accelerated at maximum speed. The missile tore through the emptiness of space on a mission to destroy their entire civilization.

"Farson," said Trill solemnly. "You have 20 seconds until it breaches the atmosphere."

There was silence on the other end. "Farson, do you copy?" asked Trill. Then the voice of Farson came over the comm lines, "Yes, sir. I'm here, sir."

"Soldier, ten seconds, let's move!"

"Sir, if we win, tell my family I'm sorry." The comm went dead. Trill watched on the holoscreen as Farson punched the fighter into maximum subliminal acceleration. Instead of trying to shoot the missile out of orbit his fighter was heading straight for it.

Five seconds left as he nosed dived out of battle and followed the calculated trajectory of the missile.

Three…

Two…

Just as the missile was about to enter the atmosphere, Farson's fighter flew straight into it on an intercepting path. As his fighter collided with the missile, it exploded in a gigantic burst of flame and smoke, which was sucked into the Esperian atmosphere.

The crew of the Draconis cheered as Trill took a deep breath and gripped his hands tight together. "That was a close call. Squad Leader Farson's sacrifice will be remembered." He composed himself quickly. "Now get those dreads."

As the remaining dreads were set to drop their payloads, four ships from Farson's squadron appeared, heading straight for the aft of the formation, firing repeated laz bolts in a frenzy of desperate fire. The bolts began connecting with the hull of the remaining dreads and they started to sputter, power systems going off line. They drifted there like sitting ducks, as the squadron flipped in a loop and reversed course for a second pass. The barrage of bolts penetrated the hull of the dread at the vanguard of the formation, blowing it to bits and sending shockwaves that killed all systems to the last to dreads. The force of the blast pushed the other dreads off of their trajectory where they were mowed down by a hail of fire from the cruisers that were engaged with the rest of the fleet above.

As the last dread was destroyed, the comms were alive with cheering.

"Phew," said Trill. "That was way too close." He activated the comm and spoke to all the ships still flying in his fleet. "Most of the carriers have dropped out of orbit. Scatter whatever you can so the ground teams have a chance. Cruisers, engage the carriers. Everyone else, let's focus on the fleet."

The cruisers began to nosedive as the last of the carriers started their planetary descent. They began firing sprays of laz bolts as they attempted to stall the progress of the carriers who had begun to pick up speed as they attempted to maneuver away from their pursuers. The cruisers were bearing down on the carriers as the upper atmosphere was alight with the dazzling colors of laz bolts being traded by both sides.

The rear carrier was hit with several direct shots and began to slow as their defenses failed. The cruisers coordinated their fire and blasted the last carrier from the rear as it exploded above the planet.

"There are two more in range, *don't let them drop!*" screamed Trill.

The cruisers sprung forward in hot pursuit. Their engines outclassed the speed of the slower moving carriers as they came in hot on their tails. The laz fire rained down, as the carriers tried to avoid the fire by banking left, then hitting their thrusts to speed off to the right. The Carchel fighters stayed glued to their asses as the Imperial carriers tried in vain to shake them off. Moments later, a second carrier was hit, flames bursting out of the side as they entered the atmosphere.

"Target that wounded duck!" yelled Commander Trill, as the carrier desperately tried to avoid further damage. After a few more direct hits the carrier exploded, fire and debris scattering into different directions. The fighters began to target the lead carrier, the last one yet to breach the ground level airspace. The fighters stayed in hot pursuit when an alert sounded.

"Sir, enemy fighters have begun chase. There are several coming in hot behind them."

Trill yelled into the comm. "Fighters, you got company, try to shake them."

The Esper fighters were pursued as they plunged through the upper atmosphere, enemy bogeys behind them laying down cover fire for the final transport. One of the Carchel fighters took a shot to their port side engine and it immediately began to malfunction, spinning the craft sideways as the crew desperately tried to regain control. It whirled around as it fell, crashing into a friendly fighter in formation behind it. Upon impact both fighters exploded in a burst of black smoke and billowing fire. Trill slammed the comm dash with his fist. "Dammit. All fighters pull back, the carrier is away. Regroup with the rest of the fleet."

"Sir, something is going on," said one of the crewmen. Trill turned to the screen and watched as the enemy fleet began to disengage. The larger ships hung back, far behind the invisible line of demarcation where the bulk of the fighting had taken place. The fighters began to alter course in mid-assault, rejoining the main fleet as if they were running into a lake with their asses on fire.

"What's happening?" said Trill. He scanned the screen for any indication of what the enemy was up to. "Bring up positional scans," he said to the crewman next to him. "I want to see how they're reforming."

"Sir, it looks like they are trying to create space between their line and ours. But why?"

"Something must be coming. Scan the damn airspace!"

The crew began to scan the void between them, looking for something they clearly were missing. It made no sense, why would the Imperial ships just retreat but not flee? Their dreadnoughts were destroyed but several transport carriers had made it planet-side and despite the scrappiness of the Carchel armada, they were still sorely outnumbered. The Imperials were poised to win the conflict despite the heavy losses they suffered. So what were they doing?

Suddenly they saw it. A single torpedo, shot from the flagship through the dense array of surrounding smaller ships that were creating a barricade between the Imperial ship and the Carchel fleet. It was moving slowly, slower than expected for a projectile that small. The projectile was physical, not a laz shot, and looked like a long cylinder with rounded edges, probably about two or three meters in length.

The crew looked at its approach with confusion. It wasn't an explosive device as far as they could tell, at least not one any of them had ever seen before. It moved along slowly at a curved trajectory, as if the target was the vanguard of the Carchel fleet. As it approached Trill began to panic. *What were they up to?*

"Sir, uh, sir — I think we have a problem," said one of the crewmen.

"What is it, do we know yet?"

"Sir, it's an orbital EMP. They are trying to disable our ship with an electromagnetic pulse."

"Oh shit!" exclaimed Trill. "Destroy it! Destroy it now!"

"A target that small will be hard to — "

"I said destroy it now!" screamed Trill, his voice laced with fear. The Carchel fleet began to fire on the slow moving projectile but the trajectory it was on was difficult to calculate. The laz blasts whizzed by it as it steadily approached their fleet.

After a few seconds of trying to snipe the EMP, Trill yelled, "Retreat! All ships retreat! Move out of range now!"

At this point the EMP had significantly closed the gap between themselves and the Imperial fleet.

"Sir, the fighters are — "

Suddenly, a sonic blast, not unlike The Harmony itself, ruptured in the void of space separating the fleets. A flash of light, like a lightning bolt, lit up the empty space as a shockwave rippled so violently he Draconis swayed like a capsizing boat in stormy waters. The fighters and cruisers stationed in the blockade and those trying to escape were thrust backwards, as if the pressure of the blast itself had disrupted their flight pattern. Trill grabbed onto the control panel as he began to float. The artificial gravity system was offline and the ship was now in zero gravity. The crewmen began to rise from their seats, holding onto whatever they could to anchor them back down to the floor.

The Draconis swayed rhythmically back and forth from the tsunami-like wave of the triggered EMP. The lights went out and they were engulfed in darkness. The holoscreen blinked off and all the lights on the command panel went dead. They sat there, like a rowboat in a storm, floating in the wake of the EMPs impact, dead in the water.

As the swaying began to slow, the emergency lights kicked on. He looked around at the terrified faces of his crew, their bodies floating away from their terminals like streamers in the wind. In the pallid dimness of the backup lights, they looked like sad, deflating balloons, slowly meandering away from the hand of a child.

All systems were offline. They were dead in the water.

Trill did his best to keep his composure. "Are the emergency backup systems damaged?"

There was a knock on the door to the bridge. Since the power systems had been disabled the doors needed to be opened manually. One of the crew floated over to the door, steadying himself with his hands like a gymnast climbing a balance beam. He got to the door, turned the manual override handle, and in floated the pit boss of the maintenance crew.

"Sir, all primary systems are dead," he said, breathlessly. "The comm is out so I had to make my way here. The backup generator is kicking in but it will take another two to three minutes to activate."

"What systems will come back online?" Trill asked, as he tried to keep himself from floating away.

"The nav system and the thrusters will come back. We'll be able to move again but it's not certain if the weapons systems have been damaged. We may not be able to fire our weapons."

"Will the holoscreen come back?" Just then the backup generator reactivated the gravity system. They all tumbled to the floor, some of them harder than others. The ship felt like it was spiraling through a dark abyss. The crew felt seasick but no one had the courage to vomit on the bridge so the few that did, did so in their mouths and swallowed it back down again. Once they got up and made sure no one was seriously injured, the crew boss made his way across the bridge and stood in front of Commander Trill.

"Sir, the artificial gravity has been restored. We won't be able to run on it long, but that's not our biggest problem. The Draconis has more sophisticated systems than most of our ships. The rest of our fleet..."

Trill looked at the young man's face. He could see the fear behind his eyes. "Our whole fleet is now just space trash. They will engage at any moment and wipe us out," said Trill, solemnly.

The holoscreen blinked back on and Trill whipped around to look at it. They had visuals again and could see the Imperial fleet just sitting there.

"Why aren't they attacking?" asked the nav crewman.

Trill looked him in the eye. "They're waiting for the residue to dissipate. It's dangerous to enter a magnetic field until all the energy has dispersed. It could disrupt their systems as well. They're waiting until it's safe to engage."

"How long is that, Sir?"

"We have five minutes at most." The command panel began to blink. "Sir, I think the comms are back."

Trill leaned over the dash. "This is Commander Trill. Status report. Can anyone hear us?"

The silence was deafening as the crew of The Draconis held their breath waiting for a response. Finally, they heard the sound of static and a voice on the other end.

"Commander, this is Yellow Squadron Leader Jaferson. My fighter is still intact. I'm trying to reach the rest of the squadron."

Just then, voices came through, one after the other, stating name and rank. After a dozen or so ships checked in, the silence continued.

"Sir, I believe we lost all of the battle cruisers," one of the Draconis crewmen advised. "None of them are responding to our hail and I can't ping them on positional nav."

An understanding started to slowly creep over the crew of the Draconis. Most of the fleet was lost and the enemy was about to pounce. Within minutes they would be destroyed, failing out of orbit like stones dropping to the bottom of a pond. This was the end. There was no chance of survival now.

Trill just stood there, looking at the holoscreen and the remnants of the Carchel fleet. As the video feeds scanned the battle space he saw most of their armada just floating, no power, no engines. The Imperials would take out all the disabled ships first, then bring their might to bear against the wounded. It will be a total loss of life.

"Can we contact Baron Carchel?" asked Trill to the communications crew.

"Sorry Sir, our long range comm system is damaged. We lost contact with Fasmouth."

This was a disaster. By now the carriers that made it through their blockade would have landed outside of Fasmouth and began their assault of the citadel. The Baron and the Fasmouth troops were isolated. Trill and the rest of the fleet could no longer aid them. They were on their own now. Even if the Baron found a way to repel them, after the Imperial fleet decimated what remained they would have a clear path to the planet to finish off any survivors. Most likely they would destroy the chaos device and kill the only people in the Imperium who could rebuild it, leaving the universe at the mercy of The Harmony forever.

"Do they know what happened down there?" asked Crewman Rathbone.

"They know," responded Trill despondently. He sighed a defeated sigh. "They know, son."

"What do you think it looks like from down there?"

"After the carrier explosions and the EMP detonation, they probably can't see much of anything. It would look like clouds on fire, as if the skies themselves are burning."

CHAPTER 46

It's Been A Pleasure

Five Imperial carriers plunged through the wispy clouds of Esper's lower atmosphere, evading pursuit by the swarming Carchel fighters. Two of the last remaining carriers were engulfed in flames and shredded metal during the breakneck race to the surface, but the bulk of the Imperial forces managed to slip through the blockade as the Carchel armada narrowed their focus on the lumbering dreadnoughts.

The carriers glided in a scattered formation, slicing through the crisp upper atmosphere as they hurtled toward the sprawling outskirts of Fasmouth. As they burst through the puffy cloud cover, the azure skies in their wake were flecked with spirals of fire and ash from the ravaged carriers, their metallic corpses crumbling as they were incinerated. The carriers collectively yanked their forward thrusters to prevent a full nosedive onto the tarmac of the cramped landing port below. With a final heave, the stabilizing stasis engines steadied their descent, allowing the ships to hover parallel to the ground before settling with a resounding thud.

The first carriers lingered above the slick tarmac before touching down one-by-one with a screech of metal. The landing port was small by Imperial standards, leaving no room for all five behemoths to settle. Two carriers scanned the surroundings, propellers whirring as they sought adequate space to land. Beyond the port sprawled an open field that bled into the ancient forest bordering the coast, the trees stretching down the rugged shoreline of the Great

Sea. The last two carriers glided over the swaying grasses of the field, pausing briefly before their bulk sank into the soft earth.

As soon as the final carrier was grounded, the doors of the cargo bays reverberated open with a mechanical grind. Armored transports rumbled down the ramps, followed by a vast battalion of troops numbering in the thousands. Mechanized exoskeletons known as Kordarmour Battle Mechs, piloted by single soldiers trained in their operation, powered on with a high-pitched whine and disembarked onto the loamy soil. As the Imperial regiments spilled out from the carriers, the formidable stronghold of Fasmouth could be glimpsed cresting a craggy hill in the distance, encircled by jagged ridges that unfurled into the ancient forest. This open tract near the landing port was the closest the hulking carriers could position themselves near the fortress.

The path winding to Fasmouth was mostly uneven dirt track, scattered with thatched fishing hamlets, all leading to the steep and serpentine main road that clung to the hillside toward the towering gates of the keep. Although Fasmouth was naturally fortified on all sides, making a direct assault treacherous, the vast numbers and advanced weaponry of the Imperial forces gave them a distinct advantage. The legions marched out, brandishing laz rifles and handguns, festooned with knives and brutal close-combat weapons, in anticipation of bloody skirmishes. The army assembled into precise military formations, standing at stern attention as they awaited their commander's orders.

Commander Levitz strode down the lead carrier's ramp, flanked by two other rigid officers. As they marched, Levitz addressed the shorter officer to his right, Commander Oratal, whose fiery red hair contrasted his pallid complexion.

"Now the real fight begins," Levitz remarked to Oratal.

"This should be over quickly," Oratal responded flatly.

"I'm uncertain about that. Carchel is keeping Jesper and the princess under lock and key. I'd relish watching them draw and quarter that weasel Jesper and mount his head on a spike, but if any harm comes to Princess Raeka, it'll be our heads on the chopping block. The Emperor shows no mercy for failure. We must be cautious."

"If Jesper's been captured, then the device is still in Carchel's clutches. Will we attempt to retrieve it?" Oratal questioned.

"I conferred with the Emperor himself after we got word of the Princess and Jesper's detainment," Levitz answered. "His orders were explicit: rescue the princess by any means. If it's possible to secure the device as well, we will. But once Raeka is safe, we are commanded to raze Fasmouth to cinders, slaughtering everyone inside."

"Yes, sir," Oratal said with a sharp salute before breaking away to address the waiting regiments. The massed battalions stood poised for combat as Levitz activated his comm and transmitted directly into the ear of each soldier.

"Attention, this is Commander Levitz. Our intelligence suggests Princess Raeka and Ambassador Manderlay are being held prisoner in the great keep of Fasmouth, just over that ridge. We will take the coastal path leading to the front gates, but expect fierce resistance from the enemy. Show no mercy. These fishmongers fight for a traitor who has chosen to shelter the Imperium's foes. They must be eradicated."

He paused, then continued. "Our orders are plain: rescue Princess Raeka alive and transport her safely to our ships off-planet. I repeat, we must find and secure the princess unharmed. The Emperor will not forgive failure. His daughter must be restored to him intact, or all our lives will be forfeit. Thus, we cannot unleash our heaviest artillery until the princess is verified as safe and away from the fortress. Once I give the command that the package is secure, we will lay waste to everything here."

Levitz flung his arms back towards the sprawling meadows and roiling ocean. "These peasants will know agony for defying the Emperor. You've been thoroughly briefed. Victory awaits at the ready."

Just as Levitz concluded his speech, a distant rumble could be heard over the whistling wind. He quickly radioed Oratal over a private channel. "Do we have a visual on the source of that noise?"

"Yes, sir. It's a local militia force. They've barricaded our path up the coast. They'll be upon us in minutes."

"How many?" Levitz tersely inquired.

"No more than a few hundred soldiers, some armored weapons platforms, a couple of hover tanks," Oratal clinically reported.

"Excellent. The first quarry of the day," Levitz remarked with icy satisfaction.

CHAPTER 47
Until The End

Andros Carchel raced down the corridor, Twila's hand clutched in his own, as the ground shuddered violently beneath their feet. It was as if the ancient keep was being ripped apart by a monstrous earthquake. Shockwaves from the deafening explosions outside rattled the walls, dislodging debris that rained down on them from above. They careened around a corner at full speed and burst into the command room where the others were gathered, clinging to furniture as the room quaked.

"Orbital communications are down. What's happening up there?" asked Jax, shouting over the din.

"Nothing good," replied Andros grimly. "We've lost contact with Commander Trill. Intel suggests their ships were crippled by an electromagnetic pulse."

Jesper's face paled. "Then the fleet is helpless above us."

Zarena rounded on him furiously. "How did you not know they had an EMP? Now our ships are sitting ducks!"

"It appears," said Jesper through gritted teeth, "that Rakeus had some surprises even I was unaware of."

Zarena threw up her hands. "Oh, whoops! We forgot to mention that minor detail!"

"There is some good news," Raeka interjected. "My father believes I'm being held captive, as we hoped. Their transmissions indicate the ground forces are under orders to rescue me before leveling the keep."

"Small comfort," muttered Andros, squeezing Twila's hand. "Did you find it?"

Andros nodded grimly, retrieving a tiny metallic orb from his tunic, no bigger than a child's ball. He placed it gently on the table. Jax eyed it warily.

"Doesn't look like much," he scoffed.

"This little trinket can vaporize a kilometer of land," Andros said darkly. "It's the last of our portable atomics, kept in stasis beneath the Keep."

Emerald paled, clutching Evard's hand. "Weapons like that deteriorate over time. What if it fails to detonate, or goes off right now?"

The room grew still, all eyes fixed on the innocuous metal ball resting ominously on the table.

Andros broke the tense silence. "The dreadnoughts have been destroyed as planned, though some carriers survived landfall. Imperial troops are engaged with our forces near the landing pad. We're badly outnumbered." His face was grim. "They've reached the coast and are advancing on Fasmouth. The villages are gone but we're still fighting."

Evard and Emerald exchanged an anguished look.

Jax spoke up. "So what now? Wait for them to seize this place and execute us while they rescue the princess?" Andros met Jax's gaze as he continued. "You must choose. We wait and they capture Raeka, killing the rest. Or..." He gestured at the metal orb. "We end this."

Twila spoke up. "But our people will die, too!"

Andros looked stricken, as if pierced by a sword. "Rebuilding would take years," he whispered.

"They'll be upon us soon," warned Jesper. "You must decide."

Andros looked as if he had been staked through the heart with a sword. "I... I... I don't know."

"The Imperial battalion is advancing along the coast. They are destroying everything in their path and slaughtering your people. If you do this you may have to rebuild, yes. But at least you'll have something to be rebuilt," said Jesper, solemnly.

Andros just stared at him, fear and indecision gripping his heart. It was Raeka who spoke next.

"Baron," she said. "In about thirty minutes they will have advanced close enough that the blast radius of this device will most likely include Fasmouth itself. By then, the opportunity to use it will be too late. I understand your hesitancy but the fate of your planet hangs in the balance."

Twila grabbed his arm and turned her head towards him gently with her hand. "My love, she is right. You may think you have a choice but you do not. Not any longer. It is this or death. Not just your death, or mine, but the very death of our culture — of our way of life. Now, you tell me, do you think that is a choice?"

Andros sighed. His arms felt like lead, his heart was full of regrets.

"Okay," he said, quietly. Twila looked at him lovingly, a tender smile touching her lips. "Okay," he said, louder. "I'll give the word. All troops fall back to the keep." He motioned to the device. "We still need a suicide team to drop it."

"I'll do it," said Jax. "I've been in sticky situations before. I'm accustomed to flying beat up old crafts. Give it to me."

Zarena grabbed him by the arm and spun him around. "No way, Jax. It's a suicide mission."

He took a step back from her and tipped his hat. "Only if you were flying it, darling," he said, with a grin. She pushed him away and stormed off to the other side of the table. Jax turned back to Andros. "I'll need someone to ride shotgun who thinks they can fire this thing. Baron, you have any men left?"

Suddenly, Evard let go of Emerald's hand and stepped forward. "I'll do it", he said with false sounding confidence.

"No way," said Andros. "Boy, you don't have any training."

Evard cut him off. "We don't have time to debate this. The princess said we have half an hour. That might be generous. Everyone is out there fighting to save our lives. There's no one left. Everyone here has a role to play, something to add. I can do this. It's the reason I'm here."

Therus, who had been watching the events of the past few minutes unfold silently from the corner of the command room, finally spoke. "He can do it. I've read his thoughts, seen his heart. He's seen more violence in his young life than most of us here." Therus closed his eyes as if he was meditating, then opened them with a flutter. "His mind is calm; he's not acting out of fear or lack of reason. He should be the one to go."

Emerald looked him in the eye and it was obvious to the rest of the group that thoughts were passing between them. She said aloud, "I know you can do this." She squeezed his hand and gave him a kiss on the lips. "I'll be in your mind the entire time. I'll help guide you."

Jax clapped his hands, startling everyone. "Okay then, it's settled. Let's go blow up some bad guys."

Ten minutes later Jax and Evard were climbing into an old, decrepit looking fighter craft on a tiny landing pad located in the back of the inner keep. Andros, Jesper, the twins, Zarena, Raeka and Emerald stood away from the ship, watching Jax and Evard get accustomed to the controls.

"You need to activate the device first, then gently place it into the firing canister. Once the light turns from red to green the payload is ready to deploy," advised Andros.

Jax showed Evard how to work the controls. "You use this lever here to aim. This old craft doesn't have a targeting system so you'll need to aim wisely."

"I think I got it," said Evard.

"You better hope you do. Otherwise we'll be vaporized in mid-air," grinned Jax. "You want to get back to that beauty of yours. All you need to do is just relax and fire.""Sure, sure. I got it. Relax and fire. Okay, I'm ready," said Evard, breathlessly.

The cockpit hatch closed, locking them inside the ship with an armed and potentially unstable nuclear weapon. Raeka grabbed Zarena's hand tightly, both of them looking at the ship and hoping for the best. Evard could see Emerald from his seat inside the ship and he reached out to her with his mind.

Hello, he thought.

Hello, she responded back.

Emerald closed her eyes and read his mind. *Don't be afraid, my love. You are brave, the bravest man I've ever known. You can do this.*

I know, he responded in his mind. *I will do it. In case I don't, you should know — I know,* said Emerald's disembodied voice in his mind. *I love you too.*

The stasis engines engaged and the craft rose steadily above the pad. Pretty soon they had risen above the keep, their friends standing down on the landing pad below watching as their craft ascended. Emerald connected to Evard again.

Don't be nervous. You need your mind clear for the best shot.

Not totally clear, he thought. *I need you with me. Until the end.*

Until the end, she responded in his mind.

Jax pushed a few buttons in and turned a dial on his right. "Okay, there they are. Man, they are pushing forward fast. We don't have much time."

"I can see the remaining militia squads retreating up the road. Should we wait until they make it into the keep safely?"

"There's no time, lad," said Jax. "Time to burn the sky."

The small craft lurched forward as Jax engaged the rear engines. He pushed the throttle lever forward and the ship took off like a laz bolt, speeding over the inner keep.

Evard could see the keep below them, all the surviving militia running for their lives up the embankment. Scores of soldiers poured in as the Imperial troops steadily advanced through the last remaining fishing village at the base of the Keep's Road. He could see the Imperial army, Soldiers and Battle Mechs marching down muddy streets, firing into abandoned buildings as they smashed through any structures in their path. The tanks and armored transports crunched wood and dirt and the bones of the fallen as they advanced through the village, leveling everything in their path. The imperial battalions on foot marched through the village streets, shooting any stragglers they came across. Death squads chased down the fleeing militia soldiers, shooting the slowest ones in the back as they hightailed up the Keep's Road toward the main gate.

Fires raged as all the remaining wooden structures burned. Fishing boats burned in the harbor, the docks barely visible through the smoke and ash. Evard was frightened by the absolute carnage he was witnessing. He'd never seen anything like it before. It was complete and utter devastation. Heaps of bodies lay in the street, some of them on fire, others rolled over by the advancing tanks. He felt a lump in his throat as they approached the fray, speeding past the fleeing Carchel troops hoping to make it into the keep before the Imperials rained oblivion down on them.

When they cleared the high walls of Fasmouth, Jax took the craft low, as low to the ground as he could, in an attempt to avoid detection. The militia men and women barely seemed to notice them hovering above their heads as they ran like a flock of wild sheep being chased by a hungry wolf.

"There they are, those bastards," said Jax. "We need to find a good spot." He scanned the area. "See that there?" he shouted to Evard. "Over by the ships. Down by the port. The Keep's Road bends there on its way up. See that group of Mechs behind that line of tanks? That's the spot."

Evard steeled himself for his shot, staring at the spot Jax pointed out and imagining himself shooting the bomb directly in the middle of it.

Good, said Emerald in his mind. *Imagine the shot first.*

"Oh, shit!" yelled Jax. "They spotted us. We got incoming!" Jax twisted the controls of the fighter and spun sideways while streams of laz fire whooshed passed their ship. "It's gonna be impossible to fly over them without getting shot down. We're fucked. Hold on."

Jax pulled the controls sharply to the left as the ship banked hard, Evard almost vomiting from the abrupt motion. He weaved the ship in and out, avoiding all of the coming fire as he brushed so close to the ground that some of the fleeing soldiers scattered to avoid being clipped by the fighter's wings.

Evard closed his eyes. "We don't have a choice, Jax. We're out of time. You need to gun it past their line and i'll take the shot."

"If we try to run right at them, they'll blow us out of the sky."

"This is a suicide mission," he said, with an eerie calm. "We were never supposed to make it back."

Jax didn't respond immediately as he piloted the small craft, banking and turning to avoid the onslaught of guns. "Yeah, I guess you're right. Looks like our time has come."

Emerald screamed in Evard's mind, No, no — you can't!

His eyes still closed, he responded, *I have to. I'm sorry, I really am. Tell Zarena I'm sorry. I love you.* He opened his eyes and grabbed the control lever for the canon. "Okay, I'm ready."

"Okay, lad. It's been a pleasure, it truly has. I'll see you on the other side."

Jax punched the throttle and the ship burst forward like a cork popping out of a bottle. A flurry of laz fire came from all directions. They pressed past the first line of Imperial troops, the foot soldiers turning to fire upon them as they zipped by.

Evard saw the spot Jax had told him to target. He focused on it while Emerald continued to scream in his mind. He severed his mindsnap with Emerald, his thoughts fell silent, and he regained focus.

The hail of laz fire began clipping the ship. They jostled in their seats as a few laz bolts ripped through the side of their hull. An errand shot caught the back thruster and the ship banked downward. Jax screamed, "Now!"

Evard steadied himself and fired. As the projectile shot out of the cannon, another bolt ripped through the bottom of the craft, knocking out the stasis engine. The ship went into a tailspin, spinning in circles through the air. It careened downward, sending them towards the direction of the beach.

Jax tried to maintain control as the ship fell out of the sky, spinning like a wooden top. He engaged the forward thrusters, the only engine segment still functional, and the ship flipped up in the air almost as if it was balancing on its nose. The ship continued to flip end-over-end as it was hurled towards the shallow water, past the edge of the rocky shore line. They impacted the water like a ton of bricks dropped from a great height, the force of the collision with the waves flailing them around like fish in a net.

The force of the impact ripped the wings clean off as Evard and Jax bounced around so hard, they thought they're skulls were about to pop off their necks. Their small craft skipped along the waves on its side, speeding past the reefs, completely out of control. It continued to skip along, like a pebble on the surface of a pond, until they found themselves out in the open deep water. Once its momentum slowed, it was caught in the swell of the ocean, coming to a stop as it swayed back and forth on the crests of the waves.

They were quite a distance off shore now. They could see the shoreline from where they landed. There was no explosion, only the methodical advance of the Imperial troops. Evard mindsnapped to Emerald again while they watched from the cockpit as Imperials continue their advance towards the Keep.

You were right, Em, thought Evard. *The bomb was a dud. I launched it in the middle of their army but it didn't go off.*

The ship began to sink as Jax and Evard struggled to free themselves. They pushed the hatch open and rolled out of the cockpit into the rough surf. They bobbed along with the current, trying to keep their heads above water when suddenly a flash of light went off on the shore, irradiating the whole sky. For the length of a breath it was completely silent. Jax grabbed Evard's arm and dragged him below the waves as a deafening thunderclap resounded through the air. They sank deeper and deeper below the waves as the entire coastline was consumed in a conflagration of brimstone and fire.

CHAPTER 48

You Did Good, Kid

Evard thought he was dead. The world was pitch black and he couldn't feel anything but pressure forcing itself inward along the entire expanse of his body. It felt like every inch of him was being pressed together. He didn't even think to move, all he could do was drift through the murkiness.

He started to feel a tug on his shoulder but thought perhaps he was imagining it. He suddenly was jerked upward as he tilted his head to see a shadowy figure in the darkness of the water hovering above him as the world started to fill with hazy light. Jax was pulling him towards the surface. His lungs began to burn from being underwater for so long. When he thought his lungs were finally about to burst, he was yanked up, breaking through the surface of the water like a breaching whale, gasping through wet and ragged breaths for air. He could see Jax floating next to him, also breathing heavy as his oxygen-starved lungs inhaled as much air as they could.

After a few deep breaths, his eyes began to slowly focus. As the fog lifted from his mind, all he could feel was pain. It hurt to breathe and he felt dizzy. Blood was starting to trickle off his body, streaking through the clear blue water like crimson streamers. He tried to take in his surroundings. He turned his head towards the shore line but all he could see was black billowing smoke and fires with flames spurting a several stories high. The blackness of the smoke shrouded the view of the keep. It looked like the entire planet had spontaneously immolated.

I hope Emerald and the rest are alright, he thought desperately, through the pain and the fog of his own mind.

Evard? A voice asked in his mind. *Thank goodness, you're alive.*

Em. I'm, uh… I'm alive. Sort of at least.

What about Jax?

He's alive. He saved me from drowning, I think.

Where are you?

Floating, in the ocean. Far… he tried to concentrate but his brain wasn't cooperating. *Far offshore. I can see the destruction from here.*

I'm coming to get you. There are a few rescue crafts. Therus and I are taking one. Just hang on.

We're hurt Em. How will you find us?

Don't worry, I'll find you.

Jax was holding onto Evard's arm to keep him afloat. "Stay right here" he said, in a breathless voice. He let go of his arm and swam off.

Less than a minute later he returned to find Evard drowsing out of consciousness, his head bobbing below the surface of the water. Jax was dragging a part of the wing of the ship that had come off during the crash. He had his arm around it, using it as a floatation device. He pulled Evard by the collar as he slowly began to sink again and threw him over the broken wing.

"Just stay put. I'm going to start paddling." Jax began to kick as he propelled them forward. After a moment he stopped. "Well, maybe not towards the shore."There really wasn't a shore left anymore. The entire stretch of visible land along the coast was drenched in flames and smoke, the sky filled with ash and debris. Even this far off shore it was getting harder to breathe.

"Don't," coughed Evard. "Just stay here. Emerald is on her way."

"Okay kid. I guess we float."

Evard was starting to lose consciousness. He kept saying to Jax, "She'll be here. She'll be here" which devolved from words into mumbles after a few repetitions.

As Evard's mind began to sink back down into the inky blackness, he heard a voice. This voice was different. It wasn't the sweet voice of Emerald, it was gruffer, harder to hear. It was as if this voice was attempting to patch through from far out of range. Only fragments of words were coming through the static. Before he let the darkness take him he thought he heard the voice of an old friend saying that help had arrived.

It was dark when Evard awoke. He was lying in a strange bed, a gurney style stretch bed in an empty room. He couldn't see much in the dark but he could feel his head throbbing. He coughed and winced in pain, grabbing his side as he did so.

He couldn't tell where he was but he could sense he wasn't alone. He struggled to get his bearing when a hand gently took hold of his own. Confused, he focused his eyes in the low light, and saw that Emerald was sitting there next to him. She patted his hand soothingly, and gave him a smile full of love and mirth.

"Welcome back," she said softly.

"Wh...where am I?" he asked. "You're in the infirmary. Well, a makeshift infirmary. A large portion of the keep was demolished during the blast."

"Jax..Is he.."

"Hey bud," said Jax from the shadows. He was sitting on a chair and leaning against the wall. "Glad to have you back."

"W-what happened?"

"Well," said Emerald. "You launched a nuclear device into the middle of the Imperial army and then crashed into the ocean. Fortunately, you crashed so far out to sea, you were out of the blast range." She rubbed his hand gently as she spoke. "You almost drowned, you have a concussion, a fractured rib, and your entire body is bruised or bleeding, but you survived. Therus and I found the two of you floating out in the ocean on a broken piece of the ship you crashed in. You've been sleeping for a few days, falling in and out of consciousness. The worst has passed now."

"They saved us in the nick of time too. The waves were starting to swell. A few more minutes and we would have drowned, for sure," chimed in Jax. He stood up and walked over to Evard's bed.

"You look like you're in better shape than me," Evard whispered, weakly.

"Luck of the draw, kid. You were the one that saved us, though. Your, whaddya call it, *mindsnap*? Calling Emerald on that psychic comm of yours helped them get a location on us. We were getting swept out to sea so without that, they probably would never have found us." He patted Evard on the shoulder gently. "You did good, kid." He tipped his hat to both of them, and said, "I'll give you some privacy."

After Jax left Evard tried mindsnapping to Emerald but the effort was painful.

"Don't," she told him. "Your concussion was pretty bad. We were worried there might have been brain swelling but the Baron's physician said you should be fine. You just need some rest. Use real words now. I'm right here." She stood up and kissed him lightly on the forehead.

"Okay, Em. I'm sorry I scared you like that." His side burned with pain. He found it was still difficult to breathe. "Don't worry. You just rest now. I'll be back to check on you soon."

She started to leave when Evard asked, "Em? Did everyone make it?" She turned around with a sorrowful expression on her face. "Zarena, the Baron, the others—they're all okay.. But most of the Baron's men are dead. All the villages were incinerated. Fasmouth sustained heavy damage, the forward ramparts collapsed and there were a lot of injuries. But it's over. For now."

Evard tried to sit up but the pain was too much. He gave up and sighed. "What about the fleet?" he asked.

A small smile touched the corners of her lips. "Well, most of the Carchel fleet was destroyed but the Imperial fleet retreated. Some unexpected reinforcements showed up."

Evard smiled a big smile. "Did they? Did they really?".

"Oh, yes. A friend of yours led the charge. He's here, on Fasmouth. Zarena used the chaos device on him and the rest. They're all back to normal now. You can see him in a little bit, after you've rested some more."

"But how, how did they…?"

"Don't worry about all that now. We'll explain everything once you're up to it. For now, just rest."

With that Emerald left him alone. He watched her go then laid back on his bed and closed his eyes, a tired but satisfied smile on his face.

CHAPTER 49

The End of the Beginning

While Evard lay unconscious, floating on a piece of debris snapped off from the hull of the ship he had only minutes before fired a bomb from, a fleet of ships came out of FTL speed on the flank of the Imperial fleet. After disabling most the ships in the Carchel armada, the Imperial ships had begun to close the line between them and their enemy, a dizzying array of laz bolt fire pouring across the empty space of no man's land as they sped towards the remnants of the planetary blockade.

A line of Carchel fighter's hung in space, floating along like marshmallows in a cup of hot chocolate as the torrent of fire rained down on them. The fighters began to take damage, several of them briefly bursting into flames that vacuumed out into the emptiness of space then disappeared as the debris from the destroyed ships began to float away like cosmic dust.

The Draconis floated amongst them, dead in the water, as the Imperial fleet bore down fast, the end of the battle in sight.

"Can we get any communications back online?" roared Commander Trill as the enemy licked their chops and advanced upon them.

"No sir," said a crewman. "But we have restored one of the backup batteries. It's doubtful comms will reach the planet but we might be able to communicate with any nearby ships that avoided the EMP."

Trill grabbed a comm from the command panel on the bridge. "This is Commander Trill of The Draconis. We are in need of assistance. I repeat, this is Commander Trill. We need immediate assistance." Nothing but static on the other end of the line.

Trill sighed, turned to his crew. He looked at the face of each person on the bridge, one by one. He could see fear and the grim resignation of inevitable death in their eyes. He didn't sugarcoat it. He owed each of them more than that.

"It looks like our time has come." He put his hand to his forehead in an old fashioned military salute. "It has been an honor to serve with you."

After everyone saluted in return he sat down again in the commander's chair and leaned back. The ship would be fired upon any second. He just sat there, making his peace with the universe, waiting for the end to come when static kicked through on the comm line. Then a garbled voice crackled through the line. Trill grabbed the comm and said, "Hello, is anyone out there?"

Nothing but silence from the other side. Then — "Hello… Commander…This is….Halbert Jonze. I'm a friend of Evard Roost. He said you guys needed some help."

Trill's heart started racing. "Captain Jonze, thank you! We were hit with an EMP. Our systems are disabled. The Imperials are about to finish us off."

More static on the other line, then the tranquil voice of Hal Jonze came through the comm again. "Just sit tight, Commander. I've brought some friends. We're going to give those Imperial bastards all they can handle."

Trill and the deck crew of The Draconis watched in stunned silence as a bevy of ships, maybe twenty or so, most of them non-military cruising vessels but armed with laz guns, swarmed the enemy's flank. They poured volley after volley of laz bolts into the port side of the Imperial line. Given the chaos that ensued it was clear the Imperials were taken completely by surprise with this unexpected ambush.

The Imperial fighters tried to turn towards the new threat but most of them were mowed down by the ambushing fleet. Hal's ships flew into the midst of the battle and Trill watched as the Imperial ships, caught completely unawares, began exploding in droves. The core of the fleet attempted to return fire but, as quickly as they could defend themselves, their perimeters were overrun by the surprise guests.

Trill watched in amazement as ship after ship was destroyed by the Immune brigade. The display was surreal. *Like a dream,* thought Trill. Maybe a better word to describe it would be 'miracle'.

"That kid did it. His friends actually came. Hallelujah!" cried Trill to no one in particular.

The Imperials were suffering heavy casualties. Trill was unaware at that very moment Evard had just detonated an ancient atomic weapon in the middle of the Imperial ground forces. The war on the ground was over.

Trill expected the Imperials to rally and begin a full frontal assault on the squad of Immune ships that just sideswiped their flanks. Instead, each of the remaining Imperial ships engaged their FTL drives and began to skip away, leaving the space above Esper empty, except for a bunch of disabled fighter ships and the squad of Immune that came to their rescue.

A voice came over the comm again. "Commander Trill. This is Hal Jonze. Looks like the Imperials up and left. Permission to space dock our ship to The Draconis, sir."

"Of course, Hal. Permission granted. I look forward to meeting you face to face."

"Likewise, Commander. I'm a pretty decent space mechanic. So are some of my crew. Let's see if we can get your ships up and running again."

Commander Trill fell back in his chair and started laughing, relief washing over him like crashing waves. "Sounds good, Hal. Welcome aboard."

A few days later everyone was assembled in the throne room of the Inner Keep.

Fasmouth had almost been turned into ruins, but many of the structures still stood intact, including the Inner Keep, which had always been one of its most secure locations. The front gate had collapsed, many of the ramparts had toppled, and there had been an avalanche that caused critical damage to the foundation. Most of the interior structures had crumbled and scores of housing needed to be replaced, but Andros was optimistic that Fasmouth could one day be restored to its former glory.

"We will rebuild Fasmouth," he declared to all assembled. "Today we won a great victory. An impossible victory against a ruthless foe. Thousands of lives were lost. Homes were destroyed. Our fleet is in ruins. But House Carchel is still here. We will rebuild from the ashes. The sacrifices today will not be in vain."

Everyone clapped as he continued the speech.

"It would not have been a victory if not for our new friends, the Great and Honorable Immune, who answered the call of one of our own, despite the great peril it placed them in." He nodded to the congregation of Immune standing to the side of the throne. Hal Jonze stood in the front, no longer sporting The Harmony smile but smiling nonetheless. Hal bowed to Andros, and Andros bowed formally in return.

"These brave fighters would not have known of our danger if not for the brilliance of Emerald Seltz and Zarena Denamonte. Together, they solved the riddles of our minds, and saved us from the fate the Emperor designed for us. Thanks to them humanity is… changing. We are unlocking potential within ourselves. Potential that was always there, lying dormant, waiting to be unlocked. They provided us with the key." He bowed to both Emerald and Zarena, who were standing next to Raeka and Evard respectively. They both bowed formally in return, Zarena doing her best to repress a mischievous smile.

"And to Ambassador Manderlay and Princess Raeka. For standing up to the evils of the Imperium and helping us win the day. We could not have done this without your assistance." He bowed to both Jesper, who was standing behind Raeka, and the princess, herself. They both bowed deeply in return, as is the custom between royalty.

"There were many heroes of the Battle of Esper. Few braver than Jaxxon Rill and Commander Trill. Mr. Rill flew a fighter craft armed with an antique nuclear weapon into the heart of the enemy's line. Commander Trill gave us the time we needed to find a path to victory. They both risked their lives and very nearly gave them. Thank you for your service." Andros bowed to both of them in turn, Commander Trill saluting in response while Jax tipped his hat in appreciation.

Andros cleared his throat and continued. "Last, but certainly not least, the youngest hero of the Battle of Esper, Evard Roost. Young Evard devised a plan to call across the stars for help in our great plight. By some miracle, his call to arms was heard. Without the support of the Immune fleet, the battle would have been lost. It was Evard who fired the weapon that destroyed the Imperial troops advancing on the beach, saving Fasmouth from certain destruction. He was gravely injured in the process. For your bravery, Mr. Roost, I award you the House Carchel Medal of Valor."

Evard, on crutches, limped from his position next to Emerald, and approached the Baron. Therus stood next to Andros and handed him a small wooden box. Andros opened the box and took out a medallion made of gold with a green patina hue. The medallion had a Kraken symbol in the center and was held by a strand of ribbon. Evard stood still as Andros placed the medallion over his head.

"Thank you, Sir Evard. You have made us all proud." Then Andros leaned in and whispered, "You would have made your family proud too."

Tears welled up in Evard's eyes, and he bowed to the Baron as best he could on the crutches, before shambling back to Emerald's side as the room erupted in applause.

"We have much work ahead before we live in a free universe again, but today we showed the Emperor how strong we are. We will not go quietly over the precipice and into the abyss. We all have a lot more living to do. Thanks to those assembled here, we can do it with our minds clear and our hearts free!"

The room erupted into fresh applause. It was the first moment of celebration many of them had had for quite some time.

Emerald, applauding with the rest of the crowd, reached out with her mind and snapped into Evard's. *You're a true hero*, she said as a voice inside his head. *I'm so proud of you.*

He turned to her in real life and gave her a warm kiss, wincing a little bit as he moved. *I'm only as good as what you've made me. Before you, I was no one. Everything I am now, I owe to you.* They continued to kiss as the Baron concluded his speech, barely hearing any of his rousing final remarks.

An hour later Andros, with Twila by his side, sat in the dining hall of the Inner Keep. Zarena, Emerald, Evard, Jaxxon, Jesper, Raeka, and Therus sat around the table with him, eating what limited food stores had survived. There was some fruit, cheese, and bread, along with some dried meats and a keg of Esperian Ale. They ate and drank and chatted about the events of the battle.

Andros turned to Jesper. "So what now?"

"Now?" replied Jesper. "Now the princess and I must take our leave. We need to return to Archlon."

"You can't!" protested Zarena. "Rakeus will kill you on site!"

"That's unlikely,, said Jesper, for what almost passed as sneer. "He has no knowledge of what transpired between us, and I will be the one to control that narrative. It's imperative Raeka returns to The Mark. Rakeus will expect us and she must be there to assume the throne when the time comes."

"How? Are you going to just kill the Emperor when you get off the ship?" asked Zarena, sarcastically.

"Leave the details to me," said Jesper. "Raeka will be safe. She will be needed at the capital in the days to come."

Emerald injected. "But the Immune are ready. They want to fight back. We have an entire resistance here at our fingertips.

Who better to lead them than the Karmarch Princess and heir to the Imperial throne."

Jesper laughed. "You're right, of course, Ms. Seltz. Still, the best course"

Raeka cut him off. "Emerald, that is very kind of you to offer but if I stand in opposition of my father that will lead only to more bloodshed. The only way to truly end this peacefully is for me to end this, and I can only do that while sitting on the Golden Throne. Our paths must diverge for now but know this, you have friends inside the Imperium. Soon, once our plans have taken root, the Imperium itself will be your friend."

Zarena, who was sitting across the table from Raeka, caught her eye and gave her a solemn smile, one which Raeka returned in kind.

"What about you then?" Andros asked Emerald and Evard.

"We may have won the battle," Evard answered. "But the war is only beginning. The Immune are strong, I think. Emerald and I will be rallying them. We've been searching for them, with Therus' help, and asking them to come to Esper. They want to help rebuild Fasmouth. They're ready to stand up to the Imperium."

Emerald nodded in agreement. "But first we are going to head back to Exalon. I'm going to rescue my mother and Jazz. We'll bring them back here and use the chaos device to fix them. Then we'll follow your lead, Zarena."

Andros clapped his hands together. "That's wonderful news."

Zarena addressed everyone gathered. "We plan to make Esper the stronghold of the Immune army. Their help will be invaluable in rebuilding the destruction here and we need a place to congregate but we can't stay on Esper forever. The Emperor, in all likelihood, is plotting his next attack. We need to liberate more worlds, and fast. We'll also need to make more chaos devices."

"House Collette may be sympathetic to our cause," said Raeka. "Especially if Zarena and Emerald can use the chaos device to liberate them and their people. Their homeworld of Vergerdan had an usually high rate of individuals affected by The Sequence. They have money and resources. They would be key allies.”

“They are also friends of your father, said Andros, with a certain pessimism.

“My father will have no friends after word of what happened here spreads,” answered Raeka. “We just need to wake them up so they can be reminded of that.”

Zarena nodded her head in agreement. “Vergerdan should be our next mission. They have a large fighting force and would make for powerful allies. We’re going to need to start somewhere.” Everyone nodded their heads in agreement, except Andros. Twila squeezed his arm and he began to nod. They both laughed.

“Okay, okay — those rich Collette bastards get freed next,” Andros agreed.

Zarena looked at Jax who was sitting silently next to her and playing with his food. “What about you?”

“Me? Well, my mercs and I intend to fight. By now we’re Imperial enemy number one, after you, of course. Can’t get left in the lurch. We’ll stay here on Esper for a bit, then head off and scout ahead. See what’s what out there. When the time comes to meet with the Collette’s just call us, we’ll be there. First though, we’re going to give Emerald and Evard a lift back to Exalon. Make sure they extract their people safely. Of course, we’ll need to find a ship. Ours was incinerated.”

Zarena squeezed his shoulder. “I’m glad you’re staying and helping the cause.” Jax said nothing but tipped his hat politely.

Jesper and Raeka stood up. “Our time to go has come.” Jesper bowed to the table and said, “Thank you Baron, for the hospitality.”

Raeka said goodbye to everyone with a wave and a smile. She walked over to Zarena, who stood up and they embraced. It was a fierce embrace full of love and fear and uncertainty. Finally, Raeka pulled away and said, “Don’t fret, Zee. We’ll see each other again soon. I promise.”

Jesper took her arm and began to escort her out of the room when Jax stood up. Jesper moved so fast Jax barely saw him move. He slid in front of Jax and looked him squarely in the eye.

"I made you a promise, Mr. Rill, that we would settle our affairs before the end. This is not the end, I fear. It's only the end of the beginning." Jax just stared at him with a seething malice.

Zarena stood up and gently took hold of his arm. "C'mon, Jax," she said, softly. "Let's finish eating."

Jesper took a step away, then turned and said, "I'll see you again Mr. Rill. You can count on it." With that he ushered Raeka out of the room.

The rest of the guests breathed a sigh of relief that more blood wasn't spilled so soon after the battle. Jax and Zarena took their seats again and Andros raised a glass.

"Well, when you all first walked into my keep I expected many things, but certainly none of the things that have come to pass. We've freed one world while also leaving it in ruin. We have a lot of work to do in the days and months ahead and there will be plenty of time to worry about it. For now, let's enjoy our victory, such as it was, and remember how much was sacrificed in its name."

"To what we lost," toasted Zarena, raising a glass.

"It's a new dawn. To House Carchel," Andros said raising his own glass. The rest of them echoed, 'To House Carchel.'

"To new friends,"continued Andros.

"To the Immune!" cheered Emerald.

They all toasted and drank down their mugs of ale, each of them finally finding a moment of respite amid the stormy seas of war.

Epilogue - House Karmarch

Emperor Rakeus sat alone in his throne room, resting his elbow on the velvety cushion of his arm rest. Lost in thought, he didn't notice one of the guards had entered. The guard waited patiently until they caught his attention.

"What do you want?"

"Commander Levitz is here to see you, sire."

"Fine. Bring him in," said Rakeus, with annoyance in his voice.

In walked Commander Levitz. His face appeared calm but Rakeus could tell he was nervous. A bead of sweat ran down his temple. Rakeus beckoned him forward with a dismissive wave of his hand. He approached the throne and bowed deeply.

"My emperor," he began. "I take full responsibility. I throw myself at your mercy."

Rakeus looked him over. He was a cowed and broken man, ready to throw himself at the mercy of his emperor. It was amusing, really.

"It was not your fault, Commander," Rakeus said leisurely. "The fault lies solely with that fop of a Baron and the traitor Councilor. Trust me when I say this, Commander. They will suffer agonies unlike any they've ever imagined. They will beg for death before the end."

Rakeus twirled his finger in the air, a gesture that unnerved Levitz even more than the Emperor's casual tone. Levitz stood still, his head bowed, waiting for Rakeus to continue his musings. Finally Rakeus asked, "What of my daughter? Did she survive?"

Levitz took a hard gulp of air, his Adam's apple rippling, sweat now pouring down his face. "Your Majesty," he said, with a cracked voice. He coughed and tried again, "Your Majesty. There has been no word. We believe she was killed when the bomb was detonated. Fasmouth was partially inside the blast radius. Much of the Keep was destroyed. There were thousands of casualties, their men and ours. We believe she was among them. Also Ambassador Manderlay."

Rakeus raised an eyebrow. "You think Jesper died as well?"

"They were together at Fasmouth and have not been heard from since the battle," said Levitz, sheepishly.

"If she was with Jesper she may have survived. It'll take more than some ancient fucking atomic bomb hidden in a rat in-fested sewer by a charlatan playing at royalty to kill Jesper." Rakeus began to laugh. It started as a slow laugh, but the pressure began to build and soon it was a cackle. He threw his head back and screamed with laughter as a mortified Levitz stared at him. After the laughing subsided, he waved his hand at Levitz.

"Out of my sight," he said coldly. Levitz immediately bowed and headed for the door. He was so scared he almost broke out into a run.

When Levitz had finally escaped, Rakeus leaned back on his throne. A dark smile began to touch the corners of his lips. He wasn't feeling quite himself today. No matter what he did, he couldn't quiet the voices in his mind. They threw barrage after barrage of insults at him, fears formulating in the dark corners of his mind he hid from the world. *You're a failure*, they said. *You're weak*, they said. *Your daughter and your bastard both betrayed you*, they said.

He couldn't help but smile. The smile grew into a grin and he began to laugh. He laughed and laughed and laughed until he was almost out of breath.

Suddenly, there was an explosion in his mind, like a million ballistics all going off at the same time inside his skull. At first he thought he was having a heart attack but then he realized he didn't feel sick, he felt great. A million neurons fired at the same time and a deluge of rage washed over him. He became so angry that he began to laugh harder as his thoughts were taken over by The Sequence, bit by glorious bit. He howled out loud, like a wolf in the light of a full moon. He stood up and screamed a bestial scream, releasing all of his pent up feelings. His thoughts were painted red, his fears gone, his hate which had been simmering all this time below the surface blissfully boiling over.

He stood up, renewed and feeling better than he had in years. He reached into his comm and said in a calm voice, "Can you please send Commander Levitz back in."

A few minutes later, Levitz nervously made his way into the throne room. This time, Rakeus stood to greet him. He walked down the steps leading up to the Golden Throne and approached a skittish Levitz with a jovial grin and a skip in his step. Levitz, confused, bowed and said, "Your Majesty, how may I be of service?"

"Oh, you can be of service, Commander." Rakeus reached into his robes and pulled out a long serrated blade. He grabbed Levitz by the shoulder with his free hand, and stabbed the blade straight through his gut with enough force it burst out his back, severing his spine in the process. Levitz began to convulse and dropped to the floor, choking his last few breaths on the blood bubbling up from his throat. Rakeus patiently watched the body of Commander Levitz spasm in the throes of death until he eventually stopped twitching. Then the Emperor cleaned the blade with his robes and sheathed the knife back underneath them. He skipped along calmly, as if he was a child visiting a fair, and after sauntering up the steps to his throne, he threw himself comically on the chair. He took his comm and called in the guards. Two guards walked in and saw the body of Commander Levitz. They both stopped in their tracks.

Rakeus said amiably, "Clean this mess up."

The guards looked at each other and started to move slowly towards the bloody pile on the floor that used to be Commander Levitz, trepidation coloring each careful step.

Impatiently, Rakeus stood up and bellowed, "I said clean this mess up!"

The guards, nearly soiling themselves, rushed over to the body and began dragging it towards a secondary door off to the side of the throne room. Rakeus sat back down and watched them. One of the guards caught his gaze and, terrified, he ventured, "Sire, we will send in a cleaning crew to, uh, take care of the mess."

Rakeus nodded amiably. "Oh, one more thing. My daughter lives, I'm certain. Bring me Commander Wentz. I must find her. Now."

THE END OF BOOK ONE

About the Author

Mark Stellan is a writer, musician, ballet dancer, martial arts expert, and sex symbol in exactly one of the infinite dimensions he inhabits—just not this one. In this universe, he is an avid reader, gamer, karaoke singer, and hibachi enthusiast. He claims to have mathematically proven the existence of aliens after a night of questionable decision-making, and he has an uncanny ability to remember song lyrics about sad breakups.  Mark once rode a toboggan down a mountain near the Great Wall of China and was nearly drowned by a beluga whale. He writes poetry in tribute to Edgar Allan Poe, though Poe has yet to return the favor. A simple traveler through time and space, his love of literature and fantasy has carried him to many worlds—most of which he still inhabits. He currently resides in the Greater New York area with his family and their telepathic dog, who insists Mark should stop trying to be funny all the time. The Harmony is the 1,317th book he has written in his head, but the first one he has bothered to publish.